TOGGENBURG – BOOK 3
Sea Holly

Michaela Francis

TOGGENBURG – BOOK 3
Sea Holly

FICTION4ALL

Chapter One

Sarah hummed happily to herself as she teased out her hair in front of the bathroom mirror. The bathroom was slightly smaller but not a bit less luxurious than the one she had bathed in the previous night. It was the one adjoining Daniela's bedroom. Sarah had left Daniela at the big dressing table in her bedroom when she had gone to take a shower. Sarah had been deeply touched by Daniela's dressing table. There were three framed photographs on it. One was of a handsome man and a truly beautiful woman and Sarah had guessed it was Daniela's parents. Another was a picture of a very pretty young girl, perhaps six years of age, whose resemblance to Daniela was striking. It could only be Daniela's daughter. The third was the newest one and it was a photo of Sarah taken on the Santis. It had torn Sarah's heartstrings to see that her picture held pride of place among the people Daniela loved most in all the world.

Sarah felt profoundly content. She had had little sleep but she had read somewhere that well-loved people didn't require as much sleep as the less fortunate and she could understand why. It seemed almost ungrateful to lose precious hours in unconsciousness; precious hours that you could share with the person you loved. The Ticino could wait. She had a whole day of Daniela to herself. That was the important thing. It was a whole day; twenty four wonderful hours to savour. This was love then; an existence for the moment; a treasuring of every priceless second, greedily feasting on every shared moment and resenting every instance of separation. She could not see Daniela for the moment but she could hear her singing at her dressing table; the lovely voice she knew would haunt her for the rest of her days.

Sarah finished brushing her hair and she inclined her head to look at herself in the mirror. She was pleased by the sight. She was beautiful and, for the first time in her life, she believed it. It had taken a woman she loved to finally convince her of the fact. Daniela had stopped singing. A moment later she padded into the bathroom with a silk gown wrapped about herself. Sarah smiled at her reflection in the mirror and was rewarded by a dazzling smile of pure happiness in return. Daniela stood behind her and wrapped her arms around her waist and nuzzled at her neck. "Hmm. You smell nice."

Sarah laughed contentedly and leaned back against her. "What time is it?"

"About half past nine."

"God we've only had four hours sleep."

"So come back to bed." Daniela was teasing at the bow on Sarah's dressing gown.

Sarah took an ineffectual slap at Daniela's hand. "Stop it Danny. We've got to get ready for work."

"Ah yes. Frau Fritzl phoned while you were in the shower. She says she doesn't need me today but she's asked if you could just help out for a couple of hours over lunch."

Sarah whirled around to face Daniela. "That's not fair!" she protested petulantly. "I wanted to spend the whole day with you."

"It's only a couple of hours Sarah."

"But we've only *got* today Danny. I have to go to Ticino tomorrow."

"I'm sorry darling. Look she only wants you from twelve till two. After that we've got the rest of the day to ourselves. I'll drive you over there."

"In your "broken" car?"

"In my suddenly and miraculously functioning automobile. I'll drive you over and while you're at work I'll cook us some lunch. The weather's cleared a bit so we might be able to eat in the garden."

Sarah pulled a face. "I... I wanted to be with you."

Daniela kissed her. "My darling you're always with me even when you're not." She eased Sarah's dressing gown open and slid her hands inside.

6

Sarah squeaked as Daniela ran a languid finger over her nipple. "Danny! We haven't much time."

"Then don't waste it by arguing about it. Relax. You don't have to be at the bloody hotel for another two and a half hours. We've time enough. I'll make us some breakfast and then I'll iron your blouse and skirt while you're putting your face on." Daniela slid the dressing gown from Sarah's shoulders and let it fall in a heap on the bathroom floor. "Now stop wriggling and kiss me properly."

Chapter Two

Two hours later Daniela delivered Sarah at the hotel. Frau Fritzl saw them arrive and rushed out to meet them. "Hello girls. Come in and let's have a coffee."

Daniela looked doubtful. "Er doesn't Sarah have to work?"

"Ach. Not for ages yet, Angie and I have already set up for lunch and we've no lunch bookings until half past twelve. I think we're going to be quiet in any case. Most of the guests either checked out this morning or they're out for the day. We've loads of time and it's lovely to see you girls." Frau Fritzl regarded them fondly. It took her about two seconds to be completely sure that her devious manipulations had not been in vain. The two girls looked happy and close. She was sure they were lovers.

She sat them down at a table in the restaurant with a cup of cappuccino each and observed them with pleasure. Daniela looked radiantly happy and Sarah blushed prettily under her frank appraisal. Many people might have been tempted to fish for information at this point but Frau Fritzl was a much more direct sort of character. "So have you two finally stopped fannying about?" she asked bluntly.

Sarah blushed crimson. "Wh... what do you mean?"

"You know bloody well what I mean. Have you or have you not finally realised that you two were made for each other?"

Sarah flapped her arms, flustered. "We... well we've become.... very close." she murmured evasively.

"So I assume that you didn't sleep in separate beds last night."

Sarah gave a passable imitation of a confused goldfish but Daniela lowered her eyes demurely and nodded in mock contrition. "I'm afraid we didn't Frau Fritzl. I'm a ruined woman."

8

"Oh Good!"

"Yes I'm sorry to say that Sarah took unfair advantage and ruthlessly seduced me last night."

"Why... you... you..." Sarah's face was a picture of outraged speechlessness.

"I'm glad to hear it." said Frau Fritzl with a satisfied grin. "I'm pleased to hear that you've got *some* sense Sarah."

"I... I did nothing of the sort." protested Sarah indignantly. "This shameless hussy lured me back to her place with a cock and bull story about her car being broken so that she couldn't give me a lift home."

Daniela ignored this outburst austerely. "Yes I was just sat on the sofa in my night dress about to watch the television when she sidled up to me under a pretext, plied me with strong drink and took advantage of my befuddled state to have her wicked way with me. I'm thinking of running away to join a nunnery to atone for my fall from grace."

"Hmmph!" snorted Sarah in derision. "Somebody had better warn the nuns. Nobody will be safe after *you* join the sisterhood."

"It was awful Frau Fritzl." Daniela continued. "She wasn't content with simply violating my purity with her bestial designs the one time. She was quite insatiable. There was no outrage or indignity to which her carnal desires did not subject me."

Frau Fritzl leaned back in her chair with a laugh. "Well, well, well. I never knew you had it in you Sarah. I always thought you were such a shy timid little thing. It just shows. It's always the quiet ones. You never can tell."

Daniela nodded in mock seriousness. "Oh don't be fooled by the nice girl image she shows to the world Frau Fritzl. Underneath that sweet little persona she's a rapacious fiend who will stop at nothing to satisfy her base lusts."

"Don't listen to a word she says Frau Fritzl." commanded Sarah in outrage. "I've never heard such unmitigated bullshit."

Daniela put down her coffee cup with an exaggerated sigh. "I'm afraid I must leave you Frau Fritzl. My lady and mistress has ordered me home to prepare her meal for her so that she may whet her appetite with fine food before turning to her darker passions and intentions upon my poor mistreated body. If her meal is not prepared on time she will doubtless beat me."

Sarah glared at her. "Just wait till I get home Miss Devin."

Daniela rolled her eyes comically. "You see how abused I am Frau Fritzl?"

Frau Fritzl chuckled warmly. "Yes well you'd better be on your way then. I'd hate to be the cause of domestic unrest."

Daniela rose with a grin and bent to kiss the indignant Sarah with a grin. "Until later sweetheart. Do you want me to pick you up after lunch?"

Frau Fritzl shook her head. "I'll drive Sarah back Danny."

"Ok. When will she be finished Frau Fritzl?"

"Two o'clock at the latest I think."

"Ok I'll have lunch ready by two o'clock. Don't be late honey or the cats can have your lunch." She kissed Sarah again and stroked her hair with a wink. Sarah found it impossible to stay angry with her incorrigible girlfriend and she forgave her with a smile. Daniela almost danced out of the hotel.

Sarah watched her go, captivated by her until she became aware that Frau Fritzl was watching her with amusement. Hastily she turned her gaze away and tried to appear business like. "So is there anything that needs doing Frau Fritzl?"

Frau Fritzl shook her head slowly. "The important job's already done Sarah. Well done honey. You finally did something sensible for a change."

Sarah blushed. "Hardly sensible Frau Fritzl. Tomorrow I have to travel to the Ticino to meet my prospective future husband. Now what am I going to say to him?"

"How about the truth Sarah? Try telling him the truth!"

Sarah frowned. "That's hardly an option Frau Fritzl. Both our families are going to be there and all our family friends. They're all expecting a big formal announcement of our engagement. I can't really just stand up and say, "Oh sorry Alan I can't marry you because I'm sleeping with another woman." It's not going to happen." Sarah groaned and held her head in her hands. "God! What a mess."

Frau Fritzl looked at her compassionately before leaning across the table and taking her hand. "Sarah I'll be honest with you. I don't really need you for lunch today at all."

Sarah jerked upright in surprise. "I beg your pardon."

"It's true Sarah. We've hardly got a single booking to be honest and there's nothing Angie and I can't handle."

"Then why the devil have you called me in?"

"Because I wanted to talk to you. First of all I wanted to see you; see if you and Daniela were... well that you had got your act together. Well I've seen all I need to. You walked in here blushing like a new bride and looking radiantly happy. That was a no-brainer of course. You've been in love with that girl from nearly the first moment you clapped eyes on her. Every time you mention her name your eyes sparkle and your skin glows. As for her... well she quite clearly worships the ground you walk on. It's an old story; girl meets girl, they fall in love; hardly original but none the worse for

11

having been told endlessly before. It's the last part I'm worried about; the "... and they all lived happily ever after." bit. That's why I wanted to talk to you. I wanted to talk to you because I'm damned if I want to see you go off to the Ticino tomorrow and make the biggest mistake of your life."

Sarah looked haunted. "Well what the hell do I do?"

"You tell the truth Sarah. You *have* to. However hard and difficult it may seem, you have to stand forward and tell the truth."

"I... I don't know that I can."

"What is the alternative Sarah?"

"I... I don't know."

"Because there isn't one Sarah. This is the crunch decision. The rest of your life depends on what you say in Ticino. You can tell the truth and get on with your life or you can lie and live a lie for the rest of your days."

"But... but I'm going to hurt people; my family, Alan."

"Not half as much as you will hurt them if you don't tell them the truth. What has Alan done so wrong to you anyway?"

"Why nothing."

"Then why would you want to condemn him to marriage with you?"

"I'm not that awful."

"You would be if you married him. You'd be the worst thing in the world; a wife who doesn't love her husband. Hurt people? You're barking Sarah. If you let your parents and Alan bully you into giving up the person you truly love for a loveless marriage you'd never forgive them. You'd end up hating them all. Your wedding gown will be a curse on your family. It will drive a wedge between your family and yourself that you'll never recover from. When the divorce papers are finally signed, you'll turn on your parents and tell them that this was all their fault. That's the sort of resentment that can last a lifetime Sarah. I've seen it happen. So are

12

you going to destroy your life and those of people around you just because you're too pusillanimous to stand up and tell the truth; tell them who you are, *what* you are and what *you* want to do with your life? What about Daniela? You know she came in here this week in tears because you told her that you were going to marry Alan. This is the woman that loves you Sarah. Can you just throw her away? She's one of the most extraordinary people I have ever met Sarah and she's in love with you. You'd be mad to let her go."

Sarah wrung her hands helplessly. "Nicole told me all the same things Frau Fritzl. You've nearly repeated everything she said."

"Sometimes people on the outside see things more clearly Sarah."

"Nicole's not *on* the outside Frau Fritzl! She... well she loves me too."

Frau Fritzl nodded sadly. "I know Sarah."

"You *know*? How?"

"I've known Nicole as long as I've known you Sarah and I'm not completely myopic." Frau Fritzl sighed. "Poor Nicole. She's the real loser in all this. You're going to have to find some solution for Nicole." Frau Fritzl shook herself briskly. "But that's by the by. That has nothing to do with your decision. The choice before you is clear cut Sarah; a life in a Zurich suburb with Alan or a life here in the Toggenburg with Daniela. Now which of those two alternatives sounds the most attractive?"

"You make it sound so easy when you put it like that!"

"It *is* bloody easy for heaven's sake. What could be simpler?"

"But I'll lose my family Frau Fritzl."

"Nonsense! Ok maybe there'll be some temporary cooling; a period of re-adjustment but in the end Sarah your parents will remember that they love you and ultimately they will be grateful that you're happy. They

13

do love you Sarah. They love you enough to never want that you live in absolute misery in a place you hate with a man you don't love. Sooner or later, they'll come around to understanding that. They'll respect you for having the courage to tell them the truth. It might even be a wakeup call for them; the day they realise that their little baby Sarah is a grown woman now and has her own decisions to make. Ok so maybe your mother won't get to throw the big society wedding she's hankered after. Well she'll have to get over it. Marriages are made in heaven not church."

"There are financial considerations to my marriage too Frau Fritzl. Dad was always concerned that I marry somebody that could support me and my children properly."

Frau Fritzl gave a snort of laughter. "So you've just hitched up with a millionairess. I think you could probably manage to ease his concerns on that score don't you?"

"I'm not *marrying* Danny."

"Maybe you should."

"*What*?"

"Sure why not? We could throw the reception here. My God! It would be the wedding of the year in the valley. The year? Sod that! The *decade*! Good God there'd be thousands to see it; national newspapers, television crews; the works. God if your mum wants a big fuck off wedding we'll give her one to go down in history."

"Er can we come back down to earth please?" asked Sarah with a touch of acerbity.

Frau Fritzl sighed with a small chuckle. "Well that's one for the future I suppose. Still it's a lovely thought."

"There's more to the financial side of things Frau Fritzl. My father and Alan's father are virtually business partners. Alan's father is investing heavily in dad's business."

14

"Not even your dad is so mercenary as to sell his own daughter to cement a business deal Sarah. You can hardly take that into consideration."

"But..."

"Listen Sarah it's one but after another. Tell me truly. Do you love Daniela?"

"Yes I do."

"Do you love her enough that you could imagine spending your life with her?"

"It's complicated Frau Fritzl. I mean..."

"Yes or no?"

"Yes."

"So what on earth is the sodding problem?"

"I... I don't know. You must be patient with me Frau Fritzl. I'm still trying to come to terms with all this myself. A few weeks ago I would have been shocked if anyone had said I was gay. Now I've just slept with a woman for the first time in my life. Now I'm in love with a woman and it's no ordinary woman either. Daniela is a celebrity. If I have a relationship with her it's going to very visible publicly. I don't know how my family is going to deal with seeing me associated with Danny in the Sunday papers. Hell I don't know how *I'm* going to deal with it. I'm still pretty uncomfortable with being gay in the first place let alone with the whole world and its grandma knowing about it."

Frau Fritzl pursed her lips thoughtfully. "Yes that is a problem Sarah. Fame can be a poisoned chalice. There can be a lot of pressure from the media around people associated with celebrities. Having said that, I must say that Daniela handles the media pressure pretty well. She's quite a private sort of person and it's characteristic of her that she lives a quiet life here in the Toggenburg. You rarely see anything about her in the papers unless she's on tour or making some sort of public appearance. She's not the kind of girl that turns up in nightclubs or swank resorts. I know when she first came here we had a few weeks when there were photographers and so on hanging around in the valley but she kept such a low profile they soon became bored and moved on. She's not a girl that overtly seeks the glare of publicity. I actually admire her for that. Many a famous singer milks the media for all the publicity they can get but not Danny. She's a girl that lets her talent do the talking for her. She's a wonderful musician and an electrifying performer but, away from the studio or stage, she pretty much shuns the limelight. I think that's why she so loves it here in the Toggenburg. It's the sort of dead end little backwater that allows her to live in relative obscurity. It's hardly like she settled for St Moritz or Monaco. A peaceful little valley where everybody knows everybody else and doesn't put on airs and graces suits her just fine.

"I was worried when I first heard that she'd come here to live to be honest. I thought we were going to suddenly become inundated with celebrities and turn the valley into a bloody circus. I didn't know her then of course. She's blended in perfectly and she's such an altogether nice and decent person that people have come to like her for who she is and not because of her celebrity status. How many other famous stars do you know that would help out a friend in a restaurant as she did last night Sarah?"

Sarah giggled. "None I guess. It was funny."

"But that's the nature of the girl Sarah. I actually think she really enjoyed being a waitress for an evening."

"Oh she did. She told me so several times."

"Well there you are Sarah. Just look at your young lady for a moment. She's not only very beautiful, extraordinarily talented, clever, witty and funny but she's also down to earth, kind, gentle and loving and a thoroughly decent human being. She's a marvellous companion for you Sarah. She fits you like a glove. Ok there may be a seven day wonder when the media gets hold of the story but that will soon blow over. It's not as if you and Danny are the sort of people to get thrown out

16

of posh nightclubs for punching photographers or anything. You'll pretty soon settle down into a quiet life together. Of course Daniela's performance obligations will take her away from home quite a bit but I'm guessing she'll soon come running home to her Toggenburg and her Sarah. You can have a blissful life together Sarah and it opens up opportunities for you as well."

"What opportunities?"

"Well it's not as if you haven't got your own talents to develop Sarah. For one thing you're the most accomplished naturalist in the valley."

"Oh I wouldn't say that."

"No you wouldn't but everybody else would. I don't know if you're aware of it Sarah but your breadth of knowledge and understanding of the local fauna and flora is nearly legendary in this valley. A few months ago I was talking to some of the local dignitaries and they were saying that it was high time that somebody conducted and published a comprehensive survey of the natural history of the Toggenburg. Yours was the name that came up."

"Me?" asked Sarah incredulously.

"Of course. Who better to document the wildlife and plant life of this valley than the person who has spent nearly her entire life studying it? Well you can't do *that* from a Zurich suburb. Seriously Sarah I know for a fact that you've been keeping diaries on the alpine plants and animals of this valley since you were a little girl. Those diaries could well be the most important record of the natural life of the valley in existence. It's criminal to keep that record to yourself. You could make a real contribution to the science of natural history in this valley. A life with Daniela would give you the time and leisure to make that contribution. It's not as if you'd be short of money."

"I... I never thought of it like that." Sarah mused. "Daniela once said that I ought to publish my natural

17

observations." Sarah creased her brow as the new thought occurred to her. To spend her days seriously studying the natural eco-system of the Toggenburg was a vision of paradise to her.

"Well there you go. Daniela would back you to the hilt I'm sure. Then again there's the problem of your name."

"What's wrong with my name?"

"Nothing at all. Fraulein Fuchs is a perfectly respectable name." Frau Fritzl leaned over the table. "But wouldn't *Doctor* Fuchs sound a whole lot better?"

Sarah blinked. "You mean do a PhD?"

"Absolutely. You've said more than once you'd like to study for a doctorate. Daniela gives you the time and opportunity. Now I'm guessing that that would go on hold if you marry Alan. I can't see you working on your thesis in the kitchen while preparing the evening meal for the hubby coming home from work. Daniela would give you all the time you wanted and as for funding... well figure it out. This one's a no-brainer. Danny would be delighted to help you. I know she would because she's told me so herself. Both of us agreed that it would be desecration to allow a brain as brilliant as yours to suppurate in some God forsaken backwater of a Zurich suburb. Eagles fly in the mountains Sarah. You can stay here and soar with the eagles or go to Zurich and gobble with the turkeys. This isn't just the love of your life Sarah. This is a career opportunity that may only come once in a lifetime. We want you here Sarah. You're not cut out to be a domestic housewife. Doctor Fuchs; eminent naturalist, published author and respected historian from the Toggenburg... that's who you're meant to be."

Sarah stared at Frau Fritzl intently. "And have you been talking about me and all this with Danny?"

Frau Fritzl nodded. "Yes Sarah. I'm afraid I have. I'm not going to apologise for it though. When Danny came in here, the day you told her you were going to

18

marry Alan, she was devastated Sarah. I've never seen her upset before but she was in bits that day. So I sat her down and we had a long talk."

"Did your two girls really have to go home urgently yesterday Elke?" asked Sarah shrewdly.

Frau Fritzl had the grace to look sheepish. "No Sarah. I gave them the night off."

"So it was all a cock and bull story to get me and Danny together in the same place right?"

"I'm afraid so Sarah. I'm sorry if it was a little devious but I was bloody determined that you were not going to go to Ticino without at least some effort to show you just how much of a mistake you were making. You're a wonderful girl Sarah but sometimes you need a kick up the arse."

"How much did Danny know?"

"Not all of it. I didn't tell her that I deliberately sent my girls away to leave myself short-handed but when I called her to ask her if she could help out I did tell her that you would be working too. She'd already told me that if I needed some help then I could rely on her but I don't think she expected me to ask her to serve in the restaurant." Frau Fritzl chuckled. "She was quite taken by the idea and when I told her that you'd be there as well she said yes straight away. It was then that I intimated that it might be a good idea if her car experienced some temporary Italian case of the vapours and put itself out of commission for the evening."

"You're a sly, manipulating, dishonest, devious woman Frau Fritzl."

Frau Fritzl grinned proudly. "Yep that sounds like me. Are you complaining?"

Sarah shook her head with a smile. "No not really. I'm glad you did it. If you hadn't I would have gone to Ticino never knowing what... well what it would be like to..." Sarah tailed off in confusion.

"And now you do know."

"Yes."

"And?"

"It was wonderful. I've never felt so happy with somebody."

"Excellent."

"But you haven't told me everything you talked with Danny about. Did you talk about all this stuff regarding a PhD and this nature project?"

"Yes I did. You see Sarah Danny's a hopeless romantic. She thinks that love is all it takes. You fall in love and everything just falls into place. Well that's all well and good but I told her that while you're a romantic too you'd have to put you on a rack to make you admit it. I told her that you'd always look to practicalities as well. I couldn't see you just being content to be the kept woman of a very rich lady. You've always worked hard Sarah and you'd pine away if you didn't have meaningful work. Let's face it, Danny isn't always going to be home. She's got major tours coming up and they'll take her away for perhaps weeks or months at a time. Now there's no point in you just being a spare part on the road with the band but if you've got your own projects on the go you'll certainly be busy. You could do a PhD easily Sarah. You finished top of your year class at uni with a first class degree. They'll bite your hand off if you apply for a doctorate with your own funding. You don't need to be at uni all that often either. You could do most of the work in your own living room. Then there's the other thing I was talking about. You could do it Sarah and with Danny's wealth then you'd have ample funds for material and research."

"I can't just live on Danny's money Elke."

"Why the hell not? Only a few days ago you were going to marry Alan and live on *his* money. Why is this any different? Anyway you won't be living on her money permanently. She can regard it as an investment. With a string of letters behind your name you'll soon be earning a whacking great salary of your own. If you're feeling that guilty about not doing your bit to cover

20

domestic costs well there's always plenty of work here Sarah. It works for me too because I'll have the best waitress I ever had just down the road whenever I need her."

Sarah smiled. "I'd like that. I like working here."

"Well there you go. Let's stick another chalk mark up under the column headed "reasons not to go and live in Zurich"."

"What did Danny say about all this Elke?"

"She thought it was a brilliant idea if it ever came to it. She was a bit uncertain that you'd go for it but she was absolutely one hundred percent behind it. She said she'd be behind you all the way. She knows that you need your own life and your own career too. She thinks you'd just be wasting your talents as a housewife. I agree with her."

Sarah shook her head bemusedly. "It's an awful lot to be thinking about."

"Well I'm glad that you *are* thinking about it. To be honest though, I don't see how much thought this requires; a brilliant future in the place you most love with a person you love and doing the things that you love: how hard can it be?"

"I still have to go to the Ticino."

"So wind up your affairs there and we'll expect you back here next week."

"If only it was so easy."

Frau Fritzl groaned. "Oh God! When was the last time somebody put you over their knee and spanked your bottom Sarah?"

Sarah looked chastened but before she could reply Angelica entered the restaurant. "Hello Sarah." she said warmly before bending to kiss Frau Fritzl affectionately.

Frau Fritzl snaked an arm around Angelica's waist. "You've come just at the right moment Angie. You can help me sort this young lady out. I was about to give her a spanking. You can hold her down while I paddle her rump for her."

21

Angelica giggled softly. "You can't go spanking the staff Elke. Think of the scandal there'd be. You can't spank them if it's not in the terms and conditions of employment; well not unless they want you to of course. Anyway what's poor Sarah done to deserve a spanking?"

"I'm trying to make the dozy little baa lamb realise that she belongs here in the Toggenburg with Daniela and not squandering her life away in a foul Zurich suburb with a waste of space for a husband and she's giving me a hard time about it."

Angelica laughed. "Is that all it is?" In a fluid movement she stepped around the table and, to Sarah's embarrassment, sat down on Sarah's lap and folded her arms about her neck. She leaned close and nuzzled Sarah with her nose. "Sarah's not going anywhere are you sweetheart? Sarah's *married* to this valley Elke. You could no more shift her from here than you could relocate the Churfirsten and she's not going to leave her Danny either. She loves her too much. Tell her Sarah. Tell her that you're staying with us and we're all going to live happily ever after."

Sarah smiled. She felt slightly uncomfortable about Angelica perching on her knee but Angelica was such a warm and uninhibitedly physical soul that it was impossible to feel put out by her displays of affection. She liked the gentle warm hearted lady immensely and it was easy to understand why her partner adored her so. Sarah cleared her throat. "It sounds like a good ending to me Angie."

Angelica kissed her gently on the forehead. "Of course it is and none the worse for having been used before. Now give me a kiss and I'll protect you from our tyrannical boss."

Frau Fritzl glanced out of the corner of her eye. "Break it up you two. I think that's the Mannsteins arriving for lunch. Come on, put her down Sarah before we have another scandal to contend with."

In the end Sarah pottered about in the restaurant for the next hour or so without any real justification for her presence. It really was very quiet and she had little to do. She enjoyed the company of Frau Fritzl and her irrepressible Angelica however. Angelica was flirting with her outrageously, much to Frau Fritzl's amusement who was completely unconcerned by her partner's predilection to flirt with anything pretty in a skirt as she put it. Eventually Sarah begged leave to depart. Frau Fritzl told her that if she waited another half an hour or so she'd drive her back but Sarah shook her head firmly and said she'd prefer to walk. She was early and it was turning into a lovely day. In any case she had some thinking to do.

Chapter Three

It *was* a lovely day. Sarah loved these days after a night's rain in the Toggenburg. There was an even more verdant feel to the valley, after refreshing rainfall, and the little brooks gurgled more enchantingly than ever with the extra water swelling their volume. It was a big sky today for great ranks of cumulus clouds stretched in procession to the horizons, against the clear blue background, and the sun lanced down between the columns, warming the landscape invigorated by the rain. There was still a stiff breeze but Sarah loved the feel of it in her hair and the scents it brought to her from the meadow flowers that seemed to have burst forth in even greater exuberance through the benediction of water from heaven. The big Ox eye daisies and umbellifers by the roadside were crawling with bees, hoverflies, beetles, moths and butterflies.

There were Ring Ousels singing from the tree line above and Tree Pipits displaying from the upper boughs. Black Redstarts sang their strange scratchy melody from the roofs of barns and farmhouses while White Wagtails flitted around the houses and compost heaps. Sarah listened in pleasure to the songs of the ubiquitous Chaffinches, the monotonous refrains of the little Chiff Chaffs, the fluty repetitions of the Song Thrushes and the cawing of the crows. There was a Whinchat perched on a fence post and small flocks of Goldfinches feeding on the thistles in the damp meadows. The valley seemed more alive than ever.

Sarah sat by the roadside for a few minutes to collect her thoughts. The air was so clear it felt as if you could reach out and touch the Schafberg on the other side of the valley. She could look down and see the yellow of the post bus as it left from Wildhaus. She was happy she realised; more happy than she could recall ever being. Tomorrow might be a dark cloud looming but today she was content to ignore it and live for this moment of deep satisfaction. Angelica was right. She *was* married to this valley. This was her home and all the home she had ever desired. How could she ever think of leaving it?

Sarah's revelry was interrupted by the chime of her mobile phone. It was Nicole. "Where the hell have you been?" demanded Nicole acerbically.

"I left a note to say I was working at the Toggenburg last night Nicky. Didn't you get it?"

"Well yes but you didn't come home."

"Didn't you see the weather Nicky? It was foul so I stayed over."

"I could have come and picked you up."

"It was late Nicky so..." Sarah hesitated but drew a deep breath and continued, "So Danny put me up for the night at her place."

"You... you stayed with Danny?"

"Yes I did."

"I see. And er did anything well..."

"Yes it did Nicky."

"Oh! Right."

"Are you working today Nicky?"

"This evening damn it. I could call in sick though if you want. We've got to have a last night together before you go to the bloody Ticino."

"I'm spending the night with Danny Nicky."

"Oh! Ok."

"I'm coming home this afternoon sometime though to pick up my things to go to Ticino if you're home."

"Well yes I should be. I don't have to work until six."

"Fine we'll have a quick drink together."

"Oh hell Sarah!" Nicole sounded wretched. "I... I wanted to spend a last evening with you. God knows when we'll see each other again."

Sarah stared out across the valley. A glint of sunlight reflected off some surface on the weather station on the Santis far to the east. "I wouldn't worry about it Nicky. I think we'll be seeing each other again all too soon."

Chapter Four

Sarah paused as she rounded the front of Daniela's house. She had been about to enter at the front door, but she'd heard music playing from around the back and Daniela singing along with the music. It was really her first chance to look at the house closely by daylight. They'd left in a hurry that morning for Daniela's amorous morning requirements had delayed them somewhat. Now, however, Sarah was able to examine the house at her leisure. The house was built of wood set on stone foundations. That was not at all unusual. Nearly every old house in the Toggenburg was built of wood. This wasn't an old farmhouse though and Sarah puzzled for a moment over the origins of the building. The clue was on the front door. Above the front portal was a venerable old sign that Sarah had not seen when they left the house earlier. It read "Edelweiss". With a shock Sarah realised that the house was an old converted guest house. It had been highly modified and there were newer extensions added on the ground floor but, now seen closely from the outside, its original function was obvious.

Nineteenth century Sarah guessed. There'd been a lot of the older hotels and guest houses built in that era when alpine tourism had first emerged. No wonder the place was so big and had so many rooms. Daniela's big living room had probably once been the main dining room for the guest house. Some of the bigger rooms on the upper floor would probably have been dormitories and the main bedrooms the private rooms for guests. The place had been brilliantly converted into a private dwelling but it was enormous.

Sarah stood back to admire the building. There was an eccentricity to it that Sarah knew would have made Daniela fall in love with it immediately and its sheltered location in the glade surrounded by small copses was charming. Sarah wondered why she had never seen the place before. It was off the beaten track to be sure but Sarah prided herself that she knew the valley pretty much inside out yet she had never come across this old place before. It was a significant building she realised. These old guest houses were a part of the history of the valley. She determined to find out what she could of its history.

The name of the guest house was no great surprise. The Swiss excelled at many things but originality in the naming of hotels and guest houses was not one of them. In Switzerland a hotel next to the post office and bus station was invariably Hotel Post or by the railway station Hotel Bahnhof. Nearly every town and resort in Switzerland had its Hotels Sonne, Sternen, Alpenblick, Steinbock or Alpenrose. Edelweiss was a common name. There had to be hundreds of them Sarah reflected. There were over two and half thousand species of flowering plants and ferns in Switzerland but only a handful ever made it onto the sign of a guest house. Likewise there were some four hundred species of birds recorded from the country but other than the odd Adler or Schwann few of them ever had hotels named after them.

Nevertheless it was deliciously ironic that Daniela lived in a house called Edelweiss for that was the flower that Sarah had given her by the Fahlensee. It also reminded Sarah that, at home, she still had the little diamond and sapphire edelweiss pendant in white gold that she had bought for Daniela in Winterthur. She thrilled at the thought of giving it to Daniela. She would hang it around her neck with her own hands this very day. It mattered not a jot that, although expensive for Sarah, its price was trivial to Daniela. Daniela would love it even if it was made from stainless steel and chips of broken glass. The one thing you learned from having a very rich girlfriend was that the value of things was not measured by their monetary worth.

28

Bemusedly Sarah walked around the side of the house where she could here Daniela singing more clearly. Obviously Daniela wasted few opportunities to exercise that angelic voice. Sarah found Daniela on a lawn at the back of the house where she was happily laying out a table for lunch. She had her back turned to Sarah and did not see her arrive in the garden. Sarah stopped to regard her in amusement. The afternoon sun had tempted Daniela into shedding clothes for she wore a skimpy bikini in sky blue. She was evidently busy in the kitchen however for she'd donned a flowery apron over her bikini. The result was touchingly comical. Sarah felt like a husband coming home from a hard day earning the household bread to find his beautiful wife, scantily dressed, happily preparing his evening meal. It was like some vision straight out of a bygone idealised fantasy of the nineteen fifties.

With a smile Sarah approached. Daniela heard her coming and whipped around. In an instance she had flown across the lawn, wrapped herself around Sarah with almost childlike delight and was smothering her face with kisses as if she hadn't seen Sarah in months. Sarah felt the heat rush to her body as she held Daniela and allowed her hands to stroke her naked back and pat her bottom. "Hey, you're early." said Daniela at last.

"Frau Fritzl didn't really need me after all so I got away early." Sarah assumed a stern face. "Are you trying to tell me that dinner's not ready? I hope I'm not going to have to discipline you."

Daniela giggled merrily. "It will be ready in no time my lady. You've just got enough time to shower and dress for dinner."

Sarah looked at her. "Is this what you call dressing for dinner?" she asked. "That pinny looks downright silly on you."

"I'll replace it with a sarong when we sit down to dine."

"What am I supposed to wear anyway?" asked Sarah. "I haven't got a change of clothes with me."

Daniela pinched her cheek. "Don't go blond on me sweetheart. Did you think I hadn't thought of that? I've laid you out a clean dress, some sandals and fresh undies. You'll have to go "au naturel" up top though because my bras won't fit you."

Sarah grinned and squeezed Daniela's breast. "Too big for me huh? I suppose I'm a bit inadequate in that department."

"You've got gorgeous tits; just the right size. I wouldn't have them any other way."

"What's for dinner?"

"You'll find out when it's put in front of you. Now come on. Get changed. I have a culinary masterpiece to look after."

Daniela led her back into the house through the back kitchen door and Sarah lingered a few moments to admire her at work. Daniela leaned across a work top to rummage among some jars of herbs and spices, exposing her inadequately clad bottom invitingly. There was a wooden spoon lying on the work top. Sarah picked it up with interest. "Is this spoon clean?" she asked.

"Yes it is. I was going to use it to...OUCH!" Daniela sprung upright clutching her bottom.

Sarah waved the spoon at her. "That was for telling Frau Fritzl a load of gumpf about my insatiable, rapacious sexual lusts."

Daniela rubbed her bottom with a ludicrously comic look of penitent contrition on her face. "Yeth ma-am." She lisped "Thorry ma-am. Thall I bend over again tho you can punith me properly?"

"Oh God don't do that or we'll never get round to eating." Sarah kissed her quickly. "I'm going to jump in the shower."

"Don't be long. Dinner is in fifteen minutes flat."

Sarah showered quickly and located the dress that Daniela had laid out on the bed. Significantly she'd laid it out on her own bed. There was no question any more of Sarah sleeping in the guest bedroom. It was a simple but high quality cotton summer dress in a pale blue, green and white print with a white belt to clinch it at the waist. Daniela had provided her with clean knickers as well; plain white but with a little blue bow on the front for a touch of frivolity. Sarah pulled the sandals on, amused at the coincidence that she and Daniela took very nearly the same size shoe.

Back in the garden Daniela looked at her appraisingly. "You look sweet." she told her. "That dress suits you. You can have it."

"Danny you don't have to keep giving me clothes."

"I *like* giving you clothes. Stop arguing and open the wine while I lay out the food."

Daniela had chosen a white wine to accompany lunch and it was chilling in an ice bucket on the table. It was a good quality Fendant from the Valais region of southern Switzerland. Fendant was the regional name but the grape was known more universally as Chasselas. Sarah was interested in the grape because it was reputed by some authorities to be a native Swiss variety although it was grown also in France, Germany, Portugal and even as far away as New Zealand now. Certainly it was the most commonly grown wine grape variety in Switzerland and usually turned into a full fruity, dry wine which was the perfect accompaniment to cheese. In many parts of Switzerland it was traditional to drink the wine in tiny thimble like glasses like schnapps glasses but Daniela preferred larger containers. She had set out a pair of crystal wine glasses with long stems. She obviously liked to set a fine table for there was expensive china on the garden table, silver cutlery and green linen napkins to match the pattern on the plates. She had placed a floral arrangement at the centre of the table; simple yet attractive.

Daniela placed the food on wooden boards laid on the table. "It's only something simple I'm afraid Sarah."

31

she apologised. Sarah didn't believe her. The food looked and smelled delicious. Daniela was experimental with salads it appeared for she had produced three bowls of different salads. There was a tomato salad in an Italian style with onions, garlic, and goat's cheese in olive oil and vinegar; an endive salad in oil, vinegar and mustard dashed with Cayenne pepper and a lamb's lettuce salad dressed in oil and lemon juice with a dash of hot mustard and garnished with a chopped hard-boiled egg. She also laid out a platter of toasted garlic bread and a small bowl of olives. The main dish she brought steaming to the table and Sarah's nostrils filled with the delicious cheesy smells emanating from it.

Sarah looked at it in delight. She was hungry. "Oh my!" she declared "Gnocchi. I haven't eaten gnocchi for ages. Where did you buy it?"

Daniela placed a hand on her hip and looked indignant. "Cheeky bitch! What do you mean where did I buy it? I made it."

"You *made* it? You mean this is homemade gnocchi?"

"Of course."

"Oh God how do you do it? I've always meant to look it up. I love gnocchi."

"It's actually easier than you think. You boil your potatoes and simmer them for about twenty minutes until they're really soft. The choice of potatoes is crucial. Some people use waxy potatoes like redskins or new potatoes but I prefer floury potatoes because you get a smoother texture when you mash them and sieve them. I use King Edwards normally. Once you've boiled them, you put them in the oven for about five minutes to dry them and then you mash them up really fine to eliminate all lumps. I force them through a sieve to get an even texture. Then you mix them with plain flour, plenty of salt, a bit of pepper and an egg to make a good smooth dough. Once you've made your dough, you roll it out in sausages maybe half an inch think and then you cut the sausages into pieces around an inch or so long. I use a special gnocchi paddle to get those ridges on the sides. Once you're done you simply bring a big saucepan of salty water to the boil and drop the pieces in and let them simmer until they rise to the surface when you scoop them out with a sieve and transfer them to a warm serving dish. Then you pour the sauce over them, sprinkle it with chives and serve. I've made a really simple Gorgonzola sauce. I just melted some butter and Gorgonzola in a pan then poured in some cream and brought it gently to the boil and added it to the gnocchi. Easy as you like."

"It looks gorgeous."

Daniela smiled and wrapped her sarong more firmly about before taking a seat. "Well let's see what it tastes like."

It was delicious. The gnocchi were soft but chewy like soft dumplings and the rich creamy cheese sauce was heavenly. The garlic bread and the crisp, fresh and tangy salads made a perfect accompaniment and Sarah ate greedily, washing the lot down with the cool dry wine. It may have been simple food but it was executed masterfully. Replete at last Sarah pushed her plate aside and took a deep breath. She had eaten too much. She gazed at Daniela in wonderment who was still picking daintily at her food. "You know something Danny?" she mused. "You are one of the richest people I know and I'm not talking about your money. Every time I think I'm getting to know you then you reveal some other hidden talent or accomplishment that I didn't even know was there."

Daniela smiled at her ironically. "That's interesting Sarah because that's almost exactly the same way I think about you. You surprise me continually. There's a depth to you I haven't even begun to plumb." Daniela laughed and raised her glass. "Here's to the two most talented women in the Toggenburg. Think what we could achieve together." Sarah swallowed but she met Daniela's eye and tapped her glass against hers. "So what do you want to do this afternoon?" asked Daniela.

"Well I have to pick up my bags from the Alpli Danny. Nicole phoned as well. I said we'd meet her for a drink before she has to go back to work this evening. We don't have to though if you don't want."

Daniela shook her head. "No I think we *have* to see Nicole Sarah. I'd guess she's probably having a bad time for the moment."

Sarah nodded sadly. "Yes. Frau Fritzl said much the same thing. She says that Nicole's the real loser in all this mess."

"I don't like it when *anybody* loses Sarah."

"Somebody's got to lose out Danny."

"Hmm maybe. What was work like?"

"I didn't have much to do in truth. Frau Fritzl didn't really need me. She only called me in because she wanted to talk to me."

"Oh! And what did she want to talk to you about?"

"You."

Daniela put her glass down and grimaced. "Oh! I see."

"Danny, she said that you and her had a long talk about me."

Daniela nodded contritely. "Yes that's true. I'm sorry Sarah. I didn't want to divulge any personal matters to her but I was pretty cut up the other day when we met at Oberdorf and she was the only person I had that I could turn to. Was she rough with you?"

"A little bit. Essentially she told me that I'd be the world's greatest idiot to leave you and the Toggenburg and go away and marry Alan."

"That's up to you to decide Sarah. Frau Fritzl is a strong minded woman and she'll have her say but ultimately it is you who decides that Sarah."

"Do you agree with her though?"

Daniela sighed. "It's not fair to ask me that Sarah. I can't advise you from a purely neutral viewpoint. I'm too involved. It's impossible for me to give an unbiased opinion. You know what I want. You must do. But it's you who must decide what *you* want."

Sarah took a breath and marshalled her thoughts. "Danny I have to go to Ticino tomorrow. Now I don't know what's going to happen there but I'll only say one thing. I'll go to Ticino with my mind open and my options open. I have to listen to what Alan has to say. I have to listen to what my family has to say. I'm burning no bridges behind me though. I'll talk to them and I'll make a judgement on what they have to say. Before I can make that decision however I need more information."

"I understand."

"No Danny you don't. It isn't only from Alan and my family I need information from."

"So where then?"

"I need to know... I need to know what would happen if I... well if I reject Alan's suit. I need to know what happens if I say no to the marriage and come back to the Toggenburg. I... I need to know what happens with *us* then."

Daniela gazed at her searchingly. "If you said no to Alan would it be because of me?"

"Yes it would."

"This is a big house Sarah. I would like to share it with you."

Sarah blinked. "Do you mean that?"

"I have never meant anything more. Please disillusion yourself of any notion that I regard our relationship as just some casual love affair Sarah. You are the woman I love. I want to share my house with you. I want to share my *life* with you. I can't put it any plainer. I have never felt this way about anybody before. If you come back to me from the Ticino I will be the happiest woman in the world. I can't ask you to do that I can only state what is the truth. I've dreamt of us making a life together in this house Sarah. You give me hope that my dream is not yet dead."

"If... if I lived here what would Nicky do? I don't think she could maintain the rent on our place in the Alpli on her own."

"She'd have the same problem if you married Alan Sarah."

"But not if I came back to the Toggenburg and I lived there Danny."

"Do you want that?"

"No... I mean I don't know. I... I would want to share with you but I'm worried about Nicky as well."

"Ok stop worrying. I'll buy the house in Alpli."

"Oh come on! Don't be silly."

"It's not silly at all. Perhaps you are unaware that your current landlady is interested in selling your house."

"Well yes... I mean she's always threatening to do so but nothing's ever come of it."

"So I'll make her an offer she can't refuse."

"But why for heaven's sake?"

"Because it's a place you love, because it gives us a solid investment in the valley and because it gives us at least a partial solution to Nicole."

"Nicole?"

"Why yes. Nicole can stay there as long as she likes. We'll charge her fifty rappen a month for rent."

"You can't just buy a bloody house so that Nicky has somewhere to stay."

"It wouldn't be just for that. It's a valuable property and liable to increase in value. It would be an investment. Furthermore we'd tie Nicole to us; part of the family almost and she won't be parted from the girl she truly loves. You'd still be close to her. Sooner or later she may find somebody just for her and then we'll help her out. She's a Chinese obligation Sarah. We have to look out for our own. Nicole's part of us Sarah. We have to look after her."

Sarah wrung her hair in agitation. "Oh God! I'll have to think about this. For God's sake don't say anything to Nicky when we see her today."

"Of course not. In any case it will all depend on what you do in Ticino."

Frau Fritzl mentioned something else you talked about Danny."

"Oh yes?"

"Yes... about... well about my career. She might have been talking a load of guff though."

"I think I know where you're coming from Sarah. We did discuss that. She was of the opinion that you ought to pursue your academic career and your studies of the natural environment in the Toggenburg. I agree with her. It would be a dreadful waste of a brilliant mind if you were not to exploit those talents. I know it's something you *want* to do as well. I will state plainly that should you choose to throw in your lot with me as it were then I will give you all the support and encouragement that I can. I will fund your studies as and when required."

"I can't let you just pay for me to do a PhD Danny!"

"Why not? I don't know what type of funding a doctorate entails in this country but I'm certain that it's not prohibitively expensive given that I've got more money than I know what to do with. Please understand Sarah. I not only love you I am also proud of you. I am proud of your brilliant mind and incisive intelligence. I want it to shine. What's the point of me having all this money if I can't use it for something I love and believe in? Don't feel guilty about it because you'll earn every penny. You're the most remarkable woman I ever met Sarah. I want you to be as brilliant as you can be."

"I... I don't know what to say."

"Well how about "do you need any help with the dishes?". If we're going to meet Nicole we'd better get our act together."

37

Sarah looked at her with a mischievous grin. She stood and walked around the table. "The dishes can wait. We've got other domestic chores to attend to."

"Such as?"

Sarah bent over her and unfastened her sarong. "This."

Chapter Five

Later they drove over to Alpli. They had the Ferrari's hood down and Daniela was looking happy and humming to herself; her face flushed a becoming pink. Sarah was watching her in fascination, still astonished at this new found ability to so please and delight her lover. She'd always felt somewhat subservient to Daniela's undoubtedly greater experience. It was thrilling to discover that Daniela became so malleable and adorably helpless under her caresses. It took but a few touches to make her whimper with mounting arousal and the slightest tease to make her moan in frustration and become frantic in her desire for satisfaction. Sarah had never experienced the feeling of being in control of a partner's pleasure before; never felt that her touch could so electrify a person's libido or cause them to virtually lose control of their senses. Sarah found she liked it very much indeed. Daniela was a walking sensual bomb and Sarah was finding, to her delight, that she held the matches to the fuses.

Experimentally she reached over and stroked a hand along Daniela's leg below the hem of her dress. Daniela jabbed the brakes hard and pulled the car to a halt. Sarah squeaked, thrown forward by the sudden deceleration. "Eek! What are you doing?"

Daniela took a deep breath. "Sweetheart, darling, if you keep doing that then we're either going to have an accident or I'm going to have to pull this car over into a quiet forestry road and tear all your clothes off. Either way we'll be late to meet Nicole. Now if we're going to make this rendezvous without embarrassing excuses I would advise a little restraint. I'm somewhat volatile at the moment so stop teasing me."

Sarah giggled and slid her hand to the inside of Daniela's thigh. "What? You mean like this?" Daniela shuddered and grasped Sarah about the shoulders to lean across and bury her face in her neck. Sarah gave her a little slap. "Behave yourself Danny. I think there's a tractor coming up behind us!"

"Bitch!" Daniela disengaged herself breathing heavily and restarted the car. "You're driving me crazy."

Nicole was sat in the tiny front garden of the house as they pulled up. She was looking quite serious and she was a little awkward as Sarah kissed her as if she didn't know how to react to Sarah and Daniela now that they had become lovers. Daniela was sweet to her but Sarah could feel her discomfort. She seemed unusually shy and reserved although she said nothing discourteous and she politely offered them drinks. Sarah felt odd, as if she'd become a stranger in her own home. Nicole was friendly but her habitual extrovert exuberance had deserted her. The most awkward moment was when Sarah went upstairs to collect her bags. It felt like a separation as if she was moving out for good. Nicole looked suddenly sad and vulnerable. They lingered until it was nearly time for Nicole to go back to work when Sarah kissed her and promised to phone her from the Ticino. Nicole nodded glumly and they took their leave; the shining day now ruined with sadness. Sarah was quiet all the way back to Oberdorf and she blinked back tears. Daniela did not disturb her melancholic revelry other than to reach out and touch her hand consolingly on occasion.

Back at Daniela's house Sarah slumped down into a chair in the garden disconsolately. Daniela took a seat by her side and took her hands. "That was rough huh honey?"

"Yes... yes it was. Poor Nicky. I feel awful."

"Perhaps it would have been better if you'd never met me Sarah."

"Don't say that."

"But perhaps it's true Sarah. Then Nicky would have never lost you."

"She would have lost me anyway Danny. She would have lost me to Alan or whoever. If I'd never met you I'd have never found out how Nicky felt about me. It was only after she discovered that I could love another woman that she was able to declare her feelings. It's not your fault Danny. It's nobody's fault really. It's just one of those things."

Daniela was quiet for a few seconds as if trying to find the correct words. "I'm not a jealous person Sarah." she said at last.

Sarah squeezed her hand. "I know you're not Danny. God anybody else would have been furious with me because I told them that I was marrying somebody else. I can't believe how patient you've been with me. I know you're not jealous of Nicky."

"Could you both love me and Nicky Sarah?"

"*What!*"

"I mean could you take both of us? It might be an option you know."

"Are you crazy? I don't believe I'm hearing this! You're not seriously suggesting that I have *two* girlfriends are you?"

"I'm suggesting nothing. You were the one that said she was keeping her options open."

"That's loopy Danny. I couldn't have two girls at the same time. How could that possibly work? What would I do? Allocate different days of the week to different girlfriends? Keep Nicky on the side for when you're away. I couldn't be unfaithful like that."

"I could handle another woman in the relationship Sarah. It could be a solution you know."

"It's nonsense Danny. It would be cheating."

"Who said anything about cheating? Why would you need different days of the week? That bed of mine is pretty big; easy room for three I would have thought."

Sarah stared at her. "You're taking the piss."

"I'm just floating ideas about Sarah. I'm just letting you know that there needn't be this sadness between you

41

and Nicole that's all. I like Nicole a lot and you love her so, she'd always be welcome in our house or, if it came to that, our bed Sarah. I just don't want you to think that Nicole would be lost from you just because you decided to be my girl. If you could love her too then so could I."

"You're serious aren't you?"

"Yes. Too serious. Far too serious." Daniela grinned and stood up. "It's time we lightened up." She held out a hand. "Come with me."

Sarah stood up uncertainly. "Where are we going?"

"Well to the bathroom to begin with where I shall divest you of every last item of clothing. After that I'm going to soap you down all over and just for fun I'm going to shave off all your pubic hairs. Following that I'm going to massage you all over with aromatic body oils seeking out every last crevice I can find. After *that* I'm going to drag you into the bedroom where I shall proceed to torment you with my hands and tongue until you beg for mercy. Any questions so far?"

"Er no. It all seems perfectly clear till now."

"Right! Come along then."

"Yes ma-am."

Chapter Six

The weather was changeable. The pleasant sunshine and fluffy clouds of the previous day had given way to grey skies and drizzle by the morning, as Sarah and Daniela sat down for breakfast. The gloomy day seemed perfectly appropriate to the mood in Daniela's kitchen, for there was little gaiety in the atmosphere and conversation was strained and subdued. Sarah was already dressed for travelling. She wore a pale blue grey suit of short skirt and jacket she had bought in Winterthur over an expensive frilled blouse that Daniela had given her; her legs were clad in fine stockings and she wore matching high heeled shoes on her feet. It was not her own choice for travelling clothes. In the normal run of things she would have donned an old pair of jeans and a shirt for a day on the Swiss railway system but Daniela had put her foot down and refused to allow her out of the house dressed like that. "You're going to see your parents." she'd insisted. "You can't just turn up looking like a tramp. I want you to look pretty and smart for them."

Sarah had been amused by Daniela's concern. "Oh yes!" she'd noted ironically, "I mean whatever would they think of my girlfriend if she let me leave the house not looking my best?"

"Exactly." Daniela had stated firmly, not in the least put out by Sarah's heavy sarcasm. "Now let's find a ribbon for your hair." Sarah had submitted to Daniela's ministrations patiently and a little touched by her obvious pride in her. When she had regarded the end result in the mirror she had realised that, once more, Daniela was subtly manipulating her. The image in the mirror had been smart, attractive and very grown up. Sarah looked like the very epitome of a mature self-confident woman who knew her own mind. Sarah knew that her parents would view her with surprise. Their little girl had grown into a woman. She was power dressed; cool and self-composed. Daniela didn't want her to turn up in the Ticino looking like a meek subservient daughter at her parent's command. She wanted Sarah to point out in no uncertain terms that she was there as an adult and equal. She wasn't there to do as she was told. She was there to negotiate.

Nevertheless Sarah was pleased at her appearance and it was true that she felt more confident dressed thus although she was a little worried about the practicalities of her dress. She doubted that she had ever tried to jump in and out of railway trains in high heels before. Daniela had attended to her make up as well and even painted her nails. Sarah felt strangely uncomfortable sitting down for breakfast so well dressed but they were on a schedule today. "It's just gone nine Sarah." Daniela pointed out. "What time is your train?"

"Oh we've plenty of time. My train leaves Nesslau at ten past eleven."

Daniela raised her eyebrows. "Nesslau? I thought you'd be catching the train in Buchs."

Sarah shook her head. "No. Oh I could go that way but there's no train connection over the St Bernardino pass and so I'd have to change in Chur and take the bus over the pass to Bellinzona. It's hardly any quicker and the bus is a bit of a pain. It's easier to go from Nesslau."

"Do you have to change?"

"Yes. I take the local train just to Wattwil and then I change to the Inter-Regio to Arth-Goldau. From there I take the Inter-City through the Gotthard tunnel to Bellinzona."

"I thought your parents lived in Ascona."

"Near to Ascona. Somebody's supposed to be picking me up in Bellinzona."

"How long is the journey?"

"A shade under three and a quarter hours. If all goes well my train is due in at two twenty three."

"Will you have time to make your connections?"

"Oh yes. I've only got four minutes in Arth-Goldau but the train pulls up on the adjoining platform and the Inter-City won't leave until it makes the connection. This is Switzerland Danny. They have railway schedules down to a precise science."

Daniela looked out of the window moodily. "It's not a nice day for travelling."

"It'll be fine once I reach Airolo Danny."

"Airolo?"

"It's the station on the far side of the Gotthard railway tunnel Danny. Once you're through the tunnel you're on the south side of the Alps and the climate changes dramatically. It's one of the most extreme climatic divides you'll find in Europe. It can be blowing blizzards and arctic conditions at Goschenen on this side of the mountains then you go into the tunnel and emerge fifteen kilometres later in blazing hot sunshine and Mediterranean climate on the south side. I checked out the weather on Google after I showered. They're predicting thirty five degrees in Locarno today."

"Jesus!"

Sarah lowered her head sadly. "It'll still feel colder and gloomier in the south though."

Daniela took her hand across the table. "It'll be all right Sarah. Things will work out just fine."

"I'm scared Danny."

"Keep it together Sarah. It'll be fine. You'll see."

Sarah lifted her head. "Look Danny I know we're ahead of schedule, but would you mind if we got going right now? Every minute I stay in your house is breaking my heart. I... I need to be on my way. I need to get this done with. Can we go?"

"Of course sweetheart. I'll just throw the dishes in the sink and deal with them when I get back. We can leave straight away. If we're too early we can have a coffee in Nesslau."

"Do you need to change?" Daniela was dressed in a pair of designer blue jeans, carefully faded, and a plain white blouse.

Daniela shook her head. "I'm only driving you to the station honey. I'm not meeting your parents. Give me a minute to pull some shoes on and we can get going."

Daniela rushed out to find shoes while Sarah bent to stroke the cats and say goodbye. She was becoming fond of them especially the scruffy little tortoiseshell female Daniela called Stevie who was affectionate and had taken a liking to Sarah; jumping up on her lap whenever she sat down. Sarah smiled at a thought Daniela's words invoked in her mind. She pictured the absurd scene of introducing Daniela to her parents. "Mum, Dad, I'd like you to meet my girlfriend...." The vision was richly ludicrous.

They somehow squeezed Sarah's bags into the Ferrari which was not an automobile particularly designed for the conveyance of luggage. "How the hell do you manage it when you're touring?" asked Sarah.

"Oh my stage costumes and wardrobe travels in the tour coach Sarah if we're going by road. I normally only carry an overnight bag in the car or I go on the coach as well."

"Well a sharp set of wheels this may be but it's not the most practical is it?"

"You're right. We need another car."

"Sorry?"

"Get in Sarah. Let's get this show on the road."

Sarah glanced back at Daniela's house nestled in its secluded glade and her heart skipped a beat. "Yes. Let's go."

In the end, Daniela drove Sarah to Wattwil which was only another ten to fifteen kilometres or thereabouts from Nesslau and avoided Sarah having to change trains. It was a fairly ugly little town of just over eight thousand inhabitants and the largest municipality in the Lower Toggenburg. It was hardly improved by the weather which was damp and miserable and Sarah's depression mounted as they found a seat in the station buffet for a coffee. Daniela ordered for them as Sarah went to purchase her ticket.

Sarah queued at the ticket office window as a little old lady in front of her plied the patient young gentleman behind the window with seemingly endless inquiries about her connections. She was apparently visiting her grandchildren in Rapperswill which was hardly a monumentally taxing journey but Sarah supposed that it was quite an adventurous day out for the lady. Eventually Sarah found herself at the window. She held out her abonnement. It was a vitally important document. For one hundred and fifty francs a year it gave her unlimited half price travel on nearly every rail service or bus service in Switzerland as well as most mountain railways, cable cars and even ships on the lakes. It saved her a small fortune in travel expenses over the year. "Eine halbes nach Bellinzona bitte schon." She requested politely.

"Einfach oder retour?" the ticket dispenser asked her. It was a damn good question; single or return.

Sarah bit her lip. "Er retour bitte."

The young man produced her ticket from the machine and smiled at her. "Bitte schon Fraulein. Eine gute Reise."

"Er Danke, danke viel mals." Sarah took the ticket feeling flustered and slipped it inside her abonnement. In the buffet Daniela was trying to look inconspicuous. It wasn't working. Several people were staring at her. She didn't look too displeased with herself however. Sarah blinked and pointed at an object on the table accusingly. "What is that?"

Daniela shrugged and looked at the wine bucket. "Moet and Chandon Brut Imperial it would seem. It was the best champagne this God forsaken dump had to offer."

"Have you taken leave of your senses? It's only a quarter past ten in the morning. I asked for a coffee."

"Don't scold me Sarah. I just wanted to toast you on your way with something a little more emphatic than railway buffet coffee which tastes like river estuary sediment."

"You have to drive back to Oberdorf I'd like to point out."

"So I'll just have a token glass."

"Oh brilliant! So I have to finish the rest of the bottle on my own I suppose."

"What's the problem? You've got all the way to Bellinzona to sleep it off."

Sarah took a seat exasperatedly. "If I fall asleep on the train and wake up in Milan my arse is toast."

Daniela grinned. "You worry too much. Come on we can have a last drink together. Did you get your ticket?"

"Yes."

"Let me see it."

"What?"

"I said let me see your ticket."

Puzzled Sarah pulled her ticket out and handed it to Daniela. "Why do you want to see my ticket?"

Daniela looked at it and an odd expression drifted across her face. "You bought a *return* ticket Sarah."

"Well... well yes of course. It's an open ended return."

Daniela frowned. "It's not good enough though."

"What are you talking about?"

Daniela stood suddenly and grasped the ticket. "Pour the champagne Sarah. I'll be right back."

"Where are you going?"

"Never mind."

In puzzlement Sarah poured two glasses of champagne. Daniela returned within a couple of minutes looking satisfied with herself. She handed the ticket to Sarah. "There. That's better."

"What have you done?"

"I've upgraded your ticket to first class."

"*First class*! What the hell have you done that for? I *never* travel first class."

"Well you are doing today. It's going to be crowded on that train and I'm not having *my* girl roughing it with the riff raff in steerage. You can travel in style today."

"That's an unnecessary extravagance Danny."

"Why? Can't we afford it?"

Sarah snorted exasperatedly. "You drive me nuts sometimes."

Daniela lifted her glass. "Shut up Sarah and let's drink a toast... to us."

Sarah was quite tiddly by the time they carried her bags out onto the platform. She had drunk most of the champagne herself. Daniela had been amused, telling her that she didn't have to try and drink it all. It was perfectly acceptable to leave some of it but that had offended Sarah's habitual frugality. Having paid so much for a bottle of champagne it seemed criminal to waste any of it. On the platform however she felt sober; sober and sad. There was still a good five minutes before her train was due to depart. It promised to be a heart rending five minutes. Daniela flung her arms about her and clung to her fiercely burying her face against Sarah's neck. At one time Sarah would have felt uncomfortable with such a public display of affection but today she didn't care and she grasped Daniela tightly to her ignoring the inquisitive stares from the other passengers on the platform. With a shock she felt the dampness of Daniela's face against her. Daniela was crying piteously. She had only seen her cry once before.

"Danny! You're crying. Stop it honey."

"I can't help it Sarah. Oh Sarah I love you so much. Please, please come back to me. I can't bear to let you go."

"Hush darling. I'm coming back I promise. I... I don't know what's going to happen down there Danny but I will come back. I just don't know when."

"I'm scared Sarah. I'm scared of losing you."

Sarah raised her face with her fingers under her chin and looked into her eyes. "Don't be frightened Danny. I've found you now. I'm not going to let go of you so easily. I may come back in bits. I may come back with my tail between my legs but I will come back." Sarah reached into her handbag. "I have something for you sweetheart. It's a present. I was going to give you it last night but I decided to wait until today so I could leave you with something to let you know that I'm thinking about you." Sarah pulled out a small box. "I bought this in Winterthur because it made me think of you when I saw it."

Daniela opened the little box carefully and peered inside. It was the little Edelweiss pendant on its chain with the cluster of little diamonds around the central sapphire. Daniela clutched at her breast. "Oh Sarah! It's beautiful. It's too much though. This must have cost you a lot of money. I can't take it."

Sarah grinned mischievously. "Why? Because we can't afford it?"

"It's a lot of money for you Sarah. You shouldn't spend so much on me."

"Perhaps you're right. I'll just take it back to the shop and demand my money back. If they ask why I'll tell them it's because the woman I love most in the world refused to accept a tiny little token from me to tell her how much I love her."

"Oh Sarah I..."

Sarah took the box from Daniela. "Just shut up and hold your hair up so I can hang it around your neck."

Daniela obeyed meekly and Sarah fastened the clasp behind her neck and straightened the pendant to hang on Daniela's breast. She lifted the pendant and kissed it and then transferred her lips to Daniela's, possessing them long and ardently. The urgings of the station master were becoming more insistent and Daniela broke their embrace, breathing heavily. "Your train's about to leave sweetheart. You have to get aboard."

"Yes damn it! God I hate goodbyes."

"Please come back Sarah."

"As quickly as I can. I love you."

"I love you too. Now get aboard."

Sarah hefted her bags aboard the train and stood in the doorway. There were a few torrid seconds when they were parted by just two feet and unable to cross the tiny gap before the station master blew his whistle and the doors clattered shut with a hiss of compressed air. The train lurched and began to move. Sarah blew her a kiss and waved. Daniela returned the gesture and, as the train pulled away, Sarah's last sight of her, through her own tears, was of a small forlorn figure staring desperately after the train and clutching the pendant at her throat. Then she was lost to sight.

Chapter Seven

It took a minute short of an hour and a quarter for the train to journey to Arth-Goldau. It seemed interminable. Sarah normally loved train journeys but she wasn't enjoying this one. She was desperately homesick within the first few kilometres and every one that she travelled took her further from Daniela. She cried the whole way and she was thankful that it was quiet in her carriage. She had never felt so wretched. The journey passed in a daze of desolation.

She had to change in Arth-Goldau. A less resolute spirit than Sarah's may well have broken under the strain and abandoned her journey here; jumping on the first return connection to Wattwil and fleeing back to her love. But Sarah was made of sterner stuff. Resolution, such as it was, awaited her in Ticino. Whatever must happen, she had to face it. Anything else was a coward's escape.

But it was hard for her and harder still that the municipality of Arth-Goldau held special happy memories for her. She had a fondness for this little town that went back to her childhood. It was a curious place split between the community of Arth on the southern shores of Lake Zug and the twin community of Goldau that perched at a slightly higher elevation on a curious mound of over grown boulders and detritus. It was a town with a tragic history. In 1806 the side of the mountain above Goldau, the Rossberg, had collapsed after days of heavy rain and the resultant landslide had all but obliterated Goldau and surrounding villages dumping 120 million cubic metres of rock on the community and burying it in places up to seventy metres deep. Four hundred and fifty seven people had lost their lives in the cataclysm.

Tragedy notwithstanding Sarah's memories of the town were happier ones. It was a pretty place and its location between Lake Zug and the nature reserves that included the Lauerzersee and the valley before Schywz was attractive. But it was another feature for which Sarah loved the place. Founded and built on top of the great landslide was what Sarah considered to be the most beautiful and charming zoo in Switzerland. The Arth-Goldau Tierpark perhaps did not have the fame or international renown of Basel zoo and, since its collection was largely confined to European wildlife, it did not boast the exotic and more glamorous exhibits of that establishment. But it was a beautiful park of landscaped natural coniferous forest that had grown on top of the rubble of the collapsed mountainside containing, within it, some ponds for wildfowl and where many of the animals were allowed to roam free within the enclosed park. Sarah had fond memories of the zoo for her parents had taken her there as a small girl and she had bought little bags of animal feed at a kiosk and fed the deer, mouflon, chamois and little baby wild boars. They had very nearly had to drag her away. Sarah had loved the place ever since. Even as a teenager she had often returned to wander around the park or sit in the shade of the woods to feed the squirrels. It was the sort of place she would love to take Daniela to.

If she now had problems with her family it did not detract from her happy memories. It was worth remembering at this moment, when she was heading for conflict with her parents, that she had them to thank for one of the greatest gifts she could have been granted; a truly golden childhood. That was a blessing beyond calculation. Sarah had grown up in a loving, protecting family in beautiful surroundings and with never a day's need in her life. Her childhood had been simply one long great adventure of discovery and wonder. It almost seemed a betrayal now to oppose her parent's wishes. She had never been the rebellious sort. She had her parents to thank for the person she had become. She must never forget that.

With these confused notions in her head Sarah boarded the Inter-city train for the Gotthard tunnel and the south. The train was crowded for there were numerous Italian people aboard; presumably going home for the weekend for the train's final destination was Milan. There were over five hundred thousand Italian people living in Switzerland, a sizeable percentage of the entire population, and this figure did not include the Italian speaking native population of the Ticino who were, of course, full Swiss nationals. It seemed a goodly number of them were on their way to their homeland to visit their relatives this day for Swiss natives seemed heavily outnumbered on the train. Sarah found a seat at last and managed to stow her luggage in the overhead racks with difficulty.

She had no sooner taken her place next to a large middle aged Italian lady than the ticket inspector arrived in her carriage asking for tickets and abonnements for all passengers joining the train at Arth-Goldau. Distractedly Sarah pulled out her ticket and abonnement and handed it to the inspector. He looked at it and blinked with surprise before shaking his head officiously. "You're in the wrong compartment Fraulein. First class is three carriages up just past the restaurant car."

Sarah clasped a hand to her mouth and blushed scarlet. She had completely forgotten that she was travelling on a first class ticket. "Oh! Oh I'm sorry." she mumbled in confusion. "I... I'll change at once."

Bizarrely the inspector was regarding her sternly as if he had caught her in some major misdemeanour. "Just after the restaurant car." He repeated, for all the world as if he was about to add "I'll overlook it this time but don't let it happen again."

Blushing with humiliation Sarah retrieved her bags from the rack feeling that everyone in the carriage was staring at her. She struggled off along the crowded gangway in the lurching train with her tail between her legs. It was sheer purgatory battling her way through the restaurant car for they were serving the midday meal and it was packed but eventually she found the first class carriages and sank thankfully into a comfortable seat. There were only three other people in the entire carriage. Sarah felt quite alien in the exclusive domain. A middle aged business man looked up from his financial paper to regard her for a second and, to Sarah's fevered imagination, he seemed to be wondering what on earth the world was coming to; they were letting any old riff raff in here nowadays. Sarah felt like poking her tongue out at him and saying "My girlfriend's the most famous rock and roll singer in Switzerland. Who the fuck do you think *you* are?" He rustled his paper and returned to peruse its pages determinedly and Sarah turned to look out of the window. She pondered what Daniela would say when she told her that she'd been unceremoniously thrown out of second class. Daniela would be highly amused. Sarah could hear her clear ringing laughter in her mind.

The train was approaching Schwyz and it was another place full of memories for Sarah. As a teenager she had once spent a holiday skiing in the nearby resort of Stoos. She had gone with Nicole and a couple of friends from school and they'd stayed in a youth hostel in the resort. It was a lovely ski village set at 1,300 metres above sea level and only reachable by cable car or the funicular railway. The gentleman who had run the hostel was a grand old character who took a liberal view when it came to serving the under aged girls beer and they'd adored him. It had been a merry holiday.

Schwyz itself was an austere although not unattractive small town. It was very consciously proud of its own history for it was the capital of the eponymous Canton of Schwyz and it gave its name and its flag to the entire country for it was the leading canton that had formed the original federation of Switzerland together with Uri, Obwalden and Nidwalden. The original charter of 1291 could still be seen in the town's museum. This was the very heart of Switzerland. She had visited the town with her father when she'd been about eleven years old and he'd had some business to conduct there. To the east the skyline was dominated by two tooth like mountains; the Grosse Mythen and the Kleine Mythen. She'd climbed the larger of the two with her father but found it rather dull for it was little more than a tourist trail to the top and highly modified to make the route as easy as possible for day trippers. She had one precious souvenir of that visit though for her father had bought her an elaborate Swiss army knife in Schwyz that had been manufactured at the Victorinox factory in the nearby village of Ibach. It had innumerable functions on it and Sarah never went for a day's hiking in the mountains without it. It was still one of her most treasured possessions.

They'd also found time to visit the little town of Brunnen on the shores of Lake Luzern just a few kilometres away and Sarah had fed the ducks in the harbour. There had been a couple of very pretty ducks that Sarah had never seen before, even on her forays to Lake Constance. She'd had to look them up because they weren't featured in any of her bird guides. They'd turned out to be an American species called a Wood Duck or sometimes a Carolina Duck. These highly attractive ducks were popular in wildfowl collections and often escaped. Sarah had learned later that the Wood Ducks at Brunnen actually bred occasionally along the stream that led to the lake at Brunnen and it was possible that they might, some day, establish a self-sustaining colony and become naturalised Swiss citizens.

Beyond Schwyz and Brunnen, the railway line hugged the shores of Lake Luzern and came at last, on its southern point, to the large village of Altdorf. It was another iconic name in Swiss history for here, legend had it, Wilhelm Tell had shot the apple from his son's head in the market place in 1307 and sparked the rebellion that led to the formation of the Swiss

Confederation. How much was true and how much fiction nobody knew but it was deeply entwined into Swiss mythology.

Lost in thoughts and memories Sarah watched the world pass the train window until, at last, they were climbing high into the mountains and the dividing watershed that separated the cool temperate climates of the north from the sultry warmth of the Mediterranean lands to the south. The Gotthard railway was one of the great engineering wonders of Switzerland. Sarah had travelled it with her father on more than one occasion and he had a liking for technical details and a willingness to share them with his impressionable daughter. Apparently there were some one thousand, two hundred and thirty four bridges along the line and its branches and something like seventy tunnels. At Altdorf on Lake Luzern the railway line climbed from 447 metres above sea level to the highest point of 1,151 metres inside the main 15 kilometre long Gotthard tunnel which had been the longest railway tunnel in the world at its opening. The track achieved this climb through a series of spiral loops cut into tunnels and these had long fascinated Sarah. You would look out of the train window at a view before being plunged into darkness as the train entered a tunnel. After some considerable distance you would emerge from the tunnel to see, to your surprise, the same view as before only now from higher up as the train looped back on itself as it climbed in altitude. Finally, at Goschenen, the train entered the Gotthard tunnel.

Sarah shivered as the train plunged into this long tunnel. She disliked long tunnels and this one was a beauty. The train spent between seven and eight minutes to traverse this tunnel but it felt longer as the dreary passage underground afforded nothing more than the sight of the walls of the tunnel flashing past, illuminated by the train's interior lighting. It was a journey of gloom and tragedy as Sarah knew well. It had taken ten years from 1871 to 1881 to build this tunnel and the lives of many of its builders. Over two hundred workers had died during construction mostly from floods within the tunnel or from accidents with the compressed air trains used to carry out excavated material from the tunnel. Even the engineer who had masterminded the project, Louis Favre, died of a heart attack inside the tunnel in 1879. There had even been murder in the tunnel for, in 1875, the Swiss army had been called out to quell a strike of workers in the tunnel and four workers had been killed by the soldiers. The tunnel lay beneath the Gotthard massif both as a triumph of human endeavour and as a monument to the tragedy of the human condition.

It was a relief to Sarah, therefore, when the train, in a sudden concussion of light, plunged out of the tunnel at Airolo. Beyond Airolo the train once more curved back on itself in tortuous convolutions as it sought to lose the altitude it had gained under the now brilliant blue sky of the south. Even inside the air-conditioned first class carriage the temperature rose noticeably. The sun blazed down on a mountain landscape different again from the lands to the north. Everything seemed different. Now all the houses were constructed of grey granite and little villages perched in impossible places high on the mountainsides clustered tightly around the grey stone churches. The vegetation changed subtly as the train descended down into the Ticino valley and there were palms planted in the villages. It didn't feel like Switzerland anymore. The whole canton was virtually surrounded by Italy and this was reflected in its architecture and culture. Sarah had once heard someone say that the canton was Italy only cleaner and where the trains ran on time. This was the most southerly canton of Switzerland; its most Mediterranean enclave; Italian speaking and steeped in the culture of the Mediterranean. This then was the place to which Sarah had come to face her doom. This was the Ticino

Chapter Eight

Sarah stepped out of the train onto the platform at Bellinzona and it was like stepping into an oven. It was baking hot on the station platform and the blue-grey suit which had seemed very smart and attractive back in the Toggenburg now promised to be a liability in the searing heat. Sarah ran a finger around the collar of her blouse and expelled air in a long "whew!" She was perspiring already. The train was pulling out of the station and the passengers, who had descended from it, were beginning to disperse. Sarah stood bemused for a moment because she was not at all sure who was supposed to be collecting her or where.

"Sarah?" the voice was uncertain and inquiring but Sarah would have known it anywhere.

Sarah span around. Her sister was standing ten metres away looking as if she could scarcely credit the evidence of her own eyes. "Hi Jess!" said Sarah with delight. She loved her sister.

Jessica blinked and pursed her lips. "Good God! It *is* you Sarah. I didn't recognise you."

Sarah blushed suddenly aware of her attire. Over the past weeks she had become so used to dressing in a feminine and grown-up fashion, due to Daniela's continual influence, that she had forgotten that her new appearance would come as a shock to her family. She glanced down in embarrassment. "Oh er... the clothes..."

Before she could elaborate Jessica had crossed to distance between them and gathered her in her arms to kiss her warmly on both cheeks. Then she held Sarah at arm's length the better to admire her. "Let me look at you." she cried. "My God! My little sister just grew up whilst I wasn't watching. You look stunning Sarah."

"Well you haven't seen me since Christmas Jess. I... er... I've changed."

"You sure as hell have. I was looking for my kid sister in her old blue jeans and a rucksack over her shoulder and out steps this elegant young fashion model in her place." She fingered the material of Sarah's suit and blouse. "Expensive designer threads no less. Have you won the lottery or something?"

Sarah grimaced in embarrassment. "No. Dad just sent me an allowance to buy a wardrobe for my engagement Jess."

"Wow! It's more than he gave me when *I* got married."

"You eloped without parental approval Jess." Sarah pointed out.

Jessica grinned wryly. "Yeah. True enough." She wagged a finger at Sarah. "Well make sure you spend it all ruthlessly. Have no mercy and take no prisoners. Dad's rolling in the stuff at the moment and once he finalises these deals with Alan's dad then he won't know what to do with all his money, so milk him for all you can get."

Sarah winced. It was not a subject she was comfortable with. "He... he's been very generous." She volunteered hesitantly. She also cringed when she thought of the other clothes in her bags. Not only were there the fine clothes she had bought herself out of her father's budget but there were also the sizeable contributions to her wardrobe that Daniela had been providing. The night before Daniela had insisted on rummaging through her luggage and augmenting her collection with several, somewhat spectacular, additions from her own clothes and deafening her ears to Sarah's feeble protestations.

Jessica nodded. "It looks like it." She fingered the pendant around Sarah's neck. "Expensive bling too." Sarah was wearing the white gold necklace and heart shaped pendant set with a single emerald that Daniela had given her in the Gade. It didn't really match her ensemble but Sarah barely ever took it off these days.

60

She was wearing her moissanite earrings too and Jessica was fascinated by them. "Wow those are serious rocks Sarah."

"Oh er they're just moissanite Jess... not diamonds."

"Still expensive though." Jessica noted. "And as for this brooch."

Sarah started. She had forgotten about the little crescent shaped brooch that Daniela had insisted on pinning to the lapel of her jacket this very morning to complete the ensemble. It was just a piece of cheap costume jewellery Daniela had assured her. "Oh the brooch." said Sarah hastily. "That's nothing expensive."

"Bullshit! It's bloody platinum and those are real diamonds for sure. You can't tell me that someone is going to put pieces of cut glass into a platinum setting. Are you sure you don't have a sugar daddy on the side?"

No thought Sarah to herself bitterly; just a sly, duplicitous girlfriend, with more money than sense, who was going to get her arse smacked when she got back to the Toggenburg. "Oh it was er second hand." Sarah prevaricated unconvincingly.

Well ok let's get going anyway. It's bloody roasting in this station." Jessica glanced down. "Are these all the bags you've brought?"

Sarah looked at her two small cases. "Yes. Why?"

"Oh nothing, it's just that mum said you'd be absolutely loaded with luggage because you're staying the rest of the summer."

Sarah frowned. "Oh *did* she."

Jessica glanced at her shrewdly. "Well come on let's go. I've got the car outside." Jessica picked up the larger of Sarah's two bags and made for the exit. As they walked Jessica turned to Sarah. "Look Sarah do you feel like pulling off the road for a drink at some congenial grotto somewhere on the way. It's absolute pandemonium in the house at the moment with mum's preparations for tomorrow's party at full battle stations. I say we skive off somewhere for an hour or two and catch up on gossip."

"Suits me. It's too hot to be getting roped into one of mum's all hands on deck party details!"

"Great! They won't miss us for a couple of hours. I know. Let's drive up to Lavertezzo."

"Oh yes!" Sarah was thrilled. Lavertezzo was a lovely little village high up in the beautiful Valle Verzasca; one of the notably entrancing valleys in Ticino.

"Away then." Outside the station Sarah blinked in surprise for, instead of her customary rather battered old Citroen, Jessica led her to a sleek silver expensive looking BMW. Jessica winked at her. "I borrowed one of dad's cars." she explained. "I couldn't be picking up the star of the show in my clapped out old banger now could I?" It was roasting in the interior of the car so they wound all the windows down and Jessica turned on the air conditioning before leaving the car park in a hurry. Sarah gripped the sides of her seat. Jessica belonged to the Nicole school of driving; a little less chaotic perhaps but just as fast and she was obviously revelling in the rare chance to put her father's fast BMW through its paces.

Jessica was rapt in her attention to the powerful automobile and conversation lagged somewhat as they roared southward down the Ticino valley towards Locarno. It gave Sarah the chance to regard her sister closely. Jessica was a warm, tall, willowy brunette that few men would have passed without a second glance. She had more of her father's looks about her than Sarah but her character, with its feisty stubbornness and mercurial moods, was closer to her mother. This was not to say that Jessica shared her mother's devotion to female vanity, although she was not above her own indulgences in that regard. Jessica, however, was the rebel in the family and the closeness in character to her mother meant that there were often fireworks between them when the two headstrong women met head on.

Sarah had long admired her sister's insistent individualism and her refusal to compromise on her principals upon meeting the brick wall of her mother's obduracy. Jessica went her own way and always had done. She adopted a more Bohemian style of dress; tasteful but guaranteed to aggravate her mother's fixed notions of haut couture who had sometimes told her to stop trying to dress like a hippy from the nineteen sixties. It was water off a duck's back to Jessica. She had broken loose of her mother's heavy handed influence long before and she was her own woman now.

Today she was dressed in a gypsy like ensemble; her wrists were covered in bangles, there were numerous chains about her neck and huge gold earrings hanging from her ears. The cheesecloth gypsy dress she wore, in white with red trimmings, and the scarlet neck scarf and shawl she wore over her shoulders was typical of Jessica. She was flamboyant and individualistic; a woman content with the person she was; artistic of temperament and revolutionary in nature. She espoused causes continually, from Third World Poverty to global warming and she could be very vocal indeed over her favoured hobby horses. She played acoustic guitar in folk clubs, had a liking for marijuana and occasionally raised hell in public places. Sarah sometimes thought that she was Nicole's mother's spiritual sister; a pair of rebels born out of time and determined to extract the maximum amount of enjoyment and hell-raising from life. It could be said that she was the antithesis of her mother but those people of a discerning mind would have been amused by that for Jessica was very much her mother's daughter; uncannily similar in temperament and, if they clashed, then it was simply because, in some curious way, they were so alike. Jessica was the reverse mirror image of her mother.

Jessica was several years older than Sarah and it was an endearing trait of her that she doted on her baby sister. She had fought long and bitterly with their brother, for whom Jessica had little time for, but Sarah had always been her darling. She had protected her fiercely as a child and spoiled her terribly and, in any clash with their mother, Jessica was Sarah's most stringent defender. Sarah took comfort from Jessica's presence. She not only worshipped her older sister she also knew that Jessica was possibly her best ally in the confrontation that might be imminent. "So how long are you staying in Ticino?" Sarah asked her as they drove.

Jessica shrugged. "Dunno really. I don't have to be back straight away because Damien's away for the next week at a big exhibition in France. I wanted to go with him but mum cracked the whip and insisted that everybody had to be home for your big party. If it had been for any other reason I'd have told her to get stuffed but I can't miss my kid sister's engagement party can I? I might stay on for a few days. It depends how much mum gets on my nerves."

Sarah reached out and touched her hand. "I'm glad you're here Jess."

"Nervous kid?"

"Yes I suppose so."

"I'd be shitting myself personally Sarah. Mum's gone way over the top on this one. She's invited over two hundred guests to your do tomorrow. We've got a dance floor laid out in the garden, a five piece band and the sort of buffet the more decadent Roman emperors would have been proud of. The whole fucking place is getting decked out in bunting and she's even decorating the place with naff banners with crossed hearts and Alan and Sarah emblazoned across them; all stupid little cupids and love hearts. This is just the engagement party. Fuck only knows what she's got planned for the wedding day."

Sarah groaned and held her head. "Oh God! Seriously?"

"Oh hell yes! She's got caterers in, a mobile bar and the florists bill alone for all the sodding roses is going to come to a small fortune. Then there's the balloons."

"What bloody balloons?"

"Four hundred of them Sarah. There're two hundred pairs of balloons, red and white, with hearts on them and your name on one and Alan's on the other. She's going to have them all released into the sky in pairs just before sunset. That's when the band are supposed to start and you and Alan have to take to the floor to start proceedings off. The whole thing is as choreographed as a sodding royal occasion. The fireworks are scheduled for ten thirty."

"Fireworks!"

"Oh yes. Mum's blowing about ten grand in pyrotechnics just in case the world doesn't know her youngest daughter is getting married by this point."

"Oh God! This is worse than I thought."

Jessica looked sideways at her. "You look like you could do with that drink kid."

"Take me to it."

Jessica smiled ironically and a minute later they turned right off the main road to Locarno and drove along a small country road to the Verzasca valley. There was a steep climb up a narrow road with innumerable hairpin bends on it, for the Valle Verzasca was a classic hanging valley, perched high above the Ticino valley and isolated geographically by the great glacier that had carved away the deep valley below, back in the ice age. Sarah caught a glimpse of the Verzasca dam as they drove. It was a formidable great concrete wall across the narrow gorge of the valley over 220 metres in height and a great favourite for bungy jumpers and base jumpers and others of like-minded extreme adrenalin rushes. It was also famous for having been used for a stunt in the James Bond film "Goldeneye". Switzerland had been the setting for many of James Bond's more eye-catching adventures.

Beyond the dam lay the Lago di Vogorno; the reservoir created by the dam. They drove along the lake, through the small village of Vogorno until they came to Lavertezzo. Jessica parked the car by the roadside and they stepped out and looked down at the river. Lavertezzo was a remarkable place. It was a typical Ticino village of stone houses clinging to the steep slopes by the river around its lovely old Baroque church. It was the river view that made the place outstanding however. The fast, high mountain stream of the river Verzasca had carved the underlying rock into a fantastic creation of convoluted striations with gushing white water giving way to deep pools lying between angled teeth of rock. Some of the pools were prodigiously deep but the clear mountain water was so transparent that you could see the bottom everywhere and the colour of them was the lovely turquoise blue of Daniela's eyes.

Even more extraordinary was the stone footbridge that crossed the river. It was narrow and leaped the river in two high arches with its centre being supported on a large protrusion of rock emerging from the river. It was called the Ponte dei Salti which translated as the bridge of jumps. It was an understandable name for, lying beneath the bridge, was a pool of such inviting coolness and profundity of depth that it must have tempted many a person on a hot day to leap from its heights into the beckoning water below. It was a treacherous allure, Sarah knew, for the waters of the Verzasca river were icy cold and the currents unpredictably dangerous. There were warning signs everywhere to caution against the folly of succumbing to the temptations of the river's beckoning.

Sarah and Jessica's destination lay across this bridge for there was a lovely grotto beyond on the far side. It was a dizzying experience crossing over the bridge for it was high and narrow and its great high arches had only knee high parapets on each side. It was often called the "Roman bridge" locally for it had something of the aura and construction of the bridges of the old Roman empire but it was a misnomer for the bridge had been constructed in the seventeenth century. Sarah took off her high heeled shoes for the crossing and walked barefoot for the stone of the bridge was rough and she dared not trip. She peered cautiously over the edge into the pool below. She saw a pair of trout wavering in the current. They were small trout which was hardly surprising in these cold clear mountain streams which held little in the way of nutrition for any trout with ambitions to grow to any great size.

On the other side of the bridge a short sandy track led to the grotto. Jessica was walking beside Sarah chatting merrily when her younger sister suddenly thrust an arm out to arrest her progress. "Whoa Jess!"

Jessica halted in puzzlement. "What's up?" In reply Sarah pointed to the track before them. A snake was curled up on the sunny path in front. "Oh shit!" exclaimed Jessica, "A fucking snake!" She took a step backwards. She was frightened of snakes. "Is it poisonous Sarah?"

"Oh yes. It's an asp."

"Asp?"

"*Vipera aspis* Jess. It's a sort of viper closely related to an adder. You can see quite a lot of them in Ticino. You can tell the difference between them and an adder by the nose. It's more upturned on the asp than an adder."

Jessica was backing away nervously. "I don't want an in-depth field identification Sarah. I just want to know if the fucking thing's dangerous."

"Oh they're very venomous; far more so than an adder. Queen Cleopatra is reputed to have committed suicide by holding an asp to her flesh. That might be just a linguistic confusion however because "asp" is also just an old name for any venomous snake. It's unlikely that a healthy adult would die from an asp's bite and most authorities think she used an Egyptian cobra. Still an asp is highly poisonous."

"Oh great! How the hell are we going to get past the thing?"

Sarah laughed. "They're not aggressive Jess. He'll be far more frightened of you than you are of it. I'll get rid of it." Sarah picked up a large rock and dropped it heavily to the ground. The snake stirred and slithered slowly off the path. "Normally I just stamp to shift them." Sarah explained. "It's the vibration in the ground that scares them off. Trouble is that I don't have my shoes on and this path is stony."

Jessica looked cautiously over Sarah's shoulder. "Is it gone now?"

"Oh yes he'll be far away by now. They're not dangerous unless you're dumb enough to try and pick one up or if you stand on one."

"Jesus you mean we could have walked on and just trod on that thing. I'd never have seen it. It was so well camouflaged. You might have saved my life."

Sarah laughed. "For God's sake Jess! Don't be such a drama queen. It was only a bloody snake."

"You scare me sometimes kid."

"Let's get that drink." The grotto was a few metres further along. The word grotto implies a cave or subterranean cavern in most parts of the world but it had evolved into a somewhat different meaning in Ticino. In times before the invention of refrigeration it had been the habit of the inhabitants of the Ticino to store their perishable foods, salamis, cheeses and wines in small caves or under shaded outcrops of rocks they called grottos. These were often artificial in construction with rough granite posts hammered into the ground supporting rock beams and rough wooden trellises which were often intertwined with growing vines to provide shade and cool the space beneath. Naturally such places became focal meeting points as people invited their friends into their grottos to eat good cheese and drink wine. Thus the name had evolved and in the Ticino now it was given to a characteristic type of rustic restaurant with a small, shaded, stone built garden for its guests. The example to which Sarah and Jessica came was typical. The tables and benches were all made of rough granite and there were vines supported by stone pillars shading the garden from the heat of the midday sun. You could even reach up whilst enjoying your drink and pluck a handful of grapes from the vines overhead and it was blessedly cool in the welcome shade.

"What are you drinking Sarah?" asked Jessica as they seated themselves on a stone bench.

Sarah pondered. In the searing heat out of the grotto her thoughts had been fixed on something cold and refreshing but now, in the comforting shade, she wanted to drink something that had long been her favourite in Ticino. "I'll have a boccalino please."

"I think I'll have the same."

"Steady on! You're driving."

Jessica shrugged. "I'll just have the one or maybe I'll just phone dad up and tell him that Sarah's got me pissed and can he come and pick us up."

"Oh thanks Jess!"

"He'd do it Sarah. You're the golden girl at the moment; daddy's little gosling about to lay the golden egg. You could get arrested for public indecency at the moment and all he'd do is grumble a bit while paying the bail."

"Bit difficult to get arrested for public indecency in Ticino Jess! I mean when was the last time you saw anybody bother to wear a bikini while sunbathing up the Valle Maggia?"

"Ah here's the waiter." Jessica lifted a hand to catch his attention.

The man drifted over wiping his hands on his apron. "Si Senora?"

"Due boccalino di merlot per favori."

"Si Senora. Prego."

69

He disappeared into the dingy interior of the restaurant. Jessica sighed. "He called me Senora." She lifted her left hand up ruefully. "They've got eyes like laser beams when it comes to spotting a wedding ring around here."

"You could always take it off if you've got a mind to flirt with the local talent!"

Jessica grinned. "Nah! It's a part of me now. I'm a happily married woman. How the hell did that happen?"

"You were pretty insistent about it as I recall."

Jessica shrugged. "Oh I've no regrets Sarah. I married a good man and it's worked out pretty well."

"Why no children yet though Jess?"

"It isn't for want of trying believe me. In fact we've got an appointment with the quack next month to see if there's some problem there."

"Oh I hope there's nothing wrong."

"Well we might be over dramatising. It's only really this last year we've been trying to have a baby. We weren't ready for one before that. There's no need to panic yet. A year's nothing."

"I think you'll be a fine mother."

"I think that's something you never really know until you're lumbered with the job. Anyway that's enough about *my* marriage. Let's talk about yours."

"Do we have to Jess? Oh look here come our drinks." The waiter carried two mugs out on a tray and deposited them on the table. Sarah looked at them with pleasure. They were absolutely characteristic of Ticino. They were glazed earthenware jugs, for all the world like rather rustic milk jugs, with a handle and a spout, and they were full of rich dark red merlot wine. They were called boccalinos and they were the traditional drinking vessels for wine in the Ticino. The first time Sarah had encountered one she had assumed it was a carafe and she'd waited ten minutes for the waiter to bring her a glass to pour the wine into before realising she was supposed to drink straight from the jug. Many of them were decorated with paintings or reliefs of bunches of grapes but this was a classic simple design in plain white but with a double band of dark blue and maroon around it; the colours of the Ticino's cantonal flag.

Jessica picked her drink up. "Ok Sarah, here's to a happy marriage and a long prosperous future."

"To the future Jess." They clunked the thick jugs together and sipped at the wine. It was rich and strong and Sarah knew she'd probably regret this later. She'd sobered up somewhat from Daniela's disgracefully early champagne but hot weather and strong red wine was a fearsome combination.

Jessica put her mug down and grinned at Sarah. "So sweetheart. Big day tomorrow huh. My God it seems like only yesterday you were running around with your hair in a ponytail and now here you are a grown woman and on the verge of getting married. Where did the years go?"

"I don't know Jess."

"Well it all kicks off tomorrow Sarah; a wedding to plan; a whole new life to plot out. You're marrying into a rich family and a handsome man. This is a big time for you. Everything's going your way. So what the fuck is the matter?"

Sarah started. "What do you mean?"

"Come on Sarah! This is Jess here; your big sister who's known you since you dribbled food down your chin. Here you are, a day before your big engagement party, about to see your boyfriend after an absence of some months and on the brink of having a fucking great rock slid onto your ring finger. You should be happy and excited. Instead you've got a face like a condemned criminal. You've been looking bloody miserable ever since I picked you up in Bellinzona. So what the hell is the matter?"

Sarah lowered her head. "I... I don't want to get married Jess."

"Oh shit!"

"I'm not ready for it Jess. I can't do it."

"Oh hell Sarah! Listen is this something you've thought through or is this just last minute nerves?"

"I've thought about it for a long time now Jess. This isn't my party tomorrow Jess. It's mum and dad's party! It's their party to marry me off into Alan's family. This is an arranged marriage Jess; a nice cosy little business deal with me as the icing on the cake. Nobody's actually asked me if I *want* to get married. Alan hasn't even proposed to me."

"You mean he hasn't asked you to marry him yet?"

Sarah shook her head. "No. The idea is, I suppose, that he asks me at the party tomorrow night and then we make it official. Everybody's assuming that it's a foregone conclusion. Well it *isn't* a foregone conclusion; not by a long shot."

"Oh hell Sarah! I thought at least you'd *discussed* marriage with Alan."

"No Jess. Alan has only talked about marriage with mum and dad and gained their approval to make a formal proposition. That's what all this bloody to do is about. Mum and dad are just tacitly assuming that I'll say yes and mum gets to plan the sodding marriage. She's even bought a wedding gown for me and picked my own bloody bridesmaids."

"Yes I knew that. I was furious with her. Christ how can a bride not be expected to choose her own gown and bridesmaids?"

"I'm being bullied into this marriage Jess. Nobody's had the common courtesy to ask if I actually want it. Well I don't want it Jess and I'm not going through with it."

Jessica leaned heavily on the table. "My God Sarah! What are you going to do?"

"I... I don't know."

"Do you want me to drive you back to the railway station Sarah? It's not too late to do a runner! I won't be far behind you!"

Sarah shook her head. "No I have to face up to it somehow. I'll see Alan when he gets here tomorrow and discuss it with him."

"Oh God if you turn down Alan on the night of mum's big engagement party there'll be fucking carnage. I'm going to keep my head down below the parapet when you drop that bombshell on mother dearest."

"Will you stick around Jess? I mean will you stay around for a few more days until things sort themselves out? I need you Jess. You're the only person I can turn to! I... I can't do this alone." Sarah was close to tears.

Jessica leaned over and took her hand compassionately. "I'll be there to back you up Sarah but Christ I hope you know what you're doing."

Sarah squeezed her hand and looked out from the garden through her tears. It was ironic because she loved the Ticino. The natural beauty of it and its fascinating wildlife entranced her. This was the first time she had ever visited the region without her binoculars and field guides. In other circumstances she would have been happy to be here. The Ticino had its own flora and fauna quite distinct from the parts of Switzerland she was more familiar with. She could happily spend hours exploring its beguiling valleys with their quaint villages high on the slopes above and rummage among the scrubby mountainsides for the bewildering variety of insect life that this region was so rich in. Even from where she sat Sarah could see the little wall lizards scuttling around on the rocks and a praying mantis perched in a bush. A big Camberwell Beauty, a spectacular butterfly, rare in the north, fluttered past. Daniela would love it here Sarah knew. But Daniela wasn't here. She was in the Toggenburg waiting for her. "I hope I know what I'm doing too Jess." she said at last.

Chapter Nine

Sarah's parents lived in a large villa on a broad terrace on the hillside, the Monte Verita; Mountain of Truth, overlooking the town of Ascona on the banks of Lake Maggiore. The villa was surrounded by a large garden complete with swimming pool and liberally adorned with palm trees and fig trees. It was a beautiful house set in a quiet and exclusive neighbourhood of scattered villas and the view from the garden over the great glittering lake below was breath-taking. Lago Maggiore was an enormous body of fresh water sixty eight kilometres long and some three to five kilometres wide, for the most part, forming a sinuous ribbon between the feet of the surrounding mountains of the Lepontine Alps. Only its northern tip lay in Switzerland where it was fed from the streams of the Ticino, Verzasca and Maggia valleys. The bulk of the lake lay to the south in Italy where it was the second largest lake in the country after Lake Garda. The surface of the lake was at an altitude of 193 metres above sea level but the bottom of the lake was well below sea level for it was a deep lake plunging down to a maximum 372 metres. It had a surface area of 213 square kilometres and a volume of 37 cubic kilometres. It was so big that it had a discernible influence on the local climate making the winters much milder, through its heat retention, and generally adding to the balmy Mediterranean climate of the towns along its shores. Lake Orta and Lake Lugano both drained into Lake Maggiore and numerous other streams fed the lake. Its sole outlet was the River Ticino which had its source in the eponymous southern canton of Switzerland, entered the lake near Magadino and left once more at Sesto on the southern tip after which it became a tributary of Northern Italy's River Po.

It was a spectacular body of water and Sarah paused to admire the view over it from her lofty perch in the front drive of her parent's villa as Jessica muscled her bags from the car boot. The prodigal daughter's return did not seem to have elicited much in the way of joyous welcome so far for there was nobody to be seen. "Where is everyone Jess?" Sarah asked.

"All around the back in the garden I should think. Come on let's dump your bags in the porch and go and find them."

Jessica was right. The preparations for the following day's party were well advanced. Her mother was busily setting up a cocktail bar by the side of the swimming pool with the assistance of two of the neighbours and her father was up a step ladder, being held by her brother, hanging lights in the trees. A small gang of men were erecting a stage and a raised dance floor at one end of the garden and some of Sarah's mother's friends were doing mysterious things with scissors and tape, surrounded by a small mountain of gaily coloured bunting. There were also two or three professionals from the catering company carrying large boxes into the back garden from a van parked in the drive and two large muscular men chivvying an outsized refrigerator into place.

Sarah's arrival in the midst of all this frenetic activity went unnoticed and Sarah felt downright deflated by her less than spectacular entrance. Her father saw her first and boomed "SARAH!" across the garden before descending from his perch hastily to greet her.

Her mother glanced up from her labours and saw her. "At last!" she cried and came around the swimming pool to meet her. She was dressed in only a pair of shorts and a bikini top but she looked as spectacular as ever. Sarah's mother was in her late forties but she was still a strikingly beautiful woman with a lithe well-toned body, with not an ounce of excess fat on it, and her long chestnut brown hair was almost the mirror image of her youngest daughter's.

Sarah had little time to admire her mother's looks however for her father had grasped her in a great bear hug. "Here you are at last." he cried in pleasure. "You look marvellous." He turned to his approaching wife. "Doesn't she look wonderful Alisha?"

Sarah's mother halted to look at her. "Indeed she does. She looks terrific. I don't think I've ever seen her so well dressed."

Sarah blushed "Hi Mum."

Sarah's mother's embrace was somewhat more restrained and formal. It wasn't that she wasn't pleased to see Sarah she was just less comfortable with close physical contact; a product, Sarah suspected, of her English reserve. Nevertheless her greeting was warm and she was obviously impressed by her daughter's appearance. "Well Sarah you do look fine I must say. I'm glad to see that you've made an effort over your appearance."

Sarah pulled a face. Her mother could even make a compliment sound like a rebuke. "Well I'm a bit overdressed for this weather mum. It was rotten weather in North Switzerland. I never expected it to be as hot as this."

"Well I'm sure you need to refresh after your journey so you can grab a shower and change. Do you have anything suitable? If not, I'm sure I can find you something."

Sarah bristled at the inference that she had only the one set of clothes that her mother might consider to be at all appropriate but at the same time she smiled to herself. Between her own purchases and Daniela's contributions she had a pretty stunning wardrobe in her luggage. Her mother was in for a shock.

Sarah greeted her brother John warmly. John lived only in the next canton to Sarah but she saw him rarely. Jessica and John fought quite a lot but Sarah had always

76

got along fine with her brother although she was as not close to him. He was a reserved man and very conservative; a man that kept his own counsel and was frugal with his words. There was a serious and sombre aspect to him that clashed with his elder sister's ebullience. He considered Jessica to be frivolous and shallow whilst she found him morose and boring. Both views were wrong Sarah knew and there was more to John than met the eye. Certainly his girlfriend thought so. Sarah knew his girlfriend Maria and liked her. She was a warm hearted, if extrovert, and attractive girl who quite clearly loved John dearly. John must have had some qualities to win the heart of such an eminently agreeable young woman. The only fly in the ointment was his continued hesitation to formalise his relationship with Maria by marrying her and this was a minor bone of contention within the family.

After greeting her brother, Sarah allowed her mother to take her arm and lead her aside. "Where are your things Sarah?"

"Oh we've just dumped them in the front porch for the moment mum. Am I in my usual room?"

"Well you are tonight Sarah but, tomorrow, I've given you the big guest suite." She squeezed Sarah's arm with a wink. "It's got a double bed in it."

Sarah stiffened. She hadn't expected this. Whenever Alan and she had stayed at her parents previously they had always had separate rooms for the conventions of propriety. "You... you mean I'm to share with Alan?" Sarah sounded shocked.

Her mother misinterpreted Sarah's sudden shock. "Oh it's fine Sarah. You are both adults now and practically married so I'm sure we can stretch the point a little. Just be a bit discreet around the guests tomorrow. People can be funny about that sort of thing."

Sarah felt dizzy. "I... I need to shower and change mum."

"Of course. Now have you got something nice to wear? Your father's taking us all out to dinner in Ascona tonight. It's our last chance to get together with the whole family and sit down to eat before tomorrow's party. Now I don't know where he's taking us but doubtless it will be somewhere posh so you need to look the part Sarah. If you like I'll see if I can find you something to wear."

"Mum I've got plenty of clothes thank you. I'm sure I won't disgrace you."

In her room Sarah unpacked her cases and hung up her clothes before taking a shower. Once refreshed and with her hair dry she sat down on the bed heavily wishing she was back with Daniela. It was the thought of Daniela that decided her choice of costume change. She leaped up from the bed and pulled a dress from her wardrobe. It was the lovely green and white summer dress she had worn on her first date with Daniela at the Gade. Wearing it made her feel closer to Daniela. She was suddenly terrified that she might somehow lose sight of Daniela's face in the confusion of her parent's home. She even still had the accessories she had borrowed from Nicole on the occasion of her date with Daniela. She had never got around to giving them back. She took time over her appearance, rebelliously wanting to demonstrate to her mother that she was quite capable of dressing elegantly without her help. She used the green sash about her waist and donned Nicole's jade earrings to match her emerald pendant before repainting her toenails and pulling on the high heeled sandals that had given her so much grief on the road up to Schwendi on that fateful day. She perused herself in the dressing table mirror thoughtfully. It was not quite perfect.

An object of the sideboard caught her eye. Her mother had adorned the item of furniture with a vase of fresh flowers. They were red and white roses. The whole house was full of them. The florists had been that very afternoon and there were hundreds of them all over and many more still in boxes and bouquets to decorate the garden for the party. Her mother had chosen red roses as a symbol of love and white roses because they were the flower of Yorkshire, their county of origin in England. With a grin Sarah took a single white rose from the vase and, with a clip, carefully mounted it in her hair above her left ear. She had read somewhere that if you wore a flower over your right ear it meant that you were single but over the left it meant you were spoken for. Well she *was* spoken for. She had a girlfriend. It was only a minor act of subtle defiance but it was an act of defiance nonetheless. She looked once more in the mirror. *Now* it was perfect.

She walked back downstairs and out through the back veranda French windows into the garden. Some crisis was brewing in the preparations. Apparently the generator her father had originally hired for the outside lighting and the band's sound system had proved defective and he was hastily trying to arrange for a replacement. Sarah couldn't understand why they couldn't just lay a cable to the house and take electricity from there but, apparently, there were technical problems with that solution. Her father frowned and muttered an epithet. "Thank God we don't have this sort of do often." He grumbled.

"Well you've only got a limited number of daughters to marry off." Sarah told him, trying to keep the bitterness out of her voice.

Her father put his mobile phone away and grinned ruefully. "I've only got one as pretty as you Sarah. You look lovely."

"Thank you Daddy. Where are mum and Jess?"

"In the kitchen getting drinks for everyone. I think we all need a break."

"I'll go find them. Sarah wandered off across the lawn. As she did she reached into her handbag. She had a message from Daniela on her phone. It was short. It read simply "*J love you*." Sarah smiled and paused to message back. "*J love you too. J'll call you later*."

In the kitchen her mother was hefting a pair of large glass jugs, full of iced tea. She paused to inspect Sarah's appearance though. "I don't know what's come over you Sarah." she declared. "Two nice ensembles in a single day. You'll start me thinking that you're actually turning into a lady."

"Oh I'd hate you to be under that misapprehension mum." Sarah remarked sarcastically.

"Well you look very nice Sarah."

"I er... pinched a rose for my hair from the vase in my room. I hope you don't mind."

"Good God no! It's not as if we haven't got enough. Here though it's a bit lopsided." She put down the jugs and wiped her hands. "Here let me adjust it for you." Sarah endured her mother's fussing for a minute before she was satisfied. "There that's better." She picked up the jugs once more. "You can help Jessie carry out the glasses if you want." Then she swept out into the garden.

Sarah turned to Jessica. "You haven't said anything to her have you?"

"You're joking! No I haven't said a word. We've been talking about the weather. She's worried about it."

"What's wrong with the weather? Seems ok to me."

"She's petrified that we're going to have a thunderstorm tomorrow night." It was a legitimate concern. Ticino was famous for its thunderstorms. Jessica laughed shortly. "I could have told her that there were plenty of squalls ahead and a frigging thunderstorm was the least of her problems but I held my peace."

Sarah rolled her eyes. "Oh God! Tomorrow's going to be the worst day of my life. I only hope that..." she was interrupted by a chime from her phone. "Oh sorry I've got a text." It was from Daniela again. "*J can't wait. J miss you*." Sarah smiled.

Jessica was looking at her strangely. "Anybody I know?" she asked.

"Oh it's just from Nicole wishing me well." Sarah lied.

"Right. Well let's shift these glasses. Has mum told you about this dinner we're going out for tonight?"

Sarah picked up the other tray. "Yes she did mention it."

"It'll be a bloody ordeal I should imagine but I suppose we'll manage."

"I think it's a nice idea. It's ages since all five of us sat down for dinner together."

"And we'll probably remind ourselves tonight why we don't make a habit of it. Come on, let's go."

The iced tea was welcome to the people labouring on the infrastructure of the party and there was general pleasure at its appearance. They all took chairs around the garden tables at the swimming pool to refresh themselves. The chairs were a new addition Sarah noted. Her parents had hired a lot of collapsible trestle tables and folding chairs for the party. Most of these were still stacked in piles to one side. Presumably they would all have to be unfolded and laid out at some point. Sarah's mother, who was clearly in charge of the proceedings, wiped her forehead with the back of her wrist and looked around. "Well it's going better than I'd hoped." She noted with satisfaction. "I think once we get the tables and chairs set out, the last of the bunting up, the stage and dance floor down and the bars set up, we can knock it off for today and leave the rest for tomorrow. We've got Jasmine coming in the morning to do all the balloons and table decorations and the florists are coming to finish off the floral displays. We need to have those buffet tables up before lunchtime tomorrow because the caterers will be here at twelve sharp. Oh yes and we've got to get the barbeque grills up." She turned to her husband. "Where were you going to put the barbeque honey?"

"I thought over by the side of the house nearest the Judas tree Alisha. That way it'll be far enough away from the bars and people won't have to choke on charcoal fumes."

His wife nodded. "Fair enough. Have we got enough charcoal?"

"Bags of it. Dino brought half a dozen ten kilogram bags this morning. We've got more than enough. Dino and his colleague from the Bella Vista are coming to do the barbeque so they'll make sure they have plenty of everything."

"Any news on that bloody generator?"

"Gianni assures me he'll have another generator here within two hours."

"He'd better have or I'll go down that workshop and kick his backside for him. We've got the band coming in the morning to set up and do a sound check so we need the power online."

Sarah's father rolled his tongue in his cheek. "I did mention that you'd be upset if he let us down Alisha." There was a general suppression of smiles around the tables. The thought of Sarah's mother being dissatisfied with one's efforts was liable to be an affective incentive to greater effort. Alisha on the warpath was a formidably intimidating prospect.

"Well I will be." she remarked grimly. "Well if everyone's finished their drink we can push on. I want us to be finished by five o'clock because I've got to get ready to go out for dinner. You too Jessie. You can't go out to dinner dressed like that."

"What's wrong with the way I'm dressed?"

"They'll never let us in the restaurant Jessie. They'll think you're pedalling clothes pegs or something. For God's sake, if even Sarah can manage to make an effort to dress nicely for a change, then you can."

Jessica was about to retort that *she* hadn't had the benefit of a generous allowance to spend on new clothes but she bit her lip. "All right I'll change into something else if it makes you happy." she ground out.

"Excellent. Well let's press on everybody."

"What can I do to help?" asked Sarah.

To her surprise her mother vetoed the very idea. "Absolutely nothing for the moment Sarah. This is your party so I'm not having you knocking yourself out in preparations. You can just relax and keep out of everybody's way." Inevitably her mother added a note of reproach. "Anyway it's so seldom that we get you looking your best and I'm not going to risk you getting your dress dirty or messing up your hair before we go out to dinner."

"Yes mother." said Sarah wearily. In the end Sarah didn't mind her exclusion from proceedings. She felt detached enough from the whole process as it was so she felt no inclination to contribute. She took a seat in a corner of the garden overlooking the panorama of the lake below and watched the scene in the garden unfolding with mounting trepidation. She texted her misgivings to Daniela and received reassuring texts in return. She willed calm upon herself and turned to watch the boats leaving white wakes on the azure waters of the lake glittering in the sunshine.

She'd been alone with her thoughts for nearly two hours when Jessica came over and joined her to escape from the others for a cigarette. Jessica was the only member of the family that smoked. It irritated her mother intensely and she was always hectoring Jessica about it. "You bored Sarah?" she asked.

"Not bored, just terrified Jess. Bloody mum's gone completely loopy over this party."

"I did warn you. It kind of puts you in a difficult position doesn't it?"

"Tell me about it. It doesn't bear thinking about."

"Well I'm glad I'm not in your shoes kid."

Sarah frowned. "You know Jess there's something I don't get."

"What's that?"

"It's this house, this land. I mean our parents are wealthy. They live like millionaires."

"Er that's just possibly because they *are* millionaires Sarah. If you own *any* property in Switzerland, you are de facto a millionaire and mum and dad own four They've got the chalet in the Valais, two town houses in Zurich and this place. How much do you think this little place is worth on the market? I mean I know it's mortgaged up to the hilt but it's still a bloody great financial investment." Jessica shook her head. "You're not very worldly are you Sarah? Mum and dad are loaded. Dad could retire tomorrow and never have to work another day in his life."

"But that's what I don't understand Jess. If they're so wealthy why do they need these deals with Alan's parents? Why am I getting sold off as the sacrificial calf just so they can make even more money that they don't really need?"

Jessica shrugged. "The trouble with a lot of rich people Sarah is that they never seem to be satisfied with what they have. Making money becomes an end in itself. They carry on accumulating wealth long after there's any rational reason for it. Now dad might be a little over extended business wise for the moment but he's hardly approaching bankruptcy. He could sell up and live comfortably for the rest of his life. There's no sense really in him working himself into an early grave just to make more money. It's just become a way of life to him. Alan's father is just the same and so is Alan. They can never imagine a state of being too rich. If you married Alan you'd certainly become a very wealthy woman too Sarah."

"I don't need his money Jess."

"I'm just mentioning it Sarah. You've got to remember honey that this isn't just about dad's business deals. Oh sure he's not above milking the cow for all it's worth but, at the end of the day, what he really wants is to see you set up for life. He doesn't want you to make the mistake he thinks I made by marrying someone without a penny to their name. I know that Damien's doing well now but we were skint when we got married and it shocked dad to the core. He'll be damned if he lets his little baby Sarah go the same way. To him this is the perfect solution. You marry well into wealth and he and mum get all the financial and prestige advantages of alliance with Alan's family. Mum is delighted with it because Alan's family is a rich and well established one and she's a social climber; always has been. Marrying her youngest daughter into a family as renowned as Alan's is beyond the dreams of avarice to a snob like mum. So it might seem as if mum is the one pushing this marriage. Make no mistake however that the real driving force is dad. If you want to squirm out then he's the one you're going to have to convince. In the final analysis he wants what's best for you. If you can persuade him that you'll be unhappy with Alan then you're half way there. You'll have your work cut out though. Dad will have a hard time believing that anyone can be unhappy with a big fat bank account."

"He didn't always used to be like this Jess. When we were little he didn't seem to be so obsessed with wealth."

"He always worked hard to make sure we never wanted for anything Sarah. I guess it just became natural to him. Maybe when he gets the last of his children settled for life he'll relax and live on his gains. Don't hold your breath though."

"He's got to understand that I want more from life than just wealth Jess."

"He wants you to be happy Sarah. The trouble is he thinks money and happiness are synonymous." Jessica crushed out her cigarette and flicked the tab into the climbing Bougainvillea on the garden trestles. "I'd better get back."

Finally, when her mother was satisfied with progress, work was adjourned for the day and the assorted members of her family retired to dress for dinner that evening. Sarah took advantage of the solitude to phone Daniela briefly and pour out her woes. Daniela was sympathetic and understanding and Sarah took comfort from her quiet support but she missed her dreadfully. Sarah told her all about her mother's preparations for the party and Daniela clicked her tongue in anxiety. The one thing that Sarah did not mention was her mother's sleeping arrangements for her the following day. That can of worms was one she didn't want to open until she could find a way to finesse it.

Chapter Ten

In the early evening Sarah's father drove his family down to Ascona for dinner. After parking the car, they all walked along the lake front. In spite of her anxieties Sarah felt a little spark of pleasure, for Ascona was one of her favourite towns in Switzerland. It was a beautiful little town of white plastered buildings, clustered along the side of Lake Maggiore, full of quaint narrow streets and little hidden plazas. Sarah adored it in the spring when the lakeside was awash with blossoming trees and the air above the lake seemed so sharp and clear. Again the feeling was of Italy and this Italianate culture was reflected in the architecture of the houses and the lovely old basilica church of San Pietro e Paulo. The waterfront was busy for Ascona was a popular resort. Hordes of people were walking along the lake side or sitting at the innumerable cafe terraces across the road. The lake itself was busy with dozens of boats and yachts upon it, from the little motor boats for hire to the larger ships carrying tourists or travellers across the lake. She watched a ship pulling up at the Isole di Brissago; the two small islands out in the lake which, with their botanical gardens were popular with tourists. As they ambled along the lake front she saw a shoal of fish feeding on the bread being thrown to the ducks by day trippers. She was familiar with the fish for they had once caused her a headache to identify. They were pigo; sometimes called Danubian Roach which, name notwithstanding, were common in the lakes and rivers of the Po basin.

In the restaurant to which Mr Fuchs brought his family they settled down to eat around a large rustic table. Sarah's father ordered for his family and there was a pasta dish as a starter which was the tradition in Italy and a delicious osso bucho for a main course, which was a dish of veal shanks on the bone cooked in a rich meat broth, flavoured with wine and with vegetables in it. The slowly braised meat fell off the bone and the broth was thick and tasty with the marrow from the bone. It was served with mounds of golden polenta, which was something of a local speciality and they washed it down with a fine quality local merlot.

If the food was superb the same could not have been said of the atmosphere around the table. Sarah's mother was babbling on about the preparations for the party seemingly oblivious to the fact that the rest of her family were distracted and looking less than enthusiastic. John was already fed up with the party and counting the days until he could return home. He was fond of his younger sister and pleased for her that she was marrying but his mother had taken the opportunity to contrast the marital status of his two sisters and his own ambiguous state.

John was always in a difficult position, being the middle child. He was dominated on the one side by a strong willed elder sister and on the other by a somewhat pampered favourite younger sister. He always tended to feel a little cut out of family affairs. He was a disappointment to his father who had originally wanted him to join the family business. But John had no head on him for the trappings of his father's business and ran a simple joinery business with his friend and colleague in Appenzell. It provided John with a steady income but hardly the sort of financial return that would have earned his father's respect. That was a little unfair for John was hard working and conscientious in his small business and if the paper work and administration of the business eluded his grasp then he had a clever and qualified girlfriend to run the office whilst he and his partner busied themselves with tools and got their hands dirty. What really ticked John off however was the continuous comparisons between his own modest ambitions and achievements and those of Alan who, it seemed, was being accepted into the bosom of the family as a surrogate son and compensation for the failures of the biological son. Privately John despised Alan for being everything his parents had wanted him to be.

To add to John's discomfort was the fact that Jessica was being particularly sharp with him. Over dinner he tried to make polite conversation with Sarah; asking her about her plans and even offering to help out should the house in Zurich require any joinery work on it. It was a case of good intentions falling on stony ground for Sarah was looking anxious and distracted and answering him in subdued monosyllables. Eventually Jessica told him to shut up and leave Sarah alone and he retreated into sullen silence. Jessica herself was looking agitated and she kept glancing at the less than happy visage of her younger sister with concern. Sarah seemed withdrawn and disinclined to converse and it seemed as if the dinner was rapidly descending into a monologue by her mother to set of morose looking children.

Mr Fuchs was hurt and puzzled by the atmosphere. He dismissed Sarah's mood as nerves over the coming event but he was deeply disappointed that his family dinner party was turning out so poorly. He had thought it would be a chance for everyone to relax, put the thought of the party aside and simply sit down together as a family to privately celebrate Sarah's forthcoming engagement. It should have been an occasion for happiness and familial bonding. It was anything but. With his wife monopolising the conversation, it was taking on all the aspect of a lecture to a particularly uninterested audience.

To compound the problem, over coffee and grappa, Mrs Fuchs pulled out a piece of paper upon which she had sketched out the order of proceedings for the following day's festivities. It was a forbidding document. It choreographed the whole event with military like precision. "Well Sarah." she announced firmly. "If you'd managed to get here earlier we could have gone over all this at our leisure but since you've decided to leave it until the last minute I'm going to have to brief you now." She consulted her list. "Now most of the party should be set up by early afternoon so you've got plenty of time to prepare. I've made an appointment at the hairdresser's for you at half past twelve and then we're picking up your outfit at the boutique as soon as we're finished there and at the beautician's et cetera."

Sarah looked up in disbelief. "You've ordered an outfit for me?"

"Yes. I've got you a beautiful maxi Grecian style evening dress by Valentino in soft rose. It's lovely. It cost me nearly two thousand francs."

"Mother I already have perfectly suitable clothes. Daddy gave me a generous allowance to buy a new wardrobe and I've put it to good use. What earthly point was there in my going shopping for clothes if all you're going to do is deck me out as *you* wish?"

Her mother tapped on the table impatiently. "Your new wardrobe won't go to waste Sarah dear. You'll have plenty of opportunity to parade in your finery over the coming weeks. Now I'm pleased so far that you seem to be developing a little more dress sense and I hope you'll keep it up because we have a busy social calendar over the next few weeks up to your wedding. Tomorrow, however, is very important and I want you to look the best you can. On your past record I could hardly trust you to look the part for such a big occasion so I've taken the trouble to make sure that you have the right outfit for what is after all one of the biggest days in your life."

Sarah leaned back exasperatedly. "Oh fucking hell!"

Her father slapped the table and frowned. "Sarah! I'll ask you not to swear in front of your mother thank you. I'm surprised at you. I've never known you use such bad language at the table."

"I'm sorry Daddy but really this is too much. I'm a grown woman. I'm perfectly capable of choosing my own dress."

Her mother held her hands up. "If you'd come down earlier in the summer Sarah, as I frequently asked you to, then you would have had all the time in the world to help me pick out a suitable gown for you."

"Sorry mother but I had other things to be getting on with."

"Such as?"

"Well a *life* for one thing."

Her mother glared at her. "Your "life" is *here* Sarah. It starts tomorrow evening in case you'd forgotten. I wanted you down here to start taking responsibility for that life instead of just idling your time away up in the Toggenburg."

"I was not idling my time away. As for coming down here…. well being dragged around every boutique between here and Milan and being told what I'm going to wear does not strike me as much of a life."

Her mother shook her head. "I can't understand you Sarah. Most girls would be delighted to hear that their mother has just bought them a fabulous designer evening gown to greet their boyfriend when he comes home."

Sarah pulled a face. "So what's next on the agenda after I'm wrapped up like a welcome home present? Do I have to visit the surgery to have my brain removed?"

"That'll do Sarah!" her father admonished. "Your mother has done her best in your absence and I'll thank you to show her some respect."

Sarah retreated into sullen silence as her mother continued somewhat haughtily. "Well then there's the manicure and pedicure obviously..."

"Obviously." Sarah muttered under her breath.

Her mother ignored her and pressed on determinedly. "We'll be on a tight schedule because we need to be back at the house before five o'clock to have the welcoming reception set up."

"Who are we welcoming?" asked Sarah sulkily.

Her mother glared at her in exasperation. "Why Alan and his family of course Sarah!"

"Oh forgive me. I had no idea. Nobody's actually thought to inform me as yet as to when my boyfriend is returning. Even Alan seems to have overlooked me when informing everybody of his plans. I don't see why I should be surprised however. I'm just his girlfriend. What do *I* matter?"

Jessica looked haunted and placed a hand on Sarah's knee. "I thought you knew honey. He's arriving with his family at seven o'clock. Hasn't he phoned you?"

"No I'm afraid he hasn't. Presumably he had more pressing *business* to attend to." Sarah couldn't help but place an emphasis on the word business.

"Well what does it matter Sarah?" her mother asked in irritation. "He *is* coming and that's the important thing. I suppose he thought that we'd tell you when he was getting here. He's been travelling a long time. He can't think of everything."

"No and especially something as trivial as his girlfriend."

"That's quite enough Sarah!" her mother told her crossly. "He's flown all the way back from America to be with you tomorrow for your big day. He'll be jet lagged and tired today."

Sarah faced her mother squarely. "Are you telling me he's already back in Switzerland?"

"Why yes. He flew into Kloten last night. He's at his parents' town house in Zurich."

"Oh so he's been back in Switzerland all day and he hasn't even had the courtesy to phone me and let me know he's arrived?"

"Well he knew he'd see you tomorrow Sarah. What's the problem? I told you he's probably tired today. I can't understand why you're being so difficult."

"I think Sarah's right to be annoyed." Her brother interjected. "However tired he was he could have spared a minute to phone her up and let her know he was back. The bloke's a self-centred prat. Always has been!"

Jessica turned on her brother. "Butt out of this John. You're not helping here."

"Sorry for breathing."

Mr Fuchs slapped on the table again. "Now listen all of you! I won't have this conversation deteriorating into an unseemly family squabble. Now I understand that you're a bit miffed because Alan hasn't called you Sarah but I'm sure he has good reasons for his negligence. I've had to endure a fair bit of intercontinental travel myself and I know how tired and unable to think straight it can leave you. It might be a little reprehensible that he's forgotten to call you but that's no justification for this childish petulance. Your mother is right when she points out that Alan has travelled thousands of kilometres to see you and it is churlish of you to take him to task for a momentary failure of attention. I can't think what's come over you this evening."

It was a mark of how Sarah was changing that she did not cower under this assault. Previously a public rebuke from her father would have had her cringing in servility. Now however her dander was up and she was refusing to bow under the assault. "Perhaps I'd just like to have a little more control over my own marriage father." she blurted out. He blinked in surprise. Sarah always called him daddy; never father.

Jessica swallowed sensing a confrontation approaching. "Take it easy Sarah honey." She pleaded.

"Why?" demanded Sarah angrily. "All I've heard since I got here is everybody else's plans and wishes. Nobody's even thought to ask me. This is supposed to be *my* boyfriend, *my* engagement and *my* bloody wedding. Fat chance! I'm not even allowed to choose what I wear. I am not informed even when Alan is due to grace us with his presence. And what's this sodding reception you're talking about?"

Her mother blinked, taken aback by Sarah's uncharacteristic outburst. "Why it's nothing honey." She said trying to mollify her angry daughter. "We're just setting up a drinks reception at the garden gate to welcome Alan back and his family. I thought it would be a nice idea if you met Alan first at the gate and offered him a drink. It would make a perfect photo opportunity."

"Oh I see. So even my reunion with my boyfriend is being turned into a ceremonial public spectacle is it? Are you sure you don't want me to kneel down with a basin of spring water and wash his feet for him when he arrives?"

"Don't be silly Sarah. It's just a nice gesture that's all."

"I think *I'd* like to determine how I greet my boyfriend after a long absence mother. I'm not here as a bloody supplicant. I've travelled myself to be here although to be honest it sounds as if you could have replaced me with a shop mannequin for all my presence matters."

"You've travelled down here very late Sarah." her mother pointed out. "It's too bad of you to complain now that you've had no say in the proceedings after you've stubbornly resisted all my efforts to get you to come here and participate in the process."

"Forgive me mother but I always thought that this sort of "process" was one that was solely between the two major protagonists involved. If Alan wanted to ask me to marry him then he knows exactly where I live. There are conventions about this sort of thing you know. It's the usual tradition for the man to ask for a girl's hand *privately*."

"Now you are being ridiculous Sarah." her mother declared. She turned to her husband. "Make her see sense for heaven's sake George."

Sarah's father lifted a hand. "I think this has gone far enough!" he stated. "Sarah is obviously tired and irritated after a long day's travel and she's understandably nervous about tomorrow so we'll table this until the morning. I think we could all do with a good night's sleep."

"But I've still got to finish briefing her on the party tomorrow."

"It can wait until the morning Alisha. You'll have plenty of time to go over the party with her at the hairdresser's or somewhere. I see no point in making a spectacle of our family disagreements in a public restaurant. Now drop it Alisha and as for you Sarah try and get a good night's sleep and wake up in a better mood tomorrow." Sarah averted her eyes defiantly and he regarded her with annoyance and concern. All was not right with his daughter and, on the eve of such an important day for all of them, that was very disturbing. The evening had not been a success.

Chapter Eleven

Sarah's father put his coffee cup down with a sigh. The morning sun was already warm in the clear blue sky. It was going to be another scorcher. He was sat at a table out on the back veranda in a dressing gown but any hope he'd had of a quiet breakfast was doomed for his wife, sat opposite pouring out more coffee in a long green housecoat, was in a fine dudgeon. "I can't think what the matter with Sarah is." she was saying for at least the twentieth time.

He glanced ruefully at the morning paper lying neglected on the table before him. The daily paper was part of his morning routine but today promised to be anything but routine. "It's just a case of nerves Alisha." He assured her soothingly. "I'm sure everything will be fine once she's reunited with Alan. We just have to be a little patient with her."

"We can't afford to be patient George. All our friends and your business colleagues are going to be here this evening. If she behaves the way she did yesterday she's going to humiliate us in front of everybody."

"She'll be fine honey." Mr Fuchs had been repeating this assurance monotonously since the clash in the restaurant the day before. He'd wanted to have a quiet word with Sarah when they'd got home the previous night but she'd taken herself away to bed as soon as they arrived back at the villa in what could only be described as a sulk. Mr Fuchs groaned to himself. "Who'd be a father?" he asked himself bitterly. He loved his children deeply but he was forced to concede that they seemed biologically programmed to make life as difficult as possible for their parents. What was really making this domestic crisis so vexing however, was the fact that it involved Sarah. Now you expected rocky shoals with John and they were an inevitability with his headstrong daughter, Jessica but not with Sarah. Sarah was always the quiet obedient little baby of the family. She'd always been the sweet subservient apple of his eye. She was his favourite and it was almost a family joke that Sarah was her father's pet lamb who always did as her father told her. Her sudden outburst of angry defiance had shocked everybody last night. It was completely out of character for her.

"The trouble is that she's been spoiled." His wife continued. "You pamper her too much George. She needs a firm hand."

"Alisha darling. She's a grown woman. I can hardly put her over my knee and spank her bottom for her."

"Hmmph! If you'd taken the trouble to do so more often when she was little perhaps she might have grown up to be less selfish and immature."

"Now that's unfair Alisha. Sarah's never been a selfish girl."

"Well she is being now. I've gone to a great deal of trouble to organise this party for her and now it's all about *her* and what *she* wants. If she'd come down to Ticino at the beginning of summer as I asked her to originally then we could have sorted all these problems out weeks ago and she could have had her own input into the organisation of things. But no! No she had to insist that she wanted to stay in the Toggenburg and *you*..." Mrs Fuchs paused to tap on the table accusingly, "You let her get away with it."

"I tried to persuade her to come Alisha. What was I supposed to do; go up to the Toggenburg and physically abduct her?"

"You could have tried being a little more firm with her. She wraps you round her little finger George and always gets her own way."

"Oh come on now Alisha. Sarah's the most obedient child we've got. You've said so yourself in the past even, if she doesn't like you dressing her up as a fashion model."

"I blame that friend of hers, that Nicole." said Mrs Fuchs, changing tack with bewildering speed. "The sooner she's out from under that girl's influence the better."

"She's known Nicole since she was six years old for heaven's sake Alisha. I haven't noticed any deleterious effect on her character until now."

"Well you mark my words. It'll be Nicole that's putting all these notions into her head. It's no good George. We can't have another outburst like last night this evening when all our guests are here. I'll die of shame if she doesn't behave herself tonight. You have to talk to her George. She won't listen to me."

Mr Fuchs heaved a great sigh. "All right Alisha. I'll take her down to Locarno with me this morning and have a quiet word with her."

In truth, Sarah was not proud of her behaviour the night before. She rose late and her head was not the best. She'd drunk too much yesterday she knew, starting from Daniela's champagne early in the morning. She was sure she'd never have dared to have such an open confrontation with her parents in public if she hadn't drunk so much. She sat on the edge of her bed miserably. Even the view from the window out over Lake Maggiore, glorious in the morning sunshine, failed to raise her faded spirits. She groaned when she thought of the dinner party but she knew the genie was at least partly out of the bottle. She hadn't said anything that she didn't believe to be true and there was no way to retract it now.

She grasped her head in her hands. What the devil was she going to do now? It had truly shocked her to learn that Alan was turning up formally for a prearranged welcoming at seven that evening. She had assumed that he would be turning up at some time during the day and that she would be able to talk to him privately. Now it seemed as if the evening was so orchestrated that she'd barely have a minute to have him to herself. Her eyes flew open in fear at a new thought.

"Oh my God! What if they expect Alan to propose to me in public; in front of witnesses? What the hell will I say?" She jumped from the bed agitatedly and paced the room. "They can't do that! Surely not."

Her sudden panic was interrupted by a knock on her bedroom door. "Are you coming down for breakfast Sarah?" It was Jessica.

Sarah stilled the wild beating from her chest. "I'll be a few minutes Jess. I'm not dressed yet." She called out.

"Ok I'll put the coffee on."

As Jessica departed Sarah turned to her choice of dress for the day. The rebellious streak in her wanted to don the most tattered pair of jeans she possessed and match them with the grubbiest old shirt in her collection. That was just childish and petulant though she realised. In any case such a minor insurrection was not an option. Daniela had vetted her travelling wardrobe thoroughly. She did have one pair of jeans with her but they were a pair of stylish designer jeans from Daniela's wardrobe. In the end, her contrary mood led her to the other extreme. She pulled out a pretty halter neck sun dress in a print of dark blue, purple, gold and white palm leaves that Daniela had given her. It was beach wear as much as anything but perfectly acceptable for a hot day in Ticino. Low cut, tied behind the neck and with a flared hem that fell to just above the knee it was pretty and flirtatious. Daniela had even provided accessories for it in the shape of a purple bangle and a string of purple and yellow glass beads although Sarah wore her white gold necklace as well. Her high heeled white sandals matched the outfit perfectly and she was pleased with the result. She wanted to push her mother's accusations about her inability to dress stylishly back in her face. She had no idea how much the dress cost but she guessed it was expensive. The material felt expensive and Daniela didn't do cheap. Dressed for battle she went downstairs in search of breakfast.

She found Jessica alone in the kitchen, drinking coffee and listening to the radio. John had already been despatched on some party business and her parents were taking breakfast outdoors in the garden. Jessica was wearing a pair of shorts and a T-shirt and spreading butter on a croissant. She glanced up as Sarah entered. "Whew kid! What is this? Are you so pissed off with Alan that you're after hunting down every warm blooded male in Ticino? You look dressed to kill."

Sarah took a seat at the table. "Don't *you* start on me Jess!"

"Oh! Bad start to the day is it? Well you look stunning anyway."

Sarah reached for the coffee pot. "I can't see the day getting any better. This is shaping up to be the worst day of my life."

Jessica pulled a wry face. "Yes I think you're probably in for a rough one. Doubtless mother dearest is well out of sorts following your declaration of war last night."

"Oh God! I'm sorry. I didn't want to start a fight in that restaurant."

"I don't see how you're going to get through this without a fight Sarah. You've certainly drawn up the battle lines."

"Have they said anything to you?"

Jessica shook her head. "No. Oh doubtless there have been high level discussions and recriminations but I've not been included in them. I'd brace yourself for a serious counter attack sometime during the day though. Come on have a croissant."

"I'm not hungry."

"Nonsense! You need all your strength on the eve of a major offensive."

"Sun Tzu said that the supreme art of war consists of defeating the enemy without having to fight Jess."

"Sun Tzu never had a bloody minded Yorkshire woman for a mother Sarah."

Sarah sighed and reached for a croissant anyway. "No I suppose not."

Suddenly Jessica leaned over to turn the radio up. "Oh I love this song!" Sarah's face froze into a mask. The song was "Blue Stone Lady"; Daniela's last single release. She tried to keep her face impassive but her fingers were trembling as she tried to butter her croissant. Jessica didn't notice the change of mood in her younger sister. She was singing along with the melody. "I really like this chick's music." she told Sarah, "I bought her CD last month."

"Oh really?" said Sarah in as neutral a tone as she could manage but her voice sounded hoarse. Fortunately she was saved by the entrance of her father. She sprung up rather too quickly to kiss him good morning. "Morning daddy." she intoned meekly.

"Morning honey. You look very pretty."

"Thank you daddy."

"Look Sarah I have to go down to Locarno to pick up a few things for the party your mother's asked me to fetch. I wondered if you'd be so good as to come along and help me."

Sarah swallowed and she saw Jessica rolling her eyes out of the corner of her eye. Her father's pretext was transparent. It was obvious he wanted a private chat with her alone. "Yes of course daddy."

"Thank you sweetheart. Take your time and finish your breakfast. I'm not going for another twenty minutes or so."

After finishing her very frugal breakfast Sarah drifted out into the garden in search of her father. Her mother was pottering about with some floral displays distractedly. Sarah half expected a serious lecture from her but she seemed somewhat reserved although she complimented Sarah warmly on her appearance. The failure of her mother to take her to task for her behaviour the night before puzzled Sarah. She guessed, rightly as it happened, that her father had made her mother promise

101

not to reopen the discussion until he had talked to their daughter.

Chapter Twelve

Sarah and her father drove to Locarno in his BMW. Locarno was the next town to Ascona and somewhat larger, separated from Ascona by the delta formed by the River Maggia as it flowed into Lake Maggiore. It was a lovely old town with an attractive lake front, a beautiful old monastery on a hillside over the town and a charming central square surrounded by arch covered walkways full of fine shops and little cafes. They finished their business quickly and loaded the items her father had bought into the boot of the car before Mr Fuchs suggested that, since they had plenty of time, it would be nice to take a coffee at a cafe on the square. Sarah set her lip and prepared for the worst.

Her father ordered two cappuccinos and stirred his cup thoughtfully for a minute whilst gathering his thoughts. Sarah sat silently and waited. A few swifts were flying overhead. Sarah glanced at them with interest. The swifts in Locarno interested her. As well as the normal common swifts there was a colony of a much rarer species, known as a Pallid Swift, in Locarno. They were fiendishly difficult to tell apart from common swifts but Sarah had taught herself the subtle identification features for they were a notable species of bird. The nesting colony in Locarno was the only one in all Switzerland.

"Sarah..." her father began at last, "I've been thinking about last night."

"Look daddy..." began Sarah defensively, "I didn't want to start a row in that restaurant last night but you and mum have to understand that..."

Her father raised her hand. "Slow down Sarah. I'm not here to tell you off. On the contrary I understand why you were upset last night Sarah."

"You do?"

103

"Of course Murmuli. I've been married to your mother for twenty six years Sarah and, love her as I do, I have no illusions that she's always the easiest person to get along with. I know she likes to take control of things and sometimes she can seem overbearing and arrogant. I know you feel that she's hijacked your wedding arrangements and you're understandably upset that you seem to have no say in the affair. You feel, quite naturally, that, since it's your marriage, that you should be the first person consulted in the arrangements."

"Daddy she's even bought my wedding dress. She's even chosen my bridesmaids for me."

"I know, I know. You'll have to re-negotiate that with her yourself Sarah but I'll do my best to persuade her that you deserve to be consulted before she makes any arrangements. It is after all your wedding." He sighed deeply. "You have to try and understand your mother Sarah. She never really had the wedding she wanted."

"I thought you married in church."

"Well we did but it was a bloody last minute rushed job I can tell you. Your mother was heavily pregnant and if we'd left it much later Jessica would have risked being born in the vestry. It's always been a disappointment to your mother that she never had a really big romantic wedding. Then when Jessie ran off with Damien she was robbed of the chance to throw a big wedding for her eldest daughter. Now she sees you as her last remaining chance Sarah. This is very important to her Sarah. I agree with you that she should have given you more say in the proceedings but all she really wants is to make sure that her daughter has the big wedding with all the trimmings she never had."

"And if I don't want that?"

"Sarah is it so much to give your mother? Does it really matter *how* you marry? If I talk to her I'm sure I can get her to see that you need to be more involved in your own marriage plans. In fact I'm sure she'd *love* you

104

to be more involved. She's been moaning all summer that you weren't there to collaborate with her. She wanted you to help choose a dress and go to be fitted but she thought you weren't interested in things like that. She'd be delighted if you joined in more enthusiastically." He lowered his head for a second. "I think she was hurt when you refused to come to Ticino Sarah. I think she felt you were distancing yourself from her. Perhaps she thought it was Jessica happening all over again. She was so looking forward to sitting down with you to plan your wedding and then you didn't want to come. I think that made her sad Sarah."

"Daddy has she already set a date?"

"Provisionally yes. She's looking at a date in the middle of September but there is some leeway in that."

"How much leeway?"

"Maybe a week or two."

"Daddy don't you think it's a little bizarre that my mother is setting a date for my marriage before my boyfriend has even got around to proposing to me?"

"Well that's hardly going to be a problem much longer is it Sarah?"

"Don't you normally start planning for a wedding *after* the bride has given her consent?"

"Well yes under normal circumstances Sarah but..."

"So what's so *abnormal* here?"

"Well because in this case there's been a long standing arrangement and..."

"An *arrangement*?"

"It's just a word Sarah... call it an understanding if you like. You and Alan have been informally affianced for two years now. A proposal only formalises a long term mutual understanding."

"And that "formality" is the object of tonight's circus is it?"

"It's just a party Sarah; a bit of a bash to celebrate your engagement. It was supposed to be a treat that your

105

mother and I were putting on for you to celebrate your engagement. It's for your benefit."

"Bullshit daddy!"

"Sarah! Your language is becoming atrocious these days. I will thank you to moderate your vocabulary and use language more appropriate to a lady."

"I'll start acting like a lady daddy when you start treating me like one and not a little baby. What you've just said has more holes in it than an Emmental cheese. This party isn't for my benefit at all."

"Of course it is."

"Oh really? I happened to glance through the guest list yesterday afternoon whilst being shoved out of the way and being told to mind my own business. I've never even heard of half of the people on that list! The ones I had heard of were mostly a mixed collection of mum's socialite friends, your business colleagues, relatives and friends of Alan's family. In fact, immediate family aside, there wasn't a single person on that list that *I* would have chosen. Conspicuous by their absence were any of *my* friends! Odd that don't you think? I notice that a couple of Alan's golfing buddies made it into the invitation list but not a single one of my own personal friends. Not even Nicole was invited."

"Well your mother doesn't really approve of Nicole Sarah."

"Oh doesn't she? Well I didn't notice her asking *my* approval for any of *her* friends. Now whose party is this supposed to be? This party is for you, mum and Alan's family isn't it? I'm just the prize exhibit."

Her father ran a hand through his hair agitatedly. "Well Yes I concede it does appear a little bit like that."

"Appearances have nothing to do with it daddy. Those are the facts."

"Look Sarah if you'd come along here earlier and joined in the process I'm sure you could have invited whoever you wanted."

"Subject to mum's approval of course!"

"Stop prickling Sarah. Yes, all right, this is a bit of a formal do for our family friends and work colleagues. That's not the end of the world Sarah. You can go through the motions and be civil to people. A lot of them are very important to us. I'm not asking you to do anything difficult; just to be polite and allow them to wish you the best. Yes there'll probably be a few stuffed shirts among them but it won't hurt you to be cordial and welcome them. If you like we can throw another party at a later date for yours and Alan's friends. You could have a more informal bash so that you young people can let your hair down a bit."

"There's another problem with this party daddy."

"Now what?"

"You're putting the cart before the horse again. This is an engagement party. *I'm not engaged yet.*"

Her father looked at her in bewilderment. "But that's the whole point of the do."

"You don't get it do you daddy?"

Sarah's father was suffering but he ploughed on bravely. "Look Sarah it's only a party. Yes I concede it's as much, if not more, for your mother's benefit as yours. But Sarah this is important to her. I'm just asking that you go along with her wishes this once. I've taken on board all your concerns and, once we get tonight out of the way, we'll address those concerns seriously. Your mother is worried that we'll have a repetition of last night's outburst in front of our guests and she's asked me to talk to you about it. I've promised that I'll ask you to maintain some decorum for the sake of our family pride. It's nothing difficult I'm asking you to do Sarah. Do it for me please if not for your mother. I think we can agree that there have been faults and wrongs on both sides. Well let's put them behind us, get tonight out of the way and move on from there."

Sarah stared at him coolly for several seconds, marshalling her thoughts. "Very well." She said at last.

"I'll do it for you daddy. There are, however, conditions."

"I've already said that we'll address your concerns Sarah."

"I require more specific guarantees. Tonight I promise I will cause no scandal or in any way bring disgrace on our family daddy. In return I require that henceforth any questions regarding my marriage be entirely at *my* discretion. There is to be no further question that any detail of any marriage of mine be decided without my consent and one hundred percent approval. There will be no wedding date set for me that hasn't obtained my unqualified agreement and there will be no details of that wedding concerning me that I do not have full control of. Do you agree?"

"I'm sure we can work something out between us Sarah."

"This is not negotiable daddy. Those are my demands." Mr Fuchs stared at his daughter barely recognising her at this moment. Something fundamental had changed in the sweet little girl he loved so much. The sweet little girl was gone. He was looking at an adult. Almost as if reading his thoughts Sarah continued. "Am I over twenty one daddy?"

"Well yes of course you are."

"Am I therefore a full adult with full legal rights as an adult?"

"Naturally."

"Do I not in that case have the full right to determine when and to whom I shall marry?"

"Well I..."

"Yes or no?"

"Well yes...."

Sarah nodded. "Thank you daddy." She picked up her handbag and rose. "Now if you'll excuse me I need to use the ladies." He watched her walk calmly into the cafe and slumped back in his seat in astonishment.

108

Suddenly he felt a mounting anxiety. There was trouble ahead.

Chapter Thirteen

To Mr Fuchs' surprise Sarah returned from the ladies, after a protracted absence, in a somewhat better humour. With relief he decided that she must have mulled over his words in privacy and been reassured by his promises to her. For a while there he had begun to worry that the difficulties that Sarah was giving him were symptomatic of some much deeper problem. Now it was plain that her ill humour was just nerves after all and a petty resentment of her mother's brow beating demanding that her own wishes and concerns be considered. There was nothing there they couldn't handle.

Mr Fuchs was an accomplished business man. He was an expert in negotiations and the way in which you manipulated negotiations to pander to the concerns of all involved toward a common goal. Sarah's unexpected resistance had been simply her way of laying out her negotiating platform. That was fair enough. You always started out from a platform some way beyond which your client was prepared to go and then, through a series of concessions and adjustments, met them along some middle route which was agreeable to both parties concerned and moved on from there.

Mr Fuchs tended to see the whole world in terms of contractual agreements. Everything in the field of human interaction was a series of compromises. He almost felt quite proud of Sarah for the way in which she had handled her side of the negotiations with skill to extract the concessions she required. She was a chip off the old block he told himself and she was growing up fast. So she had put her foot down and played hard ball. There was nothing wrong with that. He had made concessions promising her a greater say in her marriage arrangements and she in turn had met him half way and promised to do

110

nothing to upset her mother's party this evening and now they could still do business.

In fact, the reasons for Sarah's elevated mood would have caused him far more cause for concern. To begin with, Sarah had, to her own satisfaction, extracted the one concession which she regarded as fundamental; to wit the acknowledgement that she and only she could determine her future marital state. There was a major breach of understanding between them.

As far as Mr Fuchs was concerned, he had granted Sarah greater autonomy in the decisions concerning her marriage and respect for her individual wishes. He knew of course that there would have to be some adjustments and that his wife would have to be handled with delicate skill. For instance they might have to rearrange the wedding date to suit Sarah's convenience. That didn't strike him as an insurmountable difficulty. A couple of weeks here or there wouldn't make too much difference. It was really only a concession to Sarah's pride in that she would now be the one to set the date in consultation with Alan.

Then there was the wedding dress. He hoped that there would be some compromise over that. It was true that Alisha had gone a little off the tracks by already buying the dress. An important part of a bride's build up to her big day was the choosing of her own wedding dress and Alisha had effectively taken that away from Sarah. Well if Sarah was going to be stubborn on this point they might well have to give in over it. Alisha would be disappointed but she would have to bend on this one and perhaps Sarah would go so far as to allow her to participate in the choosing of the new gown. There was a chance, however, just a chance, that Sarah might bend on this issue. Mr Fuchs had seen the wedding gown that Alisha had bought and even he could see that it was sensational; an absolute dream of a fairy tale wedding dress. There was every chance that Sarah might see it and fall in love with it. They could of course allow her to

111

customise it to her own tastes and pick her own accessories but if she decided to wear it after all then it was a result much to be desired. For one thing, the damn dress had cost a small fortune and Mr Fuchs was not so incautious a business man as to wish to write off several thousand francs as a loss to Sarah's hurt feelings. It would certainly please Alisha if Sarah chose the dress and perhaps they could use that to bend Alisha over the question of the bridesmaids. This was one area where Mr Fuchs could see straight away that there was going to have to be a major concession. Sarah was miffed enough about the exclusion of her friends from the engagement party. Alisha had picked out the daughters of a couple of her socialite friends as Sarah's bridesmaids and even gone so far as to start picking out bridesmaid's dresses for them. Well there was no way that Sarah was going to go for that. Alisha might disapprove of Nicole but if Sarah determined that Nicole was going to be one of her bridesmaids then Alisha was going to have to lump it. Perhaps though, if they conceded completely on this issue, it might sway Sarah towards accepting the wedding dress.

There was one issue that hadn't even been raised yet and it was a worryingly intractable one. Alan's family were Catholic and were insisting on a Catholic wedding. Sarah on the other hand was protestant and, furthermore, she had been raised in the Toggenburg where people could be prickly over questions of religion. Mr Fuchs was a most secular man and saw no real reason in his own mind why this should be a problem. It would simply be a matter of paying lip service essentially to whatever Christian denomination the wedding took place in. It would of course mean Sarah going through the motions of conversion to Catholicism but it wouldn't really mean anything. Neither Alan nor Sarah were churchgoers and so it wasn't as if Sarah would be expected to attend mass regularly or anything. It was a conversion of convenience really. As for Alisha, although she had been brought up as an Anglican, she was even less religiously inclined than her husband. She couldn't care less what sort of church Sarah married in as long as it *was* a church. Nevertheless Mr Fuchs decided to table this one for the moment. They could iron this one out later. Sarah could have peculiar ideas on this sort of thing and she was curiously attached to the Toggenburg where people often took their protestant religion seriously. It was best not to rock the boat on this matter therefore.

Nevertheless, all in all, Mr Fuchs felt quietly satisfied now that Sarah seemed to be happier. He began to recover his confidence. There were no major stumbling blocks and they could proceed as planned. It was a magnificent self-delusion. Sarah did not see his concession in the same way at all. As far as she was concerned, he had granted her complete autonomy on the very fundamental question of her marriage per se. He had not told her that she might be able to choose her own wedding date, her own gown or bridesmaids. These were trivial details and in any case irrelevant. She had extracted a straight yes to the question that she had the full right to determine when she would get married and *to whom*. Unwittingly Mr Fuchs had given her a get out clause. In Sarah's analysis, he had conceded her right to refuse Alan's proposal of marriage outright. She had found the loophole in her arranged marriage.

Mr Fuchs would have been horrified to know that his daughter's better mood resulted from her relief in believing that she was under no obligation to marry. It had never occurred within his darkest dreams that Sarah was not simply bartering for better terms but in fact manoeuvring to escape from the marriage altogether. He had given her a priceless point of argument. If she now exercised her right of refusal she could simply trump his objections with the simple question, "When we discussed my right to determine the conditions of my own marriage, did you or did you not say..." It was a devastating weapon in her arsenal. Mr Fuchs might have reconsidered his pride in his daughter's negotiating skills. She had pulled off a brilliant coup. Without actually having to say that she did not wish to marry Alan she had nevertheless extracted the right to that option. Mr Fuchs was an accomplished businessman but he had just been outwitted by his own daughter.

There was another reason for Sarah's better mood than this triumph. Whilst in the ladies she had phoned Daniela to report on her progress. Daniela had been so completely happy to hear from her and so buoyed by the news that Sarah was actively resisting her engagement that she was nearly weeping with happiness into the phone. "Oh darling! You're so brave. I love you. When are you coming home?"

"Soon my love. Soon. I miss you."

"Hurry back to me Sarah. The world's gone grey without you here."

"I'm doing my best Danny. Just be patient. Things are delicate here."

"I love you Sarah."

"I love you too Danny."

So Sarah had returned to the table feeling much better. Her father, oblivious to his impending peril, looked at her approvingly. "Well, well." he cried. "A smile no less. I was beginning to think that I was never going to get a smile out of you today."

Sarah bit her lip. "I'm sorry if I've been so difficult daddy." she said almost girlishly. Now that she had what she wanted she was not above falling back into the role of daddy's little girl and pandering to his rose tinted perceptions of her.

He was almost pathetically pleased. "So you're going to be a good girl tonight then?"

"Yes daddy. I've promised. I'll even be nice to mum when she drags me round the hairdressers and shops this afternoon."

He smiled warmly at her. "Thank you Sarah. This means a lot to me."

"Yes daddy."

He glanced at his watch. "Well I suppose we'd better be getting back soon." Then a thought occurred to him and he grinned. He was not only a doting father but he was always a believer in putting a little sugar on any deal he was trying to close. He reached into his pocket, pulled out his car keys and laid them on the table in front of her. "I tell you what. Why don't you drive us back to the house? It's a long time since I saw you behind the wheel of a car. If you haven't got too rusty maybe next week we can take a little time out and go and see if we can't find you a little car of your own."

Sarah beamed at him hugely. She doubted if she would ever see that car but she didn't care. Daniela was waiting for her and if she needed a car Daniela would buy her one. That wasn't important though. She was in love and that love was just a little step forwards toward realisation. The desperation that had gripped her since coming to the Ticino had lifted. For the first time she could see a crack in the walls of the trap about her. For the first time she had a plan. She reached out and took the car keys. "Thank you daddy!"

Chapter Fourteen

Sarah's mother was agreeably surprised by her youngest daughter's cooperation that afternoon. Since the incident in the restaurant the previous evening she had been expecting sullen resistance at best or outright hostility at worst. When Sarah and her father had returned from Locarno, she had pulled her husband to one side and asked, "Have you spoken to her George?"

Mr Fuchs had nodded. "Yes I've spoken with her."

"Well? What's she got to say for herself?"

"Everything's going to be just fine Alisha. She's promised not to cause a scene tonight and she'll cooperate with you fully this afternoon."

"Well thank heavens the girl's come to her senses."

"Wait a minute Alisha there are some provisos."

"What provisos?"

"Well Alisha she's very upset because she thinks that you're hi-jacking her wedding."

Mrs Fuchs had bridled indignantly. "Well! I like that! After all the effort I've..."

"Shut up and listen Alisha." Mrs Fuchs had stilled her outburst with an effort and her husband had briefly outlined those areas which he perceived to be Sarah's main objections. "So you see," he had concluded, "We're going to have to give her far more say in the planning of her marriage and we've got to stop steam rolling ahead with plans without consulting her. It is after all *her* wedding and right now she feels as if she has no say in it. Now, of course, you'll still be central to the planning but you've got to at least create the illusion that she's involved in all the decision making. She's a big mass of wounded pride at the moment Alisha and we're going to have pamper her a bit. Sarah's not Jessica. She's easy to manage as long as she receives enough reassurance that her concerns are being addressed."

"Well, as I've said a hundred times, if she'd come down earlier this summer as I asked then..."

"That's history now Alisha. The fact is that she *is* here now and we're going to have to treat her accordingly."

"Does she really want that Nicole girl as a bridesmaid?"

"I would think so Alisha and we'll have to give way on that one I think. She is her best friend and if we start tampering with childhood loyalties we'll have a major rebellion on our hands."

Mrs Fuchs had groaned but reluctantly conceded. "Well I suppose the girl's not a complete disaster, appearance wise. She might scrub up quite well, I suppose. I'd more or less promised Juanita and Maria that their daughters would have the role though."

"Well consider them fired. Sarah will have her own friends as bridesmaids. I don't think that's negotiable. Come on Alisha it's only a small concession to keep Sarah happy. Sarah's a sweet obedient girl for the most part but she can be pretty adamant and stubborn on things she feels strongly about. Anyway, if we concede the point over the bridesmaids, we might just be able to sell her on the wedding dress you've bought. As long as she's involved in the process I'm sure she'll be ready to compromise a little."

Mrs Fuchs had frowned. "I think she's being very self-centred George."

"She's got every *right* to be self-centred Alisha. A wedding is the *bride's* big day. It's *supposed* to be all about her."

"All right. I take your point. Heaven knows I've wanted Sarah to be a bigger part of this thing but she just didn't seem to take it seriously up until now. I suppose I should be grateful that she's taking an interest in it at last."

"Thank you Alisha. Now this afternoon try to treat her with kid gloves honey. Make sure you get her

117

approval on her hairstyle and the dress you're getting her and, for God's sake, don't keep pointing out her past failures to dress according to your standards as you were doing last night. She's done a good job using the allowance I gave her to buy nice clothes and if you keep harping on about her past record she'll get all defensive on us and we're back to square one."

"Well I have to admit that she's been looking very well turned out so far; very pretty clothes and good labels too. I didn't think she had it in her."

"Well you can see why she was so mad yesterday Alisha. She'd gone to all that trouble to deck herself out nicely and then she finds that you've bought her a gown for this evening because you don't trust her to pick out something suitable herself. She'd probably already bought something really nice for this evening and you've gone and trumped her. No wonder she was so furious."

Even Mrs Fuchs had been able to concede the justice in that argument and she had managed to look chastened. "Yes I suppose so. It's a good point. All right George I'll let her wear what she wants as long as it's not too awful. It's a good job I haven't paid for that dress yet." Mrs Fuchs had given a long sigh. "It is gorgeous though. It would have looked stunning on her."

"Well don't give up on it yet Alisha. Take her along to see it by all means. As long as you approach it from the direction of asking her opinion of it you can still sell it. Just don't give her the impression that you're not giving her a choice in the matter. Sarah's a funny girl but, at the end of the day, she is a young girl being offered a fabulous designer evening dress costing a small fortune and she'll have a hard time turning it down. Just make sure she doesn't think she's being bullied into it."

"Ok George. I've got the picture."

"Good girl. We've got to be a little cautious with her Alisha. She's as nervous as hell and a bit volatile for the moment. We only need to pat her hand a little and

118

pander to her wishes and we'll have her purring like a pussy cat."

Mrs Fuchs had taken on board everything her husband had said and, as she and Sarah drove down to Ascona in the afternoon, she approached the subject tentatively. "Sarah," she began hesitantly.

"Yes mum?"

"I er... I didn't want to give you the impression yesterday that I'd already bought you a gown for this evening. Actually I haven't even paid for it yet. I just really wanted you to see it and decide whether you'd like it. Of course if you've already got something for this evening I'll quite understand. Even if you don't decide to wear it this evening I'd like buy it for you anyway; as a present. It's a lovely dress and I'm sure you'll find occasion for it sometime."

Sarah smiled inwardly. "I'm looking forward to seeing it mum."

Mrs Fuchs could not have been more pleased. She gripped the steering wheel and smiled. "Well I'll think you'll like it Sarah. It'll look fabulous on you. Mind you I'm not saying that you don't have nice clothes. I must say I've been very impressed by your choice of outfits these past two days. You've certainly turned over a new leaf. I like that sun dress you're wearing. Who's it by?"

"I've no idea mum. I don't tend to look at the designers. I just pick out what I like."

"Well you've certainly got a good eye." Mrs Fuchs meant what she said. After her talk with her husband, he had taken Sarah off into the garden for a cool drink and she'd taken the opportunity provided to dash upstairs to Sarah's room and rummage about in her wardrobe. She'd been astonished by what she had discovered there. She'd lifted one lovely outfit after another out and admired them. Sarah it seemed had developed a late and unexpected taste for haut couture for they were all good quality, stylish and expensive outfits usually from good labels and all in impeccable taste. Mrs Fuchs was not often impressed by another woman's wardrobe but she had been forced to admit that her daughter had surprisingly metamorphosed into a very well dressed young lady. She had felt quite a rush of maternal pride in her. Sarah was her mother's daughter after all, it appeared. Of course she was not to know that a considerable percentage of the outfits in Sarah's wardrobe had originated in Daniela Devin's collection; one of the best dressed young women in Switzerland.

Nevertheless, it was a thrill to discover that Sarah had so unaccountably taken an interest in fashion and was possessed of a fine eye for elegant clothing. She was certainly the first of Mrs Fuchs' children to have done so. John spent most of his life in a pair of dungarees and Jessica dressed in styles that horrified her mother and was outwardly contemptuous of her mother's enslavement to the conventions of high fashion. Sarah, previously, had merely endured her mother's attempts to raise her standard of dress. She had politely allowed her mother to take her shopping but she had quickly become bored and disinterested and anything her mother had pressed her into buying had usually been quickly relegated to the back of her wardrobe and immediately forgotten about. Mrs Fuchs had despaired of her but now it appeared that her efforts had not been futile after all. Judging by the current contents of her wardrobe, Sarah must have been absorbing the lessons her mother was trying to instil in her, in spite of the evidence to the contrary. Now it seemed as if those lessons were bearing fruit and, in the light of her daughter's newfound enthusiasm, Mrs Fuchs could hardly wait to take her youngest daughter shopping.

If she had one criticism to make about the collection in Sarah's wardrobe at the villa it was simply that it wasn't anything like *big* enough. If Sarah was going to be in residence for the rest of the summer, up to her wedding, she was certainly going to need a more extensive wardrobe than the one, as nice as it was, that she possessed. Well that was no problem. They would have time enough to address that issue and, with her husband in an indulgent mood and liable to be lavish with funds over his favourite, they could go on a binge the like of which this sorry canton had never seen. Good God! Milan was only a couple of hours away. They could get down there for a weekend. To Mrs Fuchs Milan was the fashion capital of the world; Gucci, Prada, Valentino, Versace, Dolce and Gabbana and Armani were all headquartered in the city. They'd have to buy extra suitcases and hire porters. It would be fun. In fact, (Mrs Fuchs made a mental calculation) they should be finished at the hairdresser's and manicurist's by about three at the latest and, since everything was now just about ready up at the house, they didn't need to back before four or half past. Perhaps therefore, they might have the time to see if there was anything else in the shop that would suit Sarah. As far as Mr Fuchs was concerned, time spent shopping was never wasted and her credit card was burning a hole in her handbag. She grinned with pleasure at the thought.

In her bubbling enthusiasm Mrs Fuchs failed to read her daughter's mood. Sarah was being almost serenely calm and her confidence was restored now that she had the germ of a plan. She was sitting in the car smiling pleasantly and ever so slightly amused by her mother's garrulous babbling. An odd mood had come over her. She felt as if she was elevated to a higher state of consciousness; detached from her surroundings and her eyes far away fixed on a goal waiting for her in the Toggenburg. Her anxieties had fallen from her now that she knew what she must do and curiously she felt a sense of empowerment; the thrill of being in control of her own destiny. This sense of power enabled her to see her mother dispassionately for the first time and she had the measure of her. She realised, with a thrill, that she was a match, more than a match, for her mother who had so dominated her life. She even felt more mature than her mother and she was able to perceive the childishness in her and how easily she could be manipulated. She felt a strange new love for her mother but it was not the subservient love of a daughter for a dominating mother but rather the indulgent affection one might have for a loquacious, precocious child. She felt strong and amused by her mother's triviality with her spirit soaring to places her mother could not touch. For the first time in her life, she was not afraid of her mother and curiously, now that her mother seemed no longer an enemy, she was inclined to forgive her for her faults.

The visit to the hairdresser's was straightforward. Sarah's hair was one of her best features and Mrs Fuchs was sensitive enough to realise that it needed little in the way of elaborate treatment. A little trimming and styling to enhance its natural loveliness was all that was required. Mrs Fuchs had hair ornamentation for Sarah back at the house to complete the desired effect. Nor did they need much time at the beautician's for Mrs Fuchs also understood that Sarah had the sort of complexion that many a woman would have sold her soul for. There was little required in the way of depilation for Sarah had very little in the way of bodily hair and, since coming to know Daniela, Sarah had been shaving those parts of her liable to show unsightly hair growth religiously. Thus her armpits were clean and blemishless and her arms and legs smooth. Her mother was slightly dissatisfied with her eyebrows and Sarah had to endure some thinning of them but otherwise her mother kept her cosmetic modification to a minimum, preferring to show off Sarah's naturally lovely, youthful complexion and the warm tan of a girl who spent so much time out of doors in the mountains. In fact Sarah had been becoming so used to wearing clothes that exposed her arms, legs, shoulders and other areas to sunlight that her tan was more complete than at any time in her life since she was a small child.

The one area that Mrs Fuchs anticipated problems with was Sarah's nails. Sarah's nails were usually a disaster. That was normal for a girl that spent so much time scrabbling around on mountain slopes with the inevitable tally of broken fingernails and neglected toenails. To Mrs Fuchs' pleasant surprise, however, Sarah's nails turned out to be nowhere nearly as bad as she had feared. For one thing Sarah had not been climbing as much this summer as in previous years and, in addition, she hadn't been working as much either, which was another knell of doom for careful maintenance of fingernails. More to the point Daniela and, to a lesser extent, Nicole had taken over responsibility for the well-being of Sarah's finger and toenails. Sarah had sadly neglected her toenails and feet over the years. Feet, to Sarah, had been things you walk on and you couldn't see them anyway in a pair of hiking boots. Daniela had completely changed that perception for she loved Sarah's feet and rarely missed the chance to play with them. She loved to see Sarah in open sandals that showed her shapely feet and she adored to rest Sarah's feet in her lap, massage them, trim her nails and paint them for her. As a result Sarah's feet had enjoyed a hitherto unprecedented level of care that summer and Sarah had begun to take a certain pride in them, knowing how much pleasure they gave to Daniela. The night before she had left for the Ticino Daniela had given her a full pedicure and manicure by the fireside in her house and the result paid dividends now.

Finally coiffed and beautified to her mother's satisfaction Sarah allowed herself to be led to the boutique where her evening gown was awaiting her. A few minutes later Sarah was staring at herself in astonishment in front of a full length mirror. The dress was a luxurious full length Grecian evening gown with a slight train to it in a simple pale rose colour, with a high waist and low cut with a single shoulder. It was stunning, show stopping and glamorous; its soft drapes cascading down her thighs sensuously. Sarah looked like a Greek Goddess. She was delighted. From the moment she saw herself clad in the fabulous gown she knew her mother had made a major tactical mistake. This was a dress to capture everyone's attention at the party. In this dress she would stand out. There was no chance of her being relegated to a position of meek servility. She could command the floor in this dress. It was exactly the power dress her budding plan required.

"Well er... what do you think?" asked her mother nervously.

Sarah stared at her reflection and allowed a beam of triumph to cross her face. "It's just *perfect* mother."

"You really like it?"

"Oh yes."

Sarah's voice seemed to ring with authority and her mother glanced at her a little nonplussed. She was pleased that Sarah liked the dress but an odd change seemed to have come over her. She seemed suddenly commanding and filled with radiant energy. She hardly recognised her daughter at that moment and a twinge of nervousness nagged at her subconscious. She pushed aside her faint misgivings and paused in her fussing with the waistline. "Right then if you're... er sure, we'll get them to wrap it for us." She paused hesitantly. "Er... since we've got plenty of time perhaps you'd like to look around and see if there's anything else you might like."

Sarah turned to smile at her. "Yes I think I'd like that."

On the drive home Mrs Fuchs felt slightly shell shocked. She had treated Sarah in the boutique but it had not been cheap. It was not, however, the expense that had so shocked Mrs Fuchs but rather her daughter's miraculously acquired penchant for high quality couture. Mrs Fuchs had picked a couple of dresses off the racks to ask Sarah's opinion but Sarah had had her own ideas about what she liked. In truth she had homed in on the sort of outfits she knew Daniela would have liked and

Mrs Fuchs was bound to concede that her eye was unerring. She'd picked two perfect summer dresses off the racks, a boldly patterned skirt and matching top, a handbag, assorted accessories and an exquisite pair of Armani high heeled sandals that cost a whopping four hundred and fifty francs. The total bill left a yawning cavity in Mrs Fuchs' clothing budget and a new found respect for her daughter's tastes. Sarah was well satisfied with herself. Revenge was sweet.

Sarah might have overplayed her hand slightly for Mrs Fuchs was a tiny bit disturbed. Her ill-defined misgivings had returned and her antennae were up and twitching suspiciously. Sarah was being just a little odd and a bit too good to be true. There was nothing concrete Mrs Fuchs could put her finger on but her intuitions were niggling at her. Sarah was up to something.

Chapter Fifteen

Back at the house Sarah had a good hour and a half to get ready before the first guests arrived. They were scheduled to arrive anywhere from six o'clock onwards. Alan and his family, as befitting the stars of the show, were due to arrive late, at some time after seven. Sarah smiled grimly at the thought. *Stars*! She'd show them who the real *star* of the show was. She hadn't been studying the public projection of one of the biggest stars in Switzerland these past weeks without learning a trick or two.

Before retiring to her room to dress and make her preparations Sarah took a quick tour around the garden and house to reassure herself that nobody had moved the goalposts. The whole garden was decked out in red and white roses and there were masses of red and white balloons everywhere, bearing her name on the white balloons and Alan's on the red ones, each surrounded by love hearts. Sarah personally found them cringe worthily gauche but she was at least satisfied that the symbolism had gone no further than merely hearts. The heart motive was continued everywhere. Even the table clothes were covered in hearts and the coasters were heart shaped. Anxiously Sarah hunted among the decorations for any other more meaningful symbolism and was relieved to find none. There were no images of brides and grooms, no linked rings, gowns and tuxedos or anything else that represented marriage. The banners hanging from the trees simply read "Sarah and Alan".

The word engagement was mentioned nowhere. Sarah had seen a copy of the invitations that had been sent out, this very morning but she had failed, at first, to recognise the opportunity that they provided. She did now though. Those small documents were her escape clause. She re-examined one of the invitations to assure herself that she had not misread them. But no they were clear; on such and such a date guest so and so was "cordially invited to attend the occasion of the reunion of Sarah and Alan following their long separation..." blah, blah, blah. Reunion! What a lovely word that was. Sarah could have kissed it. This was officially a *reunion* party. It was, of course, a fiction. The official line was that the guests were there merely to witness and celebrate the reuniting of two lovers sundered by enforced separation. There was no mention of *engagement* anywhere. There couldn't be, of course, because there had been no formal announcement of any engagement. *That* was supposed to be part of the evening's proceedings but it could not be mentioned in the invitations because it would pre-empt the highlight of the night's entertainment. At some point during the evening there would be a formal announcement but up until that point the fiction had to be maintained that this was just a party to reunite Sarah and her widely admired boyfriend within the bosom of their respective families. It was only a small point but it was the loophole Sarah needed and she intended to exploit it to the maximum.

Fortunately Sarah was able to prepare herself alone in her room. Her mother was too busy with her own preparations. Deliberately she locked the bedroom door and sat down on the bed to steel herself for the ensuing conflict. She picked up her phone and texted Daniela. "*About to go into action. Wish me luck.*"

The return text followed within seconds. "*Luck. My love.*" Sarah smiled and laid her new dress out on the bed. Carefully and slowly, she began to dress herself for the party.

By six o'clock the first guests were arriving and there was still no sign of Sarah. Mrs Fuchs, resplendent in a black and silver cocktail dress and looking every inch the elegant hostess, was becoming agitated. "I can't think what's taking Sarah so long." she muttered to her long suffering husband. "She only had to get dressed and put her accessories on. We did all her make-up and everything this afternoon."

Her husband smiled. "The biter bit. This is karma Alisha; payback for every time you've left me climbing the walls by spending hours getting ready to go out."

"It's not me leaving the guests waiting George. She should be here to welcome them. It's incredibly rude of her."

"Oh cut the girl a bit of slack Alisha. It's her big night. She probably just wants to look perfect."

"Hmmph!" Mrs Fuchs saw her elder daughter hovering in the background. "Jessica! Go and see where your sister is and tell her to hurry it up."

Jessica sighed. "Ok mum." A minute later she was knocking on Sarah's door. "Sarah are you nearly ready?" she called out through the door. "All the guests are arriving and mum's going psychotic downstairs."

"I'll just be a couple more minutes Jess. I'm nearly ready."

"Well for fuck's sake hurry it up kid before mum loses it and throws herself in the sodding pool." Jessica left and Sarah smiled to herself. She could imagine her mother's anxiety and if protocol didn't determine that she be present to welcome the guests, she would doubtless have been banging on Sarah's door herself. Sarah wasn't "nearly ready". She'd been "ready" for a long time. She was now sitting on a stool in front of her dressing table and biding her time. She glanced at the clock by the bed. It read a quarter past six. Another quarter of an hour, she decided; another quarter of an hour to rack the tension up and make her point.

She gazed at her reflection in the mirror. It was perfection. She knew she had never looked so stunning. To complement her Grecian gown, she had looted her mother's jewellery box and adorned herself with pearls; a pearl choker about her neck, a pearl bangle on her right wrist, pearl earrings and lastly a thin silver chain about her head that hung a single small pearl on her forehead. She wore her emerald pendant in her cleavage and a white rose, the white rose of York, Daniela's birthplace, over her left breast. Finally, at nearly half past six, she rose from her stool and took a last long look at herself. She took a deep breath and spoke aloud, "Let battle commence!"

Out in the garden her mother was circulating among the guests, making sure they had drinks and fielding inquiries about her daughter. "So where is Sarah?" one immaculately dressed lady asked her.

Mrs Fuchs waved a hand airily. "Oh still getting ready Diane. You know what young girls are like." She glanced nervously at the house, furious with her daughter.

"I'm looking forward to seeing her again. I haven't seen her since before she went to university." The lady chuckled. "I hope you've managed to get her out of her old blue jeans Alisha. I don't think I can recall her wearing anything else. She was always a bit of a tomboy your Sarah."

"I think you'll find she's grown up a bit since then Diane."

"When are you going to announce the engagement then?"

"After the buffet's been served and the speeches Diane."

"My word, your little Sarah getting married. I can still remember her that summer in Zinal; off up the mountain with her father in her little boots, her little pink anorak and her hair in a ribbon. She must have been what, five or six years old. She was adorable. And now she's getting married. Marrying well too. The Bergers no less! She's done very well for herself. You must be very proud."

"Oh I am Diane but I think Alan is lucky as well to be marrying a lovely girl like Sarah wouldn't you say?"

Mrs Fuchs was ever so slightly miffed at the insinuation that Sarah was marrying above her station.

The lady wafted her hands theatrically. "Oh of course Alisha. Still the Bergers are among some of the richest and most well connected families in Switzerland Alisha. Your Sarah's hooked a big one there."

"Yes quite." replied Mrs Fuchs with a tight smile, her irritation increasing. "Would you like another punch Diane?" she asked sweetly.

Sarah's entrance was as dramatic as she had hoped for. Many of the guests had not seen her for a long time and some had never seen her at all. Those that did know Sarah were quite unprepared for her startling appearance and those unfamiliar with her blinked in admiration. She glided out of the back French windows and onto the veranda in front of the swimming pool in a stately fashion becoming a princess. In truth, she admitted to herself, there wasn't much any other way she could walk in her gown. You had to walk carefully and slowly or risk tripping over the trailing hem and ruining your entrance by going arse over tit into the pool. So her progress into the crowd was slow, measured and elegant. Out of the corner of her eye she saw her father staring at her with his mouth open, quite unable to grasp that this cool regal beauty could possibly be his daughter. The chatter around the bars and pool had come to a halt and everybody was staring at her. Normally being at the centre of attention would have horrified Sarah but tonight, she knew, that that was where she needed to be. She had to command this audience, dominate them, upstage every woman or man there and leave nobody in any doubt that this was *her* party and that *she* was the star.

At the beginning of this summer she would never have been able to pull it off. But Sarah was an observant girl and a quick learner. She'd been getting a master class in the art of staging a public entrance from the person who could have written the book on the subject.

Even walking into a mountain hut in a short skirt and hiking boots Daniela could appear on the scene like a physical shock wave and bring the room to a halt. Sarah had watched in wonder as Daniela played a crowd; the way she could turn her charm onto every person and make each one of them feel that she'd been waiting to talk to them personally all day. She had watched the gracefulness of Daniela's every move; the conscious choreography of it as if she never took a step without knowing precisely where she was going to place her foot or move her hand without being completely aware of the lines and grace of its motion. That was one of the greatest lessons she had learned from Daniela; that you had to be completely self-aware of your body and movement. You had to use your body like a tool, a communication medium and hold the attention of those around you with the harmony and elegance of your movement. Daniela had learned this through the medium of dance and she had mastered it. She could, after all, walk on a stage and hold a crowd of thousands enraptured by her every move; a consummate performer. Sarah could have learned her lesson from no greater an artist but her coach would have been proud of her today.

Her mother was fussing at her side and introducing her to people but Sarah barely acknowledged her. She was gliding among the crowd and greeting the guests as if her mother had not already done so. It took a lot to upstage Mrs Fuchs but Sarah managed the feat effortlessly and the feeling grew that, now Sarah had arrived, the party could begin in earnest. Older women were fussing over her whilst their younger counterparts gazed at her enviously and hated her. The older men were pulling their paunches in noticeably and trying to be charming whilst younger men were swarming around her like bees around a honey pot. One young man snatched a glass of champagne from the tray of a passing waitress from the catering company and pressed it into her hands. Sarah accepted the drink graciously and rewarded him with such a dazzling smile that his legs threatened to buckle beneath him.

She was like a ship under sail but she was manoeuvring for sea room. Imperceptibly she was steering a course into the very heart of the enemy's fleet. Around the tables of honour were the inner clique of her mother's female circle and their spouses, her father's closest colleagues. Her mother had been affording them the honour of introducing them last and that suited Sarah in her purpose. She had swept all the lesser vessels before her so far but here, in this inner circle, she had to strike the blow at the flagship. Her father came up alongside her. "You look absolutely wonderful Sarah." he told her with feeling.

She inclined her head with a smile. "Why thank you Daddy."

A large stout man with a florid face exclaimed loudly. "By God! You're right George. I haven't seen your youngest here since she was twelve years old. My Lord what a stunner she's turned out to be."

"She takes after you Alisha." Another gentleman remarked gallantly.

"Thank you Hans." Mrs Fuchs replied, momentarily flustered. She was having a hard time coping with the novel experience of being outshone by her youngest daughter.

"Yes," the gentleman continued. "It's not hard to see where Sarah gets her looks from."

Sarah simpered disgracefully. "You're too kind sir but I'm sure I could never match my mother's beauty."

Above the chorus of protests a lady sidled up mischievously. "You must be very excited Sarah."

Sarah tacked into this new breeze sensing an opening in the defences. "Well of course I'm looking forward to seeing Alan." She said nonchalantly as if she wasn't really fussed either way. "I haven't seen him since he returned from America so no doubt we'll have a lot to talk about."

Another lady patted her hand. "I should think so. So when's the big day going to be?"

Sarah feigned a look of puzzlement. "Big day? Do you mean my graduation?"

"No silly. The big one!"

"I'm sorry? I don't follow you."

"The wedding honey. When's the wedding going to be?"

Sarah laughed as if the lady had made a pleasantry. "Oh I don't know anything about a marriage Senora Pancetti. Alan and I haven't discussed the matter." There was an awkward silence. Sarah's mother was glaring at her. Sarah didn't care. She had the wind gauge now and she was running free before the breeze. It was time to roll out the main batteries.

"Haven't discussed it?" the lady was saying in puzzlement. "But I thought you were betrothed more or less."

Sarah shook her head. "Why no Senora Pancetti. Alan's not asked me to marry him yet."

Sarah's mother opened her mouth to speak but Senora Pancetti spoke first. "But isn't this is your engagement party Sarah?"

Sarah laughed, looked at her and unleashed the broadside. "Why of course not." she laughed in a clear voice so that all could hear. "This is just a reunion party. Alan and I are not engaged. I repeat; Alan has not asked me to marry him."

There was a stunned silence. Senor Pancetti was groping for words. Sarah's mother looked profoundly shocked. "But...but..." another lady guest began, "I thought you were announcing your engagement this evening."

Sarah gave another little laugh. "I can't see how I can announce something that hasn't occurred yet Senora. Of course if Alan did ask me to marry him at some future date and I agreed then we would be able to

133

officially announce it. But that, of course, is just a future possibility. I wouldn't care to speculate on it publicly."

Senora Pancetti had found her voice. "But isn't he going to propose to you tonight?" she blurted out.

Sarah managed to look shocked at the very idea. "Oh I wouldn't have thought so."

"You... you wouldn't?"

"Why no. Such a public event is hardly the sort of forum for such a private matter wouldn't you agree? If Alan were to so honour me by asking for my hand in marriage I would expect him to do so privately and I would expect the usual courtesy in allowing me my woman's prerogative to be granted the normal symbolically honorary period of time to consider my answer. I could never entertain a proposal of marriage in such public circumstances that my right to respond to the proposal privately was so compromised by the pressure of witnesses." Sarah smiled devastatingly. "Mummy and daddy brought me up to be very old fashioned in that way."

"Mummy and daddy" were currently looking as if their champagne had been laced with strychnine at the moment. Sarah, commanding centre stage, turned to her father with beaming smile. "I see that it's nearly seven o'clock daddy. Shouldn't you and mum be seeing that the drinks reception for the Bergers at the front gate is ready?"

Her father glanced at his watch. "Ah yes of course. They should be arriving any minute." He glanced at Sarah and delivered a witheringly stern look of reproach but it glanced off the armour of Sarah's tranquillity without leaving a scratch.

Her mother made as if to intercept her daughter, doubtless to have strong words with her. But she was cut off by a crowd of ladies eagerly seeking enlightenment on this new turn of affairs. Sarah allowed herself to be detained by three or four other ladies all agog and demanding illumination. One of them took Sarah's arm possessively. "So there's to be no official announcement of your engagement tonight at all then Sarah?"

"Not with my consent Senora." Sarah told her with a pleasant smile, eager to mop up the survivors, "How could there be? I'm not engaged."

The lady shook her head. "Extraordinary!"

Sarah's father managed to detach himself and make his way over to his daughter. "If you'll excuse me Senora I must have a quick word with my daughter.

"Si Senor. Certo."

Mr Fuchs took his daughter by the arm and led her firmly aside. He looked angry. "Sarah!" he whispered accusingly, "You *promised* me."

Sarah met his eye steadily. "I've kept my side of the bargain daddy, just make sure you keep *yours.*"

"What do you mean? What game are you playing?"

Sarah raised an eyebrow scornfully. "Mum gave me a copy of her program for the evening this afternoon daddy. I see that after the buffet and following speeches and before the dance floor opens there is to be a small item on the agenda that you haven't mentioned to me."

Her father ruffled his hair perplexedly. "Why I assumed you were aware of it Sarah."

"No daddy."

"But... but... it's only a bloody formality Sarah."

"I'm not a "formality" daddy."

Mr Fuchs glared at her. "Now look Sarah I don't know what you're playing at but..." He was interrupted by a tone from his mobile phone. He pulled it out and glanced at it. "Oh bugger! That's the Bergers. They'll be here in two minutes. We'll have to get to the gate sharpish. You and I have to have a little talk as soon as the Bergers are here young lady."

"I'll be delighted to discuss any problems you have daddy. Now if you'll excuse me I have to powder my nose." She swept away regally, leaving him standing there speechless.

Chapter Sixteen

Mr Fuchs swore under his breath and dashed around to the front of the house where all the guests were now congregating around a set of wooden trestle tables that had been set up as the official reception for what was billed as the grand arrival of the Berger family; Alan together with his mother and father. This was supposed to be one of the high points of the evening; the moment when Sarah was reunited with the man destined to be her husband and the moment when the Bergers and the Fuchs' were publicly to greet each other in recognition of their enjoined family status. Jessica and John were both alongside their mother and everywhere cameras were at the ready. Mrs Fuchs had even hired professional photographers and digital cinema cameras.

Mr Fuchs joined his family with a set face. His wife was looking furious. "Wait until I see Sarah." she ground out grimly. "Where the hell is she anyway?"

"She's slipped off to the loo."

"*What*! Has she taken leave of her senses? The Bergers will be here any second. Why couldn't she have gone earlier? Why the devil have you let her go?"

"Don't snap at *me* Alisha. How the devil was *I* supposed to stop her?"

"She's your daughter George. It's time you put your foot down with her."

Mr Fuchs took on a stern expression. "Don't worry Alisha I'll give her a piece of my mind."

"If she ruins this party George I'll.... I'll..."

John interrupted his parents' tense conference. "Mum, dad, the Bergers car just pulled up the hill."

Mr Fuchs repeated the unfortunate epithet he had employed earlier. "Christ! Ok look we're just going to have to try to stall them at the gate until Sarah gets her backside out of the lavatory. Make sure the serving girls have drinks ready."

The Bergers, it seemed, had decided to arrive in style for the arriving automobile was a great, gleaming black Maybach 62 four door, luxury sedan which would have cost close on seven hundred thousand francs. Jessica turned her nose up contemptuously. She despised Alan's family for the vulgar, ostentatious way it flaunted its wealth. It was typical of them to underline their importance by turning up so late and in such a dramatically magnificent vehicle. Mr Berger and his wife emerged from the car as the chauffeur rushed to open the door.

Mr Berger was a large barrelled-chested man, virtually bald with a great domed head and broad shoulders. His livery face and paunch betrayed his dedication to good food and wine and he carried himself with the arrogance of a man conscious of his own importance. His wife at his side was a complete contrast for she was a skinny little stick who always appeared to be on the point of a nervous crisis. She had doubtless been pretty in her youth but age had not been kind to her and she looked withered and lined beyond her years. She was over-dressed and carried so much jewellery she seemed to jingle as she walked. Jessica thought that the two senior members of the Berger clan resembled nothing less than an ageing Chicago gangster and his moll straight out of the nineteen thirties.

Stepping out of the car behind his parents came Alan. Jessica didn't have a lot of time for Alan but she had to concede that he was a fine looking man. He was tall and slender with hair so dark it was almost black, a fine boned face and deep brown eyes. He looked very dapper in his tuxedo although not entirely comfortable. Alan was not an elegant man although he could compensate for that with a confidence that sometimes bordered dangerously on arrogance. He rarely seemed to be relaxed. however. There was nothing easy going

137

about him. You always had the feeling that there were things he needed to be doing. He was wired; always to some extent a coiled spring. Many women would have found this dynamic energy attractive but Jessica always wanted to tell him to chill out.

Mrs Fuchs approached the Berger delegation with a fixed, rather glassy smile motioning nervously to one of the serving girls with a tray full of champagne glasses. Her husband was at her side, looking uncomfortable and casting anxious eyes back toward the house, hoping for a glimpse of his seemingly uncooperative daughter. "GEORGE!" roared Mr Berger in a booming voice. "How good to see you." He clasped Mr Fuchs' fingers in a vice like grip from his ham like fists. Before Sarah's father had chance to respond Mr Berger turned his expansive personality on Sarah's mother. "And Alisha. Good God you look better every day." He nodded at Mr Fuchs and winked at her. "If you get tired of this old reprobate you can join my harem any day." He roared with laughter at his own feeble joke.

Mrs Fuchs' smile became slightly more waxy, if that were possible. "Er a drink for you and your wife Herr Berger perhaps?"

Mr Berger waved his hands effusively. "Of course, of course!" He grasped a glass of champagne from the tray. "What about you George? You haven't got a drink. Never trust a man who doesn't drink; that's my motto."

Mr Fuchs accepted an offered glass from one of the serving girls. "Of course Bruno. Thank you for coming. My wife and I would like to extend our warmest welcome to our house." He turned to Mr Berger's wife. "And how wonderful to see you Mary. Please be welcome."

Mrs Berger simpered coyly. "We're very pleased to be here George."

She might have expanded but her husband intervened and clapped Mr Fuchs about the shoulder flamboyantly. "We are indeed George. We have lots to talk about, you and I."

Mr Fuchs staggered under the affectionate blow. "Oh really?"

"Absolutely!" Mr Berger leaned forward with a stentorian whisper. "There're a lot of things in the pipeline George. Lots of exciting prospects coming up. The deal with the Americans looks good. I think we might be able to do business there."

Mr Fuchs swallowed. "Well that... that sounds very encouraging Bruno."

"It's more than encouraging George. This is a big opening for us. If we close this deal then we have the whole American market opening up. We're looking at mega dollars here George and I want you in on this one."

Mr Fuchs took a deep breath. "Thank you Bruno. I... I am gratified by your confidence in me."

"Nonsense! You've earned it." He batted Mr Fuchs on the back once more. "Anyway I look after my own and we're nearly family now *what?*" He beamed at Mr Fuchs.

"Yes. Yes of course." Mr Fuchs paled and shot another anxious eye toward the house. There was still no sign of Sarah.

Mrs Fuchs was desperately trying to engage Mrs Berger in trivial conversation but her efforts were growing thin. Alan was stood by his mother and his eyebrows were furrowing in puzzlement. He was holding a large bouquet of flowers in one hand and glancing around in a lost fashion. Finally he dared to interrupt Mrs Fuchs' brittle chatter. "Er where is Sarah Mrs Fuchs?" he asked

His father overheard. "Yes where is the filly?" he boomed. "I expected the lass to be here to greet us."

It was one of the worst moments in Mrs Fuchs' life. In desperation, with the eyes of the entire party upon her, she flapped ineffectually. "Oh I'm so sorry Her Berger. She was supposed to be here but I think you caught her by surprise. She... she had to visit the ladies room. I'm sure she'll be here any moment."

Timing the moment to perfection Sarah chose this moment to step out of the front door. It was the second of Sarah's grand entrances this evening and, if anything, the most impressive of the two. Theoretically she had supposed to have been present to welcome Alan at the front gate with a welcoming glass of champagne. She had dismissed the idea with contempt. "I'm supposed to be his girlfriend not his bloody serving wench." she told herself firmly. It was important, she realised, to escape being trapped into subservience; meekly stood at the garden gate awaiting her master. If she was going to retain control over this party she had to trump the notion that the grand entrance of the Bergers was a climax of proceedings. She had to destroy the impression of the Bergers' condescending arrival at the Fuchs' humble abode where they would magnanimously accept the servile offer of that family's youngest daughter, as a mate for their son, in return for their patronage. Such an obsequious deference would spell ruin. This time, she had to leave the indelible impression that she was the real prize here; a princess being sought by eager supplicants, here to be wooed, to have her suitors pile gifts at her feet and vow to worship her. Therefore the timing was critical. She had to keep the Bergers waiting at the garden gate until she should choose to descend gracefully from the front steps of the house to benevolently invite them in.

Her parents' plans had played straight into her hands. They had the entire party now gathered at the front gates where there was supposed to be a minor ceremony and photo opportunity. With everybody milling around in confusion holding cameras and waiting for the promised occasion Mr and Mrs Fuchs could hardly simply whisk their guests into the garden without Sarah. The official photographers were standing to one side looking confused and everybody's attention was diverted from the Bergers as they looked around in vain for Sarah. For one awful moment Mr Fuchs thought Sarah might have decided to forego the meeting at the garden gates entirely. That, however, would have been a deliberate affront tantamount to an insult and Sarah was playing a much cleverer game than that. She descended the few steps from the front door with unhurried dignity. Above all, she needed to avoid the perception of a love struck young girl dashing to the arms of her handsome lover returned from across the sea. She drew herself up to her full height and glided regally down the garden path with a measured tread as slowly as she dared. The crowd divided before her progress for all the world like the waters of the Red Sea parting before Moses.

Alan saw her coming and his jaw dropped in amazement. He had never seen her looking so beautiful nor ever so self-assured and serene. To his fevered imagination, she seemed to glow as she floated down the path towards him, as if she were possessed by some goddess. His mouth seemed to go dry and he felt beads of perspiration break out on his forehead. A profound silence seemed to fall across the gathered company as if it was holding its collective breath. Alan and Sarah's parents were forgotten as the crowd stood riveted watching the tableau unfold before them. Sarah drew out the agony exquisitely, her eyes fixed on Alan and with a smile on her face that her sister would later describe as being about three levels beyond the Mona Lisa on the enigmatic scale. Even the birds in the trees seemed to stop their chittering to watch what would happen next.

Sarah drew up close to Alan and smiled slowly. "Welcome back to Switzerland Alan." She said quietly. Then she raised her hand to him palm down and slightly curved.

Intoxicated by her and unable to help himself Alan bowed and kissed the back of her hand. There was a blinding detonation of camera flashes and Sarah granted him a warm smile exultantly. "Sarah!" he croaked hoarsely. "You... you look marvellous."

Sarah gave him a tiny curtsy. "Thank you kind sir." She nodded to a young serving girl stood nervously at hand with a tray of full champagne glasses. The girl hurried forward. "Shall we take a drink together?" Sarah made no move to take one of the glasses so Alan took two of them and handed one to her. "Thank you." She told him warmly and raised her glass. "To the future?" she intoned inquiringly.

Alan swallowed. "To *our* future." he corrected her.

She smiled ambiguously. "Very well then to *our* future, whatever that might be." She took a token sip from the glass and replaced it on the tray. After polite but short greetings to Alan's parents Sarah took Alan's arm demurely. "Come," she said, "let's go into the back garden and take a seat." She led him back down the path and around the house dragging the crowd behind in a bemused train and leaving her perplexed parents and Alan's to bring up the rear.

Chapter Sixteen

Sarah kept Alan close by her in the garden. Ironically, he now became her defensive shield from her parents who were, by now, thoroughly agitated by the way she had stolen the show. It was important to dominate Alan; to reinforce his deference to her if she was to keep control over events. Alan quite clearly was out of his depth not realising how he was being manipulated. It was certainly not the welcome he had anticipated. Apart from the gallant peck to the back of her hand he had not even kissed her. Yet he was mesmerised by her. He had always thought of Sarah as an attractive girl but never one of such feminine allure. There were all sorts of good reasons for wishing to marry Sarah but, hitherto, he had not counted stunning beauty among them. He was quite entranced by this new Sarah but a little frightened of her. He had always been the dominant one in their relationship and that had pleased him for he was a man that liked to be in control. Now, however, he found himself literally tripping at her heels and he was not at all sure he liked the situation. He graciously presented her with the bouquet of flowers he had brought and Sarah thanked him prettily before handing the flowers to one of the hired servants to place in a vase. She even stood at the table and waited for him to offer her a chair before seating herself. She knew that sooner or later Alan would attempt to reassert his dominance but she had to make sure that that was at a time and an occasion that suited her.

Therefore she had to limit the amount of intimacy with Alan. Whilst keeping him close she nevertheless was careful to engage other guests gathered around in conversation; restricting Alan's opportunities to discuss private matters with her. She was ably abetted in this by the large number of guests wanting to be in close attendance on the happy couple and her efforts to take centre stage at the party were bearing fruit. It was important to avoid, at all costs, giving Alan any time to take her aside and declare his intentions. Even when her father protested to the eager crowd around them that perhaps the young couple might value a little space she continued to belie that claim and to socialise with the guests. Her father had asked her to behave herself in front of the guests and Sarah knew that he could not, with any justice, find any fault with her in that respect. Maintaining her central role she was a gracious hostess completely outclassing her mother's apparent supporting role. She usurped Alan by answering any general questions on their behalf before he could respond. Occasionally however a question was directed at Alan personally. One lady winked at him and said, "Don't you think your Sarah looks lovely tonight Alan?"

He cleared his throat hastily. "Yes! Yes I do. I've never seen her look so stunning."

Sarah smiled and patted his hand patronisingly. "I'm sure you're all being too kind. Actually I was thinking that Alan looks very handsome in his tuxedo. I'm so used to seeing him in casual wear or a business suit. I've never seen him in formal evening wear before."

"Well I think you make very good looking couple." Another of the circle of ladies, attached to them like glue, observed. "You look fabulous in that gown Sarah."

"Thank you." said Sarah. "But I'm sure you're exaggerating. I don't normally dress up so grandly. My mother always tells me that I look like a disaster and Alan here has often chided me for not dressing in a more ladylike manner. I'm not much to look at in the normal course of events but then I suppose you could dress up any old plain Jane in this dress and make them look nice."

"You're no plain Jane Sarah." protested the lady. "In fact I was just saying to your mother earlier what a beautiful young lady you've grown up to be. You must get it from your mother."

Sarah simpered and fanned herself with a coaster. "Oh really Senora. You're flattering me. My mother was a model in her younger days. I've seen loads of her photographs and she was gorgeous. I'm not even in the same class. I've always been the plain one in the family. My sister Jessica is much nicer looking than I am."

There was a chorus of protests and another lady leaned forward in a conspiratorial manner. "Well I think you're a lovely young lady Sarah and I can't wait to see how you look in your wedding dress."

Sarah laughed heartily. "Oh God! What a thought. I can't imagine. I'd probably look awful in a wedding gown. I'd be scared to death that I'd get all tangled up in it and fall over and disgrace myself."

It wasn't the response the lady had expected and she looked nonplussed. Her fishing was not going well. Sarah wasn't biting. One of her friends was more direct however. "So we're not to have an official announcement tonight then Sarah?"

Sarah replied with dignity. "I think I already made my views clear on that Senora."

Alan looked mystified. "What views? What's going on?"

Sarah grasped his hand and affected an apologetic smile. "I'm sorry Alan but some of the guests were under a misapprehension that we were engaged to be married and they were expecting an announcement to that effect this evening. Of course I told them that we'd never discussed the matter and naturally therefore there was no question of our announcing any such thing publicly this evening."

Alan was taken aback with shock. "But, but..."

Sarah intervened smoothly and addressed the company. "I'm sorry if there's been a misunderstanding ladies but, as I said earlier, Alan and I haven't discussed

145

marriage and I think you'll agree that any such discussion should be a private matter between us."

"So it's true that you haven't asked Sarah to marry you?" the Lady pressed, addressing Alan directly.

"Well I... I mean I..." Alan was flustered.

Sarah stepped into the breach hastily with a laugh. "Really Senora you're embarrassing my boyfriend. Don't try to paint him into a corner. He's probably not finished sowing his wild oats as yet." There was a round of laughter from the attending party and Alan looked bewildered.

"But you are going to get engaged sometime?" the lady asked insistently and Sarah began to feel irritated by her persistence.

"Senora I have already stated that this is not a matter for public discussion." Sarah allowed herself to blush prettily. "I'm sure that if Alan has any... inclinations regarding marrying me then he will approach me privately at some future date and discuss the matter at length with me away from the pressures of outside influence. We could then both decide if such an important step was in both our interests and act accordingly. I'm sure that Alan here would not like to feel pressurised by public coercion in making such a serious decision and neither would I." *"There"* thought Sarah to herself. *"I can't throw the gauntlet down any clearer than that."* She raised her head and looked across the pool. "Anyway it looks as if the buffet's opening. Shall we ladies, Alan..."

Alan took her arm and they joined the queue at the buffet. Alan was quite clearly furious. "What's all this garbage about Sarah?" he muttered under his breath. "We're supposed to announce our engagement this evening."

Sarah took a deep breath. "What engagement is that Alan?"

"Our bloody marriage engagement Sarah. That's what all this bloody circus is supposed to be about."

146

"Really? I wasn't aware that we were engaged Alan. I'm sure I can't have forgotten. I feel certain I would have remembered if you'd asked me to marry you."

"Don't be bloody pedantic Sarah. You know damn well that we're practically engaged."

"You can't be practically engaged Alan any more than you can be practically a virgin. You haven't formally asked me to marry you and until such time as you do, and assuming I accept, I will not acknowledge any announcement of our engagement. I certainly will not entertain such an announcement this evening. A girl likes to be asked Alan, not just taken for granted."

"What the hell are you playing at Sarah?"

"This is not a game Alan. This is the rest of my life I'm talking about. That's important enough that I think I deserve to be consulted about it don't you?"

"What do your parents say about this?"

Sarah turned to look at him in the eye. "I am twenty one years of age Alan and thus legally an adult. My father has stated firmly, and perfectly correctly, that I, and only I, have the right to decide when and to whom I marry Alan. If you have any concerns about the fairness of that judgement I suggest you consult with him about the matter."

"I bloody well shall."

"Excellent!" Sarah turned back to regard the buffet. "In the meantime, however, look at all this food." The catering company had done a wonderful job. The tables were groaning under the weight of the magnificent cold spread. "Aren't you hungry Alan? I am. I'm going to have some of that smoked salmon and maybe some of that Graubunden ham."

"This is no time to be discussing food."

"I disagree. I'm famished."

"We've got to talk about this Sarah."

"Oh I agree but not now Alan. I'm sure we'll have leisure to discuss the matter more fully in the coming days."

"I'm only here tomorrow and part of the day after Sarah. I have to be back at the office after that."

"Well I'm sure you must be able to find a little more time in your busy schedule to discuss a matter of such paramount importance with all the due consideration it deserves. I mean we don't want to hurry into any decision now do we?"

"We need to talk right now."

"Alan, the matter is closed. I do not wish to hear anything more about it tonight. There are times and places to discuss these things and this is not one of them. That's my final word."

"Like hell it is."

She faced him squarely, her eyes flaring. "Do you want to turn this into a public row Alan?"

"No, no of course not."

"Then I strongly advise you to drop the matter."

He set his face grimly. "I'm going to have a serious talk with your parents Sarah. They're not going to let you get away with this."

She turned away sadly. "As you wish Alan. I believe they're over by the bar talking to your mother and father. Now if you'll excuse me I'd like to take some food." He glared at her and walked away briskly. Sarah sighed. It was not true she was hungry. In fact all her appetite had deserted her. She felt terribly lonely and sad. She placed a few morsels on her plate for appearances sake and then, whilst everybody's attention was on the food she slipped away seeking solitude. Dusk was setting in and the lights were beginning to twinkle around the lake below and a pair of fireflies were already winking softly in the rhododendron bushes. She found a quiet spot on a garden bench away from the crowds and rested her chin in her hands. "Oh God!" she prayed, "Tell me I'm doing the right thing."

She knew that she had now placed her parents in an impossible situation. After her firm declaration that she did not consider herself to be engaged and that the party

148

was not the forum to accept a proposal of marriage or any announcement of a non-existent engagement, she had narrowed their options to a no-win scenario. They could, presumably, simply scratch the idea of announcing the engagement at all this evening and defer the matter until such time as Alan was able to ask Sarah for her hand privately in accordance to her wishes. That was probably the cleverest thing they could do but Sarah realised that it would hardly present itself as an attractive option. For one thing, it would be a complete surrender to her position and still with no guarantee that Sarah would accept the proposal. Sarah, for her part, would have gained time and the high moral ground to consider the proposal on its merits completely on her own terms. It left the question of the marriage dangerously ambiguous and would be seen as deliberate delaying tactics.

There was another reason why the idea was unattractive. This was, the fiction of the officially stated purpose notwithstanding, an engagement party. Whatever Sarah's protestations might be, the majority of the guests had come expecting an engagement. Certainly the Bergers had come officially in anticipation of that event. If the engagement was *not* therefore announced the whole party would be reduced to the point of farce and social disaster. It would be unthinkable. Her mother would never live down the humiliation. An announcement had to be made.

Therefore, somehow, by the end of this evening, Sarah had to be officially engaged. Now they could get Alan to take her aside and formally propose to her. That was easily finessed. She simply had to reiterate to Alan that this was not the time and place to hear his proposal and request a more private meeting at a future date and they would be back to square one. Otherwise they could have him make the proposal publicly, probably during the speeches. That was a more likely scenario but it was a terrible risk. Sarah had already publicly stated that she

149

would not entertain any proposal in front of witnesses or in any way that was not private. It would therefore be in clear contravention of her stated wishes and she would be quite clearly within her rights to protest that she was unable to respond to the proposal at this moment. Worse yet she might haughtily reject the proposal outright. Either way the risk of a scene in front of everybody was immense. They surely wouldn't risk it.

That left the unappetising option of simply announcing the engagement anyway without obtaining the formality of Sarah's consent and hope for the best. They'd presumably believe that, once confronted with a fait accompli, then they could turn her around and persuade her that was what she wanted after all. It would certainly seem like the most plausible way out of the impasse. They'd throw the ball firmly into her court and dare her to toss it back. A few months ago such a gambit would have almost certainly succeeded. They were dealing with a far more formidable Sarah now though.

"There you are Sarah!"

Sarah looked up. It was Jessica. "Hi Jess. Were you looking for me?"

"Dad sent me to find you. They're having the speeches and toasts in a few minutes."

"They can wait." Sarah was feeling perilously rebellious.

Jessica drew a breath and sat down beside her, tapping a cigarette from her pack. "Jesus kid you're playing a dangerous game here. You've really set the cat among the pigeons."

"What are mum and dad saying?"

Jessica lit her cigarette. "They're in a big pow-wow with Alan and his parents. Alan's all outraged victim, old man Berger is huffing and puffing indignantly and his wife's flapping her arms and looking like she's ready to faint. Mum's looking ghastly and dad's trying to do diplomatic damage control. It's the funniest thing you ever saw. I still don't see how you're going to worm out

150

of this Sarah but you can take it from me that the opposition is nicely softened up. You've just been fantastic. God I felt like cheering the way you kept the riff raff cooling their heels at the garden gate before condescending to grace them with your presence. You were magnificent. Nobody can say you didn't go down without a fight."

"I'm not finished yet Jess."

Jessica nodded. "Tell me about it. I don't know what your next move is kid but it'll have to be a whammy. I've got to warn you. Our dear parents and the Bergers are planning to steam roll you. They're going to put you right on the spot."

"I figured as much Jess."

"Well what the hell are you going to do?"

"I've stated my position clearly and unequivocally Jess. I don't suppose there's anybody left at this party that doesn't know my stance by now. If mum and dad and the Bergers choose to ignore that stance publicly then this marriage will have been exposed for the sham it is for all to see and on their own heads be it."

Jessica looked at her as if seeing her for the first time. "Jesus you scare me kid."

"I'm scaring myself too Jess. I just have to be brave; just a little while longer." Sarah took a deep breath and stood. "Come on then Jess. Let them do their worst."

Chapter Seventeen

The party crowd were gathered around the tables at the centre of the back lawn, replete with food from the cold buffet and awaiting the next development in nervous anticipation. The barbeque was scheduled to open later, to accompany the more serious drinking and dancing, which would continue until the early hours. This pause in the schedule however, between the feeding of the guests and the starting up of the band for the later entertainment, was earmarked for speeches and there was not a person present any longer that was unaware of the greater significance of it. It was now that it had originally been expected that the engagement between Alan Berger and Sarah Fuchs would be officially announced and toasts proposed to the happy couple. By now though everybody was equally aware that such a smooth scenario was no longer to be expected. Most people were cognisant that there had always been an element of arrangement in the forthcoming nuptials; that it was in fact a familial contract between the Bergers and the Fuchs with Sarah as the sacrificial pawn to cement the alliance. It had always been assumed that the compliant Sarah had fully acquiesced in this arrangement and was completely consensual to the marriage. Now it seemed, judging by her remarks, that she was anything but. There was a delicious whiff of scandal in the air. Everybody was expecting trouble.

Sarah quailed inside as she saw the scene laid out before her. Alan had already taken his place at the head of the top table. She was expected to sit next to him with their parents on the corresponding sides on each side. The crowd was staring at her as she approached and the tension in the air was palpable. As Sarah approached her father cut her off and held her to one side for a moment. He had a look about him that Sarah recognised. It was the look he adopted when he had cast hesitation and doubt to one side and made a firm decision. He was a man with a fixed plan to proceed and Sarah's heart sunk. "Are you going to be all right Sarah?" he wanted to know.

"I've been all right all night daddy."

"Stop playing games Sarah. You know what I mean. Are you going to conduct yourself properly?"

"I'm sorry if my conduct has not met your approval daddy. I thought I was doing my best to behave in as graceful and as courteous a manner as possible."

"I mean are you going to stop all this nonsense you've been telling people and behave yourself?"

"I haven't told anybody any nonsense daddy. My opinions and my concerns remain the same. I have said nothing that I am ashamed of and I had hoped that you had respect for my concerns."

"Your concerns can wait Sarah. We can discuss them later at our convenience. Right now though, this is an important moment and I shall expect you to conduct yourself appropriately."

"Oh I shall daddy. I shall be *very* appropriate."

Mr Fuchs groaned in exasperation. "Why are you being so difficult Sarah?"

"You mean as opposed to being *easy*?"

"You know damn well what I mean. Don't quibble over etymology with me."

Sarah looked at him sadly. "I love you daddy."

Mr Fuchs blinked. "Eh? What?"

"I said I love you daddy. I love you and I love mum too but I'm afraid daddy. I'm so afraid that you're about to make a terrible mistake; a terrible mistake for all of us."

"What's this nonsense Sarah? You know that everything I do is only because I think it is the best for you."

"You do everything but listen to what *I* think is the best for me daddy. I just want you to know that I love

153

you. I love you and I'm grateful for everything in my life that you've given me; sacrificed on my behalf; all the care and love you've devoted to me; all the protection and help you've afforded me. I'm truly grateful. I don't want you ever to forget that." A tear rolled down her cheek.

Mr Fuchs was shocked. "Sarah! Don't cry for God's sake. This is supposed to be a happy occasion."

Sarah shook her head. "No daddy. It's one of the saddest moments in my life."

"Why for God's sake? Whatever is the matter?"

Sarah dabbed at her eye. "Nothing daddy. Well nothing we can do anything about. I guess we're all in a trap." She composed herself and looked at the gathering ahead. "Come on daddy. The vultures are congregating. Let's not deny them their feast."

Sarah was ushered into her seat next to Alan. He glanced at her sharply. "Listen Sarah I've spoken to your parents and..."

She held up a hand. "Don't say any more Alan. You don't want to ruin the surprise now do you?" He retreated into subdued silence. She glanced around the table. Mr Berger was resting his chin on his chest in ponderous thought whilst his wife, at his side, had her face frozen in a glassy smile. Sarah's mother was staring at her intently but Sarah ignored her. Lower down the table Jessica was biting her lip and looking anxious and even her brother seemed perplexed by the nuances in the air. Her father took his place with his brow creased in worry. Sarah looked, oddly, the calmest person present. Waitresses were topping up champagne flutes in front of all the guests and even they seemed somehow gripped by the underlying tensions in the air.

After a decent interval, Mr Fuchs rose and tapped a spoon against a glass to command the company's attention. Sarah had never seen him look so nervous. When he had silence (and an unbearably tense silence it was too) he addressed the guests. "Ladies and gentlemen

I'd like to thank you all, first of all, on behalf of my wife and I for being present tonight for this happy occasion in bringing together my daughter Sarah and her young gentleman, Alan. This is, of course, a momentous occasion and one that makes me very proud and deeply gratified. I'd like particularly to welcome Herr and Frau Berger here tonight and, before I proceed any further, I believe that Herr Berger would like to say a few words so I yield the floor to him.

There was a polite round of applause. Mr Berger took the cigar from his mouth and eased his ample bulk, to rise heavily to his feet. "Thank you George." He growled. "My wife and I would like to thank you for your hospitality naturally and express our satisfaction that these two youngsters are brought together at last. Your daughter is a fine young lass Alisha and George and I'm sure everybody will agree with me that she looks a grand picture tonight." There was an outburst of enthusiastic applause and Sarah nodded shyly. "Yes Alisha and George," Mr Berger continued. "Your daughter is an admirable young lady and a credit to you both. I know that Alan has been chafing at the bit to see her again these past months and I'm sure he's not disappointed." Mr Berger paused to chuckle. "I had to tell the lad to stop drooling when he saw her tonight." Even Alan managed to look embarrassed by his father's tasteless joke. "Alan has had to be away unfortunately." Mr Berger told the audience. "He's been away in America attending to business; important business I might let you know; business that will be important to both our families in the days to come. I know it's hard on our womenfolk when we men of affairs are called upon to be absent from home on matters of business but, sad to say, that's the way of the world. I know my own dear wife has shown great patience and resilience over the years when I've been required to be away for prolonged periods on important matters. I'm sure, therefore, that this young lady will quite understand that

Alan, in his turn, will be asked to be parted on occasion from his nearest and dearest in the interests of their common good. After all that's what puts bread and butter on the table, and sometimes a bit of jam to boot. I think we can all admire our good ladies for their understanding of these facts of life and their unstinting efforts to maintain their households during their husband's absence and I'm sure Sarah here will be no different. Anyway, here they are, back together at last and I think it high time that we saw them commit to a more solid future together. My son is a fine young man and I'm proud of him. He is a very astute businessman for a young man of his age and he has fine prospects in front of him. I think therefore, Alisha and George, that I can guarantee that my son will be more than capable of providing excellently for your daughter and securing a most prosperous and safe future for whatever grandchildren they may bring us. Furthermore it is a great pleasure to me that, through this union, our two families, with so much in common and with so many mutual interests, should be brought closer together in what I confidently expect will be a prosperous and mutually advantageous partnership." Mr Berger paused to raise his glass from the table. "I propose a toast therefore. To Alan and Sarah and a happy and prosperous future together."

The company raised glasses and intoned the words of the toast as Mr Berger resumed his seat with a small grunt. Sarah's father stood once more and glanced nervously at Sarah whose face was fixed in an impassive mask. "Er thank you Bruno. We too are delighted to see Sarah and Alan reunited at last and of course we admire all the qualities you have mentioned in your son. Certainly we have come to recognise those fine qualities over the years that he and Sarah have been together and I know that both Alisha and I are delighted that our beloved daughter should have found such an admirable soul mate.

"It is always difficult for a father to contemplate the loss of his daughter and I am certainly no exception. Sarah is the baby of the family and I've often been accused of being overly protective of her. I can still remember the first time that Sarah stayed out late as a teenager. I was nearly a basket case by the time she came home and I grounded her for three weeks." He paused to allow a soft ripple of laughter. "Fortunately such incidents were very rare for Sarah was never a wild or rebellious child. Indeed..." Mr Fuchs paused to glance at his elder children with a smile. "and with all due respect to Jessica and John here, Sarah was probably the most obedient and well behaved of all our children. Both Jessie and John raised a little hell during their formative years and are probably responsible for a considerable number of the grey hairs I now possess. Now however they have both settled down and turned into fine young adults and I see that all my fears were groundless after all.

"Sarah was always a little different however. She was always a quiet, sensible and more serious girl. She was never a girl for wild parties and late nights, she took her school studies seriously and she inherited from me a love of the great outdoors, becoming, in her later years, respected by the people of the Toggenburg for her expertise in and local knowledge of the mountains she grew up amongst. Sarah has also just finished her bachelor's degree at Bern University with distinction. Now it may be that her university studies may only be of limited value in her future life but, nevertheless, I am proud of her academic achievements. In fact I am proud of Sarah in every respect. She has never been anything other than a dutiful and loving daughter and I am sure that she will carry those qualities with her as she leaves the nest and sets out into adulthood to the lasting gratification and appreciation of her future husband.

"It is always important for a father, as I have said, that a daughter, which he so loves and cares about, sets out into the world with every advantage possible and with every chance of a happy and secure future. Naturally, therefore, a father will regard any young man with intentions on his daughter with the utmost of scepticism. The worst nightmare for any father is in seeing his daughter fall into the clutches of some predatory young stud quite unsuitable as a mate for her. He lies awake at night wondering what kind of horror she's going to bring home. I needn't have been concerned about Sarah though. With great maturity and sense she found a young man of fine family, with exciting prospects before him and who cares about her deeply.

As far as I know, Sarah has never had any other serious boyfriend than Alan. She saw early that he was the man for her and she has single-mindedly remained devoted to him even when circumstances dictated that they be separated for prolonged periods. Such separations may well have sundered two less committed young people but neither Sarah nor Alan have wavered from their mutual devotion and now stand to reap the rewards of their patience and forbearance. Certainly the question of their partnership has never been in doubt. It has long been an unspoken understanding that they were destined for each other and that one day, when all circumstances permitted, that they would take formal vows before God and, dare I say it, start to live happily ever after. I think we can now all say that that day is nearly upon us. It is an old cliché, but nevertheless a true one, that when your daughter marries you don't lose a daughter but you gain a son. I think Alisha and I have regarded Alan as virtually a son for some time now and we could not be more pleased that he is to become our daughter's husband."

Mr Fuchs paused to take a sip of his drink and clear his throat. "Now some of you may be a little confused regarding some of Sarah's remarks earlier this evening." He gave a small chuckle. "There is a ready explanation.

Sarah has stated that she is not formally affianced to Alan and was therefore a little confused herself when people asked her if she was to announce her engagement this evening. How could she? She wasn't engaged. This technically is true. Alan had, quite admirably in my opinion, declared that he would not formally ask for my daughter's hand in marriage until such time as he could demonstrate to me that he was in a position to satisfy my demands regarding his ability to care for my daughter financially and prove his future prospects to continue to maintain my daughter in security and prosperity. I am delighted to tell you that he has more than satisfied those requirements and I have formally granted him permission to pursue his suit. In fact, the engagement between Sarah and Alan has been an informal understanding for some considerable time now and we are even in an advanced stage of planning for the actual wedding. All that remains, in fact, is to merely formalise a long standing mutual agreement.

"To this end we had planned a little surprise for Sarah. We had billed this party under the somewhat fictitious heading of a reunion party for the separated couple whereas, of course, it had a much more serious purpose. In order to surprise Sarah and make this a genuinely romantic occasion, we were perhaps less than candid with her and the net result was that she was somewhat confused when other people, more in the know, talked about her engagement. Perhaps when she realised the true purpose of the festivities she became nervous for Sarah is a very private person and eschews the limelight. She may have feared being embarrassed in public even though I don't think there is anybody here who wishes her anything but the best. However, both my family and Alan's are agreed that the young couple have waited too long and it is time that their dreams came true. I apologise to my daughter if we seem to be putting her on the spot but all we want to do is grant her that which we know has been in her heart from the first; her betrothal to the man in her life, our unqualified approval of that betrothal and our profound happiness that she has found a man to love and care for her for the rest of her days. With the deepest satisfaction therefore I would like to hand proceedings over to the young man to whom I also grant my daughter's hand. Ladies and gentlemen; Alan."

There was a warm applause and Sarah conceded, ruefully, that her father had done a remarkably good job of damage control. He was saying "Take no notice of what Sarah said. She's a bit confused because we were trying to surprise her. We're just doing what is best for her and what she wanted anyway." It was a brilliant speech, Sarah thought. Her father had a fine reputation for diplomatic smooth talk to soothe over differences in the business world. She could understand why.

At her side Alan rose to his feet. Sarah took a sip of her drink and tried to calm her heart hammering in her breast. "Thank you Mr Fuchs." He began. "I'd like to thank you indeed for your hospitality and kind words More than that I'd like to thank you for a gift so precious it means more to me than anything in the world; the hand of your beautiful and wonderful daughter. All the time that I've been in America I have counted the days to when I could hurry home to be reunited with the girl I most care about. Those months have been a torture for me and I cannot begin to express my happiness in being with Sarah once again. All those months I had but one thought in my mind; to finish my business and dash home to make this lovely girl my wife. I have known for years that the only person I wanted to marry was Sarah. I knew however that sweet words and flowers were not sufficient in themselves upon which to base a marriage. Marriage was a serious business and when the champagne bubbles had vanished and there were bills on the kitchen table it would take more than endearments to ensure the success of our marriage. So I waited. I waited and I worked hard. I worked hard to try and ensure that I would have the wherewithal and the prospects to give Sarah and I a solid foundation for our future. That future was always a motivation to me. I worked long into the nights and seven days a week when necessary and if I was tired I could remind myself what the reward was. The reward is sat next to me and finally I can confidently say that I have earned her. I would not dream to accept Mr Fuch's daughter's hand were I not able to assure him with complete confidence that he was delivering that hand into safe keeping. I believe my toils have borne fruit and that now I can accept the hand I cherish with a clear conscience. I gratefully do accept that hand therefore Mr Fuchs and I thank you once again for the gift of it."

There was an approving applause. Sarah was quite surprised. Alan's speech was eloquent and moving by his standards. She hadn't known he had it in him. Presumably he had been well coached. Once the applause had subsided Alan reached down and took her left hand. He looked at her fondly for a second before addressing the audience. "This then is the culmination of my dreams ladies and gentlemen. All the hard work has been worth it. I ask Sarah's forgiveness if I am embarrassing her but I want to state now that there is nothing in the world I want more at this moment than the hand of this beautiful lady at my side. I ask her forgiveness too if I have not until now firmly and formally declared that I desire nothing more than to take her as my wife. I hope she understands that I have never had anything other than an intention to marry her and that I am now only stating publicly what has been understood between us privately."

With a flourish Alan reached into the pocket of his tuxedo and drew out a small box. He opened the box to reveal a ring of platinum set with a cluster of diamonds and whose central stone was so large it drew gasps from the audience. "As a token therefore of my commitment," Alan continued, "I bought this in America and counted the days until I could set it in its rightful place on the finger of the lady I cherish. With your permission then ladies and gentlemen I will proceed to do just that." Mesmerised Sarah watched him raise her hand and slide the ring onto her ring finger. It didn't exactly slide. The ring was a little too small and there was an embarrassing moment when he had to exert some force to ease it over her knuckle. He looked relieved when the object was finally in place. "With this ring," he declared, "I accept the hand of Sarah to be my future wife and I vow here, before witnesses, that I will do everything in my power to make her happy and keep her in cherished security as long as I draw breath." With that he stooped and kissed her quickly.

Before Sarah could react, her father jumped to his feet. "A toast!" he called. "Ladies and gentlemen. The happy couple." The audience rose as a body to raise their glasses. "The happy couple." Sarah remained seated. She was staring at the ring on her finger. The enormous diamond at its centre flashed iridescently with refracted fire. She seemed hypnotised by it. Her father was shaking Alan's hand and her mother was embracing Alan's mother. Mr Berger came up and patted her patronisingly and people were crowding around to congratulate her. Sarah nodded in shock barely hearing them. She saw Mr Berger clap an arm around her father. "Well George." he boomed. "It's a pleasure to do business with you. Come along let's get to the bar and have a proper drink. Bloody champagne gives me gut rot. You and I have things to talk about."

Sarah's mother called for attention amid all the excitement. "Just to let you know ladies and gentlemen that we'll be starting the music in a few minutes and then we can all get our dancing shoes on. Hopefully our happy couple will lead us out onto the floor and show us all how it's done." Released from the speeches the crowd were dispersing to the bar excitedly. Sarah remained where she sat still staring at the ring. She felt unutterably sad. Alan glanced at her nervously. "Er can I get you a drink Sarah?"

She shook her head. "I've already got one thank you."

He hesitated in indecision. "Well I'll just grab something for myself then."

"Of course. Please feel free." Her voice was flat and monotone. He departed nervously but Sarah watched his confidence return as he was surrounded by well-wishers at the bar. Her mother approached and kissed her. "For heaven's sake Sarah!" she muttered vexedly. "Try to smile. You've just got *engaged* for crying out loud."

"So it seems."

"What on earth is the matter with you? This should be one of the happiest days of your life."

"Yes you're right. It should."

"Well for heaven's sake put a different face on. You're supposed to be leading off the dancing in a few minutes."

"I'm sorry mother but you'll have to make excuses for me. I'm afraid I don't feel up to dancing. You can tell your friends that I'm temporarily overcome with emotion."

"What nonsense Sarah. Of course you can dance."

Sarah looked at her coldly. "I'm sorry mother but I am not going to be made a spectacle of any more tonight. I am not going to dance and that's flat." Sarah rose from her seat. "Now if you'll excuse me I need a few minutes to myself. She turned and walked away decisively. Her mother stared after her in annoyance.

Chapter Eighteen

Sarah found a dark quiet corner of the garden where she could look down across Lake Maggiore. The lake was pearly under the rays of the newly risen moon. It reminded her of the night she had watched the moon rise with Daniela over the waters of the Fahlensee. The lights of the towns and hamlets around the lake sparkled invitingly and she could make out the lights of cabin cruisers on the water. She felt lonely and sad. She looked once again at the ring on her finger. She had won after all but she knew the terrible price it would cost her.

Suddenly she stiffened. On the other side of some bushes she heard voices approaching. Two ladies had slipped away for a quiet cigarette and they were talking in Swiss German. Sarah remained still and melded into the darkness to listen. "Well they got hitched up after all Andrea and you said they wouldn't." one of the ladies was saying.

"I wouldn't be too sure of that Gerty."

"Well the girl's got a ring on her finger now so I can't see how you could think otherwise."

"Oh yes she's got a ring on her finger and downright put out about it she looked as well. That young Berger lad jammed that ring on her finger like he was ringing a bull. I didn't see him asking permission before claiming her for his own property."

"Oh come on Andrea. You always have to look at the black side of things. I think they make a lovely couple."

"Oh yes? So did you see the bride to be looking radiantly happy Gerty? She looked like she was being sentenced to death from where I was sat."

"He just caught her by surprise that's all. I'm sure she'll be happier once it's had time to sink in."

"Oh Gerty you can be so naive sometimes. Everybody knows that this is an arranged marriage. It's just the Fuch's trying to cement a cosy business deal with the Bergers with their daughter as the icing on the cake. She's being forced into a marriage she's clearly not happy about and it shows. That's what all that theatre was about earlier when she was insisting that she wasn't getting engaged. She was kicking and trying to squirm out of it. Hasn't done the poor girl an iota of good however. They've shanghaied her. All that rubbish from George about her being a dutiful and obedient daughter was just him cracking the whip and telling her to do as she's told. Then they rammed a ring on her finger before she had time to protest."

"Surely they wouldn't force her into a marriage she's not happy about?"

"You mark my words Gerty. There's trouble ahead. I think George and Alisha have seriously underestimated that daughter of theirs. Sarah's grown up a lot in the last year or two and I don't think she's going to be so easy to whip into line as she once was. She looked mighty displeased when they bulldozed that ring onto her finger and I think they've got a fight on their hands. I don't blame the girl for kicking. I wouldn't want any daughter of *mine* married to the Bergers."

"What's wrong with the Bergers? They're a wealthy respectable family surely."

"Hmmph they're wealthy enough but I don't know about respectable. Do you know how old man Berger made his first fortune?"

"Wasn't it something to do with the defence industries?"

"That's a nice way of putting it. He was exporting arms to Third World countries and dodging his way through some pretty dubious legal loopholes to do so. The man's a glorified gunrunner when all's said and done Gerty. There're a lot of skeletons locked away in his private bank accounts. The Fuchs must be mad

165

allying themselves with someone like him." She flicked her cigarette end into the bushes. "Come on. We'd better get back."

After they had parted, Sarah sat alone in the darkness for some minutes. Her loneliness and melancholy seemed to wrap around her in the solitude of the dark. She pulled her mobile phone from her handbag and looked at her messages. There was a text from Daniela. *"J miss U! Life is sad and grey without U. Where are U now my love? Pls don't leave me. J am so sad alone without U. Come home my love."* Sarah stared at the message the tears on her face illuminated by the soft electronic light of the display screen. Jessica approached quietly from behind and saw her sitting, lost in her solitude. She took a breath. "Sarah?" she inquired softly. "Are you ok?"

Sarah stirred and turned to look at her sister. "Not really Jess."

Jessica came and sat beside her on the small bench. "Somehow I didn't think you would be. That was a pretty shabby trick you got pulled on you there."

Sarah shook her head. "No Jess. I was the one that pulled a shabby trick. I... I'm ashamed of myself."

Jessica put an arm around her. "Sarah kid! *You* haven't done anything wrong. Our parents and Alan and his Godforsaken family are the ones that should be ashamed. I nearly died of humiliation when they pulled that number on you. I just can't believe dad. I expected some pompous bullshit from Alan's sodding father but I thought dad was better than that. I've never heard such sanctimonious, hypocritical crap in my life. I can't believe he treated you like that. After all you'd said previously, he just completely ignored your own concerns and wishes and essentially told everybody publicly that you were just a silly little girl who didn't know better and that daddy knows best. God Sarah! Why didn't you throw something at him?"

Sarah rested her head on Jessica's shoulder. "Don't be angry with dad Jess. I painted him into a corner. I left him no choice."

"He could have chosen to respect you Sarah. He could have treated you with the due respect and deference due to a grown woman. Instead he treated you like a child."

"Oh Jess I'll always be a child to dad. He can't see me any other way. Fathers are like that with their daughters. Their sons grow up and challenge them but their daughters are always the little vulnerable things they doted on. Their sons grow up to be equal with them but never their daughters. We just break their hearts."

"Your heart looks pretty close to breaking Sarah."

"Yes it is Jess. I've done a terrible thing."

"For God's sake Sarah. What have *you* done?"

"I've broken my family apart Jess. I thought I had good reason. I *do* have good reason but it hurts anyway."

"How the hell have you done that? Seems like the family is pretty much made up about things. They've got what they wanted after all. They've just dressed you up, wrapped you up and delivered you on a silver platter to the bloody Bergers. They've got you engaged and that was the whole point of this bloody exercise."

"Oh Jess I'm not engaged."

"Er sorry? Did I miss something? There *is* a sodding great rock stuck on your ring finger as far as I can see. Now I'm no gemmologist but if that fucking thing's a milligram under three carats or cost a franc less than fifty grand then I'm a fucking cadet on Starship Enterprise."

"It's a piece of metamorphosed, crystalline carbon Jess. It's meaningless. It could cost fifty million and it still wouldn't mean anything."

"Er I thought it meant that you were engaged."

"Did you hear Alan humbly ask me to consent to be his wife Jess?"

"Well not as such but..."

"Did you furthermore hear me grant that consent Jess?"

"Well no but..."

"Ergo I am *not* engaged Jess. All that has happened is that I have had a vulgar item of jewellery forced onto my finger without my consent in a publicly humiliating fashion and had it announced that I am therefore betrothed to be married, against my publicly expressed wishes, before witnesses. I knew that something like this would happen Jess. In fact I *engineered* it. I forced father into a position in which he had to defy my wishes, and overrule my objections, to betroth me to Alan. The person that has been publicly humiliated is dad. The marriage has been exposed in front of all his friends and colleagues and mum's too. I didn't want to do it Jess but I was in a trap too. I nearly begged dad this afternoon to give me a loophole. I made him promise to grant me the final say over when and whom I shall marry. He has chosen to ignore that promise. Maybe he just thinks that I don't know my own mind; that I'll come around and accept the inevitable. He's wrong Jess. He's handed me the moral high ground. I can walk away from this now and be ever able to say that I was being forced against my wishes into marriage. That's my decision to make now and only mine. But it will cost me Jess. It will cost me my family." Sarah paused to wipe away a tear. "Oh God Jess. I feel terrible."

Jessica stared at her in the twilight of the garden. She was astonished. She drew a deep breath. "Whew Sarah! Dad's not the only one that hasn't realised how much you've grown. I'm guilty too. I've always thought of you as my kid sister and now you turn around and flatly state that you've manipulated mum and dad in public into making a farce out of their wedding plans for you. God that's genius!"

"It's not really Jess."

"But it is. I see it all now. All you had to do was to state that you didn't want to get engaged tonight and thus force dad and mum into giving you away anyway. You couldn't have pointed out that this was an arranged marriage without your consent more forcibly. Now nobody can blame you if you hand the ring back. You never asked for the damn thing. You can walk off with your head held high and dad won't have a leg to stand on. That's brilliant Sarah."

"I don't feel brilliant Jess."

"Oh Sarah! I know what's bothering you."

"You do?"

"Yes. You think that mum and dad will never forgive you if you walk away from this marriage. You're wrong you know. Oh they'll be mad all right. They were mad with me when I married against their wishes. I had to take a year or two in the wilderness. But, in the end, they'll remember that you're their daughter and that they love you. Of course things will never be quite the same but that's always going to happen. Parents have to learn that their children grow up and they have their own lives to lead. They have to learn that their children have their own minds and that they make their own decisions in life. They can't tell them what to do. You always had a disadvantage Sarah because you were always their favourite."

"Oh Jess they loved you every bit as much as they loved me."

"Hey Sarah, I'm not jealous. All I'm saying is that you're the youngest and however much parents don't want to show it there's always one child who is the favourite. It's unfair to that kid because they cling onto them for too long. It was even worse when I left the nest in such acrimonious style and when John drifted on his own way. You were all they had left and they clung to their little baby like glue. You're an adult woman now but they still haven't got their heads around that yet. They will do Sarah. You'll have to give them time but they'll realise it sooner or later. You *do* have your own life to lead after all."

169

"Yes. I do."

"What *are* you going to do?"

"I want to continue my academic career Jess. I'd like to do a doctorate."

"That's going to be difficult without dad to pick up the bills Sarah."

"It would be even more difficult while keeping house for Alan in Zurich Jess."

"That's true. But how would you finance it?"

"I'll find a way."

"I believe you. So what are your immediate plans?"

"I don't know really. I have to sleep on it. I'll have to make a decision in the next couple of days."

"Sarah sweetheart I'd love to stay and give you moral support but I have to go home the day after tomorrow. Damien will be back then and I have my own life to lead."

"I know Jess. I'm just grateful you're here. I'll make up my mind before you leave."

"What is there to make up your mind about? You don't want to get married. Bang! Your decision. You hand Alan his ring back and go home to the Toggenburg where you always wanted to be in the first place. What's the problem?"

"You've no idea Jess. If only it was so simple."

Jessica peered at her in the dark shrewdly. "There's something else isn't there Sarah; something you're not telling me?"

"Why do you say that?"

"Because something has changed with you Sarah. You're not the meek little girl you used to be; that Alan used to dominate or that mum and dad used to be able to command at will. You've become somebody new."

"I've been three years at university Jess. It teaches you to think for yourself."

"Hmm maybe. I think it goes a bit deeper than academia though. There is something you're not telling me isn't there? This isn't just about telling mum, dad and

Alan that you don't feel ready to marry is it? There's something else going on."

Sarah sighed. "You don't know the half of it Jess. It's not something I can talk about; not even with you."

"Why? What is the matter?"

"Drop it Jess. I think we'd better get back and join the others. I don't want to be accused of spoiling the party!"

Chapter Nineteen

Mr and Mrs Fuchs rose late the next morning and took breakfast out in the garden as was their usual habit during the warm weather. The garden made a sorry sight this morning for the debris of the party was liberally scattered around. That afternoon, Mrs Fuchs had a serious clean-up operation to organise. Fortunately she had a small army of helpers coming along to assist but it would still be a formidable undertaking. It wasn't however the first time Mrs Fuchs had had to return her house and garden to its usual pristine state following a night of festivities. She was known for the lavishness of her garden parties. She poured some more coffee. "Are you going into the office today George?" she asked her husband who was buried in the International Herald Tribune.

"Oh I wasn't going to Alisha. There's nothing that requires my immediate attention. If they need me they'll call me up. I'll stick around and help dismantle all this stuff." He waved his hand vaguely at the infrastructure of the night's party; the stage, the dance floor, the bars, barbecues, tables and chairs. It was going to take half the day to pack it all away for the hire companies.

"Oh good." said Mrs Fuchs with appreciation. "We need all the hands we can get. We can get John and Jessica to help out as well thankfully. Alan won't mind giving a hand as well, I'm sure, and Sarah can atone for some of her wretched behaviour last night by pulling her finger out and helping to clear up as well."

Mr Fuchs sighed. "She wasn't *that* bad Alisha." He protested.

"She damn well was George. She damn nearly ruined the whole party with her prima donna behaviour until the engagement announcement and then spent the rest of the evening sulking about it. She refused utterly to dance with anyone and she was barely civil to Alan for most of the evening. I can't think what's got into the girl. If a man declares his devotion to you and proves it by putting about fifty thousand francs worth of precious stone on your finger, most girls would have been delirious with joy about it. Good God she's waited over three years to marry the boy so why all this sudden procrastination?"

Mr Fuchs rubbed his chin in concern. "I was a bit taken aback by that ring to tell you the truth Alisha. I know the Bergers like to flash their cash but I think that ring was a bit over the top. I'm not happy with the thought of Sarah carrying about so much money about on her finger. She's unworldly with such things Alisha. It would be just like her to go and lose it or get it stolen or something. I hope that they had the sense to insure the thing."

"I'm sure Bruno wouldn't forget that simple precaution George. Anyway you're changing the subject. I was talking about your daughter's inexcusable behaviour last night."

Mr Fuchs frowned vexedly. He had a mild hangover and was not in the mood to tackle his mercurial wife with a bee in her bonnet. "Why is she always *my* daughter whenever you're annoyed with her Alisha? I seem to recall that you've got at least half a share of parental responsibility here."

"Stop beating around the bush George and stop making excuses for her. She was being a little madam last night and you know it."

"Well she was miffed with us Alisha for dropping the engagement on her like that after I'd promised to involve her in the process more. I think she felt pressurised."

"Well, for heaven's sake, what choice did she give us? We had to announce the engagement last night. That's what all the guests had come to celebrate, for God's sake. Did she honestly think we could postpone her engagement while she flapped her hands and pretended to be hard to get? The girl's got no sense of responsibility."

Mr Fuchs shrugged. "Well she'll get used to it Alisha. As you say, she's waited three years and I'm sure she'll see things a bit differently now. Doubtless she'll feel that we've not consulted her again and we'll have to put up with a bit of ill humour from her but once she realises that we've only pushed ahead with what was a foregone conclusion in the first place, she'll come around. I told Alan to give her a little extra loving care and attention last night. If he's done his job properly, they'll have kissed and made up in bed. You watch, she'll probably be purring like a pussy cat this morning."

Mrs Fuchs frowned. "I hope the pair of them were sensible enough to take precautions."

"Whatever for? They're practically married now for heaven's sake Alisha. Don't you want grandchildren?"

"Of course I do. Not that any of our children seem in any hurry to provide us with any. Jessica's been married for years now and devil the sign of any offspring from her. I asked her once when she was going to have children because she wasn't getting any younger and she near as damn it told me to mind my own business."

"Well what's the problem then? I'd have thought the quicker that Sarah's pregnant the better. She'll settle a lot faster into her new life in Zurich if she's got a baby to care for." Mr Fuchs allowed himself a chuckle. "Mind you that's going to be really weird. It seems almost yesterday she was just a little girl. I can't imagine her carrying a child of her own."

"Well it's a matter of timing George. I've been thinking things through. If Sarah really is in a bit of a mood about being precipitously flung into engagement and she's still insisting on having her own say about the wedding plans well our original provisional date might be a little ambitious. If she's going to want to choose her own dress, bridesmaids, guest lists and what have you we're going to have to make all sorts of readjustments. It'll be a rushed job to arrange it all by the end of September. It might be a good idea, in that case, to postpone it for a few months. That way we can get Sarah more fully onboard and take our time to plan the thing properly."

Mr Fuchs looked at her in surprise. "I thought you were all for an early wedding."

"Well I was originally but the more I think about it the more sense it makes to put the date back a bit. I mean, if Sarah had come down here at the beginning of summer, the earlier date would have been feasible since we'd have had all that time to plan it together. Now I don't think that provisional date is practical."

"So what kind of date were you thinking about?"

"Well I thought the first week in April would be nice. It's lovely in Ticino in early April with all the flowers and blossoms out and we could throw a really beautiful wedding."

"So this is why you're suddenly concerned about Sarah's contraception is it?"

"Well yes. I mean we wouldn't want to have to make last minute adjustments to the wedding dress or have Sarah lumbering down the aisle looking as if she's about to break waters in the vestry."

"Well I'm sure they'll have taken all due care and precaution Alisha."

"Are you sure George? I mean they might have thought, well we're practically married now so what the hell and, anyway, Alan's Catholic and they can be funny about things like that."

"Well they've been together for some years now Alisha and I'm sure they haven't just been holding hands. Sarah hasn't come home with a bun in the oven yet. She's sensible about things like that at least." Mr Fuchs put down his paper and poured himself some more coffee. "But I think you're idea is a good one Alisha. I was worried myself that the early date was going to be a bit of a rush. We'll have to canvas Alan about it though. He might be very keen on an early marriage."

Mrs Fuchs looked smug. "I already have. I pulled him aside last night and asked him if a date in early April would be satisfactory for him. He was quite enthusiastic about the idea. Apparently there's a fair bit of work to do on the house in Zurich and the later date would give them more time to get it ready before they move in. He sounded quite relieved about a later date to tell the truth. I think he felt a little under the gun having everything ready so quickly."

"Well that's fine by me Alisha. It would take some of the pressure off and if Alan's agreeable then I'd say yes. We'll have to ask Sarah of course."

"Oh I'm sure she'll agree George."

"Well let's make no assumptions on that score Alisha. She's been kicking enough because she thinks her own wedding is out of her control so, for heaven's sake, let's not precipitate another insurrection by arbitrarily going ahead and setting a wedding date without consulting her. She has to give her full agreement on the date. Having said that, I think she'll probably be all too pleased to have the thing postponed for a few months. That'll take some of the pressure off her too. The only thing that concerns me is that she'll take the revised date as an excuse to bugger off back to the Toggenburg for the winter and we'll be back where we started."

"Oh she can't do that George. We'll just have to insist that she stays here for the winter or at least with Alan when he needs to be in Zurich."

"Well we'll have to be careful how we tread Alisha. Sarah's not taking kindly to our insistences at the moment. Hopefully, now she's engaged, she'll reconcile herself to the fact and want to be near Alan. Also we'll point out to her that if she wants to make it her wedding then she's going to have be here. I think she'll see the sense in that."

"Why is she being so difficult George?"

"Oh I think I can understand it honey. Getting married is a hell of a big step. She's always had a lot of freedom and now she thinks she's losing it all. She's just scared Alisha. I know *I* was before I married you. She's jumping into unknown territory. All this stuff about wanting to make her own decisions about her marriage is just her grasping at straws to try and regain some freedom and control over events. She feels under pressure. That's why I think your idea is a good one. She can help Alan out with the house for one thing. She's barely ever set foot in that house and it's supposed to be her new home. It'll feel a lot more like her home to her after she's spent half the winter decorating it and choosing curtains and carpets. I think this could work out rather well. I think we've got a far better chance of a happy bride in the spring than we do now."

"Well maybe we could tackle her on the subject today George."

"Yes we can have a family pow wow this evening when we get all this stuff out of the way. I thought it would be nice to have a family dinner in tonight. It'll be our last chance for some time. Jessie and John are both going home tomorrow."

"Yes that's a good idea. Oh look. Here comes Alan."

Alan had emerged from the house, casually dressed and looking subdued. Mr Fuchs waved him over and indicated a chair. "Good morning Alan. Pull up a seat and grab some breakfast."

"Thank you. Good morning Mrs Fuchs and you sir."

Mrs Fuchs pushed a cup over to him and plied the coffee pot. "Did you sleep well Alan?"

"Yes. Er yes thank you. I've had better starts to the day before though. I think I drank a bit too much last night."

Mr Fuchs chuckled. "Well I didn't get out of bed feeling on top of my form either. You didn't disgrace

177

yourself anyway and you've got a young liver. You'll be as right as rain by lunchtime."

Mrs Fuchs intervened smoothly. "George and I were just talking about what we discussed last night Alan; you know, about postponing the marriage until April."

Alan nodded sombrely. "Well it's perfect by me. I don't know what Sarah will say though."

Mrs Fuchs smiled. "Oh we both think she'll be fine with the idea. We think it'll take some of the pressure off her and give her more time to plan the marriage properly. We think she'll be a lot happier with a later date for the wedding."

Alan rubbed his chin doubtfully. "Hmm. To be honest, she didn't seem happy with the idea of any marriage, whatever the date, last night."

Mrs Fuchs looked at him sharply. "You two haven't had a row have you?"

Alan shook his head. "No. Actually I think I would rather have had a row. That way we might have been able to thrash the matter out about what was wrong with her. But she just remained a bit aloof and didn't want to talk about it."

Mrs Fuchs waved a hand airily. "Oh take no notice of her Alan. She's just being a bit of a drama queen because we stole a jump on her with your engagement. She'll soon come around. I'll say one thing for Sarah. She can be moody sometimes but it never lasts. She's not the kind to sulk for days on end. Now Jessica, there's another matter."

"Where is Sarah anyway?" asked Mr Fuchs, "Is she still getting dressed."

Alan shrugged. "I've no idea. I haven't seen her yet."

Mr and Mrs Fuchs blinked in surprise. "But... but isn't she with you Alan?" asked Mrs Fuchs perplexedly.

"No of course not Mrs Fuchs. I presume she's in her own room."

178

Mr and Mrs Fuchs glanced at each other in consternation over this new intelligence. Mrs Fuchs regarded Alan seriously. "But Alan we made up the guest suite for you and Sarah especially. I told Sarah yesterday. Are you telling me that she slept alone in her own room?"

"She never mentioned to me that we were supposed to be sharing Mrs Fuchs. She told me late last night that she was tired and wanted to retire and that was the last I saw of her. I didn't think anything of it. We've always had separate rooms when I've stayed here before."

"Yes but you weren't engaged to be married before Alan. I thought... well I thought that we could bend the rules a little since you were all but a married couple bar the shouting so I told Sarah that you and she could take the guest suite together." Mrs Fuchs looked flustered and embarrassed. "Perhaps... well perhaps she forgot."

Alan raised an eyebrow. "I wouldn't have thought that that was something a person would *forget* Mrs Fuchs."

"No, no quite. I... I don't know then. She did have quite a bit to drink though and... well Sarah's not got a good head for alcohol."

Alan pulled a face. "She seemed sober enough to me; stone *cold* sober I would have described her as."

"Well I'm sure she has some explanation Alan." said Mrs Fuchs hastily.

Mr Fuchs snorted. "I wouldn't worry about it Alan. She was in a foul humour. It was probably just her way of spanking you for dropping your engagement on her like that in public. I'm sure she'll be fine in the clear light of day. You might have to get outside of an unappetising dish of humble pie for lunch. She just needs a little careful handling and a bit of loving care. Alisha's right. Sarah's not a girl to carry grudges for long." Mr Fuchs thought for a moment. "In fact Alisha do we really need Alan and Sarah to help clear up today? I mean we've got enough help surely."

179

"Well I suppose we could spare them."

"Excellent." said Mr Fuchs with satisfaction. "In that case Alan why don't you take Sarah off somewhere and spend a little time on your own together today. Take her out to lunch somewhere nice and spend some time catching up. You didn't have a minute to yourselves last night and you haven't seen each other for months. Treat her gently, coddle her, tell her how you feel about her and I'm sure she'll be her old self in no time. What do you say?"

"Yes I'd like that Mr Fuchs. Thank you." Alan put down his cup. "In that case I'd better check up on things now and make sure everything is ok at the office. Do you mind if I borrow the use of your desk top to check my e-mails Mr Fuchs?"

"Go right ahead son. Take your coffee with you."

"Thank you sir." Alan departed looking much happier.

"What the devil is Sarah playing at?" hissed Mrs Fuchs furiously. "The poor boy's been yearning for months to see her again and she snubs him and makes him sleep alone. She's got some bloody explaining to do."

Mr Fuchs nodded at a figure emerging around the corner of the house. "Here comes Jessie. Maybe she can shed some light on her sister's behaviour."

Jessica walked across a lawn and approached them airily. "Hi mum, hi dad. Is there any more coffee in that pot?"

Mr Fuchs smiled. "Sure Jessie. Have you had breakfast?"

Jessica took a seat. "Oh yes I've already eaten. I've been up for hours. I could use a coffee though."

Mr Fuchs interrupted agitatedly. "Jessie have you seen Sarah this morning?"

"Oh yes. She got up the same time as I did."

"Well where is she then?"

"Out."

180

"*Out*?"

"Yes she's gone out for the day. I drove down to Ascona this morning and I dropped her off at the bus stop on the way. I told her I'd pick her up this afternoon if she called me to let me know where she was."

Mrs Fuchs looked furious. "Really Jessica! How *could* you?"

"How could I what?"

"How could you just let Sarah go off like that without telling anyone?"

Jessica rolled her eyes up in mocking puzzlement. "Er am I mistaken here or isn't Sarah really an adult woman. I think you'll find she's over twenty one and she doesn't need your permission, mother, to do as she wants."

"Well where the hell has she gone?"

"I've no idea and it's her business in any case. I did however drop her at the bus stop on the route up the Centovalli and she was wearing beachwear and carrying a big bag so my guess is that she's going to spend a few hours dossing around the river at Intragna."

Mrs Fuchs had gone pink in the face. "She can't do that. Alan's supposed to be taking her out for the day."

"Oh yes? And does Sarah know this?"

"Well no but..."

"Ah so she *doesn't* know."

"Well we've only just decided and..."

"So, in fact, you've made another decision about what Sarah is going to do without having the decency to ask her first."

"That'll do Jessica." her father reprimanded. "We've done no such thing. Alan just wanted to take her out for the day and we told him that we didn't need the pair of them to help clear up here."

"Did you put her up to this Jessica?" demanded Mrs Fuchs angrily.

It was Jessica's turn to look angry. "No mother. I don't put people up to things. I assume that once a person has reached adult age then they're quite capable of making their own decisions and it's not my business to meddle in their affairs. You might try adopting the same attitude occasionally."

"Jessica!" said Mr Fuchs sternly. "I won't have you talk to your mother like this."

"Then my mother had better remain civil to me father and not instantly assume that, just because her youngest daughter is showing some degree of admirable independence from her continual interference, it's something to do with me. I'm not responsible for Sarah's actions. She's old enough now not to require a babysitter and it's not my place to tell her what or what not to do. If you have issues with her decision to go out for the day I suggest you take it up with her and don't be surprised if she tells you that what she decides to do is her own affair and to mind your own business. She's a grown woman now father and the quicker you and mother realise the fact the better."

"There's no need to raise your voice Jessica." her father admonished.

Jessica's eyes were like flints. "Don't you think so? Well I think it's high time somebody did."

Mrs Fuchs squirmed anxiously in her seat. "She's gone to Intragna you say Jessica? Well we'd better go down there and see if we can find her. Can you phone her up and find out exactly where she is?"

Jessica heaved a profound sigh. "You're still not getting it are you mum? It's not my business where she is and neither is it yours. She's doing a Greta Garbo on us. She "vonts to be alone". So why don't you respect that and leave her be?"

"But what about Alan?" her mother protested. "He has to leave to go back to work tomorrow. Surely he's entitled to spend a little time with her in the short period he's got."

Jessica looked unimpressed. "I don't think he's entitled to the time of day personally."

"Don't talk nonsense Jessica." said her mother outraged. "He's waited months to see her, flown all the way back from America to get engaged to her and now she dumps him for the day just so she can go off and sulk on her own. He's only got today to be with her."

"Oh really?" Jessica remarked cynically. "If he was so desperate to spend some time with her why didn't he bother to take some more time off work? Sarah, I might point out, left her own home and her job back in the Toggenburg to come and see him just so that he can slip out of the office for a few hours to conduct his business with her only to dash off back to the action as soon as he's concluded the deal. Job done! One wife signed up nice and quick; handshakes all round, now let's get back to the fun."

"That's a monstrous way to put it Jessica." Mrs Fuchs protested.

Mr Fuchs intervened hastily to try and mollify the beginnings of a monumental row between his strong willed wife and his equally opinionated eldest daughter. "Now settle down the pair of you." He demanded. "We're not going to solve this by throwing accusations around." He turned to Jessica. "Jessie stop bristling. Your mother and I are just concerned about Sarah that's all. We're not trying to interfere. We just want to know why she isn't happy. We are her parents after all and we cannot help but be concerned if something is clearly bothering her. We had thought that these couple of days would be the happiest days of Sarah's life and we tried our best to make them perfect for her. Well clearly they're not and she's upset about something. She's had some kind of rift with Alan obviously and all we're trying to do is get to the bottom of it and clear the air. You can't accuse us of interfering simply because we're worried about her."

Jessica looked at him disbelievingly. "A rift?" she asked sarcastically, "She's had a rift with Alan?"

"Yes. She's obviously a tad annoyed with him and she's in a bit of a huff."

"So this is what you think this is dad; just a lover's tiff, a little minor domestic squabble you can mend with a few endearments and a bunch of carnations? God! Open your eyes dad."

"Sarah didn't even share a room with Alan last night." Mrs Fuchs pointed out. "She went off to her own room and made him sleep alone."

"I'm not in the slightest bit surprised mum." Jessica observed. "Personally, after the way he publicly humiliated her last night, if I was her, I wouldn't speak to the bastard again as long as I lived."

"Jessica!" her father exclaimed. "That's a terrible thing to say."

"Oh come off it dad! Let's stop pretending shall we? However many roses you put around the place and however many hearts you bedeck the bloody furniture with you can't keep up the pretence that this engagement is a sodding love match. Sarah told you yesterday; she told everybody yesterday that she did not want to become engaged last night and you went right ahead and bulldozed her into it anyway. I don't suppose you could do much else with old man Berger there wanting the deal signed. I notice that after your daughter had been pedalled off publicly you didn't even bother to congratulate her. You just went off with Berger senior to the bar to talk business."

"What are you trying to insinuate Jessica?"

"I'm not insinuating anything dad. I'm saying it plain. This marriage is a bloody arranged marriage; a business arrangement and always has been. I know that, you know that, Sarah knows that and, after last night's bloody performance, the whole Ticino knows that now. I have never been ashamed of my family before but I felt humiliated by last night's degrading spectacle. Everybody at that party was talking about it. The Fuchs have sold their daughter to the highest bidder. I'll never dare show my face in this canton again."

"That's an outrageous suggestion Jessica!" her father declared heatedly.

"Really? So we didn't hear all that guff about prosperous and mutually advantageous familial ties in those speeches? We heard a heap of crap about financial security and prosperity but I didn't hear the word "love" once. Personally I'd never heard such a pile of pompous, sanctimonious, patronising bullshit in my life. Here we are doing our best for little Sarah here who is far too silly and unable to know her own mind. So you deliver her on a plate to the bloody Bergers against her own expressed wishes for the whole world to see. How she sat through that I'll never know. I felt terrible for the poor girl. What has she done to deserve that?"

"Jessica!" her father choked at last. "I will not have you talk like this."

"You'd better get used to it dad because that's what half of this bloody canton is talking like now."

"It was an *engagement* party." Mrs Fuchs declared. "How could we have an engagement party without an engagement?"

"Wake up mum." Jessica told her. "You haven't *got* an engagement."

"What do you mean?"

"I mean that Sarah does not consider herself to be engaged. She was shanghaied and everybody there saw it."

"But of course she's engaged. She's wearing Alan's ring."

"Which doubtless she'll be asking Alan to thrust up a famously, badly illuminated back orifice at her earliest convenience. She does not consider herself to be under any obligation of betrothal. She has not been asked if she wants to marry Alan and she has certainly not given her consent to that effect. As far as she's concerned she had a vulgar lump of metamorphosed crystallised carbon

185

jammed on her finger whilst under restraints against public protest. She was not given a fair chance to speak or even the common courtesy of being allowed to consider her response. Right now she is one very pissed off girl and I doubt if she would marry Alan if he was the last remaining repository of XY chromosomes on the planet and the future survival of the human species depended on it."

Mrs Fuchs was suitably agitated. "Oh God! We've got to talk to her George. Make her see sense."

Jessica leaned back in her chair. "I think sense is what you might get unfortunately mum. Sarah is actually showing some sense; sense enough to take control over her own life, sense enough to walk away from this marriage and sense enough to want to have nothing to do with the Berger family!"

"What are you talking about Jessica?" her father asked in vexation. "What has the Berger family ever shown her other than the greatest consideration and affection?"

"So it's irrelevant dad is it that old man Berger is an arms merchant; a gun runner on an international scale?"

"Don't talk nonsense Jessica. Mr Berger is a perfectly respectable business man."

"Who just happens to make his money pedalling weapons dad?"

"You're being ridiculous Jessica. I know that Mr Berger has had some interest in defence contracts before but that's a perfectly legitimate business concern."

"So the federal investigations into certain irregularities in his defence interests were just fairy stories were they dad?"

"Where on earth have you heard these ludicrous tales from Jessica?"

"Oh Sarah happened to overhear people discussing them last night dad and I heard a few rumours myself. This morning I phoned a couple of friends who know about these sorts of things. They were very informative.

They were unanimous in their opinion that Herr Berger has had his fingers in some pretty dodgy pies; buying up large quantities of arms from the Czech Republic, certain Middle Eastern deals that don't bear close scrutiny and sales of sensitive military technology from American concerns. It seems quite a lot of people have taken an interest in your new business associate's more obscure transactions."

"That's absolutely absurd Jessica. Of course there were federal investigations. There always are if a person is involved in defence matters. It's simply a matter of security protocol. Anybody who has any involvement in such sensitive areas will be scrutinised for security purposes. You are simply listening to uninformed gossip and speculation. Mr Berger has never been found censurable for any irregularity or misappropriation."

"Which I suppose has nothing to do with the small army of lawyers he employs or his undue influence in high places huh dad?"

Mr Fuchs lifted a finger in caution. "Jessica these are very serious accusations you are implying. I would suggest that you desist from them."

"Oh right! Ever hear of "Farstar Innovations" dad?"

"Yes of course! Mr Berger has taken an interest in them recently. It's a relatively small British based aerospace technology company that builds satellites. You can hardly see anything sinister in them."

"Do you know what kind of satellites they build dad?"

Mr Fuchs frowned uncertainly. "Well it's not my field but apparently they design and build small, cheap low orbit satellites, designed to observe with cameras, sophisticated large satellites and examine them for any signs of damage and so on. You could apparently use them to examine the exterior hull of things like the International space station or low orbit telescopes at a fraction of the cost of expensive manned missions."

"Well that's the publicity blurb dad."

"What are you suggesting Jessica?"

"There's another kind of expensive, sophisticated satellite in low orbit dad."

"What are you getting at Jessica?"

"Think it through dad. These satellites they're building are small and relatively simple; cheap to build and easy to launch on small unsophisticated rockets." Jessica spaced out her hands. "They're about that big dad; about the size of a good sized biscuit tin. All they've got on them are sensors, a small command computer and manoeuvring rockets. You can launch them in clusters aboard simple earth to low orbit rockets and throw them like shotgun pellets out along orbital trajectories. All they can do is obey simple commands and manoeuvre to intercept other satellites in low orbit; reconnaissance satellites for instance."

Mr Fuchs stared at her. "What are you trying to say Jessica?"

"I'm saying that they're anti-satellite sats dad; smart bombs designed to take out reconnaissance satellites in low orbit."

Mrs Fuchs looked bewildered. "What do you mean they're bombs? You're not telling me that they're full of explosives surely?"

Jessica shook her head. "They don't need explosives mum. At orbital velocities, kinetic energy does all the work for you. You just steer one of these cheap little expendable satellites into the path of your target and pouf; a billion dollars' worth of spy satellite disintegrates instantly."

Mr Fuchs shook his head determinedly. "This is nonsense Jessica. I'm sure Mr Berger would have nothing to do with such a system."

"Dad "Farstar Innovations" held a sales symposium last year apparently. Their most interested clients for their new technology included such nations as China, Syria, Libya and North Korea for God's sake. Now I don't know about you but if ever there was a rogue's gallery of nation states with a vested interest in a cheap technology to stop American spy satellites flying over their territorial space several times a day then that's it, right there."

Mr Fuchs stared intently at her. "Are you sure of these facts Jessica?"

She shook her head. "No dad I'm not. It might be hearsay and speculation as you've suggested. But surely you've got enough contacts of your own to check out these rumours. It might be purely conjecture but I think Herr Berger is a merchant of death and that's the kind of man you just sold your daughter to!"

"You're being overly dramatic Jessica!" her father cautioned.

"Perhaps dad but are you sure?"

"But even if there is something a little dodgy about his father what's that got that got to do with Alan?" Mrs Fuchs wanted to know.

"Oh mum! Alan is his father's puppy dog; always has been. He's knee deep in daddy's business."

Her father drew a deep breath. "Jessica I think this has gone far enough. If there is anything at all untoward about Mr Berger's business dealings then my own contacts will inform me of such. In the meantime I forbid you to speculate whatsoever on them. For one thing such accusations are actionable."

"Ok dad. I'll hold my tongue. It's not my business anyway. I'm not the one jumping into bed with the Bergers."

Mr Fuchs paused for a moment; his furrowed brow reflecting his concern. "That doesn't solve the immediate problem. What are we going to do about Sarah?"

Jessica pulled a wry smile. "Wrong question dad. What we should be asking is what is Sarah going to do about Sarah."

Chapter Twenty

In one respect at least, Jessica was completely right. Sarah *had* gone, that day, to the river banks at Intragna. That was not, in fact, a deduction on the Hercule Poirot scale of brilliance for Jessica well knew that Sarah loved this little corner of the Ticino and it was the kind of place Sarah would instinctively seek when in need of peace and solitude to make hard decisions. Intragna itself was a typical, charming Ticino village of stone houses clustered around its church whose tower was reputed to be the largest in Ticino. Perched high on the steep valley side, the village held a lofty position over the confluence of two streams.

To the north of the village a smaller stream flowed out of a gorge to meet the main stream to the south. To the south of the village the wild River Melezza drained the Centovalli region, a name which translates as hundred valleys for the numerous side streams that poured in cascades from the steep sides of the gorge of the main valley. Together the two streams formed a larger river that eventually joined the River Maggia flowing out of the Maggia valley. Few rivers of such a short length could have boasted such a variety of climatic conditions along its course for the Maggia had its source, high on the mountains to the north-west, in high alpine tundra conditions at the foot of a glacier only to end its journey a mere forty kilometres later across the plain of Ticino where it flowed into Lake Maggiore between Locarno and Ascona and surrounded by semi-tropical palm trees. On the southern side of the confluence of the two streams at Intragna there was a little sunny sanctuary of exquisite charm. The innumerable inundations of the two rivers had left a beach of pure white sand along the southern flanks of the rivers dotted with granite boulders, striated rock formations and bordered by patches of scrub and low bushes. The River Melezza here formed a series of deep pools of deep azure; treacherous invitations to foolhardy bathers for the water was icy cold and the rivers themselves had an evil reputation for the speed with which they rose with flood water from any rainfall. The corner of sand though held a magnetic attraction for those who knew of it for it was secluded, away from main roads, invitingly sunny and sheltered. It was a favoured location for sunbathers seeking a quiet spot to bask in the rays of the hot Ticino sun especially those sunbathers with an inclination to dispense with the formalities of wearing bathing suits. It was also ironically (although it must be said that Sarah was completely ignorant of the fact) known among connoisseurs as a meeting spot for the more discerning members of the gay community. This is not to say that it was exclusively gay and it was certainly not as notorious as some of the more overtly gay beaches in Ticino but it did have its own discreet scene among those in the know and oddly this scene extended to both male and female members of the gay brother and sisterhoods.

Sarah was completely unaware of this secondary characteristic of this beauty spot. She was not alone in this for few people outside of the most cognisant of the local gay community were at all aware of it and, in any case, Sarah was hardly the person to discern this secret since she had, until recently, been entirely separate from the alternative world of the gay community. Even now she could at best be described as a newly born gay herself and totally naive regarding the inner workings of that society. She certainly did not go to the beach at Intragna with any intention to meet any other people of gay inclinations or indeed with the slightest iota of knowledge of the clandestine nature of her chosen location. To Sarah, it was just a nice place by the river that she had discovered quite by accident when on holiday visiting her parents in Ticino and suitably quiet and discreet for her purposes.

In fact, Sarah's reasons for visiting this beach were complex but they were not without a certain degree of sexual stimulation. The evidence for this could instantly be discerned in Sarah's choice of dress for the day. Sarah would have quite flatly refused to believe a few months ago that she would ever in her life dare to step out of the house dressed as she now was. She was wearing the white and pink bikini overlaid with the matching beach sarong that Nicole had bullied her into buying in the sport shop in Lisighaus earlier in the summer. She had been horrified on that occasion to walk abroad so scantily dressed and yet she remembered it as curiously stimulating. It wasn't any particular titillation that she found so stimulating but rather a sense of liberation. Nicole, by making her break a lifetime's habit of shy modesty, had set a part of her free and it was that sense of liberty she sought today as she strived to free herself from the constraints of the last two days. It was true that Ticino was somewhat more liberal in matters of dress than the Toggenburg and, with its hot Mediterranean climate, a person walking abroad in beachwear was not at all unusual but nevertheless it felt daring and adventurous to appear in public dressed so and Sarah was a girl in need of daring this day.

The worst part was the bus ride. Jessica had dropped her off at the bus stop on her way into Ascona and Sarah had felt downright silly waiting for the post bus with just a flimsy sarong over her bikini and sandals. She had a large bag over her shoulder into which she had thrown a bath towel, a few sandwiches, some sun cream, a litre bottle of Fanta, her purse, her mobile phone and a few other sundry items. Missing completely was any change of clothing. In a spirit of devil take the hindmost she had set off with only the barest minimum of clothes on her back. If it decided to rain she was in trouble! She also wore her sunglasses, Nicole's string of beads and

Daniela's emerald pendant about her neck. Absent however was her new engagement ring. She hadn't felt at all easy about wearing it. Even if she had not had such negative feelings about it the very thought of going alone to a beach with perhaps fifty thousand francs worth of diamond on her would have filled her with horror. The offensive item was safely locked away in a drawer.

In the end, Sarah had to wait over twenty minutes for a bus, during which time she felt as if half the inhabitants of the neighbouring village had passed her by and perused her. She was joined at the bus stop by an old lady and a young man. The young man was casting admiring glances at her and she was conscious of the fact that her bikini was easily visible through the thin fabric of her sarong. It was a relief when the bus finally arrived but it was a new challenge climbing aboard to pay the driver, with the gaze of the other passengers on her. She hunkered down in a front seat and placed her shoulder bag defensively in front of her. It was not a long trip up to Intragna however and soon she alighted at the village and took to the little back road that led down the hill to the river. She walked slowly enjoying the cool soft breeze that stirred her sarong and congratulating herself, now that she was alone, on her choice of light clothes, for the day was already hot. She began to relax and there was pleasure too in a beautiful cock Redstart hopping about at the side of the road, the quicksilver little wall lizards on the dry stone walls, a Red Backed Shrike with a handsome black mask hunting from atop a large bush, a praying mantis in some shrubby vegetation, a Great Sooty Dryad butterfly fluttering heavily along a shaded part of the lane and an Icterine Warbler singing loudly from the scrub as she approached the river.

She had to cross the River Melezza by way of a high stone bridge just wide enough to permit the passage of a single car at a time. She paused to look over the bridge into the deep pool below. There were several pigo swimming in the pool and towards the tail she could see a small barbel. This was not the same species of barbel Sarah was more familiar with in the rivers north of the alps but a smaller species with dark brown blotches you found in this region. There was some confusion as to the exact species, Sarah knew, because she had spent some time researching them before. Originally she had assumed them to be Southern or Mediterranean barbel, *Barbus meridionalis,* but the taxonomists had assigned the population of this species that inhabited the rivers leading into Lake Maggiore to a sub-species *Barbus meridionalis caninus.* Now however, because taxonomists never seemed to be able to make up their minds, the newest thinking was to assign them a specific status of their own and they had become simply *Barbus caninus* and local to the rivers of Ticino and Northern Italy. Whatever their classification it was a rare sighting for Sarah and a small but welcome boost to her morale.

At the far side of the bridge, Sarah left the road, climbed a style and found herself on the sandy sweep alongside the river. She walked along the riverside on the sand until it neared the confluence with the Maggia River and then looked for a place to lay out her towel. To her surprise, she seemed to have the beach nearly to herself. She was not disappointed by this. On the contrary she welcomed the solitude. She picked a place quite far back from the river where a few bushes gave her some shelter and there was a patch of luxurious fine sand between a pair of boulders. She placed her bag under some shade and laid out her towel in the sunshine. She sat down on the towel and ran her fingers through the sand wistfully. She had some hard thinking to do.

Jessica had been spot on in deducing Sarah's destination for the day but possibly less than accurate in describing her younger sister's mood. Sarah was more saddened than angry about the events of the previous day and by no means as determined about her course of action as her sister may have given the impression of to her parents. Jessica had stated, pretty brutally, that Sarah did not consider herself engaged and that she was liable to reject any suggestion that she was. That was reasonably accurate, as far as it went, but, of course, it missed the one big problem which Jessica of course was not party to. To Jessica, Sarah's dilemma was merely to escape from an unwelcome arranged marriage. By exposing that marriage for what it was Sarah had already effectively secured her escape clause. But it wasn't that simple. It was one thing to walk away from the marriage on the grounds that it was a marriage that she was being coerced into against her will but quite another to walk away from it and straight into the arms of another woman.

Sarah knew that she had been less than honest with her family and she knew that it was cowardice. The rift with her parents would be monumental enough if she was to reject Alan. God only knew what would happen if she was to reveal that she was not only entangled in a lesbian relationship but in a relationship with a famous rock star which would prove probably impossible to keep secret. The explosion would be staggering. Surely there'd be no coming back from that. Even Jessica would have a hard time accepting that. Her parents would never come to terms with it. So she had big decisions to make and she had promised Jessica that she would make them today.

She fell back on an old trick of hers when faced with a series of agonising choices. She would mentally list all the possible courses of action and then draw up all the pros and cons of each one and see if she could find some sense out of the equation. Very well then, as far as she could see, she had four, possibly five, different options open to her.

A) She could relent and marry Alan after all. This might seem derisible at the moment but, up until this summer, it had been her most likely course of action and it was after all still an option.

195

B) She could hand Alan back his ring and simply return to the Toggenburg to carry on her life as she had before she had met Daniela.

C) She could do the above but continue her relationship with Daniela albeit covertly.

D) She could reject the marriage and return to the Toggenburg and live openly with Daniela.

The first scenario was tempting to dismiss out of hand. After all, she had gone some considerable way to discrediting her marriage to Alan and it would seem bizarre now to change her mind and embrace it after all. There were positives to such a course of action however. The biggest positive was that there would be no rift with her family. Mother would get her big white wedding after all and Father would be happily tied into Mr Berger's business empire. Everything would be prosperous for everybody. Even Sarah herself would be well off under the Berger patronage and there would be no hard words to be said or tears to be shed. Her father would be proud of her again.

In fact, now that she had asserted her independence, it might even be a more attractive option than before, for she had re-established her authority to have more say in her wedding plans and future. It mattered not that her parents had defied that authority last night since she had deliberately placed them in a situation where they could do little else. She was still in control and it would only take the frightening possibility of her throwing Alan's ring back at him to make everybody bend over backwards to grant her concessions. She could well imagine the consternation that her absence today would bring in the household. Her parents would be terrified of her taking drastic measures. She had them over a barrel. At the very least she could demand a postponement of the early wedding date. That would certainly give her more breathing space. Also she might be able to negotiate some compromises on her future married life. The least she would want would be some acceptance that she could delay the starting of a family whilst she pursued her academic interests. She could even ask for a second residence in the Toggenburg. Alan was getting the bloody house in Zurich, more or less free, as a dowry from her. It would be well within his capabilities to maintain a second house, possibly rented, in the Toggenburg that she could flee back to whenever his business took him away from home. If she got them running scared enough, there was no end to the concessions she could extract. Ok if they wanted an arranged marriage she'd give them one but, this time, she would arrange it to *her* convenience. She'd stake out her position and if Alan truly wanted her then he was going to have to come up with some powerful bargaining chips.

The key to that plan would be to establish a strong enough bargaining platform. She could go home today and coolly inform Alan and her parents that she did not consider the announcement of her engagement binding in any way since she had not been asked but merely publicly coerced into it. She had enough moral high ground by now to make it stick as well. She could haughtily announce that she was returning to the Toggenburg until such time as a full and proper proposal of engagement was presented to her after which she would require some time to make her decision. She might even carry out her threat and return to her home in the Toggenburg and wait for Alan to come running to her. The effect would be devastating. Faced with the unthinkable prospect of having their public announcement of the engagement revealed as a farce everybody would be crawling on their hands and knees to pander to her wishes. She could then sit down and do some hard bargaining. If she was getting sold into a marriage she wanted her cut of the profits and she'd show them how *she* wanted the marriage arranged.

Such a course of action would be sweet revenge and there was a pragmatic side of Sarah that found the prospect quite appealing. She quite fancied playing the role of the hard headed negotiator and she might enjoy haggling over the details of her marriage. But there was one major stumbling block. That block was Sarah's romantic side. She still felt you had to marry for love. In the days before she had stared that elusive emotion in the face it had been fairly easy to pretend to herself that she was in love with Alan. She had after all barely known any other relationship but that which she had with him to judge her emotional attachment by. Now she knew she did *not* love him. It had come almost unnoticed upon her but, like a cold dousing of water; she now knew that to be fact. His performance over the last day or so had been pretty wretched. He hadn't even managed to say he loved her. She wondered, in fact, if he did. He was not demonstrative in that respect but even so, after such a long absence, she could at least have expected him to spit it out. But then she was just as guilty wasn't she? She hadn't told him she loved him either. When she really thought about it she was hard pushed to remember any time that they had declared their love for each other. Sarah frowned and drew small circles in the sand with her fingers. It was a disturbing thought. Perhaps Alan was as much trapped in this marriage as she herself was. She had never thought of it like that before. Were they two people being doomed into a loveless marriage by the wishes of their families? Alan had never expressed any doubts about that but then neither had she. They had both just drifted along accepting the inevitability of it all. Even that bloody engagement ring Sarah realised was paid for by Alan's family.

The truth was she didn't love him though. If she was truly honest with herself she found him quite irritating on occasion. How could that ever be a firm foundation for a happy marriage? Her negotiations, however much in the way of concessions she might extract, could not gloss over that fact. They would, in fact, simply be a practice run for the divorce proceedings.

She simply could not envisage Alan as a life partner. Her relationship with him had only been tolerable because of their protracted absences from each other. If she had to see him every day, spend her whole life with him....she shuddered at the thought. There were no concessions that could compensate for a miserable life with a man she did not love.

So what about plan B then? The thought of returning to the Toggenburg and resuming the status quo as it had been was beguilingly attractive. In the end, Sarah didn't need Alan's wealth or that of his family. She didn't even need her own family's wealth anymore. She had enough foundations about her to make her own way in life. She had work whenever she wanted it in the Toggenburg and, with a degree under her belt, good prospects of a future career. Doing her Masters or her PhD might have to wait until she was more firmly established financially but at least she would the mistress of her own destiny. She would still be living in her beloved valley, she still had the house she shared with Nicole and she would still have the country lifestyle that suited her. She had some money in the bank and her needs were small. It sounded like a return to the halcyon days when she and Nicole shared the little house in comradeship and lived a simple life of austere obscurity beholden to no-one but themselves.

Of course there would be problems. To begin with she would have to hand Alan back his ring but that already seemed inevitable. There would be the unavoidable monumental row with her family. Doubtless there would be a serious falling out but possibly not a permanent one or an insoluble one. Her mother would be furious, her father disappointed and probably out of pocket but they might come to accept her decision in time. Jessica, after all, had also undergone a long period of estrangement from her parents, as a result of her defiance over their wishes in regard to her marriage, but she had become reconciled with them, if on a somewhat more equal basis. It was not inconceivable that they would forgive Sarah too in due course.

In the short term, Sarah would have to absorb a financial setback. For one thing she would have to pay her father his twenty thousand francs back. He had given her that to buy herself a wardrobe for her upcoming marriage and she could not, with any decency, now reject that marriage and still retain that money. The trouble was she had already spent a sizeable chunk of it on new clothes. It wasn't an insurmountable sum of money to find. She had enough reserves in her savings account to more than cover it but it would be hard to accept taking a dent in her rainy day money which she had nurtured and kept safe for so long. Still it was a moral obligation and find the money she must.

Even with such an obligation, Sarah felt confident that her own financial position was robust enough to carry her until such time as she could embark upon a new career. In fact it was quite an exciting prospect. There was an adventurous feel to the challenge of setting out on her own way into the world without the safety harness of her father's wealth to fall back on. For the first time in her life she felt confident that she could do it as well. For the last three years she had lived independently albeit largely on her father's largesse. It was a small step to take to cut the familial ties altogether and set out her own stall in the market place of the world. She had a degree and that high qualification alone gave her a solid starting point should she wish to use it. Admittedly it was a degree in history and there were not too many careers in which that specific knowledge was applicable but *any* degree was a qualification. Then again, she had the starting qualifications as an alpine guide which perhaps she could expand upon. Failing all that she had experience and a solid reputation in the hotel business. She could automatically assume work available in the Toggenburg in that respect. Frau Fritzl alone could guarantee her that. She didn't have to remain a humble waitress. She could think about the clerical side, receptionist for example, or even the managerial side. With her experience and references, it would be easy to work her way through the system. She could be managing her own restaurant within a few years. She was multi-lingual as well. She spoke fluent English, German and French and her Italian was not bad. In her spare time over the last couple of years she had even tried to learn a little Japanese which would be a boon considering the high volume of Japanese tourists that Switzerland attracted. Work for interpreters was well paid and her linguistic skills would be precious in the tourist industry.

Sarah frowned as one negative detail came to mind. She didn't have a car. If she followed this course of action she could say goodbye to the car her father had promised her. She would remain dependent on public transport and the occasional use of or lift in Nicole's sadly degraded Renault. Could she afford to buy a little car? Second hand cars were not prohibitively expensive in Switzerland largely because the wealthy population tended to buy new vehicles and there was not a great demand for second hand automobiles. Sarah didn't need anything too extravagant. She could probably pick something up for a few thousand that still had a good deal of mileage in it. Simon might be the man to ask there. He seemed to know a lot about cars. It would mean another hole in her reserve funds of course but they were there for just such eventualities as this. She had squirrelled away her money for emergencies and, all of a sudden, life had become an emergency.

It was getting hot and Sarah shed her sarong. Sitting there in her bikini, the bikini Nicole had picked out for her, reminded Sarah of the major stumbling block in this attractive sounding scenario. Yes she *could* do it on her own. The only problem was that she *wasn't* on her own. She could not now return to the Toggenburg and simply erase the events of the past summer. She couldn't turn the clock back and rewind to that day she had returned from university. Too many things had happened since. She could not even return to her old relationship with Nicole; merely return to their shared house and continue in their old platonic relationship as house mates. Her relationship with Daniela had changed all that. It had blown open all the doors and let the light into all the secret corners. It had forced Nicole to declare her love for Sarah and their relationship could never be the same again. Of course she could simply move out and find her own place to live but that would be a cruelty bordering on betrayal. She was walking away from her family: she couldn't similarly walk away from everybody else she loved simply to assert her independence. She had to find some accommodation with the new reality and that meant confronting her own sexuality.

Because of course there was still Daniela. How could she return to the Toggenburg and tell Daniela that she had rejected marriage with Alan and was equally rejecting life with her? Well she couldn't, essentially. She didn't even want to and that was the crucial point. The only way that such a move would make sense was if she were to reject the notion that she was gay and that would be a hard point to make after her performance over the summer. She would be saying that her only motives for not marrying Alan were because she did not love him, did not want to have her marriage arranged with him and was in fact waiting for the right man to come along. She would be saying that all the feelings that she had for Daniela were just some aberration and that she was simply a heterosexual girl in waiting. Could there yet be a man she could fall in love with?

This was a hard call for Sarah. She knew very little about the realities of homosexual awareness. She had always assumed that gay people were simply born gay and grew up with no other viewpoint. They were gay and had always known it deep down. Until this summer she had never considered herself gay. Perhaps she had suppressed the notion within herself or had simply not understood it. Had she ever really considered herself heterosexual on the other hand? It was another difficult question. Her sexual fantasies had been enigmatically ambiguous to say the least and Sarah realised that she could easily have replaced any man in them with a woman. Since meeting Daniela, however, virtually all her erotic thoughts revolved around her and even more so now that she had experienced the delights of intimacy with her. Alan, essentially the only other lover in her life, seemed bland and dull compared with the excitement of her female lover. Daniela had awakened her sexuality in a way nobody had before. It went further than Daniela too for it had stimulated her interest in her own sex. Now she dreamed about the silky softness of a woman's skin, the gentle caresses of their hands and the gorgeous luxury of their hair. Oddly enough, this awakening had even changed her view about Nicole. She had always loved Nicole dearly but for the first time she admitted that she found her desirable too. She had shared a bed with Nicole many a time. It now seemed to her bizarre that the two of them had never made love, especially now that she knew that Nicole would have welcomed it. Her life might have changed a lot earlier if they had have become lovers before Daniela had dropped like a bomb into the mix.

But that missed opportunity was irrelevant now. Daniela *had* come along and life was never going to be the same. So that brought her to the other options. Should she go back now and become Daniela's lover without further prevarication or doubt? This was what her heart was telling her to do but Sarah determined to subject the option to the same cold logical analysis as her other options. The drawbacks were huge, she knew. It meant an open acknowledgement that she was gay. This alone would guarantee that the division of her from her family would be a far more serious matter than simply her objecting to marrying Alan. Her mother

203

would never be able to accept it and her father would be shocked to the core of his being. He would never be able to believe that his little daughter was anything other than perfectly straight. He would be convinced that somebody had tampered with her; used undue influence on her to corrupt her; he might even blame himself. There would be no question of her parents accepting her relationship with another woman. She would never be able to bring her girlfriend home to meet them. She doubted if they'd ever wish to speak to her or even acknowledge her existence. They would probably go into denial and never even mention the subject. Sarah would become a stranger in her parent's home.

Of course Sarah didn't need to tell them but that was, at best, a temporary solution. A major drawback about her relationship was that it happened to be with a very famous person. They might conceal the relationship for a while but, sooner or later, it would become public news. Sarah would be faced with the agonising decision whether or not to tell her parents before they read it for themselves in the newspaper. Daniela's fame was a large negative on the list. Sarah had no desire for fame or notoriety but her quiet life in the Toggenburg would be seriously threatened if she were openly Daniela's girlfriend. It was almost too late to conduct a clandestine relationship with Daniela though. The whole Toggenburg by now must be aware that there was something going on between them. In any case, Sarah hated the idea of an undercover relationship conducted in secret, almost as if she were ashamed of it.

She guessed that Daniela wouldn't particularly like it as well. Daniela was a very private person but not one to lie about her own orientation. The girl in Winterthur, Charmaine, had told her that Daniela had even played a set at the Gay Pride festival in Zurich. There was nothing there to suggest that Daniela was at all inclined to conceal her sexuality. She certainly had never made the slightest effort to hide her affection for Sarah in public.

On the contrary, she had revelled in it. She was quite overtly proud of Sarah and couldn't seem to care less that the world knew she adored her. She would hardly favour a surreptitious affair. She might not advertise it directly to the media but neither would she be inclined to deny it once it was known. Daniela saw absolutely nothing wrong with being in love with a woman. She might be puzzled or even hurt if Sarah tried to deny her feelings for her.

Daniela's fame and career was therefore a seriously problematical item on the balance books. High profile stars were notoriously unstable as partners weren't they? Their relationships were often mercurial and short lived and they went through reams of different partners if you believed what you read in the tabloid papers. Could Sarah give everything up for something that might in the end prove ephemeral? She had to consider it. What if Daniela had come into her life, turned it upside down and then left her with nothing? That was always a risk in any relationship, of course, but, with a person like Daniela, more of a risk than ever for such a scenario would be played out in public. Sarah would forever be branded the girl that was Daniela Devin's former lover.

Should Sarah then move in and live with Daniela or retain her own independence. That was an awkward one. The alternative was to carry on living in the house with Nicole but that alone was difficult since it would appear to favour Nicole over Daniela. Sarah groaned to herself. It was hard enough to contemplate even having one girlfriend let alone be in an apparent love triangle with two of them. Yet Daniela had quite openly declared that she would like Sarah to share her house. She was that serious about their relationship. But it would be a huge move Sarah knew; tantamount to a declaration of marriage. Daniela had not asked her to move in on a temporary basis. She had made a proposal; long term and committed. The moment that Sarah hung her clothes up in the wardrobe they would, to all intents and purposes, be a married couple. That was the commitment required of her; as binding as ever the house in Zurich with Alan would be. Sarah would be overtly and unequivocally living as a gay woman in a long term relationship with her female partner. Did she want that?

Sarah forced herself to think logically. She had to put to one side all the pleadings of her heart and think of the thing rationally. She would allow herself to examine her emotional responses only after she had considered every aspect from a purely pragmatic viewpoint. She returned to her theoretical balance sheet. So the disadvantages of a relationship with Daniela were clear; an overt declaration of her homosexuality, the possible public notoriety of a relationship with a famous celebrity, complete isolation from her family even to the extent that it might mean their disinheriting her, the uncertainties of life with a rock star, the absences necessitated by Daniela's career, the loss of her privacy under public scrutiny, the ruination of her reputation in the Toggenburg and the general label that would ever be attached to her name as Daniela Devin's lover. To this depressing litany she might even add the loss of her maternity. One of the few things that had attracted Sarah to marriage was the thought of children. In that aspect she was clearly a woman; a woman with an instinct for motherhood. Would motherhood be possible in a lesbian relationship? At the very least it would be complicated.

So were there any positive advantages to set against this imposing list? To her surprise, Sarah realised that there were a lot and not simply those of purely emotional gratification. For one thing, and a very important thing it was too, she would be setting up house with a very wealthy woman. Sarah allowed herself an ironic chuckle. Her father's pompous declarations to the fact that he was concerned about the future prosperity of his daughter and therefore obliged to scrutinise the prospects of any possible suitor for her hand would be deliciously funny, in retrospect, if she rejected his chosen suitor for a woman who made Alan look like a pauper. Alan might have the considerable financial patronage of his father and would undoubtedly himself be one day a well to do man but, as yet, he could not match the earning power of Daniela's musical career.

It was sometimes easy to forget that Daniela was a multi-millionairess for she lived a relatively simple life. True she was generous and easy with her money, she dressed well and expensively and owned a big house, furnished and decorated well if not lavishly. Yet for all that she was not given to the vulgar excesses of your average rock star with too much money and too little sense. Her house was big and comfortable but by no means ostentatious. In fact her parent's villa on the Monte Verita here in Ticino was far more redolent of the nouveau riche than Daniela's old converted guest house. You couldn't imagine Daniela throwing wild parties in her rustic back garden with its carpet of wild meadow flowers and old wooden tables and benches. She didn't even have a swimming pool. Her only servant was a cleaning lady who came in a couple of times a week to help or who looked after her cats when she was on tour. Daniela could afford to have her every need delivered to her door and yet Nicole had told her that she had first met Daniela when she was pushing a shopping trolley around Migros in Wildhaus. Daniela lived a comfortable but nevertheless an admirably quiet country life. The only trapping of rock star fame she affected was her Ferrari and she didn't even like it. It was this embracing of the rural life in the Toggenburg that had endeared her to the local population. The Toggenburg was coming to accept Daniela as its own. It was probably already a legend in the valley that its most glamorous inhabitant was not above pulling on a pinny and rushing to help out as a waitress in a friend's restaurant when need arose. For all her wealth and fame, she lived a life of simple rural harmony and it was a lifestyle that suited Sarah very much indeed. Given the choice between a city life in the house in Zurich with Alan or the country life in her beloved Toggenburg in Daniela's charming old house, there was simply no competition.

Daniela's wealth might not be immediately apparent but it had far reaching consequences nevertheless. Of decisive importance was the conversation she had had with Daniela the day before she had left for the Ticino. Daniela had given promises of great seriousness that she would support Sarah's wishes to continue her academic career and also that she would favour Sarah's natural history projects within the Toggenburg. Her support would not only be moral but financial as well and, she was not only in favour of Sarah pursuing an independent career, she was actively encouraging it. Furthermore she had raised the prospect of buying Sarah's current rented house both to ensure Nicole's future residency and as an investment in a second house within the valley. Sarah didn't even have to mourn the loss of her father's promised present of a new car for Daniela had casually noted that they would certainly need at least one new car. The Ferrari was all well and good for gadding about in the summer with the hood down and the wind in their hair but it was hardly a vehicle for practical everyday use. They might even need two new cars for if Sarah was to pursue her own career she was certainly going to need her own transport. They had enough garage and parking space at Daniela's house for half a dozen vehicles if they had so wanted them. In fact, if you looked at it dispassionately, Daniela had put together a far more attractive package as a proposal than Alan had ever managed to come up with; a wealthy, comfortable life in a beautiful house in a place she loved and with the means and leisure to do the things she loved. If you looked at it from that point of view then Alan's marriage proposal, such as it was, was pretty feeble in comparison. Sarah would not even be separated from the people, other than her family, she cared about. There was a discernible emerging kernel of close friends and allies that would be of moral support in the dark hours of her estrangement from her family; Peter, Simon, Nicole, Elke, Angelica and others. She and Daniela would not be alone. There were people that loved them.

Children? Why not? Charmaine had mentioned some of the solutions gay people found to have children. Even Daniela had mentioned once that she would be more than happy for Sarah to have a child of her own. Daniela, after all, was already a mother. There was nothing to stop a lesbian from having a child other than biological practicalities which were easily overcome with a certain flexibility in your moral scruples. Sarah giggled to herself. Maybe Peter could provide the sperm sample. Simon could help him collect it. They could make a party out of it.

As she thought of the good points to a future with Daniela, Sarah found herself smiling. They were the first happy thoughts she had had all day. She looked around her in pleasure. The Ticino was not her Toggenburg but it was a region she loved; a region of towering mountains surrounding great glittering lakes under the gentle balm of southern sunshine, dotted with lovely towns and villages, rich in wildlife and with a relaxed and contented population. It was as if somebody had taken Switzerland and Italy and extracted the best from both of them to create this little haven on the southern side of the Alps. She'd once heard somebody describe the Ticino as having the scenery of Switzerland and Italy combined and where the food and culture were Italian but where everything was spotlessly clean, people were polite, didn't pinch your car stereo and the trains ran on time. That was perhaps simplistic but it was nevertheless a beautiful and civilised corner of the world and probably Sarah's favourite part of Switzerland after the Toggenburg. She wished she could show Daniela it. Daniela would love it. She would like to walk with Daniela down this river bank, hand in hand, and find some shade from the sun in a little cosy grotto or make love to her on the soft sand by the river bank.

It was thoughts such as these that made her realise that all her pragmatic reasoning was, in the end, meaningless. In purely practical terms it was, as Elke had phrased it, a no brainer. Life with Daniela offered so much more in terms of career, personal fulfilment and wealth. So it all boiled down to love and her sexuality, and that, she realised, was what she should have been looking at in the first place. She no longer doubted that she loved Daniela. She had heard Daniela state in the plainest and firmest terms that she loved her in return and wished to spend her life with her. So Sarah's decision was simple. Everything else was pure distraction. Was she or was she not ready to commit herself to Daniela; was she in fact ready to *marry* her? That in simple terms was the question. Daniela had made a proposal; a proposal that was equivalent to a proposal of marriage. Was she going to accept it?

Chapter Twenty-One

As she pondered her options, Sarah suddenly started from her reverie. She was not alone. Walking across the sand, a few yards away, was a young woman, perhaps her own age or a couple of years older. She was walking languidly carrying large bag in one hand and with a beach towel draped over one shoulder. Other than that she was completely naked. That was hardly unusual here of course. Sarah in her bikini was over dressed by the conventions of this particular enclave of sun worshippers. However this girl would have stood out if she'd been dressed in a nun's habit in a convent for she was extraordinarily beautiful. She had a slim perfectly shaped body whose complete biscuit coloured tan suggested that she had never possessed a bathing costume in her life and her mane of long dark brown hair hanging down her back was luxurious and inviting. She had perfect firm breasts and a flat, well-muscled belly above the tiny wisp of dark hair above her sex. Her legs were long and slender and her bare feet padding along in the sand were appropriately slender and becoming. Sarah admired her graceful hands and her square shoulders supporting a long thin neck above which was perched the most exquisitely pretty face with soft lips, over which flickered a smile, a pert well-shaped nose and entrancingly lovely dark brown eyes. She was the kind of girl who would have caused traffic accidents on busy interchanges or made the most devout of priests reconsider the virtues of celibacy as a career move. Sarah found herself staring.

The girl stopped. With a shock, Sarah realised that she had seen her staring at her. The girl smiled at her and nodded a greeting. Sarah averted her eyes hastily and blushed. The girl smiled once more, tossed her head and walked on but her walk was slower now and more measured. Sarah dared to peer out of the corner of her eye as the girl walked away and quickly dropped her gaze once more as the girl glanced back over her shoulder as she walked. Soon the girl disappeared behind some boulders. Sarah drew a breath. There had been more in that smile than a friendly greeting; more in that nod than a polite acknowledgement. The girl had appraised her and her look had been interested. There'd been an invitation in that smile. For a second, Sarah had been sure that the girl was attracted to her.

She shook her head. She had to be mistaken she thought. She'd been thinking about Daniela and her own sexuality and along comes a pretty girl and she straight away imagines that the girl had eyed her up. It was almost certainly her imagination. The girl was probably just being friendly after all and making a passing comradely nod to what was apparently the only other person on the beach that day. She was obviously quite uninhibited by the fact that she was naked but that, given the context of the location, wasn't surprising. The girl, judging by her lack of bikini lines, was certainly used to sunbathing in the nude and perfectly comfortable with it.

And yet Sarah wasn't sure. The girl had looked at her and smiled just a little bit longer than the conventions of civility required and the way she had glanced back over her shoulder was suggestive. She had certainly known that Sarah was looking at her but she hadn't seemed in the slightest bit offended by it. She'd looked pleased, if anything, and she'd slowed her walk almost as if to afford Sarah a protracted view of her. Was that just narcissistic exhibitionism or was the girl deliberately trying to entice her? Was she, in fact, gay and had her antennae detected possible prey alone on the beach? Suddenly Sarah wanted to know.

Nervously, she squatted up on her knees and peered cautiously over a rock in the direction the girl had departed. Disappointingly, she could see no sign of her. She must be in among the rocks closer by the river.

212

Sarah wanted to see her again. That in itself was telling to Sarah for she knew immediately that she'd been attracted by the girl. It wasn't as if she was contemplating being unfaithful to Daniela of course. The girl, pretty as she was, was no Daniela. But any side of her emerging sexuality interested Sarah. It was always a shock to her to find that she found girls attractive. It was even more of a shock to think that they might find her attractive too and there'd been just enough in the girl's behaviour to suggest that that might be true. How could she find out?

Well she could follow the girl. Sarah cringed at the idea of making such an overt move. Then she thought about it. The girl must be sunbathing somewhere down near the river. Sarah could casually saunter that way, perhaps to dip her feet in the river, and "just happen" to pass the girl on the way. Surely nobody could make anything of such an innocent move. She had to wait a few minutes though. She mustn't appear as if she was running straight after the girl. She stilled her impatience and waited. After a few minutes she decided that she had left the diplomatic pause long enough and stood up. Automatically she bent down to pick up her sari. She held it for a moment, biting her lip, and then daringly put it back down again. Modesty was of little avail now. The girl had already seen her in her bikini.

Hesitantly, she began to walk slowly in the direction the girl had taken. She was terrified by her audacity and yet curiously excited. She peered cautiously around the rocks as she walked but without luck. The beach seemed to have swallowed the girl up. Puzzled, Sarah walked on. The girl had vanished. Slowly Sarah drifted toward the river. She seemed quite alone. She felt disappointed. It appeared as if she was on a wild goose chase. Perhaps the girl was just passing through and simply walking down the river. She could be miles away by now. Sarah frowned. That seemed unlikely. The girl hadn't been wearing a stitch of clothing. That was all well and good on the beach but the trail down the river soon left the beach behind and skirted the little hamlet of Golino where complete nudity might not exactly prompt the local inhabitants to call out the police but it would raise eyebrows certainly. Surely the girl had to be on the beach somewhere.

The trouble was that, with all the odd boulders and convoluted rock structures dotted around, there were hundreds of places to hide. She might have passed the girl by and not even seen her. Perhaps the girl was watching her from cover even now. That was a disturbing thought. Sarah was creeping around so surreptitiously that she would appear suspiciously like somebody with base intentions on their mind. Hastily she tried to look casual and uninterested; a not successful piece of acting as she confessed to herself. She had the sudden feeling that there were eyes on her from every nook and she was consciously aware of her dress. She might have been wearing the most modest of bodily covering by the standards of a nude beach but she had never felt more naked.

She walked down to the river in indecision and wincing as the pebbles along the river bank bit into her bare feet. She squatted down at the water's edge and lifted a couple of the rounded granite stones from the stream bed to examine in an affected manner. A splash of colour caught the corner of her eye. She glanced around. The girl was sitting on a bright red and yellow towel up against a rock some hundred metres away. It was a perfectly concealed little nook for it was only viewable from Sarah's current position. Sarah must have passed within ten metres of the girl on her way to the river. With a certainty, Sarah knew that the girl was watching her. With her heart beating, Sarah turned back to look at the rock in her hand trying desperately to look as if she was fascinated by it. It was a perfectly ordinary granite cobble rounded smooth by the erosion of the river water and Sarah had exhausted the possible areas of interest in it after about five seconds. Still she had to try and look as if there was some completely alternative reason as to why she had decided to walk down to the river.

Perhaps she could try to appear as if she was simply coming down to bathe. That was an uninviting prospect. From past experience Sarah knew that the water was so icy cold that even dipping a toe in it was agonising. Still pretences had to be maintained. In trepidation Sarah paddled out into the shallows at the river edge. The water came barely above her ankles but it seemed to chill her entire body with its glacial tendrils. Gritting her teeth she squatted down on her heels and dabbled her fingers in the water marvelling how anything on such a hot day could be so cold. The water was literally only a couple of degrees above freezing point which was hardly surprising since it was likely that it had within the last hour or so formed part of an ice sheet a few madcap rushing kilometres upstream.

Sarah glanced covertly at the girl. She had changed position. She was now kneeling upright and her face was turned toward Sarah. Sarah felt her heart thumping loudly and considered furiously her next step. She was quickly going to start looking foolish dabbling around at the water's edge and in any case she could barely feel her feet anymore. She was going to have to retrace her steps back to her bag and towel and that meant passing very close by the girl's position. She'd have to try and look as casual as possible and look surprised if the girl caught her eye. She had to affect a look of weary boredom as if she were merely pottering about in a desultory fashion out of a lack of anything better to do. Sarah was not known for her Thespian skills. It is probably true to say that her performance at her parent's party, the night before, had represented the highlight of her acting career but that had been well planned and mentally rehearsed in advance. She was never going to pull off an impromptu improvisation like this.

215

In the event, the matter was taken out of her hands. An insect was about to intervene and it was no ordinary insect. With her attention divided Sarah never saw it coming and only at the last second was she aware of the sudden angry sounding buzz approaching. An enormous black, shiny bee with iridescent violet wings collided heavily with the side of her face. Sarah squeaked in alarm, lost her balance and sat down heavily in the shallow water. The water was cold enough on her feet and hands but the sudden shock of its chill on her tender nether regions was excruciating. Casual dignity abandoned, Sarah scrambled to her feet sucking in air in a gasp. The perpetrator of the outrage was already zooming away along the river bank. Sarah recognised it and felt even more foolish.

It was a Carpenter Bee, a spectacular solitary species that nested in dead wood that you often saw in Ticino. They were formidably large bees, bigger than bumble bees, and with a loud, aggressive sounding buzz. Even more alarming the males were very competitive and spent their time aggressively chasing away anything that might be a rival for the females. Sadly they seemed unable to discern the difference between a rival male and almost anything else and thus they were liable to ram into anything that might conceivably be a threat to their sex lives. They were the bull in a china shop of the insect world. It was all macho bluster and show however for they were completely harmless and the males couldn't even sting. Nevertheless, a rampant male with sex on its tiny mind could create chaos on a crowded restaurant terrace along the waterfront in Ascona by barging around madly and leaving a trail of hysterical women and furious arm flapping in its wake. Sarah liked the silly little things and admired their brilliant metallic hues but she couldn't take them seriously. She felt downright humiliated that one of them had managed to make her look quite such a prat at such a delicate moment.

She floundered ashore and sought privacy behind a large outcropping of rock. Suddenly overcome with the giggles she leaned against the rock and laughed helplessly. Somehow it reminded her of the first time she had met Daniela and she'd been hopping up and down on one foot with a boot in one hand and a sock in the other. She had a propensity, it seemed, for looking like a complete idiot when confronted with startlingly attractive females. Mastering herself, she emerged from behind the rock and began to make her way back. She stopped in surprise. The girl was gone. Her towel was still there, and so were her bag and other possessions laid out on the sand, but the owner had completely disappeared. With her brow creased in puzzlement Sarah picked her way slowly across the sand between the stone outcroppings. Where had she gone? This girl was like a will o' the wisp with her uncanny ability to vanish at will. The she saw her again. She was another hundred metres away from her original position and she was perched in a sitting position on top of a large rock. It must have been quite a scramble to get up there but she enjoyed a panoramic view over the terrain and Sarah felt her eyes on her.

Sarah smiled to herself. This was starting to feel like a game and she was beginning to enjoy it. She sauntered along as slowly as she dared and then randomly cut off among some boulders. Once she knew she was out of sight she darted aside and found a perch herself up on a rock with the side of it shielding her from view from the direction she had come. Excitedly she crouched down and waited. Within two minutes the girl appeared some way off to the right. She didn't see Sarah and Sarah grinned in delight as it was obvious now that the girl was looking for her. She was glancing around with a puzzled air and Sarah had to stifle a giggle as she saw the girl creep cautiously to a patch of low scrub and peek surreptitiously around it. The girl had lost her. The game was getting funnier and Sarah was delighted to have turned the tables. She waited a few seconds until the girl turned in her direction and then she casually descended from her perch, tossed her hair and walked back in the direction from which she had come. Out of the corner of her eye she saw the girl looking in her direction and she walked slowly past the rocks and out of sight.

Once again hidden from view she bit her finger in rising excitement. What should she do next? Should she dash off somewhere again and then reappear at random further along? Would the girl follow her immediately or wait a minute or two? The risk was high that the girl might follow her straight away and then, if Sarah rushed away too quickly, it would be obvious she was playing with her. She had to take it slowly, yet not too easily. She had to give the impression that she was just wandering about quite oblivious to the girl's attention. She had to make it difficult for the girl to intercept her yet not so difficult that it would seem like a deliberate attempt to evade her. She followed a convoluted route through the rocks and patches of scrub, weaving about and at one point turning back on herself yet without hurrying. After some minutes of this random weaving there was no sign of the girl. Sarah stuck her tongue in her cheek and rested her hand on her hip. Had the girl lost her or was she teasing her?

Her wandering had brought her close to the river once more. Supposing the girl was off to the right somewhere then she might follow this route along the river back to her belongings. Sarah chose a flat slab of low rock an hundred metres from the river and lay down upon it, resting on her elbows, in plain view of the river. She waited for two minutes, just long enough to wonder if she had miscalculated, before the girl appeared once more. She was sauntering along the river bank and although Sarah saw her glance quickly in her direction, she affected not to notice Sarah laid languorously along the rock. "She must have seen me." thought Sarah excitedly. She must have seen Sarah and chosen this very route in order to pass her by. The girl stopped at the water's edge and squatted down to dabble her fingers in the water. She was mimicking Sarah's previous actions perfectly. She even picked up a stone and pretended to examine it. It was a delightful ploy. She was telling Sarah that she had watched her every movement and that she was aware that Sarah was watching hers. Lazily she stood up and walked on until she was out of sight once more.

Sarah giggled in pleasure. So the ball was back in her court now. This was fun. She wondered if all gay people made such elaborately theatrical games out of their stalking. It was a delicious mix of teasing, subtle signals and play acting. They were both now completely aware of each other and circling around, daring the other to make the next move. What was she going to do now? Inspiration struck her. Casually she meandered out once more, her eyes casting around for her prey. The large rock that the girl had sat on before was only a hundred metres away. Sarah would duplicate the girl's mimicry. It was quite a scramble up the rock but now Sarah had the high ground: a vantage point from which she could survey the terrain. From her high position she saw the girl almost at once about a hundred and fifty metres away. With delight she realised that the girl had not yet spotted her. She was walking slowly and pausing often to look behind her as if anticipating that Sarah was following her. She stopped by a large rock and squatted down behind it peering over in the direction from which she had just come as if waiting in ambush unaware that Sarah was watching her every move. When Sarah did not appear from the expected direction the girl stood once more looking puzzled. She started to retrace her steps but as she did so she caught sight of Sarah atop the large rock and halted. She faced Sarah and placed a hand on her hip and rubbed the back of her neck with her other hand as if unsure as to how to proceed. There were several seconds as the two girls looked at each other openly in stalemate. Then Sarah languidly slid down from the rock on the far side from the girl and out of sight.

Sarah was breathing heavily in excitement. The tension was mounting in the game and she had a notion to raise the stakes once more. Trembling at her own audacity, she untied her bikini and draped it over a rock in plain view. Then, nervous over her nakedness, she scuttled back to her belongings. Hastily she wrapped her sarong around her, sat down on her towel and waited. If the girl followed her around the rock she would see Sarah's bikini and assume that Sarah had deliberately removed it and was now walking about naked. That should bring her running. Sarah hoped she wouldn't be too disappointed to find her modestly clad once more. Sarah waited.... and waited. Twenty minutes passed and Sarah realised in disappointment that the girl was not coming after all. She must have overplayed her hand and the girl had given the game up. She sighed heavily. She had been enjoying the silly little game. Frustrated she stood and walked back to the rock to retrieve her bikini.

At the rock she came to a shocked halt. Her bikini was gone. She stared at the place she had left it in horror. The rock was unmistakeably the same one and it was mercilessly quite unadorned by her pink and white bikini. Somebody, probably the girl, had taken it. Now what was she going to do? Her sarong was quite flimsy and revealing and it was now, other than her sandals, the only clothing she had left to get home in. That was unthinkable. She'd have to phone Jessica and tell her to fetch some clothes when she came to collect her. Jessica would doubtless be highly amused to hear that she had lost her bikini and she would certainly rib her about it. She'd never hear the last of it.

"Ciao bella!" Sarah jumped at the sudden voice behind her and spun around in shock. The girl was laid out seductively on a flat rock behind a large boulder only ten metres away. Sarah hadn't seen her at all. She was grinning at Sarah triumphantly as well she might for she had checkmated Sarah decisively. She was wearing Sarah's bikini. "Have you lost something caro?" she asked innocently.

"You.... you're wearing my bikini." Sarah stammered.

The girl laughed softly. She had a deep, attractive chuckle and her eyes danced with playful amusement. "You left it here. I thought you had finished with it so I tried it on. Do you think it suits me?"

Sarah grinned in spite of herself. She knew she was being teased. Daniela would love this girl. She raised an eyebrow and looked at her directly. "Actually I thought you looked better without it."

The girl tossed her hair and laughed luxuriously. "You were looking at me caro. Do you always stare at strange girls?"

Sarah laughed in her turn, enjoying this lovely girl's teasing. "Only beautiful ones and especially ones with no clothes on!"

The girl looked at her in shockingly overt appraisal. Her mouth opened slightly and her dark eyes seemed to grow smoky. "Do you have a name caro or are you just a nymph that lives in the river?"

Sarah smiled, charmed by the imagery. "I'm Sarah, Sarah Fuchs."

"Schwyzerdutsch?"

"Only half. I'm half English."

"English!" The girl raised her eyebrows. "I like to speak English." The girl changed from Italian into English flawlessly with a beguiling lilt to her accent. "My name is Rozella."

Sarah nodded with a smile. "It's a lovely name Rozella. It suits you."

Rozella smiled and rested back on her elbows seductively. "So Sarah, Sarah Fuchs, what are you looking for down by the river today?"

221

"My bikini actually. Can I have it back please?"

"Oh so you want your bikini back?"

"Yes please. Apart from this flimsy sarong it's all I have to get home in today."

"Then you should be careful where you leave it Sarah, Sarah Fuchs."

"I shall be more careful in future Rozella. Now can you give me it back please?"

"No!"

Sarah blinked. "I beg your pardon."

Rozella slid a finger under the strap of Sarah's bikini top and ran her tongue lightly over her lip. "If you want it you will have to take it back."

Sarah laughed. "You're a bad girl Rozella."

"Not me. I am an innocent. I am just here by the river today to take the sun and a wicked siren of the river is hunting me. She leaves her clothes on a rock to lure me and when I fall into her trap and try them on she pounces and demands them back so she can leave me naked at her mercy."

Sarah laughed deliciously. "That is a pretty liberal interpretation of events Rozella."

"Ah but so much more fun don't you think?"

"So how am I supposed to take my bikini back Rozella?"

"Why easy. You just have to take it off me." Rozella raised a finger with a wicked grin. "There is one... how you say it in English... one catch though."

Sarah pulled a wry face. "I thought there just might be. Come on then... what is it?"

"You have to put it back on."

"Well of course I'm going to put it back on..."

"Now.... here... in front of me! You can't put it back on with that wrap Sarah Fuchs so you have to take it off before I let you have your bikini back. You have staring at me when I am naked... now I am wanting to see you naked."

222

Sarah grinned and sat down on the rock beside Rozella. "I could just let you keep it Rozella. My sister is picking me up in her car and I can easily go home in my beach wrap."

Rozella looked into Sarah's eyes. "Yes but then we both lose Sarah Fuchs. What a poor way to end our little game."

"How did you want to end it Rozella?"

Rozella reached out and drew a languid finger down Sarah's bare arm. "This I think you know. We are quiet here and there are places no one can see. You are beautiful Sarah Fuchs. I want you."

"Oh I'm so sorry Rozella but that is not possible."

Rozella frowned and looked uncertain. "Why so? You are gay are you not? I am also gay. I desire you and you desire me. Is this not true?"

"I have a girlfriend Rozella."

"Merda! This is true?"

"Yes Rozella. I'm sorry."

"She is as beautiful as you this girlfriend?"

"Oh more Rozella! She is the most beautiful girl I have ever seen and I love her."

"Then why are you out hunting here today?"

"I wasn't Rozella. I came here today to be alone and to think. I didn't expect to meet anyone else especially somebody as lovely as you."

Rozella's eyes lit up with hope. "Ah so you do desire me? Perhaps your girlfriend need never know huh Sarah Fuchs?"

Sarah shook her head. "I would know Rozella. I'm sorry but I can't do that."

Rozella lowered her eyes sadly and shrugged. "I thought you wanted me Sarah."

"I do Rozella... I mean I find you beautiful and desirable. When I saw you I was excited and I wanted to see more of you. I don't know many girls that are gay Rozella and I was sure that you were attracted to me. It's the first time I've ever done that... I mean gone out to

223

hunt a gay girl I found attractive. I'm very new to all this. Until a few weeks ago I didn't even know I was gay. I'm even engaged to be married Rozella: married to a man! My engagement party was last night. But I don't love the man I'm engaged to. I love my girlfriend and now I know that I'm gay. If I wasn't sure before I am now. I'm sure now because of you."

Rozella looked puzzled. "Because of me?"

"Yes Rozella. Ever since I met my girlfriend my world has turned upside down. Before that I was expected by my family to marry the son of my father's business associate. I was just an ordinary straight girl obeying her family's wishes to marry the man they approved of. But then I met my girlfriend and suddenly I felt things for another woman that I had never felt for my fiancée before. Last night my parents threw a big party to announce my engagement and now I am officially engaged. But I no longer want to be married. I came here today to try and think what to do. But that meant having to face up to being gay Rozella. It's something new to me. If I had to leave my fiancée and live with my girlfriend instead, I had to be sure; be sure that I was gay; be sure that it wasn't just a wonderful woman who had turned my head. Then along came you and suddenly I'm excited by the view of a beautiful naked girl and one who is attracted to me. Now I cannot deny my feelings anymore. I'm gay. You've helped me to see that. Thank you."

Rozella laughed suddenly. "It is my pleasure Sarah, Sarah Fuchs. Does this girl love you too?"

"Yes she does."

"Then I had better give you your bikini back."

"Thank you."

Rozella sighed and untied the strings of Sarah's bikini. When she was naked once more she held the garment out to Sarah. "There you are and now you have the advantage of me."

Sarah smiled slowly and unfastened her sarong, letting it slip onto the rock, and held out her hand for her bikini. "There now I have fulfilled my side of the bargain."

Rozella's nostrils flared and she squirmed closer. "You are so beautiful Sarah. Damn your girlfriend. Let us find a quiet place among the rocks."

Sarah held up a hand and shook her head. "I'm sorry Rozella, but I can't. But let's both get dressed and I'll take you for a bottle of wine in the grotto in Golino. I would like to hear your story Rozella; your journey to this place and I will tell you mine in return. I can't be your lover but I would dearly like to be your friend. Would you like that?"

Rozella smiled ruefully. "Yes Sarah that at least I will take but I want a kiss first; just one kiss before you put your clothes back on."

"One kiss I can grant you."

The kiss was sweet and lingering and Sarah felt her body respond at the touch of Rozella's naked body against hers. For a moment she thought she had pushed her luck too far and that she would not be able to resist if Rozella began to make love to her. Oddly though, it was Rozella that broke the kiss with a long sigh. "Madre de Dio! Your girlfriend is a very lucky girl Sarah Fuchs. Come let us find my clothes and we will take that wine you promised me and I will hear how God has cheated me of my prey this day."

Chapter Twenty-Two

It was odd, thought Sarah, how different gay women were from each other. Perhaps she'd had some sort of fixed image in her mind about lesbians; some kind of clichéd idea as to how they would appear and act. It was becoming quite a shock to realise that they were just as varied as any other people. Of course, if she'd stopped to think about it, that was hardly surprising. She wouldn't have expected heterosexual people to conform to a single identifiable type after all so why should gay people do so? People, after all, were people in spite of their sexual inclinations and they came in all the rich variety of humankind. Nevertheless she had to concede that the gay women with whom she had become acquainted with over the summer were all remarkably contrasting characters and expressed their sexuality in markedly different ways.

There was Frau Fritzl, Elke's self-assured, completely unapologetic embracement of her sexual orientation, dominant and persuasive; almost a matriarchal figure who was not above manipulating those around her if she considered it her responsibility to do so. She was overtly gay but without any sort of expressed intent to demonstrate the fact. She was just simply herself and her sexuality was merely a part of her and not the defining identity of her character. Yet there were complications in that simple acceptance of her sexuality. She was so at ease with her gay nature that it was easy to forget that it had not always been so. Elke after all had been married for many years to a man. She had come to a recognition of her true sexuality very late in life. Perhaps that was why she felt no real urge to be particularly demonstrative about her sexual feelings and why most people who did not know her well would have been surprised to learn of them. Hers was a sexuality born of bitter experience and forged into wisdom through trial. Hers was the sagacity of age and hard bought victory; a happiness won against long odds and fiercely defended. She had passed through the rapids and found the calm waters beyond and there she would stay and offer that tranquillity as a sanctuary to those still floundering in the torrents.

She had become an important figure in Sarah's life; a mentor in fact; a guiding hand through Sarah's own stormy passage and it was a role she played well, having been through the maelstrom herself. She was almost becoming a surrogate parent; the one older person with whom Sarah could honestly talk about her feelings with. She was strong minded and decisive, apt to be impatient with trivialities and irrelevancies, cutting through them to the important factors. Her philosophy was straightforward. If you're gay then you're gay; live with it; enjoy it and don't make the same mistakes that she had made. Life was too short to squander it in agony over your sexual preferences. It was the philosophy of someone who knew the terrible price you paid for dishonesty; half a lifetime wasted in misery through a failure of courage to face up to one's true nature.

And that, thought Sarah, seemed often to be a defining issue for any gay person. How well and how soon did you come to an accommodation with your sexuality? Happiest were those who found acceptance of this fundamental aspect of themselves. Elke's partner, Angelica, was a case in point. Sarah knew enough now about the relationship between Elke and Angelica to realise that it was Angelica that had brought Elke to the point she had now reached. Angelica was a person who just had a serene acceptance of everything about herself. There was no front to Angelica. What you saw was what you got. Angelica saw no reason to explain herself; no sense that she had to rationalise her sexuality. She was, in effect, a simple person; one who didn't waste time with painful self-examination. She loved Elke and saw

227

no point in questioning whether that was right or wrong. It had been Angelica's simple embracement of her love for Elke that had brought Elke to her own final acceptance. Elke might have been the more strong willed and flamboyant of the two but it was the bedrock of Angelica's straightforward love that was the foundation of the happiness between the two women.

Angelica had probably found an easier passage to her own sexuality Sarah thought. Perhaps she had had parents and friends who were more tolerant, sympathetic and understanding for she seemed to have emerged from the crisis of her exposure relatively unscathed and with her fundamental goodness intact. Many were not so lucky. Sarah thought of Charmaine. Reading between the lines Sarah suspected that Charmaine had had a far more difficult passage. Charmaine had told her that she had suffered a six month alienation from her parents upon her announcement that she was gay and that there had been a certain coldness ever since. She had also passed through the heartbreak of a doomed relationship with a married woman and she was a girl that had known discrimination and social ostracism because of her sexuality. It had radicalised Charmaine; politicised her even and left her passionate about the civil rights and social respect due her sexual orientation. Sarah worried that she herself was not more concerned about the gay rights movement on a personal level. In fact she knew little about the issues and had no really strong feelings about them. Dispassionately she considered that gay people were due the same respect and tolerance afforded to any member of society and were certainly worthy of equal treatment under the law but the matter had not touched her in a way to excite any strong passion. She supposed that was because she had never really been exposed to the problem before and, since she had never been openly gay, she had never had to experience the sort of discrimination and intolerance that Charmaine had obviously faced. She had never experienced it until now that was. She had the feeling that she was about to become far more acquainted with it from here on.

It was called "coming out" in the gay world wasn't it? The term meant that moment when you publicly announced your sexuality and came to terms with it. In this respect, everybody's experience was different but generally speaking everybody found the transition difficult. Angelica perhaps had had the easier ride but Elke and Charmaine certainly hadn't. It was about honesty Sarah realised; the moment when you stopped living a lie and confessed to your true nature. Any gay person had to confront that moment if they were to live happy and fulfilled lives. God only knew how difficult that transition was. There was still so much shame and fear attached. Sadly some people never made it. Their courage failed them and they lived on in sad lives of regret and dissatisfaction for the want of that courage. But it was a demon that you had to face. Sarah thought of Nicole. Nicole! The last person on earth that Sarah would have thought gay. She had lived with her for years and never known. Even Nicole had eventually had to find the courage in her; the courage to declare that she loved Sarah and always had done. Poor Nicole. She had come out too late. If ever there was a lesson to be learned about the perils of self-suppression then Nicole's story was surely it. For Nicole was deeply suppressed. She had almost aggressively pursued men and denied her true sexuality. Sarah saw at last that Nicole's sorry tale of ephemeral and failed relationships were truly the net result of a girl in denial of her true feelings. She had lived alongside the true object of her deepest feelings since childhood and never found the courage to say so. Sarah had never known. She was not proud of that fact. Others had seen it more clearly than she had. Of course Sarah had been pretty much suppressed as well but surely she should have seen it in her best friend. Almost painfully Sarah realised just how much it had cost

Nicole to declare her feelings for her. And it was too late. Sarah was already in love with another woman.

Then of course there was Daniela. She was different again. Sarah had never really talked with Daniela about her own journey but Sarah realised that it had been a tricky one. For one thing Daniela had come through a broken heterosexual marriage too and for another she even had a child. Daniela had obviously had had her own demons to face. It was especially difficult for Daniela as well because she was a public figure; a celebrity whose own painful adjustment had been carried out under the unforgiving scrutiny of the public eye. Curiously, however, it seemed to have failed to scar Daniela in any fundamental way. She was at peace with her sexuality; serenely accepting it without any need to assert it.

Daniela was almost pure love Sarah knew. To Daniela, there was nothing more important than her expression of her love. In a sense, her sexuality was almost irrelevant when set against the imperatives of her love. Sarah suspected that Daniela could have loved a man with the same intensity and devotion with which she loved her. The object of her love happened to be a woman. Another woman could have fallen in love with a woman because they were gay. In Daniela's case she was gay because she had fallen in love with a woman. Love ruled Daniela. Of course she was inclined to homosexuality. She was after all an iconic figure to the gay community and she had quite openly declared her sexuality in public. But, somehow, that seemed secondary to Daniela. Ultimately she just wanted someone to love and there was always the sneaking feeling that that person's gender was relatively unimportant. It didn't mean necessarily that Daniela was bisexual. It just meant that Daniela's sexuality was defined by her love. Daniela didn't seem to make distinctions between gender orientation. You loved somebody then you made love to them; end of story.

230

That didn't mean for an instance that Daniela regarded sex as unimportant. Sarah knew that without question. Daniela's passion in love making had taken her breath away.

So all Sarah' gay acquaintances were different and Sarah was coming to understand that the personal journey of each of them to their accommodation with their own sexuality played a large part in their gay characteristics. And her new friend, as Sarah observed as she sat across the stone table from her in the grotto at Golino, sipping wine and nibbling at pieces of Ticino salami, was different again. Rozella was a far different creature. Rozella had little interest in the political and social issues of gender orientation. Rozella was not the sort of person to agonise over her own sexuality. Rozella just liked sex and she just happened to like sex with women. You might have found her at a Gay Pride festival but that would only be because that was a happy hunting ground for hot gay girls! She was unabashedly, openly and without conscience a sexual predator.

Sarah suspected that she was hyper sexual and probably shamelessly promiscuous. She was a voyeur of pretty girls and, at the same time, narcissistic and exhibitionist. She flirted with Sarah continuously and was given to outrageous suggestions and innuendos. There was a prudish side to Sarah that considered that she ought to disapprove of Rozella but Rozella was a very hard person to dislike. She was outrageous, shocking, completely uninhibited and enormous fun. She would be a nightmare as a girlfriend Sarah realised. You would never be sure of keeping her in her own bed! But as a friend or even an occasional dalliance she was great fun: titillating and stimulating: the sort of wicked person you kept on your address book as a companion for those occasions when you felt like letting your hair down and having a really wild night out on the town.

Rozella, it turned out, was a graduate from university where she had completed a degree in film and media studies. She was carving out a career as a fashion photographer: a profession that would suit her to the ground if it meant the opportunity of photographing attractive girls with preferably not many clothes on! She was also a part time model herself, she told Sarah, and she'd supplemented her income at university by doing a little modelling on the side. Well she certainly had the looks for the part but Sarah, reading between the lines, suspected that her modelling experience was some way away from the area of advertising household products. Rozella was a bad girl. It was a good job that Rozella had not brought her camera along to the beach that day thought Sarah wryly. As it was, she was attempting to cajole Sarah into modelling for her one day and Sarah was under no illusion that the sort of photo shoot that Rozella had in mind would be the kind that she would be able to show her parents.

"Listen Rozella." Sarah told her with a laugh, "If I'm going to pose naked for a portrait it'll be for my girlfriend, all right?"

"Well ok then I take some photos for your girlfriend's pleasure. She is so beautiful as you say then maybe I photograph you together no? Maybe she like that. I won't even charge you."

Sarah laughed. "Oh really? That's terribly decent of you."

Rozella leaned forward across the table. She had pulled a tiny thong and an indecently low cut short skirted summer dress over her nakedness before they had retired to the grotto. Leaning forward she was exposing a generous view of her upper body endowments. "Please caro. You are so beautiful. I want to photograph you. I want to see you naked."

"You have already seen me naked." Sarah pointed out with a grin. "And furthermore I have already seen *you* naked. There's nothing under that dress I haven't already seen Rozella so stop flashing your tits at me."

Rozella grinned wickedly and reached up to squeeze her own breast with her hand. "You don't like them?"

"They're very nice Rozella and don't you just know it. Now stop playing with them."

"You would like to touch them perhaps?"

"You're absolutely incorrigible aren't you Rozella?"

"What it mean... incorrigible?"

"It means that you're a very bad girl."

"So what do you do with bad girls?"

Sarah guffawed. "Well if you were my girlfriend I'd take you down some place quiet on that beach, cut half a dozen birch twigs and thrash your backside until you pleaded for mercy."

Rozella sat up sharply with a huge grin. "Ok! Let's go."

Sarah patted her hand. "But I'm *not* your girlfriend Rozella. I'll leave that job up to the poor woman who is lumbered with the thankless task of keeping you in line. God knows she'll have her work cut out."

Rozella leaned back looking disappointed. "So who is she then this girlfriend of yours who is so beautiful?"

"She's a wonderful woman Rozella and I love her deeply."

"So what does she do?"

Sarah hesitated. "Er I'm not sure I can tell you that."

Rozella lifted an eyebrow quizzically. "Why not? Is there some secret? She is married perhaps? She not want people to know she is gay?"

"Oh no. No she's openly gay Rozella but she's a bit of a public figure and well our relationship is not in the public domain."

"She wants to keep you secret?" Rozella looked puzzled. "I don't understand. If she is gay and she is out, why she want to hide you? You are beautiful. Why she be ashamed of you?"

"She's not ashamed of me. On the contrary she is proud of me. I don't think she'd care *who* knew about our relationship."

"Ah so then *you* are ashamed of *her*?"

Sarah bit her lip in uncertainty. It was a telling point. "No Rozella I'm not ashamed of her. She's the most amazing person I've ever known. It's just that...." Sarah tailed off not sure how to continue.

Rozella looked at her shrewdly. For all her apparently one tracked mind Rozella was by no means lacking in astuteness. "So it is you that you are ashamed of then Sarah Fuchs?"

Sarah nodded miserably. "Yes. Yes I suppose it is. I... I'm only just coming out myself Rozella. My family have no idea that I'm gay. My girlfriend... well she's famous. If it gets around that I'm her girlfriend then sooner or later it will be in the newspapers and my family will see it. God knows what they'll say then."

Rozella snorted. "They going to find out sometime Sarah. What you going do? You love this woman so you go tell her that you not see her anymore because your parents go find out? You best go tell them."

"It's not as easy as that Rozella."

"Sure it is! Everybody gay have to do this sometime Sarah. Best get it over with quickly and move on."

"How did you tell your parents Rozella? Was it difficult?"

"Hmmph not so hard. I not have much choice. They find me in bed with someone."

Sarah laughed. "I might have known. How old were you?"

"Sixteen."

"*Sixteen*! God you started early!"

"Poof! That not early. I kissed my first girl when I was eleven. I always knew what I was. My best friend at school let me put my hand down her pants when we were fourteen." Rozella paused for a moment wistfully. "I was in love with her. It was my first love."

234

"Oh what happened?"

Rozella shrugged. "She like boys more. She married now with two children."

"Oh! Oh I see." Sarah didn't know whether it was appropriate to say sorry or not.

"You tell me on the beach Sarah that you are engaged to marry a man."

"Yes. Ever since last night Rozella. Last night was my official engagement party."

"You are not going to marry this man?"

"How can I? I'm gay."

"But your parents they think you go marry this man?"

"Yes. In fact they more or less arranged the marriage."

"Why you say you marry this man when you know you cannot Sarah?"

"Oh hell there's a long story behind that Rozella."

Rozella picked up the wine bottle and regarded the diminished contents critically. "So we best order another bottle then."

Over the second bottle of wine Sarah told Rozella her story omitting only the identity of the woman who had come into her life and so markedly turned it upside down that summer. To her surprise she found that Rozella was a patient listener and rarely interrupted her. When she did interrupt it was usually to ask for clarification or to make some pertinent observation. These observations were concise and perspicacious. Rozella had a way of cutting through the dross to the meat of the matter. Sarah realised that she had underestimated her new friend. Whatever you might say about Rozella's morals there was no doubting the incisiveness of her intelligence. They were half way through the second bottle of wine by the time that Sarah had finished her tale. Sarah felt liberated by telling her story to another person as if the recounting of it had clarified all the details and arguments in her own mind.

Suddenly she was very interested in what Rozella would make of her tale. "So what do you think I should do now Rozella?" she asked nervously.

Rozella looked surprised. "You don't know?"

Sarah shook her head. "Well no; not really."

Rozella laughed shortly. "You are intelligent girl Sarah. Why you make big problem out of small thing? Go back to this man and say I am gay and I can't marry you. Then tell your parents same thing. Then you go pack your bags and go home to your girl. Where is problem here? Go home to your girl! She must be missing you."

"Just like that?"

"Yes! Just like that." Rozella smiled. "You say I am bad girl Sarah. Well maybe you right. Maybe I get a lot of trouble because I am bad girl. But I am honest Sarah. I am what I am. I am not going lie about it. Maybe I get trouble for being too honest but better that than I get trouble for lie. You have not be honest Sarah and look at trouble it cause you. You're a good girl Sarah but you got to stop telling lies. Try be honest. Maybe things better than you think."

"I don't know if I can tell my parents Rozella."

"So you tell them now or you tell them when the divorce happen. Now which you think is better?"

"Oh God! If you put it like that..."

"You not tell me the whole story Sarah."

"I thought I did."

Rozella shook her head. "You have not tell me the name of this famous woman; this woman you love."

"I... I don't know if I ought to Rozella."

"So this women she go be mad you tell people you love her?"

"Well no I don't suppose so. I think she'd be pleased."

"You ashamed to tell people you love her?"

"Well no but..."

"You can't hide Sarah Fuchs. Somebody go find out sometime. You scared that I might tell people? Let me tell you something. Maybe I'm bad girl but I have principles too Sarah. I tell nobody things somebody tell me private." Rozella grinned. "Anyway I not need principles for that. You got a name for telling tales and nobody go want to sleep with you. I know lots of secrets Sarah Fuchs but I keep my mouth shut."

Sarah grinned back at Rozella. She liked this girl. Rozella was precious. "You're quite something Rozella!"

Rozella picked up her wine glass with a smug smile. "Maybe. So you try being honest now Sarah. Tell me the name of this woman. She so special she deserve girl like you I want to know who she is." Rozella lifted a finger in warning. "I tell you though. If she not special enough; if she not good enough for you then I go take you away from her."

"Oh she's special all right Rozella." Sarah grinned.

"I know lots of famous people Sarah. Some just think they are special. Not many impress me. This lady friend of yours got to be really special I don't steal her girl from her."

"She's called Daniela; Daniela Devin."

Rozella's eyes flew open in shock and she stared at Sarah for long seconds. "Danny? Danny Devin? It can't be true?"

"I'm sorry. Don't you believe me?"

"Madre de Dios! Yes I believe you. Now it all make sense Sarah Fuchs. *Incredibile*! This is the woman who wait for you back home?"

"Yes. Yes she is."

"And you sit here not knowing what to do? You crazy in the head Sarah Fuchs? You go let your parents try to marry you to some horrible man and you go have Danny Devin? You need go soak your head in river Sarah Fuchs."

"I take it that you consider my girlfriend special enough then Rozella."

"Oh she special Sarah. She one of the most special people I know. Didi is a wonderful woman."

"Didi?"

"It what I call her. It from her initials; DD. She always laugh when I call her that."

It was Sarah's turn to be astonished. "Wait a minute. Are you actually telling me that you know Daniela personally?"

"Naturalmente! I know her well. Who you think take the photos for her album covers?"

"You! You mean you took those shots of her on her albums?"

"Precisamente. She is one of my best clients."

Sarah sat back on the bench in shock. "I don't believe this. I love those pictures of Danny on her albums. I even have a blown up copy of one on my bedroom wall. Those pictures are beautiful. You're a fantastic photographer."

"Thank you Sarah Fuchs. Now maybe you go let me photograph you."

Sarah laughed heartily. "Well maybe I will. God this is amazing. I had no idea Wow!" Another thought occurred to Sarah and she frowned. "This doesn't mean that you... I mean that you and Danny..."

Rozella shook her head decisively. "No Sarah Fuchs. She is my client. All very professional." Rozella grinned wickedly. "Of course I tried. I be crazy not to. But Didi she choosy." Rozella took a long appreciative look at Sarah. "Oh she choosy all right. It look like she choose well. I just bad girl Rozella. I'm no Sarah Fuchs. I'm please for Didi. It time she find girl like you good enough for her."

"You're flattering me."

Rozella shook her head. "Not me. You forget. I am honest. You special girl Sarah Fuchs; maybe more special than you know." Rozella tossed back her hair

238

with a laugh. "Now I just got to shoot you and Didi. Madre de Dios! What I could do with the two of you together. We make the cover of every magazine in Europe."

"Whoa! Slow down. I'm not sure I want my photo emblazoned across a magazine cover."

"Coward. What better way to tell the world you love this woman?"

"Oh God!" Sarah groaned. "I don't think I'm ready for this."

"Hey maybe you and Didi get married no! You go hire me to take the wedding photos?"

"Er... I.... I'll get back to you on that. I think there's a bit of work to do before that."

Rozella became suddenly business like; reaching into her handbag and pulling out her mobile phone. "Yes of course. First of all we got to get you home." Rozella started keying buttons on her phone.

"What are you doing?" asked Sarah in puzzlement.

"I'm googling SBB." Sarah frowned in confusion. SBB was the acronym for the Schweizer Bundesbahn; the Swiss national railway system. "Hmm." Rozella mused. "You say you caught the train at Wattwil no?"

"Well yes that's where I caught the train to come to Ticino."

"So it is now half past two in the afternoon. You have train nearly every half hour from Bellinzona. There is train at six minutes past seven and another at thirty six minutes past. It the same though because they both arrive at same time in Wattwil. You miss them and you have train at eight thirty six. So you got plenty time to get back to your parents and pack your things. You think maybe your sister go give you lift to station in Bellinzona?"

"Just a minute Rozella. I can't just fly off like that."

Rozella looked at her soberly. "Yes you can Sarah Fuchs. You must. Your lady is waiting for you. She is one of the most desirable gay women in all Switzerland

239

Sarah. Don't keep her waiting. If you love her; if you really love her, then go home to her; go home tonight. Only few times in a life, maybe only once, does chance like this come Sarah Fuchs. Don't hesitate. Fly to her arms tonight Sarah. Ask her forgive you that you ever thought marry this awful man. Tell her that she the only one for you. Take her for your own Sarah Fuchs. Take her tonight. Life too short to waste Sarah. Make your lady yours tonight."

"But...but... I just can't. If I take a train at half past eight it'll be past half past eleven before I get to Wattwil and I'll have missed the last bus back to Unterwasser."

"You have phone no? So call her. Tell her that you're coming home. You think she won't come to Wattwil to pick you up? Of course she will. Just tell her that you're coming home. Tell her that this time you coming home for good."

"Oh God!" breathed Sarah. If it could only be. But then, why not? Suddenly Sarah felt a deep wrench of longing and homesickness in her belly. She knew in a flash just how much she had been missing Daniela and it was a sharp pang of pain and an aching sense of loneliness every minute she was separated from her. To do what Rozella was urging was instantly the thing which Sarah desired more than anything in the world at that moment. To rush home to her tonight; to ease the pain and misery of these past three days in her arms this very night; to feel once more at peace and free under her loving caresses. She could do it as well. Rozella was right. It would take her less than half an hour to change for travelling and pack her belongings. Jessica would run her to the station in Bellinzona. Her parents' objections wouldn't phase Jessica for an instance. Even if she wouldn't, however, there was always the local bus service and she could catch a connecting train in Locarno. She had hours to catch that train in Bellinzona. It was easily enough time.

But she couldn't could she? She couldn't just announce she was leaving and then breeze out of the house. There'd be uproar. Her parents would forbid it. Alan would be outraged. Sarah pulled a face at the thought. It would be hypocritical of him. He was due to leave himself in the morning. Presumably abandoning her was more acceptable. Her parents' objections were more formidable. But then they were inevitable anyway weren't they? She now knew for a certainty that she was not going to marry Alan. Therefore a clash with her parents was unavoidable. If she feared to face that clash then she was no further ahead. It was the fear of defying her parents' wishes that had got her into this mess in the first place. So do it now. Do it today. Take control of her own destiny and tell her parents that she was not prepared to marry and tell them that she was going home. Home! What a lovely word. The Toggenburg was her home. That was where her roots were. That was where she belonged. How dare anybody try to tell her where she should live or how she should live? To the devil with an awful suburban house in Zurich. She was a Toggenburg girl. Nobody was going to take her mountains away from her. This was her life. Nobody had the right to dictate her conduct of it. Home was the Toggenburg; home was where Daniela was. Let her parents object. There was no point in hanging around in the Ticino was there? There was no point in dragging out the recriminations; of tiresome argument. Her mind was made up. There was nothing more her parents could add to change her decision. Sooner or later you had to cut the apron strings and take a step out into the world on your own. This moment had arrived. Further procrastination was pointless. She was going home.

Rozella was looking at her questioningly. "You hesitate Sarah Fuchs."

Sarah smiled. "Not any longer Rozella. You're right. I'm going home. There's nothing more for me to do here. Thank you for helping me to see it."

241

Rozella smiled at her. "It was my pleasure Sarah Fuchs. You had better make a move no?"

"Yes. Yes I should. I'll phone my sister to come and pick me up."

"Then I will leave you. Maybe it better you not have to explain me to your sister."

"Oh but where do you live Rozella? How are you getting home?"

"Do not worry about me. A friend go pick me up in Intragna."

Sarah raised an eyebrow. "A friend? A *girl* friend?"

Rozella laughed. "Maybe. I see! Maybe she consolation prize no; consolation for day when I nearly take Danny Devin's girlfriend from her!"

Sarah shook her head in amusement. "You're quite a girl Rozella."

"So are you Sarah Fuchs!" Rozella reached into her handbag and pulled out a card. "Here is my card Signorina Fuchs. It has my mobile number on it. You phone me when you are on that train ok?"

"Yes... yes of course."

Rozella picked up her belongings and rose to stand by Sarah to stroke her hair. "It is small world Sarah Fuchs and people pass through each other's lives all the time. I am thankful you pass through mine. Thank you for the wine. We shall meet again!" Rozella bent suddenly and kissed Sarah on the mouth letting her lips linger teasingly. Then she straightened up with a triumphant grin. "Until we meet again. Arrivederci Sarah Fuchs." Then she turned and was gone. Sarah stared after her breathlessly.

Chapter Twenty-Three

Jessica came quickly in response to Sarah's phone call but it was gone three o'clock before she arrived at the grotto in Golino. Sarah had not been idle however. She needed to sort out her obligations and clear her decks for action. To that end she had phoned Nicole briefly to ascertain her whereabouts that evening. Nicole was working from six to eleven o'clock. It was perfect. In the worst case scenario of Daniela not being available Nicole would be able to pick her up in Wattwil or, if that was too much of a problem, in Nesslau. Sarah had remembered that, although there was no bus at that hour all the way to Unterwasser, there was at least a late bus connection between Wattwil and Nesslau. It would be nearly midnight by the time she got there but she hoped Nicole would not mind. If the worst came to the worst she could always call a taxi in Nesslau. It would be expensive but she would pay it gladly in order to get home tonight.

To hedge her bets Sarah checked on the train connections between Locarno and Bellinzona just in case Jessica baulked at abetting her in her dash for freedom. That was no problem. Three trains an hour left Locarno for Bellinzona and the journey only took between twenty and twenty five minutes. There was a train that left Locarno at just past eight o'clock that arrived in Bellinzona in time to make her connection. That might be cutting it fine though she thought. She'd better take the train at a quarter to eight if circumstances required it. Hopefully it wouldn't be necessary. The one person she didn't call was Daniela. Things might still go wrong she realised and she hesitated to state firmly she was coming home tonight if it was still possible that she would have to let Daniela down after all. Instead she confined herself to a brief message of love which was quickly answered. She texted back. "*R U home tonite?*"

"*yes y?*"

"*Tell U later. Luv U.*"

"*J luv U 2*"

Sarah glanced nervously at her watch. Where was Jessica? Now that she had made her mind up to leave Sarah was chafing at the bit. No sooner had the thought crossed her mind than Jessica walked into the grotto. Sarah smiled in relief. "Hi Jess. Thanks for coming out for me."

Jessica took a seat with a grunt. "Hmmph no imposition there. The atmosphere around the house is so full of crap that if I'd needed to pop out to have a tooth pulled I would have welcomed the chance to get out of the place."

"Oh God! Is it rough?"

"You're not even close. Mum's been walking about, rending her hair and wailing about ungrateful daughters, Dad's been sat around looking disappointed and pontificating about duty and responsibility and Alan's spent the day looking like somebody took his toys away from him and sulking about it. You really got under their skins this time kid."

"Not half as much as I'm about to Jess."

"Oh God! You're going to throw another whammy into the mix aren't you?"

"I'm leaving Jess. I'm leaving tonight. I have a train at half past eight. I intend to be on it."

"Jesus!"

"I'm sorry Jess. I was going to stay longer but I don't see any point in it anymore. I'm not going to marry Alan now so I don't see why I need to hang around and listen to mum and dad berating me for it. I want to go home."

"Wow! Talk about throwing down the gauntlet."

"I'm sorry if you don't approve Jess."

"Who said I didn't approve? I think it's the best thing I've heard all day. Let's both get the fuck out of here. If you're leaving I'm damned if I'm staying behind to reap the whirlwind. We'll both do a runner."

"Can you give me a lift to Bellinzona Jess?"

"Better. I can drive you back across the Gotthard if you want. I could drop you at Brunnen or Schwyz or somewhere if you like. You could catch your train from there."

Sarah shook her head. "No Jess it's not necessary. I have a return ticket and, in any case, you can't drive back through the Gotthard as quickly as the train. Just a lift to Bellinzona would be fine."

"Are you sure kid?"

"Yes Jess. I'll stick to my original plan but thank you."

Jessica ran a hand through her hair agitatedly. "Well ok then. Actually it would be stress for me to drive back tonight anyway. I was going to leave in the morning. Maybe I'd better stick to that after all. I suppose it might be quite diverting watching mum and dad come apart at the seams."

"Oh God Jess! Do you think I'm doing the right thing?"

"Hmmph! My only question about it is why you aren't on that train already. I would have been after last night's performance. Mind you I *am* pissed off with you."

"Oh! Why?"

"Because *I'm* the one that's supposed to be the rebel in the family, not sweet little Sarah who always does as she's told. You're stealing my thunder."

Sarah laughed. "I'm sorry Jess."

"Don't worry about it. At least I can aid and abet the insurrection."

"Thank you for that Jess."

"Well come on then if we've got an escape plan to execute let's get on with it. We've got a window of opportunity to strike while the guards are otherwise engaged."

"What do you mean?"

"Mum and Dad are out. Dad got called into the office and mum's had to go down to Locarno for something. We've got at least two hours before they're back. If we don't hang around you can get all your stuff packed without them breathing down your neck. Hopefully by the time they get back we'll have your things in the back of the car and be able to roll at a moment's notice if the scenario calls for a quick getaway."

"What about Alan?"

"I'm sure you can handle Alan Sarah. That fucking toe-rag's out of his league messing with my kid sister. He's about to get an object lesson in the consequences of pissing off the female line of the Fuchs clan."

Sarah grinned. "Ok let's get this show on the road sister. Should we give a rebel yell?"

"One for all and all for one. We shall overcome! Death to the establishment! Long live the revolution! Let's rock."

Chapter Twenty-Four

At least they didn't roll... the car that is, which, considering the way that Jessica drove back to the house in a squeal of tortured rubber, Sarah considered to be a miracle. Jessica seemed to have taken her role as accomplice a little too seriously. It was like being in a live version of Grand Theft Auto Sarah thought. "For God's sake Jess!" Sarah pleaded, "Slow down! I'm supposed to be escaping on a train not in a bloody hearse." Finally they pulled up at the house.

"I'll leave the car out on the street." Jessica remarked. "That way dad won't be able to block us in the drive with his car."

Sarah smiled at her sister. "I think you're being a little overly dramatic Jess."

The house and garden were much improved from the scene earlier that morning for the clean-up crew had done sterling work in eradicating the debris of the previous night's party. One or two people from the hire companies were still busy at work but the major part of the work was done. Sarah's parents were still absent and there was currently no sign of Alan. Jessica discovered that he was in her father's study borrowing his computer for some work of his own. He hadn't noticed the two sisters' arrival back at the house. "Quick go and get packed kid." Jessica told Sarah. "I'll run interference on Alan for you."

It took Sarah literally minutes to change her clothes and pack, and she thanked providence that she had not fetched a great deal of stuff with her. One problem did occur. The clothes her mother had bought her in Ascona preyed on her mind. On the one hand it seemed downright silly to abandon them since they were fitted particularly for her. What would her mother do with them? Take them back? Give them away? She agonised for a few minutes but in the end she couldn't bear the thought of being beholden in any respect and so she left them out. It was painful however because they were lovely and, in particular, Sarah regretted having to say farewell to the beautiful dress she had worn to the party the previous evening. She would have loved Daniela to see her in that.

Once her packing was complete, Sarah took a deep breath and rummaged in the drawers of her dressing table for stationary. She located letter paper and, seating herself at the dressing table with a pang of fear, began to compose a letter to her parents. This task took her half an hour and a good deal of soul searching but, such as it was, the short letter was completed. Sarah was dissatisfied with it but it would have to suffice. It was the best she could do. She lacked the courage to tell her parents to their faces. With a sense of crossing the Rubicon she sealed the letter in an envelope. Finally she vetted her appearance in the mirror, picked up her bags and made her way downstairs. Jessica was sat out in the garden together with a visibly agitated Alan. Sarah deposited her bags on the veranda and walked out to meet them.

Alan jumped to his feet as she walked out. "Where the hell have you been?" he demanded to know imperiously.

Sarah regarded him piteously. "Out!"

"Out? Where for heaven's sake? I've been waiting for you all day."

"So chickens fed, hogs swilled?"

"I was supposed to be taking you out for the day Sarah."

"Oh really? That's worrying. I'm far too young for an onset of Alzheimer's disease yet I seem to have completely forgotten about it. I suppose it is beyond credibility to believe for one minute that you omitted to consult me on the matter."

"It was your parents' idea."

"Oh of course. How silly of me. I completely overlooked the fact that my parents are the final arbiters of my daily schedule. How lucky I am to have such considerate parents that relieve me of the necessity of making any decisions for myself."

Jessica smothered a guffaw. "I'll go put your things in the car Sarah."

Alan blinked in consternation. "What things? What are you doing?"

Sarah regarded him levelly. "I'm leaving Alan. I'm going back to the Toggenburg. Jessica is taking me to the station. I was going to take the half past eight train but we seem to be running ahead of schedule so I might catch an earlier train."

Alan staggered in shock. "You can't do that."

Jessica rose. "Er... I'll leave you two to it. I'll see to your things Sarah."

Alan ran a hand through his hair in bewilderment. "You can't just leave like this Sarah. We're supposed to be dining with your family tonight."

"Alan I'm sorry but I'm through with doing what my parents expect me to do. I repeat. I'm going back to the Toggenburg."

"But you can't." he repeated. "What about us? This evening might be the last chance we have to see each other for a couple of weeks or more."

"You might want to sit down Alan. I have something to tell you."

Once Alan was seated in agitation Sarah reached into her bag and pulled out the little box containing her engagement ring. "I'm sorry Alan; I truly am, but I have to give this back to you."

"What?"

"The ring Alan. I'm sorry but I can't marry you."

"What the hell's all this about? We're bloody engaged."

Sarah shook her head. "No Alan we're not. Jamming a ring on somebody's finger at a moment when they are unable to protest due to social obligations does not constitute a proposal of marriage. I have given no consent to marriage Alan and you have at no time afforded me the courtesy of requesting such consent. Nevertheless I shall assume that a proposal has been made and this is my answer. I cannot marry you Alan. My decision is final and I hope you will respect that decision. I am sorry if this is painful to you but I think it is the best decision for both of us."

"This is crap Sarah! You can't back out now."

"I have never backed *in* Alan. All that has happened is that a formal announcement of our engagement has taken place without my being asked to consent to it. Well I withhold that consent. There will be no marriage."

"Has your fucking sister put you up to this?"

Sarah's eyes flashed angrily. "I will thank you to moderate your language. There is no need to descend into vulgarity. As to my sister I resent the presumption that I am incapable of making my own decisions. Jessica was as surprised as you are by my decision but she at least respects me enough to accept that I am capable of making my own mind up."

"Well I refuse to accept it. You can't just walk away from this thing Sarah. There's too much riding on this marriage."

"My consideration Alan, my only consideration, is whether or not you and I would be happy in such a marriage. I have thought about it carefully and I have concluded that we would not be. Therefore, regretfully, I have decided to terminate our relationship. I'm so sorry Alan but it really is for the best."

"Why for God's sake? I'm offering you everything you could wish for."

"Apart from love Alan."

"What?"

"Love Alan. Without that no marriage can work. I'm sorry but I do not love you."

"Why for heaven's sake? What's the matter with me?"

Sarah shook her head sadly. "There's nothing the matter with you Alan. Actually I think you are a good man and you'll make some woman a good husband but I'm afraid it can't be me. I have my reasons for thinking that, Alan and some of them are personal but, after searching my heart, I know now that I do not love you or ever can. I regret that Alan but I will not condemn you or me to a loveless marriage. One day you will find some other woman more worthy to wear that ring Alan and you'll know then that I saved both of us from a wretched fate. I don't wish you ill Alan. I hope that you'll find happiness with a woman who truly loves you. I'm sorry that I am unable to."

Alan stared at her in shock. "Have... have you told your parents this?"

"No Alan. In courtesy I am informing you first of my decision since really this whole matter is only between you and I."

"They'll never let you get away with this."

"I'm sorry Alan that you still believe that I am completely controlled by my parents' wishes. That I'm afraid is what brought us to this point in the first place. Our parents decided that we should marry Alan. This was an arranged marriage from the start; a cosy little business transaction between our families with no consideration as to whether it was in the best interests of our future happiness. I think if you stand back and look at it dispassionately Alan you'll realise that you're as much a victim of this arrangement as I am. I don't love you Alan but I do like you and respect you. I hope you think the same about me. If we are coerced into this marriage however we would end up despising each other. The divorce would be messy in the extreme. I won't let that happen. It's best, best for both of us, if we walk away from it now."

"I can't let you do this Sarah."

"I'm sorry Alan but you can't prevent me."

"You... you don't mean this."

Sarah rose sadly to her feet. "Once again I am sorry Alan. I *do* mean it. I know you must be upset and in denial about it but I implore you to think carefully about it and I think in time you'll see that this is the wise decision. I see no point in protracting this painful conversation. I think it better that I just leave now. I have written a short note to my parents informing them of my decision and I've abrogated all blame from you. I hope you will forgive me in time. I wish you all the best."

"You haven't heard the last of this Sarah."

"Goodbye Alan."

Sarah walked away in finality feeling sad. For all that she knew it to be the right decision she was still leaving a part of her life behind her. Jessica met her near the gates to the drive. "Job done kid?"

"Yes." Sarah leaned heavily against the gate post. "Oh hell! Let's get out of here."

Jessica pursed her lips. "Shit! Too late!" She nodded. Their father's car was pulling up the street. Presumably their father had picked up his wife on the way back for their mother was in the passenger seat.

Sarah took a deep breath. "Are my bags in the car?" she asked Jessica with a murmur.

"Yep! All stowed away. Do you want to make a dash for it?"

Sarah shook her head. "No I have to talk to them. I was going to wait until they returned before leaving in any case. I can't just run away."

"Ok! I'll duck down in a shell hole once the incoming starts flying."

The car pulled into the drive way and Mrs Fuchs stepped out briskly and confronted her daughter without preamble. "Where on earth have you been all day young lady? It's too bad of you just to take off for the whole day without so much as a by your leave to anybody. Poor Alan has been sat around waiting for you all day. He's only got today to be with you after all. He has to go back to work tomorrow. He was going to take you out for lunch and an afternoon to yourselves but you just go swanning off without a word to anybody. I'm ashamed of you."

Sarah's father emerged from the car to join his wife. "Your mother is right Sarah. It was reprehensible of you to just up and abandon Alan for the day. You knew he only had a limited amount of time to be with you. I think you owe him an apology and an explanation."

Looking at her parents bristling with indignation before her Sarah found a curious emergence of courage. Once she would have quailed at such a collective front of parental disapproval but her new sense of purpose over rode her habitual deference to their wishes. In a sudden clarity she saw the drive way beyond her parents as the road to freedom leading back across the Alps to the north, back to her Toggenburg and back to her Daniela. Nothing was now going to deflect her from that road. Her parents were just a last squawking pair of obstacles blocking her way. Seen that way, set against the terrible urgency of her purpose, they did not seem formidable at all. Of course, as she would later admit to herself, the two bottles of wine she had consumed with Rozella helped somewhat as well.

"I'm sorry if I wasn't available for Alan to take me out daddy." Sarah responded haughtily. "However, since nobody thought fit to inform me, I can hardly be blamed for missing an engagement I was unaware of. Perhaps in future you might like to consult with me before deciding upon my itinerary for the day."

"Where have you been anyway?" demanded her mother. "Jessie thought you might have gone out sunbathing up the Centovalli. Sunbathing for God's sake. Poor Alan sat around kicking his heels all day and you take off to go sunbathing. Where on earth is your sense of responsibility? I can't think what's got into you. Your father and I didn't raise you to be so selfish and lacking in respect."

Sarah felt a flash of anger rise to her cheeks. "No mother but you did raise me to be so lacking in self-respect that I would nearly allow you to sell me in marriage to the highest bidder without a whimper of complaint."

"That is quite sufficient Sarah!" her father protested angrily. "You will desist from this foolishness immediately. I realise that you have some issues with the timing of the engagement and possibly the manner in which it was announced but that is no excuse for talking to your mother in such a disrespectful manner. You are not being sold as you put it. You are simply engaged to be married to a fine man who deserves a little more respect than this childish petulance."

"I beg to differ father."

"I beg your pardon."

"I said that I beg to differ. I disagree with your analysis of the situation. I have spoken to Alan. He is in the back garden. I'm afraid you may find him a little upset. That is because a few minutes ago I had the painful duty of handing him back his ring and informing him that I felt unable to consent to be his wife."

"*Sarah!*" her mother cried.

Her father stared at her in shock. "Is this true Sarah?"

"Yes daddy I'm afraid it is. Of course I would have preferred to have informed him privately before our engagement was so prematurely and erroneously announced but the events of last night have made that impossible. I regret that naturally. I would have wished that Alan was spared the humiliation of having our engagement announced publicly when no such engagement was in fact agreed upon. However, the way in which the announcement was made last night has left me no option."

Her mother was wringing her handbag in dismay. "Sarah! How... how could you?"

"I could do nothing less mother. I do not love Alan, I do not wish to marry him, I do not wish to live in Zurich and I do not wish to leave my home. I went away today to be on my own to consider my future and my plans for my future and I have concluded that a married life in Zurich, with a man I do not love, is incompatible with those plans. Therefore I have informed Alan of my decision and have wished him well in whatever separate future he may have."

Her father seemed shell shocked. "You can't do this Sarah."

"Alan said much the same thing daddy. I must say I find it rather tiresome that people cast aspersions on my ability to make up my own mind. I *can* do it. Not only can I do it; I already have."

Sarah's mother was nearly in tears. "How can you be so ungrateful Sarah? After all we've done for you."

"I'm sorry mother. I *am* grateful. I'm grateful that you and daddy brought me up so well and granted me a happy childhood and everything I needed. I love you both. All I'm asking now is that you make the last sacrifice for me; the one all parents must make, and let me go to live my own life the way I wish to live it. My decision is final mother. This is not an impetuous decision. I haven't made it in some petulant fit of pique. I have been thinking long, hard and rationally about this all summer. I agreed to come to Ticino so that I could clarify my thoughts on the matter and perhaps hear what Alan had to propose for me. I protested from the start that I deserved to be asked my opinion on my marriage but my opinion was ignored. My consent was taken for granted and I was not granted the respect due to me to make my own decision. Nevertheless I *have* made my decision. I do not consent to this marriage."

Mrs Fuchs turned on her husband. "For God's sake talk some sense into her George."

255

Mr Fuchs looked grave. "The Bergers could sue you Sarah. There is such a thing as breach of promise."

Jessica, who had been maintaining her silence with an effort until now, snorted in contempt. "What bloody promise is that Dad? The whole bloody world and its grandma saw how Sarah was bullied into getting engaged without her consent last night. I didn't hear Sarah say yes and neither did anyone else at that party. It'd get laughed out of court."

Mr Fuchs turned to his eldest daughter vexedly. "Butt out of this Jessie. I'm addressing Sarah here."

"Yes that's right Jessica!" Mrs Fuchs agreed. "You've done enough damage for one day."

"What the hell have *I* done?"

"I'm sure you've been putting Sarah up to this. You've never liked Alan or his family. I bet you couldn't wait to put the boot in."

If Sarah had been angry before, now she was furious. "*That's enough*!" she cried loudly. "Leave Jessica out of this. I repeat. This is my decision and my decision alone. If you cannot respect the fact that I know my own mind then this conversation is at an end. As to breach of promise father.... how *dare* you? The day before yesterday you made solemn promises to me; promises to respect my opinions and not to proceed with anything regarding this marriage with first obtaining my agreement. Last night you broke every one of those promises. For the record father, I am not your chattel. I will not have you sell me as such to cement your business affiliations. I am a grown woman over the age of twenty one and under the laws of this country I cannot be forced into a marriage to which I do not consent. *I know my own mind!*"

Mr Fuchs staggered under this uncharacteristic onslaught from his youngest daughter. He ran a hand through his hair and glanced around nervously. "This is no place to have an argument like this Sarah. Let's go indoors and talk about this rationally."

Sarah shook her head determinedly. "That is not an option father. I have told you of my decision. Further argument is useless. I'm leaving now. I'm catching an evening train back to the Toggenburg. Jessica is going to take me down to the station in Bellinzona."

"You can't leave Sarah." her mother squealed in horror.

"Yes I can mother. I have waited out of courtesy to inform you and father of my departure but now I am eager to be away. I see no further point in protracting this disagreement. There is nothing more to talk about. I want to go home."

"This *is* your home."

"No mother. My home is in the Toggenburg and always has been. If you'd understood that from the beginning it might have saved us all a lot of grief."

Mr Fuchs, still in shock, tried desperately to mollify his daughter. "Sarah for heaven's sake honey. Let's not do anything rash. Let's just all sit down and talk about this sensibly."

Sarah shook her head but sadly this time. "No daddy. I can't. I just want to go home. The time for talking is past. There's nothing more to be said. I'm sorry if you think I've let you down but I'm convinced that I'm doing the right thing. I hope you'll forgive me in time but right now there is nothing more you can say to change my mind. I'm going home."

Mrs Fuchs bit her lip and seemed on the verge of bursting into tears. "Stop her George."

Sarah looked at her in pity. "I'm sorry mummy. I know you're upset but it's the best thing believe me. I love you mummy. I didn't want to hurt you." Sarah blinked back her own tears. "I... I've left the clothes you bought me in my room mum. I'm sorry but it wouldn't be right of me to accept them now." She turned to her father. "Oh and yes daddy I will be phoning the bank in the morning. I'm returning the twenty thousand francs you so kindly loaned me. You leant me that to buy a wardrobe for my engagement commitments so I cannot in all consideration possibly hang on to it. Would you oblige me by consulting with your bank to make sure that the transaction has been completed successfully? If there's any problem please inform me and I'll take the necessary measures."

Mr Fuchs, for the first time in his life, felt out of his depth in dealing with this daughter of his so resolute in her determination. "Sarah I implore you. Don't just walk out of our lives like this."

"I'm not walking out of your lives daddy. I'm just walking into my own. I should have done this a long time ago daddy. Perhaps I might have saved us all a lot of heartache. You told me this summer that I had to grow up. Well I have done. It's time to cast off the apron strings daddy. I know it has to be done but it hurts anyway." Sarah turned to Jessica. "Can we get going now Jess?"

Jessica nodded solemnly. "Sure kid. Whenever you're ready."

Sarah reached into her handbag and pulled out an envelope. "Mummy, daddy, I've written you a short letter explaining the reasons for my decision. I'm sorry but I lacked the courage to tell you those reasons to your faces. I hope you will forgive me. Perhaps you will never want to speak to me again. If so, then that is your decision. I just want you both to know that I love you and I always will. Thank you for everything. I know this is hard but I think there is always a time when a parent must let go of their child and let them out to make their own way in the world. I know you thought to do that in a church but I think it's the same anywhere. There's always sadness in it as well as joy. I'm not a bad person and all the things that are good about me I have the two of you to thank for. I could not have had better parents. I hope when you read this you will be understanding and not blame yourselves for anything. You may congratulate yourselves that you sent a good person out into the world and that you raised a daughter of intelligence, respect, tolerance and moral principles. Any wisdom I may have gained I gained from you. Please forgive me and remember that I love you."

Sarah handed over the letter to her father. He looked at it almost fearfully. "What's in this Sarah?"

"The truth father. Nothing less." Sarah nodded to Jessica. "Come on Jess. Let's go." There were tears in Sarah's eyes as she walked to the car. As she belted herself into the passenger seat she glanced back. Her parents were staring after her numbly. Her father was still clutching the letter unopened in his hand. He suddenly looked like an old man.

Chapter Twenty-Five

They drove down the hill from the Monte Verite; the mountain of truth, and Sarah was crying. The truth she had left in her father's hands was terrible. It might break her father for good she feared. Jessica took a deep breath. "God that was rough kid." she observed. "I thought you handled it brilliantly though."

"Just shut up Jess. I'm not proud of it."

Jessica lifted a hand off the steering wheel. "Ok, ok! Don't snap at me. I'm on *your* side remember."

"Oh Jess! There aren't any sides here. Nobody wins in this case."

Jessica nodded acknowledging the sagacity of the statement. "Ok kid. What the hell have you put in that letter anyway? It sounds like a pretty formidable bombshell."

"Let's not talk about it for the moment please Jess. Doubtless you'll get the full account when you return to the house." Sarah gave a short bitter laugh. "I should imagine it will be an interesting evening's drama in the family household tonight."

Jessica shook her head. "I can't get over the way you've changed Sarah. You're almost a different person."

"I'm sorry if my new persona doesn't meet your approval Jess."

"But it does kid. I'm delighted with my new sister. You've always been my kid sister and I love you to bits but now you seem so much more well... grown up and sure of yourself. I always used to think of you as I suppose a bit of a wimp... daddy's little girl... butter wouldn't melt in her mouth and all that. All of a sudden you're this strong woman with her own mind and devil take the hindmost. I admire that. You've come a long way kid. I never thought you'd have the guts to face down mum and dad like that. I'm proud of you even if you aren't."

"Great! I've just alienated my parents possibly forever and you think it's something to be proud of."

Jessica nodded. "Yes I do. I don't think you've alienated mum and dad forever kid. They'll come around. What you did do was stand up for what you believed was right. You did what you believed to be the right thing and then you stood your ground in the face of what, let's face it, is pretty formidable opposition. That's nothing to be ashamed of kid. That's laudable!"

"It doesn't feel like it Jess. I feel terrible."

Jessica patted her leg compassionately. "Don't worry kid. It'll all turn out all right. Look, what time did you say your train was?"

"It doesn't really matter Jess. There are trains every half an hour and we're way ahead of schedule." Sarah nodded at the clock on the car dashboard. "It's only six o'clock now. The trains run at six minutes and thirty six minutes past the hour. I was originally planning to take the last one at eight thirty six but that gets me back very late so I can take an earlier train now."

"Well how about you catch the seven thirty six? That gives us time for a last drink together in Bellinzona. I'd like to have a last drink with you. Way of saying goodbye and all that. Anyway, after that confrontation in the driveway, I could do with a drink. You might be the bloody ice queen of the Ticino for the moment but I need a drink."

"Oh right! Ice queen!" Sarah pulled out a tissue to dab her eyes and blow her nose. "Not exactly living up to the role am I? I'm in bloody bits here."

"You're allowed to come apart a bit at the seams after your heroics today kid. Let's have a drink together in the buffet and then we'll get you on your train home."

"I... I'd like that Jess. Thank you for supporting me these last few days."

"My pleasure sis. I am so very proud of you."

261

They took the main road to Bellinzona in relative silence. Jessica seemed thoughtful as she drove. There was something on her mind. Finally they pulled up outside the station in Bellinzona. They unloaded Sarah's bags at the terrace of the station buffet. "Get me a beer please kid while I go park the car." Jessica requested. Sarah took a seat on the terrace. She wondered if her parents had read her letter by now. Suddenly she was gripped with panic. She didn't want to discuss the matter with them now. Deliberately she removed her mobile phone from her handbag and switched it off. The sun was sinking toward the horizon but the air was still filled with the muggy warmth of a Ticino summer's day. The mountain tops were glowing in the slanting rays of the late afternoon sunshine. Sarah ordered two beers and a few moments later Jessica reappeared. "God it's a bitch finding a parking spot round here." She nodded at one of the bottles on the table. "That one mine?"

"Yes."

Jessica poured out a measure of beer into her glass. "Here's to sisters in disgrace kid. Almost a rite of passage in the Fuchs clan; pissing your parents off."

"Give it a break Jess."

Jessica laughed. "Ok! Anyway how are you getting home from Wattwil?" Jessica raised a quizzical eyebrow. "Somebody picking you up?"

"I don't know. If I'm taking the earlier train I might still catch the last bus to Unterwasser. The last bus is at 22.35 today. That gets me to Unterwasser at about ten past eleven. I should be able to make that."

"Yeah right. So that gets you stuck at Unterwasser post at some time past eleven with all your bags and a bloody great long walk up the hill to the Alpli in the middle of the night."

"Well Nicole might come and pick me up."

Jessica took a deliberate swig of her beer and rolled her tongue in her cheek thoughtfully. "Yeah Nicole. Right. How silly of me. I'd forgotten about Nicole."

Sarah raised an eyebrow. "What are you insinuating Jessie?"

"Oh nothing. Do you need to get a ticket?"

"No I have a return ticket Jessie."

"Oh so you weren't contemplating a long stay after all."

"Er no I suppose not." Sarah grimaced. "Don't let me get in the wrong compartment Jessie. I've got a first class ticket and, on the way here, I forgot and got into second class. I thought the ticket inspector was going to spank me for slumming it with the riff raff."

"A first class ticket? You? You never travel on first class."

"I thought I'd do it in style this time."

Jessica placed down her beer glass slowly and deliberately. "Ok Sarah it's time to stop shooting a load of guff. Who is he?"

Sarah blinked in surprise. "What are you talking about?"

Jessica leaned back in her chair. "Don't come the innocent with me Sarah. I've known you ever since your major mode of locomotion was on hands and knees and your vocabulary was limited to unintelligible gurgles. You might be able to pull the wool over mum and dad's eyes but not me. There's somebody else isn't there?"

"Why would you think that?"

"I'm not entirely dumb Sarah. You're in an awful hurry to get back to the Toggenburg. That tells me somebody's waiting for you. Then there's your dress. All your life you've been perfectly content in a pair of jeans and a shirt and now, all of a sudden, you're dressing up every day in stylish sexy clothes and covered in expensive bling too. You're wearing expensive jewellery; bloody diamond brooches and an emerald necklace you haven't taken off since the minute you arrived. You're not going to tell me that they're not gifts; gifts from someone special. Then there's your phone."

"What about my phone?"

263

"You're using it. For years I thought you considered a mobile phone to be an auxiliary wristwatch for telling the time. Now every time I see you you're texting on it or reading messages. You suddenly seem to have an awful lot to say to somebody. I said right from the start that something was different about you. Sarah, the old Sarah, would never have had the bottle to tell Alan and mum and dad to go take a hike! Not unless there was somebody else in your life; somebody important. I don't know if you realise it but your performance this last couple of days has been the classic manifestation of a woman in love! You could do everything you just did because you didn't really give a damn did you? There was somebody else and they were far more important to you. This is why you're dashing back to the Toggenburg isn't it? You've found someone else."

Sarah lowered her eyes and nodded meekly. "Yes Jessie. You're right."

"I knew it! I just knew it. God no wonder you didn't dare tell mum and dad that to their faces. God they'll go bloody ballistic. I'd love to see their faces when they open that letter. Everything makes sense now."

"I wouldn't be too sure of that Jessie."

"But of course it does. Now I know why you gave Alan the bum's rush. You've fallen in love with someone else. Damn it Sarah! Why didn't you tell me?"

"I didn't know whether you'd understand Jessie."

"Why the hell wouldn't I understand? Is there something wrong with him? Is he a convicted criminal or something?"

"No, no. It's nothing like that."

"Then what then? He must be rich at least to keep you decorated with expensive jewellery. Come on Sarah. Tell your big sister. What's your new fellah like?"

"I haven't got a new fellah Jessie."

"Er what? Rewind a minute. You just admitted that you're seeing someone else."

"Yes I am."

264

"Well why the hell are you contradicting yourself?"

"I'm not. I'm seeing someone else but it's not a fellah Jessie."

Jessica's eyes sprung wide open. "What are you saying Sarah?"

"I'm seeing a woman Jessie."

Jessica stared at her speechlessly. "But... but..."

Sarah nodded fatalistically. "I should have told you before. It's what I've written in that letter to mum and dad. I'm sorry Jessie. Your kid sister is gay."

Chapter Twenty-Six

If there were one thousand, two hundred and thirty four bridges along the Gotthard railway line then Sarah felt as if she was burning every one behind her, as the train carried her back to the north. It was almost deserted in the first class carriage she was riding in. The only other occupant was a well-dressed man several rows further down the aisle who was fast asleep. Evening was falling in, the sun sinking low behind the mountains and plunging the steep sided valleys into deep shadow. It would be dark by the time the train crossed the great divide into the north. The encroaching dark seemed to fit Sarah's mood for she was in tears. Her practical side had not deserted her completely in these desperate hours and she'd prudently bought a packet of paper tissues in the station buffet kiosk at Bellinzona. She was working her way through the tissues at an alarming rate.

In her wretchedness Sarah asked herself why she was so miserable. After all she had achieved everything she had set out to do. She had made her bid for freedom, escaped from a marriage she knew would have been the death of her and struck out independently into the world. But freedom can be a lonely place. In the words of the old song, freedom was just another word for nothing left to lose and Sarah's freedom had cost her dearly indeed. All her life her family had been the single most important element in her existence. Now she had lost them. Of that she was certain. It had been bad enough to see the terrible disappointment and even despair in her father's face when she had told them that she was leaving. Even her mother's sudden impotence in the face of her daughter's terrible resolve had seemed to make her appear suddenly vulnerable and desperate. Sarah's family had been a bedrock of reliable stability her entire life and yet in a few words she had destroyed that fundament, reduced her parents to helplessness and made them seem frail and irrelevant.

She was haunted by the look of hurt in father's eyes when she had told him that she was returning his twenty thousand francs. It had been a terrible thing to do, she saw now. He had prided himself that his children should want for nothing in life; prided himself for the protection he had erected over them. Yet, each in their own way, his children had walked away from that umbrella of protection. First of all Jessica had walked out, taking a man of which he did not approve and forging a life for herself that excluded him from it. Even John in his quiet way had proved that he could live a life without his parent's interference and that he did not fit into his father's notions of a suitably ambitious son of a successful businessman. If his two eldest children had disappointed Mr Fuchs' aspirations for them it was nothing compared to the hurt that his youngest and most beloved child had just inflicted on him. Sarah had always been the one for whom he felt the greatest parental affection and the most devoted desire to protect. His dedication to that purpose had clouded his own judgement of her. She had always been his own little Sarah who he would defend and succour so long as he ever drew breath. As such it was almost impossible for him to comprehend that she had grown up. She was always his little baby girl in need of his protection and support. It was a fundamental reality of his existence; it gave him purpose to his life. And then she had coolly returned his twenty thousand francs and told him that she didn't need him after all.

Her mother too, Sarah realised, must be devastated by the turn of events. She had been cheated of the weddings she had wanted for her other children. Sarah's wedding had become of overwhelming importance to her. As Sarah's father had pointed out her mother had long lamented the fact that her own wedding had been so unsatisfactory. Those frustrated hopes of a great romantic wedding she had transferred to her children. Jessica had married privately in a registry office without parental approval. Her mother hadn't even attended. John seemed in no hurry to marry at all and had scoffed at the idea of a big wedding. In any case such a wedding would be arranged by the bride's family. His mother would be a fairly irrelevant guest. Sarah however was another matter. Here at last was the big wedding Mrs Fuchs could throw and that to a man who met all the requirements for a son in law. Now that wasn't going to happen. Mrs Fuchs' dreams were shattered.

They would be even more shattered by the letter Sarah had penned. Sarah admitted to herself that she had been a coward in writing that letter. It had been difficult enough to tell her parents that she was not going through with the marriage to Alan. Sarah knew she could never have faced telling them in person that she was gay. Of course she didn't have to tell them that at all but that would have been even more cowardly and, moreover, only a temporary measure at best. She had tested her courage to the utmost in writing that letter nevertheless. It was the final blow. She had already fled from the womb of her family. That letter would cut the umbilical cord definitively. She had cast herself out into exile. There was no going back now. She was on her own and she had never felt more lonely.

It was getting dark now and in the long first class compartment Sarah's sense of isolation grew gloomier by the minute. In desperation she reached into her handbag for her telephone, suddenly needing to know that she was still loved, still wanted. Her eyes were filled with tears and didn't seem to be able to focus properly as she keyed the buttons on her phone. She tapped in the number praying that there was an answer; a sympathetic voice on the other end. Her heart seemed to stop beating as she listened to the dialling tone at the other end. "Hello?" Sarah's breath escaped in a gasp of relief at the sound of the lovely modulated voice on the other end. She had never heard anything so beautiful.

"Oh Danny! It's me!" she sobbed.

"Sarah? Sweetheart! What's the matter? You sound awful."

"Danny do you love me?"

"Of course I do Sarah! You know that."

"Say it please Danny. Tell me you love me."

"I love you Sarah. I'll always love you. What's happening? Tell me."

"Oh Danny I feel so alone."

"You're not alone Sarah. I'm here and I love you. Now tell me what's happening."

"Oh Danny I've lost them."

"Lost who? What do you mean Sarah?"

"My family Danny. I... I told Alan that I wasn't going to marry him and I've told my family I'm gay. I... I've left Danny. Oh God! What am I going to do now? I'm so lonely. Please tell me that you still want me Danny. You're all I've got left."

"Where are you Sarah?".

"I... I'm on the train Danny. I'm coming home." Sarah was sobbing piteously.

"What time is your train due in?"

"I get into Wattwil at half past ten Danny."

"I'll be there!"

"Oh there's no need. I can catch the last bus."

"Listen to me Sarah; listen carefully. I'll be at that railway station at half past ten. Stop crying now and just get yourself home. You're not alone Sarah I'll be waiting for you. Just come back to me and everything is going to be all right. You've been a brave girl. Just be brave a little longer. I'm not going to leave you. I love you. Just come home to me."

Sarah sniffled and wiped her hand across her nose. "Yes Danny."

"Good girl. Now dry your eyes my darling. Everything's going to be fine."

269

"I love you Danny."

"I love you too. Just get yourself home. I'll see you in Wattwil."

As soon as the connection was broken Daniela bit her lip in anxiety. Making a quick decision she opened her phone book. She had some calls to make. The first of these was to the Hotel Hirschen in Wildhaus. When the call was answered at reception she asked to be put through to the restaurant. "Hello, could I speak to Nicole please?"

Chapter Twenty-Seven

As she sped through the mountains into the encroaching night Sarah might have taken some consolation from the effects of her startling revelation. Whatever the devastating effects of her announcement might be on her parents, one member of her family at least had taken the news rather well. Jessica, driving back to her parents' house, had passed through shock and incredulity and she was still striving to come to terms with her younger sister's astonishingly unsuspected homosexuality but at least she was not repulsed or morally judgemental about it. Jessica had lived all her life on the fringes. She had a number of gay friends and she was by no stretch of the imagination homophobic. She was astounded to learn that her sister was gay; completely amazed that she had never before detected it in her but she certainly did not disapprove.

Of course she could not imagine her sister with another woman. That was a reality leap too far for her for the moment. It was one thing to know that one's friends were gay but quite another to grasp the fact that a person you had known ever since she was a baby was as well. Jessica had always prided herself on her astuteness and perception but it had never even occurred to her to question her sister's sexual orientation. Yes it was true that there had always been a bit of the tomboy about Sarah with her penchant for outdoor pursuits and her dress sense that seemed to be limited to blue jeans and shirts but there had never been any hint of masculinity about her. She knew of course that it was hopelessly clichéd to expect a gay woman to show masculine traits. There was absolutely no reason whatsoever that a perfectly feminine woman could not be gay. In spite of that, however, you couldn't help but look for underlying male traits almost as if it was an instinctive means of coming to terms with such a fundamental difference to your own sexual proclivity.

Yet, paradoxically, over the past few days, she had never known Sarah be so overtly female. The change in Sarah from the lovable little tomboy she had always known to the elegantly well-dressed young woman she had picked up in Bellinzona just three days ago was remarkable in its own right. She could probably have counted the number of times she had seen Sarah in a dress or skirt over the last five years on the fingers of one hand. Now she seemed to wear nothing but. Even her mother had been taken aback, albeit pleasantly, by this seeming flowering of Sarah's femininity. Then she goes and tears the rule book up and announces that she's gay.

That all beggared the question of the identity of this mysterious girlfriend of Sarah's. Sarah had been reticent on this subject and refused to disclose much in the way of information. She had told Jessica that this girl lived in the Toggenburg but she was relatively new there and it was certain that Jessica had not previously met her. Well that ruled out Nicole who otherwise would have been a logical candidate given that she had shared a house with Sarah for some years. Sarah confirmed this and told Jessica that Nicole had been as shocked as she was to learn of Sarah's sexuality. So it was someone else; someone Jessica had never met. Why then was Sarah so reluctant to divulge her name? Was she afraid that Jessica would pass on the intelligence to their parents? If so why was she afraid of her parents being in possession of that information? Did she fear that they might appear in the Toggenburg to confront this woman who had seemingly corrupted their daughter?

It was by no means an ungrounded fear. If she, Jessica, was having such a hard time believing that Sarah was gay then their parents would never accept the fact. Their immediate reaction would be to assume that Sarah had fallen into the clutches of somebody who had contaminated her with homosexuality in contravention of her natural instincts. Sarah's newfound femininity would not be lost on them either. They would be picturing some dreadful butch dyke that liked their little girl to dress up in girly clothes for her titilation. Even Jessica could not shake off the suspicion that Sarah's girlfriend was liable to be on the masculine side of the lesbian spectrum. That somebody like Daniela had come into Sarah's life was not even beginning to impinge itself on the fringes of her imagination.

Jessica found herself eager to get back to her parents' house. She had previously been dreading this evening when all that would have been under discussion was Sarah's refusal to marry Alan. Now however it was a completely different matter. Jessica was not above enjoying a delicious whiff of scandal when it in no way reflected on her. For that was one thing. Whatever their parents' reaction might be, they at least could not lay the blame for *this* one at Jessica's door. In a way that was a pity. The rebel in Jessica almost envied Sarah's bombshell; as if she almost wished that *she'd* thought of that one. It was going to be an interesting evening.

Arriving back at the villa, she found the scene of devastation almost complete. Her mother was sat on the sofa weeping piteously and wringing a handkerchief in her fist with the comforting arm of her husband about her. Alan was sat opposite nursing a stiff whisky and looking grim whilst John hovered in the background rolling his eyes in disbelief over the ensuing drama. Sarah's letter lay like a curse on the family name on the coffee table. Jessica's entrance was greeted with an almost pitiful lifting of momentary hope as if she was about to announce that the whole thing was just a bad practical joke and that Sarah was undisputedly heterosexual after all. She set her face grimly. "Well I see you've all read Sarah's letter then." she said soberly.

"Where *is* Sarah Jessica?" her father asked in a tone of voice that brooked no dissension.

"Unless she's jumped out at an intervening stop she's still on the train I imagine dad. I saw her on to the train about an hour ago."

"I can't get her on her phone."

"I should imagine that's because she's got it switched off dad. She was pretty upset when I left her and I don't think she relished the idea of a nice cosy family chat."

"How could she do this to us?" wailed Mrs Fuchs in anguish. Jessica suspected that her mother had been repeating that question monotonously for some time now.

Her father threw an accusing hand at the letter on the coffee table. "Did you know about this Jessica?"

Jessica shook her head. "No dad. Sarah told me at the railway station in Bellinzona. I had no idea she was going to do something like this."

"You must have known something Jessica."

"Dad! I'm as shocked by this as you are. I had no idea."

"Well you seemed to know the contents of that letter."

Jessica placed her hands on her hips determinedly. "Dad I only know the gist of what's in that letter because Sarah told me about it just before she got on the train. I don't know the details and I certainly had no inclination about any of this until Sarah told me at the railway station. I don't know what you're trying to insinuate dad but surely you can't accuse me of complicity in my sister's sexual preferences."

Mrs Fuchs sniffed tearfully and placed a hand on her husband's knee. "No George, leave Jessica alone. This isn't her fault. I know we've had our differences before but at least Jessie's not *queer*."

Mr Fuchs nodded sombrely, acknowledging the justice of this. "What did Sarah tell you Jessie?"

Jessica ran a hand through her hair and took a breath. "Not much more than she says she's put in that letter dad. She told me she was seeing another woman and that she's gay. Much more than that, I can't tell you. She didn't want to go into details dad. I think it was hard enough for her to say that much. She was pretty upset."

"*She* was upset?" squawked Mrs Fuchs shrilly, "How does she think *we* feel?"

"I think she probably thinks that you're going to be pretty upset as well mum." said Jessica gently. For all the conflict that had passed between them, at a fundamental level, Jessica still loved her mother. She had never seen her so distraught and in tears before. She was shocked. "I'm sorry mum. I guess this must be pretty painful for you."

Mrs Fuchs buried her face in her hands and sobbed. "How could she do this?" she repeated.

Jessica bit her lip unsure as to what to say. She turned to Alan. "Alan I know your need is pretty great but I'd appreciate it if you didn't hold on to that whisky bottle. I could do with a stiff drink too." Alan nodded. He seemed numb with shock but he passed over the bottle. Jessica poured herself a shot and took a seat. "Can I have a look at this letter dad?"

Mr Fuchs nodded. "Yes of course Jessica. Help yourself for what it's worth!"

Jessica scanned the letter briefly. It was not a great letter she had to concede. It was hastily penned and somewhat awkward. Sarah could write good coherent English prose, as her high marks at university would testify, but expression of personal feeling and emotional content were not her strong points. Also she had written the letter quickly and under considerable emotional stress. As such the letter was short and concise almost to the point of bluntness. Sarah had explained that the reason she felt unable to marry Alan was because she had discovered that she had strong feelings for a woman. She had repeated the statement that she was gay several times as if she wanted to be certain that there was no ambiguity about the fact. It sounded as if she was protesting too much. She was at pains in the letter to state that she loved her mother and father and the fact that she was gay did not alter that. Jessica couldn't see why it would alter it but it was plain that Sarah was desperately trying to hold on to the love of her parents and by no means sure that she could. Sarah stated that she was just the same person that she always had been. She hadn't changed into something else just because she was gay. She was sorry that she had not had the courage to tell this to her parent's faces. She was sorry if this upset them. Jessica counted the word "sorry" seven times in the letter. Sarah hoped that her parents would understand and accept. She loved them and didn't want to hurt them but she felt unable to continue to lie to them. She would understand if they were upset and angry with her. She wanted them to know that it wasn't their fault but that she was what she was and she couldn't do anything about that. She hoped they would forgive her. Jessica put the letter down with a sigh.

"What do you make of all that Jessie?" her father asked.

"Well it's pretty much to the point dad. I think she could have expressed herself a little better but she did write it in a hurry. In any case she has covered all the salient points."

"Do you know who this woman is Jessie; this woman she's supposed to be seeing?"

"No dad. She wouldn't tell me. She just said that she was wonderful and that she's in love with her."

"Is it that damn Nicole girl she shares with?" demanded Mrs Fuchs with a sob.

Jessica shook her head firmly. "No mum. She was emphatic about that. She told me that Nicole was as shocked as anyone to learn she was in a relationship with another woman. Anyway, from what I know about Nicole, she likes boys far too much. She's got a bit of a reputation in the Toggenburg."

"So we don't know who this woman is?" asked Mr Fuchs for confirmation.

Jessica shook her head once more. "She said it was someone I didn't know dad. That's all she said."

Mr Fuchs set his face determinedly. "There must be some way we can find out."

Jessica blinked. "Probably dad, but why? I mean why is it imperative to know?"

"I think we have a right to know who's done this to our daughter Jessica."

"Done what dad?"

"Got her claws into Sarah of course. You don't expect us to take this lying down do you?"

"I'm not quite following you dad. Are you suggesting that this woman, whoever she might be, is to blame for my kid sister being gay?"

"What other explanation is there? We know Sarah isn't gay. She's never been lesbian until now. She's been in a perfectly normal relationship with Alan here for years and then along comes this mysterious woman and her head turns and now all of a sudden she starts to think she's a lesbian."

Jessica picked up the letter and held it by one corner in the air. "Er sorry dad but she seems pretty emphatic in this letter. She states quite clearly that she's gay. No ifs, buts or maybes about it. It's not deathless prose but I can't see where it leaves any room for interpretation dad. Your daughter is gay. She's put it down in black and white."

"Sarah's not gay!" cried Mrs Fuchs in a shrill voice. "I'm her mother! I think I'd know if my own daughter was a lesbian."

Jessica shook her head compassionately. "No mum. I'm sorry but statistically you're wrong. Parents are nearly always the last people to know that their children are gay. That's almost axiomatic. It's always the hardest thing in life for a person to tell their parents that they're gay and it's just as hard for their parents to believe it."

"I know that Sarah's not a lesbian." declared Alan. "I know better than anyone. I've been in bed with her."

Jessica regarded him with irritation. "I don't think that the fact that a person has performed acts of heterosexual love is considered to be conclusive proof of their basic orientation Alan. Many people are in denial about their own sexuality. It's not unknown for people to be married to a person of the opposite sex for many years before finally coming to an acceptance of their homosexuality. I know this must be tough for you but I'm afraid that your once prospective wife is gay. It's better you found this out now and not after you'd been married to her for a few years. Sarah is gay. Live with it Alan."

"If Sarah is gay as you say Jessica," her father asked. "Then why has she never said anything until now? Why has she proceeded with a relationship with Alan for the past years without saying anything to us? Why leave it until now and why can't she say it to our faces and not through a cowardly letter?"

Jessica ran a hand through her hair in frustration. "Damn it dad! Would you have even listened if she had? She's been trying to tell you all weekend that she doesn't want to get married but you go and hitch her up without her consent anyway. Can't you understand how hard this must be for her? She's probably been agonising about this all summer; years maybe. Think about it. How many boyfriends has Sarah ever really had? Only one that really matters. Even when she was at school she never really dated boys. I never thought much about it but it seems pretty significant in the light of this now doesn't it. When I was a teenager I was always fawning over one boy or another. Not Sarah though. She never seemed interested in them. She just wanted to go off hiking in her bloody mountains. The only boyfriend she's really ever had is Alan here and that was because you and mum favoured him and as near as damn it pushed them together. Sarah always did as you and mum wanted her to. I always wanted her to bring home some completely inappropriate boyfriend just to show some sodding

278

independence for a change but she never did. She was probably gay all along. Nobody saw it. Knowing Sarah, she probably never even realised it herself. Now she meets a girl, falls in love and realises that her whole life has been one long lie. That isn't a cowardly letter dad. That letter is probably the bravest thing she's done in her life. I've seen Sarah climb up cliff faces in the mountains I would have pissed my pants on. They didn't frighten Sarah but having to come along and tell the parents that she loves above all else that she's different.... well that scares her. I can't begin to imagine the courage that took her. You should respect her for her courage and honesty dad; not berate her for it."

"You seem to know a lot about being gay." said Alan accusingly.

Jessica rounded on him. "That's because maybe I'm a little more sensitive and understanding Alan. I don't know what you're suggesting but I happen to be very happily married to a wonderful man that I love dearly. My heterosexual credentials are indisputable. That doesn't mean however that I cannot sympathise with and understand somebody who happens to have a different orientation to mine."

"But you know what dykes are."

Jessica's anger flashed dangerously. "Yes! They're an ancient engineering system utilised in drainage and flood control; very prevalent in Holland I believe."

Support came from an unexpected quarter. John, who had remained silent until now, rose to his feet. "I agree with Jessie here. If our Sarah's gay then she's gay. I'm not going to lose sleep over it. It's her life." He stabbed a finger towards Alan "And if you ever fucking well call my sister a dyke again I'll take one of those guns your dad peddles and blow your fucking balls off for you."

Mr Fuchs rose hastily. "That's enough! Sit down John. *Sit down* I said!"

Alan rose angrily. "I don't see why I should have to sit here and take this kind of abuse."

Mr Fuchs tried desperately to calm the volatile situation. "Alan please calm down. We won't get anywhere letting our emotions get the better of us."

But Alan had taken as much as he could. "This is all bullshit!" he stormed. "I *know* Sarah's not lesbian. I don't know what game's going on here. As far as I'm concerned there was an official commitment made; a commitment to a marriage agreement. I don't know what's going on here but all this is crap. Sarah is my fiancée. There have been solemn promises made to that effect. Sarah can't back out of this now. I don't know who's put her up to this but I expect you to talk some sense into her Mr Fuchs. I've invested far too much time and money into this marriage. I'm not prepared to just let it go like this."

John looked at him contemptuously. "Oh we'd hate you to have a poor return on your sodding investment."

"John!" cried Mr Fuchs. "I forbid this petty bickering."

"Well then tell this prat that my kid sister is not a negotiable asset in his fucking business portfolio. Who the fuck does he think he is?"

"That will do John!" Mr Fuchs intervened, standing between the two angry young men. Jessica was taken by surprise. She had rarely had much time for her brother, regarding him as fairly innocuous and bland. She knew that he didn't like Alan and that he disapproved of Sarah's proposed marriage to him but she had had no idea that his feelings were so strong on the matter or that he felt so protective of his youngest sister. She had underestimated him.

Alan was backing down in the face of this sudden hostility. John's face was flushed with anger and his fists were balled. John was a big man, as tall as Alan and much more heavily built. Mr Fuchs had placed himself between the two men but he looked almost small against the intimidating bulk of his son. "This will be quite enough." he was saying. "I suggest we all calm down and talk about this sensibly."

Alan was retreating. "I refuse to listen to any more of this." he declared hotly. "I think it best if I conferred with my father over this. I assure you he will not be best pleased."

John took a step forward. "Are you threatening us?"

"John please!" pleaded Mr Fuchs.

Alan turned and walked from the room. "You haven't heard the last of this." he announced in parting and then he was gone.

Mrs Fuchs redoubled her sobbing on the couch. John glared at the door through which Alan had departed. "And you were going to let that arsehole marry our Sarah dad?"

"You've said quite enough for one day John! Why the hell can't you keep your temper in check? You've probably gone and mortally offended the Bergers now."

"Good riddance to the bastards!"

Mr Fuchs collapsed heavily onto the sofa. "Oh God! What a mess. The Bergers will be furious. Why the hell has Sarah done this to us?"

Jessica cleared her throat and tried to sound calm and rational. "I don't think she had much choice dad."

"She's chosen to do *this* Jessica."

Jessica shook her head. "No dad. I don't think she did. I don't think she chose to be gay. It's just what she is; wired into her system. I don't think you make choices about things like that. It's just the way you're made."

"Your mother and I didn't make Sarah that way!"

"Dad it's not something to apportion blame about. It's not something to be ashamed about. Sarah's not an aberration; somebody that's gone wrong. She's your daughter! She's got brown eyes, chestnut coloured hair and happens to be gay. Big deal! She's still a human being. She's still your *daughter*. She's my sister. I'm not ashamed of her just because she happens to like girls more than boys. I love her to bits and I'm proud of her."

Mr Fuchs shook his head confusedly. "I don't believe it Jessica. I can't believe it. Sarah a lesbian... no I just cannot accept it."

"Don't you think that you're saying just the very same thing nearly every parent says when confronted with their child's homosexuality dad? Your reaction is hardly original. I imagine every parent goes through this stage of denial."

"This is your fault George." wailed Mrs Fuchs. "Encouraging her all those years to gad around in the mountains like a boy. I always wanted her to behave more like a girl but you let her have her own way. I could never make her wear a dress when she was younger."

"Mum!" protested Jessica. "There is no blame here. Nobody knows what makes a person gay. I was a tomboy too when I was young but it didn't make *me* gay. I don't see how what you wear makes any difference. I notice Sarah's been dressing up pretty ladylike these past few days. That doesn't seem relevant to the fact she's gay. Maybe her girlfriend, whoever she is, likes her to dress like that but I don't know. But the fact is that she's a woman. She's not a man or a pseudo man mum. She's a woman. She just happens to be a woman that likes other women. Her gender isn't in question, merely her preferences."

Mr Fuchs looked grim. "I want to know who this other woman is."

Mrs Fuchs wrung her handkerchief distractedly. "Oh God! I bet she's some awful butch woman that's got her hands on Sarah."

"We don't know that mum." Jessica protested again. "We shouldn't make suppositions about somebody we don't know. Doubtless Sarah will tell us the identity of her girlfriend in due course."

Mr Fuchs nodded. "We might have to rely on you here Jessica."

"In what way dad?"

"You know the Toggenburg better than we do nowadays Jessie. You'll be able to find out who this woman is better than us."

Jessica blinked. "You mean you want me to go and sniff out who Sarah's girlfriend is dad?"

"Well yes. I can hardly go up to the Toggenburg and start asking questions like that now can I?"

Jessica leaned back in her chair and stared at him. "I'm sorry dad. I can't do that."

"Why ever not?"

"Well, for one thing, it's none of my bloody business. If Sarah wants to tell me who she's seeing then all well and good but I'm buggered if I'm going to snoop around in the Toggenburg prying into her private life. It would be an unforgivable intrusion. You can't ask me to do that."

"Don't you think we have a right to know?"

"No I don't dad. It's Sarah's business. Yes it would be nice if you did know but you don't have a right to that information. Sarah is over twenty one and her private life is her own business."

"Well how are we to find out otherwise?"

"Well you could try asking Sarah. If she wants to tell you then fine. Otherwise you should respect her privacy. Anyway what would you do if you knew the identity of this woman; go up to the Toggenburg and confront her; make a scene; demand that she stops seeing Sarah and surrender her so that she can marry Alan after all? How's Sarah going to take that dad? My guess is that she'd be mighty pissed off about it. I know I would be. Sarah seems pretty volatile for the moment. You'd risk alienating your daughter forever dad. You don't want to do that."

"You can't expect us to just do nothing."

"Just what is it you *want* to do dad? Are you after persuading Sarah that she's not gay after all? Have you got some way of suddenly reversing her sexuality? Do you think it's just going to take a few stern parental words to show her the error of her ways and convince her to return to the heterosexual fold? She's *gay* dad. That's not something open to negotiation. It's what she is."

"Well what are we supposed to do?"

"Well here's a really radical notion dad. Why don't you just accept it and try to understand it? Yes I know it's not easy. God knows *I'm* having a hard time coming to terms with this and *I'm* just her sister. It's going to be a whole lot harder for you and mum as her parents. One day soon I hope I'm going to be a parent as well. I don't know what the hell I'll say if one of *my* kids comes home one day and tells me that they're gay. I hope that I'll be understanding and supportive. I know that it must be a very difficult time for a person when they have to come out and confess their homosexuality. I should imagine that Sarah is going through agony right now. She was pretty upset when I left her. I think if ever there was a time when she needed your love and support mum and dad it was right now."

"It's unnatural!" cried Mrs Fuchs in distress. "It's against the laws of nature and God."

Jessica sighed. "I don't buy that mum. There are countless millions of gay people in the world. They don't seem to be contravening any fundamental law of nature to me or there wouldn't be so many of them. They say people are born gay. I don't know. You're on a minefield of dispute arguing for a genetic basis for a trait that by its very nature is unlikely to be passed down through the generations. What I do know is that gay people are just people; no more natural or otherwise than anybody else. Nature must have some purpose for it or it wouldn't exist. As for God, well I don't pretend to know what He thinks about it and I think it would be

284

downright presumptuous of me to even assume that I could. I don't think gay people are evil or that God loves them any less than straight people. I, for one, am not going to be one of those awful Christian fundamentalists that walk around holding placards saying, "God hates faggots!" That's pretty sick to me. Let the bloody priests argue this one. If we're going to argue religion about it though we'll be here all night. I notice religion didn't get a mention when Sarah was supposed to abandon her protestant faith and convert to Catholicism in order to marry Alan so I think it's a bit late in the day to start invoking God in the discussion."

"But it's not right." Mrs Fuchs insisted tearfully. "It can't be right."

"I'm not going to make moral judgements mum. Sarah is just the same person today as she was yesterday. I didn't think she was wrong or bad or anything then and I'm not going to change my mind because I've learned something new about her. It's not as if she's out to harm anyone. She's done nothing other than find it in herself to have the courage to tell you something about herself that you didn't know. I'm sure she's terrified of losing your love and respect for her but she's outweighed that by realising that she respects you too much to continue lying to you. This can't be easy for her. I think we should applaud her for her courage and honesty and not make moral judgements on something she can't really help. I think she deserves our love and our support in a difficult time."

Mrs Fuchs dabbed at her eyes miserably. "I... I tried to be a good mother." She moaned. "God knows I tried. Where did I go wrong?"

Jessica regarded her compassionately. "You *were* a good mother mum. You brought three kids up into the world and there's nothing fundamentally wrong with any of us. We're all decent, intelligent and well-adjusted human beings. You did just fine."

"But... but Sarah...."

"Sarah is just dandy mum. She's probably the most intelligent of all your kids. She's a caring, devoted, loving person and well-liked by everyone who knows her. You couldn't wish to know a kinder, gentler girl. She's a good hearted and sensible person mum. You ought to be proud of her. You haven't done a damn thing wrong with her. I guess all parents start to blame themselves when their kids tell them that they're gay but the truth is that it's nobody's fault. It's just one of those things mum."

Mr Fuchs frowned. "You seem all too ready to just accept this Jessica but you don't know what it's like having the responsibility of parenthood yet. We can't just let our daughter run off into the world like this, into the clutches of some unknown woman who might be exploiting her vulnerability. We tried to ensure that our daughter's future was amply provided for. Marrying Alan would be perfect. He is a well to do young man and with an extremely promising career ahead of him." Mr Fuchs ignored the snort of disgust from John. "As parents your mother and I have the responsibility to ensure that our children set out into the world with every possible advantage. If Sarah were to marry Alan she would have everything she could wish for."

"Except happiness dad." Jessica reminded him quietly. "Happiness! If you'd married Sarah to Alan she would have been miserable for the rest of her life. You couldn't wish that for her. You just couldn't."

"I have the responsibility to make sure she is provided for Jessica."

"I don't think you do dad. When I left home to marry Damien you said much the same thing I recall. You were convinced that Damien wouldn't be able to support me. You thought we would end up living in poverty."

"You *did* end up living in poverty."

"Yes for a couple of years or so we had it tough dad; rented bedsitter, hardly any furniture, taking any jobs we could to make ends meet. They were the happiest days of my life dad. We were free, we had each other and we had a life to forge. Well we came through in the end. If we had to fight to have what we have now well that was no bad thing. We know now never to take anything for granted and know that everything we earned was through our own effort. We're doing just fine dad. You worried unnecessarily. You rowed with John too when he went off to do his own thing in Appenzell. You feared it would never come to anything. Well look at him now. He's got his own successful small business doing something he loves, a nice house, a good woman behind him. John's doing just fine as well. So why were you worried?"

Mr Fuchs lowered his head. "I concede that you and John exceeded my expectations. I'm not a man that is unable to admit that he was wrong Jessica. I'm pleased and proud that both John and you have managed to do so well."

"Well then why are you still so worried about Sarah? We all have to cut the apron strings at some point dad. Sarah has her own life to make."

"Sarah's different Jessica."

Jessica shook her head vigorously. "No dad she isn't. It's just that she's always been the baby of the family. She's always been your little baby girl. You can't see her properly dad. You can't look at her and see a grown woman dad. You still think she's the little baby girl that needs to be looked after all the time and coddled. But she's not. She's a grown woman with her own mind and with her own stall in life to set out. You've got to let her go. You've tried controlling her life and it doesn't work. Let her get on with it."

"A few minutes ago you were saying she needed our *support.*"

"Yes dad. Support; not control. I mean she needs support in the moral sense. She needs to know that you still love her even if she's gay. She needs to know that you still care for her even if what she decides to do doesn't meet your approval. She'll make her own way in life whatever but she needs to know that you understand and stand by her. Right now she's thinking she's lost her family for good. I know what that feels like dad. It's not nice."

"We've made our apologies for that a long time ago Jessica. We made a mistake and we've freely admitted to it and tried to make amends."

"Then for the love of God dad don't make the same mistake with Sarah."

"You didn't run off with another *woman.*" Mrs Fuchs pointed out tearfully.

"No mum I didn't. I *did* run off with a man that might have been the bloody Anti-Christ if you were to believe half the things you said about him though."

Mr Fuchs held up a hand. "I've already said that we were wrong Jessica. Damien is a fine man and we were mistaken about him. I don't think we should let this current crisis dig up all the old wrongs and past mistakes in the family."

"I'm not digging up the past dad, merely pointing out the parallels with the present. Here's another radical notion for you. What if it turns out that this girlfriend of Sarah's is a *fine* woman? What if she is not a demon or some awful predator that wants her wicked way with your baby daughter but in fact a good decent girl that happens to be gay, loves your daughter and only wants to make her happy?"

Mrs Fuchs groaned comically. "Don't say things like that Jessie. I can't imagine my Sarah with another woman."

Mr Fuchs looked unconvinced as well. "What if she's just some infatuation Jessica? Sarah is, after all, relatively inexperienced. You've said yourself that she's only ever really had the one boyfriend. She might just be experimenting with this woman. I don't know much about homosexuality but I do know that it's not unknown for otherwise perfectly normal straight people to have affairs with people of their own sex, especially when they're very young. Sarah might be throwing it all away for some misguided infatuation."

"Then that's *her* problem dad. She's old enough to make her own mistakes and hopefully learn from them. I don't think this is just some childish fling though dad. Sarah seems awfully taken by this girlfriend of hers and she's not the kind of girl given to rash impulses dad. She's not the impetuous type. She's probably the most cautious and conservative of all of us when it comes to affairs of the heart. She seems very in love to me and I've never seen that before with her; long term relationship with Alan or not. You may have to brace yourself to the fact that this is serious. I think she's serious; very serious."

Mr Fuchs rubbed his temples with his knuckles. "This is absurd. How can Sarah possibly be considering a relationship with a woman?"

"Er... because she's gay possibly dad?"

Mr Fuchs shook his head decisively. "She's hardly in a position to have *any* sort of independent relationship. What's she thinking of doing? Moving in with this woman? Ridiculous! She's only just out of university. She's got no full time job, no career prospects and, apart from a small legacy from her grandmother which won't last long, no capital. She's nearly penniless for God's sake. She's been living off the allowance I've been paying her to get through university. She can't possibly expect me to continue financing her while she sets up house with a lesbian woman."

Jessica leaned back with a sigh. "Oh dad! You know for such a clever man you can be really gormless sometimes."

"What are you trying to say Jessica?"

"I mean dad that you're not very observant. I don't know who this girlfriend of Sarah's is dad but, reading between the lines, I can tell you a few interesting things about her."

"Such as?"

"Well she's not hurting for money for one thing."

"On what grounds do you base that assumption?"

"Well I know that Sarah's been doing some part time work as a waitress in the hotels in the Toggenburg but I also know for a fact that she can't afford the sort of designer threads she's been wearing the last few days on the sort of wages that would bring her."

"There's a ready explanation for that Jessica. I sent her some money to outfit herself for her engagement and the social program of events that we'd planned around it."

"Yes dad. Sarah told me. You sent her twenty thousand francs." Jessica leaned forward and tapped on the coffee table. "Twenty thousand francs that she's paying you back into your account dad. She doesn't *need* your money. I bet she hasn't even touched the brass you sent her. She's got money enough of her own to deck herself out in expensive clothes or at least her girlfriend has."

"A few new clothes hardly indicates a new found source of wealth surely Jessica."

Jessica rolled her eyes. "Bloody men! You've no idea. Tell him mum."

Mrs Fuchs paused in her sniffling dramatics to look uncertain. "Well yes I suppose so. She's certainly been well dressed these past few days and I looked in her wardrobe. She had some lovely clothes and expensive too. She must have spent a lot of money on them."

"Not to mention the bling." Jessica pointed out.

"Bling?" Mr Fuchs looked confused. "What the blazes is bling?"

Jessica groaned. "Oh dad! For the benefit of those people who haven't managed to emerge from the dark ages yet, bling is twenty first century slang for jewellery."

"Oh I see. What about her jewellery? I did see she had some kind of necklace on and earrings I think."

"She was wearing a white gold and emerald necklace all weekend dad that she didn't pick up in a charity shop not to mention expensive moissanite earrings and a platinum and diamond brooch that must have cost thousands."

"Oh God yes!" cried Mrs Fuchs. "And she had a string of good quality pearls and a gold bracelet in her jewellery box. If she's not using the money you sent her George then where is it coming from?"

"There's another thing too." Jessica continued. "Did you know that Sarah travelled down here on a first class ticket on the train?"

Mr Fuchs raised an eyebrow. "Really?"

"Yes I saw it myself when I put her on the train in Bellinzona. First class! Sarah! I've *never* known her travel first class. She's always been cautious with her money, even a bit mean but now she just jumps into first class without a care in the world. She's hardly acting like somebody that's penniless dad. She's throwing the stuff around like there's no tomorrow. I'm guessing that this girlfriend of hers is loaded. Sarah's found herself a Sugar Mammy."

Mrs Fuchs grasped at her throat in horror. "Oh my God! Are you saying that Sarah's having an affair with some rich middle aged dyke Jessica?"

"I'm only joking mum. Sarah says her girlfriend is a bit older than she is but not by very much. I gather she's in her mid-twenties or thereabouts. Still she must be rich and that poses a few questions about her doesn't it? Maybe she comes from a wealthy family. I don't know. She's no pauper though."

John chuckled in the background. "Bloody hell! Wouldn't that be a joke? All this talk about marrying our Sarah off into a rich family to keep her in the means to which she's accustomed and all the time she couldn't give a flying fuck about the Bergers' money because she's got a rich girlfriend hiding in the wings. Maybe you ought to reconsider your strategy dad. If this lass' family's got money to burn maybe you ought to think about brokering a marriage deal with them and the Bergers can go fuck themselves."

"Thank you John. That'll do! I think we're making presumptions here on very flimsy evidence."

"Well that's an improvement at any rate dad." Jessica remarked. "At least we do *have* some evidence. Earlier in this conversation you were jumping to conclusions and making presumptions about Sarah's girlfriend without a *shred* of evidence to back them up."

"You can't be serious John!" Mrs Fuchs gasped in a horrified whisper. "Sarah can't marry a *woman*."

"Why not? It's legal now isn't it? Well sort of. Don't they have civil partnerships for gay people now? I'm sure I've read something about it."

Mrs Fuchs glared at him. "Stop it John! It's not funny. The very thought...."

"All right mum. Don't take me seriously. I was only joking. Still it's a thought though isn't it?" John laughed aloud. "We wouldn't have to change the wedding plans at all would we? All we'd need to do is change the names on the invitations from Alan to Susan or whatever and we're ready to roll. There might have to be a few adjustments regarding the bridesmaids and so on of course. I mean do lesbians *have* bridesmaids? Do you have two brides or what and what the hell is the lesbian equivalent of a best man? Jesus dad! When you're escorting Sarah down the aisle will her girlfriend's dad being ushering the other bride alongside? Think of the protocol problems that's going to bring up."

"That'll do John!" said Mr Fuchs exasperatedly. "This is no laughing matter. You're upsetting your mother. She was looking forward to Sarah's wedding. It was very important to her and this is all very distressing to her."

John had the grace to look sheepish. "I'm sorry mum. I was only joking." He took a deep breath and affected a casual demeanour. "I'm sorry if I upset you but you've still got a wedding to look forward to."

"I will not have a daughter of mine marrying a lesbian." Mrs Fuchs cried shrilly. "It's a terrible thing to suggest John."

"I wasn't talking about Sarah's wedding mum. I was talking about mine."

There was a shocked silence. Mr Fuchs seemed to be struggling to articulate. "John..." he began at last. "Are you serious?"

John nodded. "Yeah dad. I was going to tell the whole family tonight over dinner in any case until all this blew up. I didn't say anything before because this was supposed to be Sarah's weekend and I was going to leave it until we could all sit down together. I know this isn't the best time right now and Sarah's not here but I might as well tell you anyway. Me and Maria have decided to get married. We've been living together for over two years I know so it won't seem like much difference but well we want to have kids and all that so we thought we'd best make it official."

Mrs Fuchs' face lit up with renewed hope. "Oh John!" she gasped. "That's wonderful."

Mr Fuchs rose to grasp his son's hand warmly. "Well finally *some* good news has come out of this wretched weekend. Well done John! Maria is a fine young woman. I can't tell you how pleased I am."

John grinned in embarrassment. "Thanks dad."

Jessica embraced her brother warmly as well. She liked Maria. "Congratulations John. When are we going to have this shindig?"

"It'll be springtime now. We thought about late April or May."

Mrs Fuchs was drying her eyes and smiling for the first time that evening. "Oh John! This is wonderful news. Thank God one of my children is showing some sense today. Thank you. Thank you for bringing *some* joy into this house today."

Mr Fuchs was rocking on his heels and beaming. "Well this is a turnaround in events. This calls for a celebration."

Jessica laughed. "That's a good idea dad. Where's that whisky bottle? Let's all have a drink."

Mr Fuchs raised a finger theatrically. "The devil with that Jessie. I have a bottle of fine champagne in the cooler. I was saving it so we could all toast Sarah and Alan over dinner tonight. Well I see no reason why we should let it go to waste now."

Mrs Fuchs looked devastated. "Oh George I haven't started dinner. All this happening with Sarah just put everything else out of my mind."

Jessica put her arm round her mother. "You've got all the stuff haven't you mum?"

"Well yes everything's ready to go and all the cold foods are prepared but I haven't put the meat in yet."

"Well come on and I'll help you. Save the champagne for later dad. We can all sit down for dinner after all. Let John and dad get the wine out and set the table. We'll handle the food."

"What... what about Alan Jessie?"

Mr Fuchs frowned. "I'll go and talk to him. Maybe I can smooth things over."

Jessica shook her head with a grimace. "I think you're too late dad. I think he's already left. I heard his car in the drive not long after he walked out."

Mr Fuchs looked sombre for a moment. "I see. Well I'll see if I can't talk to him tomorrow. I'm afraid we may have some major repair work on relations to do there." He straightened up. "Still we'll not worry about that now shall we? Let's not allow that to spoil John's good news." He clapped his son about the shoulders. "How about a glass of good cognac John, while the girls get busy with dinner?"

Jessica laughed and took her mother's arm. "Come on mum. It looks like we're being relegated to the kitchen while the men folk set about getting inebriated. Some things never change. You'd think the female liberation movement had never happened."

Mrs Fuchs gave a watery smile. "That's men for you Jessie. Thank God at least *they're* predictable. Do you think you could be getting the salad together whilst I see to the meat?"

"Of course. I whip up a mean salad." As she led her mother away Jessica paused to think of her sister. In the sudden outpouring of joy and bonhomie in the Fuchs household, the youngest daughter, alone on her train in the darkness of the northern Alps, was momentarily forgotten.

Chapter Twenty-Eight

The journey seemed interminable to Sarah. Darkness had fallen and there was not even the distracting view from the train windows. It would have been a gloomy view in any case for, as the train emerged from the Gotthard tunnel, it was evident that the fine weather of Ticino was confined to the southern Alps. There were streaks of rain and sleet across the windows and up at Goschenen, at the highest altitude of the journey, there were even patches of newly fallen snow. Sarah wrapped her arms about her and huddled, miserable and lonely, just wanting the journey to end. A young man came by with the buffet trolley and Sarah bought a cheese sandwich. She was hungry. She'd eaten nothing, other than the rustic salami and a piece of bread she'd shared with Rozella in the grotto at Golino, since breakfast. The sandwich did little to raise her spirits. It was a plain baguette with a single slice of cheese in it, dry and unappetising. She ate it distractedly and without pleasure. It filled her stomach but left her dissatisfied. She was still alone other than her sleeping fellow traveller in the first class carriage. She wondered if it would have been better if she'd travelled second class. At least there might have been someone to talk to.

She changed trains at Arth-Goldau. The station was nearly deserted and it was cold on the platform with rain falling steadily on the roof. She shivered and hurried to her connecting train. Only two other passengers alighted and the train was nearly empty. Now that she was so close her impatience with the journey increased. But the inter-regional train was slow and stopped frequently. Every pause felt like an ache and she felt like whimpering in frustration. She was in a bad way she realised. Her desperate longing was growing by the minute and the only thought in her head was to salve her longing in Daniela's embrace; to banish her loneliness in the arms of her beloved; to lose her sadness in reunion. Nothing else seemed to matter now. She dared not let herself think of anything else; dared not let her mind linger on that which had passed lest it mire in regret or quail at the consequences. The deed was done and now she only sought the oblivion of comfort in her lover's soothing tranquillity. Her mind was fixed on Daniela. She just wanted her to be there. To be there and to hold her and everything would be all right.

Now the train was half an hour away from her destination and she urged it on in her mind cursing the distance that still separated her. With arrival due in twenty minutes she was staring fervently out of the window as if she thought to glimpse some distant view of her destination through the dark gloom. At ten minutes before the scheduled arrival she had already taken her luggage down from the rack and was pacing the aisle of the carriage in agitation. What if something had gone wrong? What if Daniela wasn't waiting for her? She couldn't stand it. As the train made its final approach to Wattwil she was already stood at the door peering anxiously through the dirty rain streaked glass in the door. It afforded her a poor view for as the train pulled into the station she could see little of the platform and that which she could see appeared to be completely deserted. She felt a thrill of fear, bordering on terror, course through her. Daniela wasn't there. As the train halted and the doors wheezed open she flung her bags to the platform and leapt out, darting glances about her almost in panic.

And then, gloriously, she saw her. Daniela had evidently misread the arrival point of the train in the station for she was at the far end of the platform and hurrying after the arriving train with the wind whipping at her golden hair. Sarah let out a sob at the sudden dart in her heart, so sharp it seemed to pierce her to her very soul, and then, abandoning her luggage where it lay, she was flying down the platform. Then she was in her arms sobbing frantically, tears coursing down her cheeks and burying her face against hers. Daniela was clinging to her tightly and swaying her from side to side in her arms almost crooning in pleasure. A gust of wind blew a spattering of cold rain across them but there was only the warmth of their bodies against each other. "Oh Danny, Danny!" Sarah was sobbing. "I didn't think you were here. I couldn't see you."

"Of course I'm here. Where else in the world would I be? I told you I'd be here my love." Incredibly Sarah realised that Daniela was crying too. Their tears were mingling on each other's cheeks. "Oh God I've missed you Sarah." she said. "I was so frightened. I was frightened that you wouldn't come back to me."

"Hold me Danny! Don't let me go. I'm back and this time I'm back for good. I love you Danny." She smothered Daniela's face in kisses and gripped her so tightly she bruised her flesh. "Tell me you love me Danny. Promise me you'll never let me go again."

"Never! I love you! Oh God thank you! Thank you for bringing my Sarah home. Don't leave me again Sarah. These past few days have been torment."

"Kiss me Danny!" And she did, fastening her lips to Sarah's frantically as the wind tangled their hair together.

They were startled by a discrete cough behind Sarah. Sarah whipped her head around. The station master was stood holding his baton and shuffling his feet uncomfortably. He looked somewhat embarrassed. "Er excuse me Fraulein but are those your bags on the platform back there?"

Sarah blinked and looked back up the platform. Her luggage lay forgotten next to a growing puddle under the lights of the station over a hundred metres away. "Oh er yes... yes they are."

"Well I'd move them if I was you Fraulein. I wouldn't want your things to get wet in the rain."

Daniela laughed through her tears. "Come on sweetheart. Let's get your bags and get the hell out of here."

They recovered Sarah's bags and struggled through the wind and rain across the station car park to Daniela's car. "God! This weather's awful." Sarah declared.

"It's been crap ever since you left honey. I bet it was gorgeous in Ticino wasn't it?"

Sarah dropped her bags and grasped a hold of Daniela. "Oh Danny the weather was just fine but the sun's shining right here as far as I'm concerned."

"Only metaphorically Sarah darling. Let's get in the car. We're getting soaked."

In the car Daniela turned the ignition and the powerful engine growled into life. Soon they were on the road out of Wattwil. Daniela drove slowly for Sarah's head was on her shoulder. They were overtaken by man in a little Fiat and they even saw his face behind the side window of his car in the street lamps as he looked astonished at them. Sarah supposed that there were not many times in his life that he had managed to overtake a Ferrari F430 Spider convertible in his little car.

Sarah sighed heavily. "Oh Danny, thank you for being here to pick me up. I was so lonely and missing you. I don't know what I'd have done if you weren't there."

"Sweetheart I'd have driven all the way down to Ticino to pick you up if you'd asked. In fact I nearly did. I was that desperate without you that half a dozen times I was on the point of just driving down to Ascona to throw myself at your feet and beg you to come home. I suppose that wouldn't have been too diplomatic of me."

Sarah shrugged. "Maybe you should have done. It might have saved an awful lot of complicated explanations."

"Have you really told your parents everything Sarah?"

Sarah nodded. "Just about. I told them I'd finished with Alan and was no longer going to marry him. I wrote them a letter which I gave them when I left telling them that I was gay and had a girlfriend. How pusillanimous was that? I didn't even have the guts to tell them to their faces."

"Don't beat yourself over the head about it darling. It's not the easiest thing in the world to tell your parents. It was brave of you to be so honest at all."

"Well they know everything now anyway; everything that is but the identity of my girlfriend. I never told them your name."

Daniela glanced at Sarah compassionately. "That's not something you're going to be able to keep from them forever Sarah."

"I know Danny but let me do one thing at a time huh. It was hard enough to tell them I had a girlfriend at all, let alone who you were. They're probably spitting fire and brimstone as it is. They'd have coronaries if they knew you were somebody famous. My dad would probably try to sue you."

"Has it been rough... at your parents I mean?"

Sarah nodded miserably. "You've no idea Danny."

"You don't have to talk about it if it upsets you."

"No I need to tell you Danny. I need to tell you everything." So she did. As they drove slowly up the valley Sarah recounted every event of the past three days. Once again she observed that precious trait of Daniela's; that blessed ability to know when to keep your peace and simply listen. Daniela nodded in understanding but only interrupted to request clarification. It was a soothing balm to spill out her woes to such a tranquil listener for Sarah; sharing her lonely anxieties in the warmth of the car's interior as the rain spattered against the windows. She felt cocooned; safe and protected by her lover's gentle sympathy. Most important of all she knew she was not alone.

300

Only once did Daniela make any remark over Sarah's story and that was when Sarah told her about her chance meeting with the girl on the beach at Intragna. She put her head back and laughed at Sarah's account. "Oh! So there have been some moments of compensation then." She slapped Sarah playfully on the leg. "Oh my! I'm going to have to start keeping you on a chain. Simon told me about your little encounter in Winterthur as well. It seems like every time I turn my back you're off chasing skirt somewhere."

"I was not chasing skirt."

"Well no but that was only because she wasn't wearing one or anything else for that matter."

"Well it's an FKK beach. Hardly anyone wears any clothes there."

"And you.... what were you wearing?"

"Well I..." Sarah blushed furiously.

"Aha! A guilty conscience I see! I think we can table this one until we get home and have time to discuss the matter at our leisure. You can be telling me all about it while you're bent over the back of the sofa with your drawers around your ankles waiting to have your backside paddled for you."

"You're hardly in a position to criticise *my* behaviour Miss Devin. You've had your clothes off in front of this girl as well."

"What the hell are you talking about?"

"You *know* the girl. She's called Rozella. She told me that she took the photos for your last album cover."

"Rozella! You're kidding me!"

"The very same. Is it true? Did she take those pictures?"

"Yes. Yes of course. Rozella is a very talented photographer. I've worked with her for years."

"Yes so I can't see why only I have to get my bottom spanked. If you were wearing anything in those photos other than a happy smile then it eluded my attention."

"What the hell is Rozella doing in the Ticino?"

"She comes from the Ticino she told me."

"Yes I know but she lives up north. She's got her studio in Solothurn."

"Maybe she's visiting her family."

"Maybe or maybe she's just down there working. Rozella gets about a lot."

Sarah snorted. "She didn't seem to be working from what I could see."

Daniela laughed. "Oh Rozella can always find time for quality leisure. She believes that any minute not spent in persuading pretty young things to divest themselves of their clothing is a minute wasted. My God! I really am going to have to keep you on a leash if I've got the likes of Rozella Fangio sniffing around you. She's not exactly known for the blemishless purity of her motives."

"She seems like a nice person."

"Oh she is. Rozella's a gem. She just has this terrible failing in that she can't keep her knickers on to save her life. To be fair, she doesn't pretend to be anything else. What you see is what you get from Rozella."

"I told her that you were my girlfriend. Did I do wrong? I did ask her to be discreet."

Daniela shook her head. "No honey. If you told her something in confidence she'd never spread it around. It's not a discretion entirely based on high moral principles, I'm afraid. Rozella learned long ago that people who have a reputation for kissing and telling don't get to sleep with many people and Rozella would never do anything to queer her pitch in that respect."

"It was Rozella that told me to come home Danny. I...I was hesitating and didn't know what to do. She told me to stop pissing around and get on the train tonight. She even looked up my train times for me."

Daniela smiled. "Bless her! That sounds like Rosy all right. She's a girl who believes in direct immediate decision; especially when there's a woman involved."

"She said I was crazy in the head for going away and even thinking about marrying a man when I had you Danny. She was right. I don't know whatever I was thinking of. Can you forgive me?"

"Darling there's nothing to forgive. You've come back to me. Have you any idea how happy that makes me?"

"I've been really stupid Danny."

Daniela shook her head firmly. "No darling. You haven't been stupid. Nobody expects this sort of thing to be easy. I think you've been incredibly brave and I am so, so proud of you. You're home now. Stop beating yourself around the head. I know it's been tough darling but you've done the right thing."

"What happens now Danny? I mean where do we go from here?"

In response Daniela stabbed on the brakes of the car and pulled over by the side of the road. They were on a quiet, dark part of the road just short of Alt St Johann. Daniela switched on the interior lights of the car, the better to look Sarah in the face, and took Sarah's hands in hers. "Sarah," she whispered with a croak in her voice. "We go where we must; where we were meant to go. We go into the future... together. Everything we talked about before you left for the Ticino is still there. I want you. I want you more than anything than I have wanted in my life. I want you in my house; in *our* house. I want nothing more or nothing less than to share my life together with you... forever. In these few days I have come to understand exactly what you mean to me. You mean everything to me! I had to stare the possibility that I would lose you when you went away and that's not a place I want to see any more. When you phoned me tonight to say you were coming home it was the best moment in my life Sarah. I have been so miserable without you. I know now, without any further question of doubt, that you are the woman I want to spend the rest of my life with. I love you. I have never felt this way with anyone before. I cannot bear the thought of losing you again."

Tears were streaming down Sarah's face. She caught her breath trying to articulate her emotions. "Danny... oh Danny! I... I don't know what to say. I love you too but how can somebody as wonderful as you fall in love with a foolish girl like me?"

"Because you're *Sarah*; the most amazing girl I've ever known. You're beautiful, kind, considerate, loving, brilliant and... Oh God... just everything I ever wanted. Have you no idea how remarkable you are?"

"I'm nothing compared to you Danny."

"Oh God! Don't *ever* say that Sarah. I'm nothing *without* you. I could be a global superstar Sarah. I could be rich beyond the wildest imagination; have fame and wealth in every nation on earth but it would all be meaningless now without you. Believe me Sarah. This isn't some big, rich rock and roll star talking now. This is just me; the woman behind the media hype; the simple woman who knows in her heart how lonely and desolate life would be without you. I'll trade all the fame and wealth in the world for a life in a little house, with our own garden, raising chickens in the Toggenburg with you my love. I could spend the rest of my days being nothing more than Sarah's girl and count myself rich beyond my dreams. Believe me Sarah. Stay with me Sarah. Please don't leave me again."

Sarah choked on the overwhelming love that rose like an unstoppable wave from the inner kernel of her being. She gripped Daniela's hands so hard that she bruised her palms. It was a cusp moment; the moment when you threw yourself from the cliff and damned the future to do its worst. "I'll never leave you again Danny. I will love you forever. I swear it! You are the person I will spend my life with. How could I have been so stupid?

How could I have ever have thought that there was anyone else? How could I ever have thought to lose you?"

Daniela swallowed and lowered her head for a second. When she raised her eyes again they were damp with tears. "And I swear this Sarah. I swear that as long as I shall live I will love you, nurture you, cherish you and count myself blessed that I was privileged to love you. I swear that from this moment forth only death will separate you from my love."

Sarah felt a thrill of horror. "Don't *ever* say that Danny. Don't talk about death. We have a *life* to make."

"I'm sorry sweetheart. Yes you're right. Let's talk about life. We're not going to die yet."

"So what are we going to do Danny... I mean, right now, as a practical immediacy? Do we just carry on as we have been doing?"

Daniela paused to consider for a moment. "I've talked to Simon." She said at last.

"Simon?"

"Yes he knows a man with a van."

"Van?"

"Yes he wants to help with the move."

"Move?"

"Sarah darling do you think you could possibly put your brain into gear and refrain from these monosyllabic questions?"

"I'm sorry Danny but I'm not following you."

"Let me put it this way Sarah. Are we together or not?"

"Yes, yes... of course we are!"

"Are we committed together or aren't we?"

"I've said so yes Danny."

"Do we love each other?"

"Of course we do. Why do you ask?"

"So how do you want to go forward Sarah? Do we live on opposite sides of the valley and see each other on Wednesdays and Fridays?"

Sarah lowered her eyes and shook her head. "No Danny. I haven't thrown all my past life away just to go back to uncertainty. When I got on that train tonight it was a commitment; a commitment to you. I don't want to just date you. I want to live with you."

"Then we need the man with the van. You'll need to move all your stuff up to my place."

"What about Nicky?"

"I've already talked to her Sarah."

"Seriously?"

"Yes honey. I took her out to dinner last night and we had a long talk. I told her that if you came back to the Toggenburg that I wanted you to live with me. She understands Sarah. She understands what we have between us and she's cool with that. I know she loves you but I think she accepts the situation. To be honest I think she'll be relieved that you're coming back at all. Last night we weren't certain. We both got a little teary at the thought of you marrying that awful man and leaving both of us for good. Perhaps she is a little sad that you're moving in with me but I think I was able to reassure her in some respects."

Sarah frowned. "What respects?"

Daniela took a deep breath. "I... I told her that I understood how she felt about you. I told her that it wasn't a problem for me. I would not be jealous if she wanted quality time with you. In fact I'd be pleased. I told her that our house was open to her any time. I also told her that we wanted to keep the little house that you and she shared and that she was to consider it her home as long as she wanted. I said we'd take over the finances of the house and, if necessary, buy it. I said that I hoped that we would always be welcome there. Of course she agreed."

Sarah grasped Daniela's hand and shook her head in bewilderment. "I... I don't understand Danny. Were you telling her that you were willing to share me with her?"

Daniela sighed. "I don't really know Sarah. All I know is that somehow we have to find a solution for Nicole. We can't allow you and she to break up in acrimony. Nicole was your first love after all."

Sarah blinked. "We weren't in love!"

"Yes you were Sarah... you just didn't realise it. Actually you're still in love. I can't come between the love you have for each other. It would destroy us. Therefore I'm prepared to make compromises. I'm not a jealous person. I know that if you and Nicole are alienated from each other it would make you deeply unhappy. I never want to see you unhappy. Nicole is important to you. You should never lose her."

"Danny.... Danny... I... I've never made love to Nicky."

"Then it's probably high time that you did."

"You're joking!"

"No I'm not Sarah." Daniela paused to gather her thoughts. "Listen Sarah. This summer I've had a fair bit of free time. It isn't always going to be that way. I have major commitments coming up. I'm going to be away on tour; I have serious recording contracts to honour; I'll have television appearances to make; overseas trips to make and God knows what else. We're planning a tour in America and another in the Far East. I'm going to be away a lot honey. I don't think you'd be happy just tagging along on tour. You're happiest just where you are; here, in the Toggenburg. I think that this valley is your natural habitat and I think this is the place where you can shine." Daniela paused to run a hand through her hair. "I told you once that I fell apart on our last tour Sarah. Do you know why?"

"You said it was the strain Danny."

"There's all sorts of kinds of strain Sarah. The one thing I missed, missed for a long time, was a home. You feel rootless and lost on tour if there's nowhere to go back to. The world takes on a sense of unreality. You don't belong anywhere. That's why I took a house in the

Toggenburg in the first place. I needed a retreat. More than that, I needed a home. There used to be another place that was special to me that I used to run away to when things got too much. I went and hid there when all the stuff about my being gay came out and my marriage was falling apart. But that was different. It was a good place to hide away for a few weeks but it wasn't a practical sort of place to make a home out of. The Toggenburg was ideal. So I took my house here and called it my home.

The only trouble is that a home is far more than a house however much you love a house. I could come "home" to the Toggenburg and still be lonely Sarah. All the guys in the band are pretty much scattered all over Switzerland and they have their own lives to lead when we're not working. I've worked so much over the last few years that I've had very little contact with people outside of the music business. Now I know hundreds of people in the business and many of them I like a lot but mostly they are not close friends. However much they would want to be otherwise there is always the constraint that I'm a successful artist. It's tough to find people who will just take you the way you are; people who couldn't give a monkey's toss whether you're famous or not. You know that was the first thing I loved about you. You hardly knew who the hell I was. You even couldn't remember my name the first day we met. That was just adorable."

"You're taking a heck of a long time to get to the point Danny!"

"I know honey. What I'm trying to say is that I had a house in the Toggenburg but I didn't yet have a home. The best thing that happened to begin with was my cats. I've always loved animals but a life on the road is hardly conducive to having your own animals. Within a few months of setting up house in the Toggenburg I'd accumulated a gang of cats. I don't even know quite how it happened. They're all strays from one place or another

308

and somehow they all seemed to settle on me. Now I'm lumbered with them but I love them all. Cats don't watch prime time television. Cats don't read scandal mags. Cats don't care how famous or rich you are. Cats just want a nice warm house, food on demand and a comfy lap to sit on while they get stroked. My cats were my family."

"You have a daughter Danny." Sarah pointed out.

"Yes I know Sarah but not here. I think that was another reason to have a home. On the couple of occasions that my daughter came over here to visit me I was nearly always somewhere on the road. A hotel room is not the best environment for a young child. Now I have my own place properly then maybe she can come over more often to see me; maybe even spend a summer with me or something. I would like that. I miss her."

"I would love to meet your daughter Danny. I'm betting that she's wonderful."

"Oh she is. That's not just maternal pride talking either. She's a very smart, talented kid."

"We've gone off the point again though Danny."

"Yes we have but, in a way, it's all related Sarah. It's what I'm trying to get to. Home is more than a house; it's where your people are; the people you love. I never had that until I met you. You make the Toggenburg my home. I could travel all over the world Sarah and never have to sit alone in a hotel room in misery again if I knew that, back here, in the home that we both love, you were waiting for me. I'd have my roots; my certainty; a home of love. That is so important to me. But it's not just about me. I can't travel the world and expect you to sit home alone waiting. I wouldn't want you to. There are people you love as well and people that I am coming to love. Nicole is one of those people. Simon and Peter are two others and so are Elke and Angelica. These are important people to us Sarah and we must cherish them. Now Nicole is very special. She's a big part of your life. I want to be her friend not her rival. If she ends up in bed with you on the occasions that I'm away I won't worry about it as long as I know that you still have a place for me in your heart. I don't want her to take you away from me of course."

"God! Did you say that to her?"

"Yes I did. She seemed to think it was funny. She thought she had no chance of taking you away. I told her she was wrong. She was your first love. I laid my heart on the table Sarah. I told her how much you meant to me. I asked her for her blessing on our relationship if you returned to the Toggenburg."

"Oh my God! What did she say?"

"She granted me that Sarah. In some ways I think she was relieved. Nicole hasn't exactly emerged from the closet herself. Since we've been seeing each other she's had to confront her own demons. She might never have told you how she feels about you if you hadn't thrust your own sexuality in her face. Now she has done and it makes for a hell of a dilemma for her. If I were to disappear from the scene she would have to contemplate the pretty daunting prospect of coming out herself and being openly gay. I don't think she's ready for that. In some ways this is an ideal solution for her. She still retains an intimacy with you but she doesn't have to declare her hand openly. Most importantly she hasn't lost you. Hell she even says you should keep some of your stuff at the cottage in the Alpli in case you wanted to stay over when I'm away. That's fine by me."

Sarah sighed. "Poor Nicky. I think you're right though. It's going to be a hard call for her to come out as gay. She's always been a girl with a bit of a reputation for getting around the boys."

Daniela nodded. "I guess she never found what she was looking for with a boy."

Sarah smiled sadly. "Maybe we could find her a girlfriend!"

"Well we could always unleash Rozella on her."

Sarah laughed. "Oh God! That would be funny." Sarah shook her head in amusement. "I think Rozella might be a bit over the top for her. I tell you who she might click with though; Charmaine, the girl I met in Winterthur. She's just the kind of girl Nicky might hit it off with."

"Either that or we clone you and give her Sarah Two."

"God! Don't even say that."

"Anyway honey we can't sit here all night. We'd better go."

"One thing though Danny. I have to tell you something."

"What's that darling?"

"I'm broke. Well I'm not completely broke. I still have some money in my savings account if I absolutely need it but my normal current bank account is just about dead in the water. I'm going to have to give my dad the twenty thousand francs he gave me back and I'm afraid it'll just about clear my account out. I did have about seven or eight thousand in there before he gave me that money but I spent so much on new clothes and so on that giving him the money back will just about bankrupt me."

"Ok we'll sort that out in the morning. We'll shift some money to your account. You should have your own spending money."

"Wait a minute Danny. I wasn't asking for money."

"Well what's the problem?"

"I... Well I'm not comfortable just living off your money Danny. I don't want to be a kept woman. I want to earn my money."

"You will do darling. Look we're both going to have to work hard to make this work. We *have* gone over this ground before. I'm not keeping you. You've got your own career to forge. Let's just be thankful that money isn't a problem. If you don't want to take my money outright then I'll lend you it. I know damn well you'll pay me back and with interest. We've got enough work on our hands making a future together honey. Bloody money is the least of our problems."

"I don't want people to think that I'm just your girlfriend for your money Danny."

"People will think what they will Sarah, but you know it's not true and I know it's not true as well. We've got enough money; not me or you, *we* have enough money and that's an end to it. Now come along let's go. We're late."

"Late? Are we in a hurry?"

"Well we ought to get going. We are running later than I said."

"Said what? What are we late for?"

Daniela smiled and restarted the car. "You'll see."

Chapter Twenty-Nine

Sarah blinked in surprise. "Why are we stopping here?" she asked. They had driven up the hill from Unterwasser to Schwendi, on the way home, but Daniela, instead of continuing on the road around to Oberdorf, had pulled in at the Hotel Toggenburg. The hotel looked cheerfully welcoming with its bright lights in the dark, miserably rainy night.

Daniela turned off the car and kissed Sarah swiftly. "Just thought we could do with a drink honey. I told Elke we'd pop in for one on the way home. She's looking forward to seeing you."

Sarah was taken aback. "Oh! Oh I see."

"We don't have to stay long if you don't want to."

"No, no that's fine."

"Come on then."

In the hotel Daniela led Sarah into the restaurant. In one corner of the restaurant a large table was set. Sarah gaped in astonishment. The table was decorated with candles, flowers and balloons and there was a hastily contrived banner hanging from the beam over the table. It read "**Welcome Home Sarah.**" Even more astonishing was the gathering around the table. Elke and Angelica were there and so were Peter and Simon. Last but not least, still in her working uniform and grinning in pleasure, there was Nicole. As Sarah stared dumbfounded, the party jumped to its feet and, cheering loudly, rushed to embrace her. The next couple of minutes were delirious as Sarah was hugged, kissed and, in the case of Angelica, virtually danced around the room in glee. Nicole grasped Sarah tightly and smothered her with kisses, laughing through her tears. "Oh Hell Foxy! I thought you weren't coming back."

Elke beamed hugely. "Of course she was coming back Nicky. As if she'd do anything else. Now come along. She's back now so let her catch her breath. Angie. Where's Magdalena with the bloody champagne?"

Angelica grinned delightedly. "I'll go find her. God it's good to have you back Sarah."

"I've only been gone a few days." protested Sarah feebly.

Elke wrapped an arm around her waist. "It felt like years Sarah honey."

"How the hell did you know I was coming back? I only decided myself this afternoon."

"I told everyone Sarah." Daniela confessed. "As soon as you phoned me I called around everyone to arrange a little welcome home party."

Sarah shook her head in bewilderment. "But that was only two or three hours ago."

"Yes well we've had to improvise on the run." Elke told her. "It's a bit of a rushed job I'm afraid Sarah but Danny didn't give us much notice."

Sarah blinked back her tears. "I... I can't believe you've done all this for me. It... it's wonderful. Thank you."

Elke kissed her fondly. "Only the best for our Sarah. Are you hungry?"

"God yes! I'm famished. All I've had since breakfast is a bit of salami and a cheese sandwich on the train."

"Well I'm afraid the chef's finished for the day so it won't be anything elaborate. We're having a fondue if that's all right with you."

"What one of your cheese fondues?" Sarah's stomach seemed to jump up and start nibbling at her throat. The Hotel Toggenburg was renowned locally for the excellence of its cheese fondues.

"That's right; Fondue fromage au poivre, the house speciality. We'd have put out a nice buffet if we'd had time but we couldn't do it at such short notice."

"Fondue sounds just wonderful Elke."

"Good. Come on then. Take a seat."

314

Peter intervened smoothly. "Allow me." Gallantly he held a chair out for Sarah in place of honour at the head of the table.

Sarah swallowed and took her seat as gracefully as she could. She placed a hand on Peter's and looked at him seriously. "Oh Peter. Don't be mad with me. I'm sorry."

"Whatever for Sarah?"

"I... I've finished with Alan Peter. I've told him that I'm not going to marry him."

"I know Sarah. Good for you."

"Excuse me."

"I said good for you Sarah."

"But...I thought you'd be angry with me."

"On the contrary. If you ever think about marrying that arsehole ever again I shall personally ask Daniela's permission to put you over my knee and spank your backside until you squeal for mercy."

Sarah stared at him in confusion. "I thought you wanted me to marry Alan Pete."

"I was wrong Sarah. I'm man enough to admit that."

"I don't understand Peter. How do you know anyway? Has Danny told you?"

Peter shook his head. "No Sarah. Alan told me."

"Alan? I don't understand! What's going on?"

Simon, listening to the exchange, intervened. "You're not up to date on developments Sarah. Whilst you were on the train coming home your delightful ex called us up."

Sarah clapped a hand to her mouth. "Oh God! What did he have to say?"

Peter looked grim. "He had quite a lot to say, Sarah, and most of it unwelcome."

Sarah blanched. "Oh my God! What did he say?"

Peter eased himself into a chair next to her. "Apparently he'd just come from your parent's house. He said you'd left him and taken a train home and that

315

you'd left a note saying that you were gay and seeing a woman. I don't want to upset you Sarah but he said your parents were devastated. He said he'd had an argument with your brother and sister and left in disgust. He asked me if I knew this woman you were seeing."

"Oh God! Did you tell him?"

Peter shook his head. "No Sarah. I told him that I was aware that you'd been seeing a woman although I was unsure how serious it was. He demanded to know the woman's name. I told him that I could not tell him the name of the woman because that would be a breach of confidence and that if you wished him or your parents to know her identity then doubtless you would inform them yourself."

"Oh God! What did he say then?"

"I'm afraid that he became threatening and abusive Sarah. He suggested that Simon and I had something to do with your being gay in some way as if we'd corrupted you. He called us deviants and said it was typical for queers to stick together. His language became so offensive I put the phone down."

"Oh Peter…. I'm so sorry."

"Please do not apologise for that man's bigoted and foul behaviour Sarah. It's not your fault. I was upset, I'm afraid, but I tell you something; I might be queer and a nancy boy as he called me but if he'd said the things he said to my face he'd have been going home in an ambulance."

Simon nodded in agreement. "I'll second that. If that bastard ever shows his face in this valley again I'll make it a point of honour to kick the living shit out of him. Nobody talks to my partner like that."

Sarah lowered her head. "I'm sorry boys. I seem to have made trouble for everyone."

Peter shook his head vigorously. "No you haven't Sarah. Don't ever say that. You're well rid of the man. I'm just so happy that you saw it before I did. We're just so happy to see you back. Forget the bastard. He's filed and receipted as an insufferable arsehole. Thank God you've found somebody better."

Sarah gripped Peter's hand. "Thank you Peter. Thank you for your support."

Daniela came to stand behind Sarah's chair and to rest a hand on her shoulder. "Everybody supports you Sarah. Us queers stick together."

Peter smiled but became serious once more. "Listen Sarah and you too Danny. I think it's better if you two don't advertise your relationship for the moment as it were. Alan was threatening to take action against your girlfriend Sarah. Now Simon and I are agreed that he won't learn Danny's identity from us. In fact we're resolved never to talk to the bastard again. We think, however, that perhaps it would be better if Danny was kept a little secret for the moment. Alan's family is pretty powerful and influential. They could yet do you some harm."

Daniela snorted contemptuously. "Hmmph! I'm not frightened of those bastards."

Peter took a breath and looked disturbed. "You should be Danny. You're a public figure after all and Alan's family could find all sorts of ways to attack your reputation. I don't want that to happen."

Daniela smiled slowly. "We're not going to live in fear of them Peter. I'm not saying that we announce it to the world but I'm not going to crawl back into the closet and lie there quivering because of those people. I know some pretty powerful people myself Peter. If they want to make a fight out of it, then I'll make them rue the day."

Sarah bit her lip in agitation. "Oh Danny! Don't antagonise them. Peter's right. The Bergers are not people to mess with."

Daniela gripped her shoulder. "Don't be frightened my love. I'm not going to start a war. On the other hand I love you. I'm not going to hide that Sarah. I'm through with hiding and pretence. You're the girl that I want and if anybody tries to tear you away from me they're going to find out that I've got teeth."

Simon nodded but weighed in with a word of caution. "I appreciate that you're not frightened of the Bergers Danny and nor should you be. I think Pete might be being a little overly paranoid but nevertheless he has a point. There's no need to make an issue out of this. I realise that you're never going to keep it a secret forever, and why should you, but there's still no point in flaunting the situation under the Bergers' noses. You don't want to make your private life the subject of immediate public speculation in any case. Ok, if the media gets hold of the story, then we'll take it from there. Nobody's saying you have to carry on clandestinely but, on the other hand, I'd try not to announce it publicly. It's nobody's business but yours for the moment. Let things settle down for the moment. At the very least, let's not precipitate a conflict until we have some ammunition in reserve if it comes to a fight."

Sarah looked at him in puzzlement. "What are you trying to say Simon?"

Simon pulled a wry face. "Well I don't want to say too much Sarah but Alan's family is not the only one with power and influence. I come from a fairly influential family myself and I know for a fact that there are certain people that have taken a good deal of interest in the Bergers' rather unconventional business associations. I don't want to go into details at this moment but I kind of doubt if the Bergers would want some of the details of those associations to become part of the public domain should they wish to question Daniela's public reputation."

Peter blinked in surprise. "You've never mentioned this before Simon."

"I didn't want to worry you Pete. I was never happy about enlisting Alan's advice in the first place and I'm even less happy about it now. I made a few inquiries. The Bergers' money is dirty Pete. Ok that's not anything particularly new in this country but there's an even more unusual amount of muck sticking to *their* financial background. Ironically Daniela's public persona is to our advantage. They'd have to attack her publicly. It would be a different matter if they could just intimidate somebody who was an ordinary, unknown person. In Daniela's case they'd risk going through a law court. Give me a couple of months to dig around and the Bergers won't dare to have showdown in public. There'd be too many skeletons hopping out of the closet."

Sarah was looking at Simon frantically. "Oh Simon be careful for heaven's sake. We don't want a public fight with the Bergers."

"Relax Sarah. I'm not after starting a fight either but I think it would be prudent to have a few guns loaded in case they want to make an issue out of it. As I say, I don't think they'll cherish the thought of a public confrontation either. They're not a family concern overly comfortable with the spotlight of publicity on them. They'll soon back down once we unmask the batteries."

Frau Fritzl clapped her hands together decisively. "And that, I think, will suffice on this issue for tonight. I refuse to have Sarah's homecoming spoiled by the intrusion of the bloody Bergers into the conversation. I hereby declare this subject closed. Tonight is for rejoicing so let's all sit down and soak up some bubbly."

Angelica was already opening a bottle of fine champagne and Magdalena was placing baskets of fresh crusty brown bread, cut into rough bite sized cubes, in the middle of the table. Each place setting was simplicity itself with merely a plate and a long handled, thin tined fondue fork. A large oil burning heater, set into a metal stand, was occupying pride of place at the centre of the table and there was a delicious scent of melting cheese emanating from the kitchens. Before Sarah could turn her mind completely to the immediate business of food and drink however her telephone sounded. With a frown she extracted the unit from her handbag and peered at the display screen anxiously, prepared to sever the connection without answering should the caller be anybody she did not wish to speak to. It was Jessica. Taking a deep breath Sarah thumbed the connection. "Hi Jess."

"Hi kid. You got home alright?"

"Yes, yes thank you. I... I'm back in the Toggenburg. Where are you now?"

"Still at mum and dad's."

"How... how are they?"

"They've gone to bed now Sarah. I'm just sitting up having a drink with John. How are you doing?"

"I...I've had better days Jess."

"Well you were well out of it here kid. I'm afraid your letter precipitated a glorious display of drama and histrionics."

"Oh God I'm sorry Jess."

"Hey don't be. Actually it was so pathetic it was funny. I suppose we just about went through every worn out cliché in the book; mum wringing her hands in tears denying that her daughter is gay one minute and asking where did we go wrong the next; dad fuming that some evil dyke had corrupted his darling Sarah and moaning that now there'd be no man to look after her. Alan seemed to take the whole thing as an affront to his masculinity and John threatened to punch his lights out for him for making opprobrious remarks about his kid sister. It was better than soap opera. A fine time was had by all."

"Oh God! Well I expected it I suppose."

"Well it was the best bombshell we've had in many a long year. I was quite envious actually. I've always prided myself as the family rebel and you've nearly made me look respectable. Maybe I ought to think about turning bi and having an affair with an airline stewardess or something."

"Stop it Jess. It's not funny."

320

"Sorry Sarah. I know this must be hard for you. I was just trying to lighten things up."

"Are they totally furious with me?"

"It's a bit of a shock for them Sarah. You've got to understand that. Oh I know I make fun of them but it can't be easy for them either. You're just going to have to give them a little time on this one. It wasn't too bad in the end because John suddenly announced that he and Maria are getting married and everybody got back to some semblance of normality."

"John's getting married?"

"Yep! He dropped it on us right in the middle of the family crisis. Mum looked pathetically grateful. Talk about clutching at straws."

"Oh I'm pleased about John. I like Maria a lot."

"Don't tell John that. He might think you fancy her."

"Jess!"

"I'm sorry. That was insensitive of me. No it's good though. I like Maria as well. Anyway, after John's announcement, the drama decreased markedly and it turned into a celebratory family party after all. Alan wasn't there. He stormed out of the house earlier."

"I know. He's been phoning my friends demanding to know the identity of the girl I've been seeing."

"Bastard didn't waste any time then did he? Watch your back there Sarah... a man scorned and all that."

"Is my name mud then Jess?"

"It's a bit grubby for the moment kid I'm afraid. At dinner mum forbade anyone to mention your name. She said she didn't want John's happy news spoiled by any further reference to your unforgivable behaviour. I'm sorry Sarah... they were her words not mine. I think you might have to accept being persona non grata for a while."

"I expected nothing less."

"Don't worry about it. They'll come around in time. Isn't this sort of thing more or less par for the course after somebody has the temerity to inform their parents that they're gay? There are even support groups for families whose children have come out aren't there?"

"Oh Hell Jess! I can't see mum and dad attending parental awareness evenings run by the LOS or somebody."

"No, you're probably right. That's maybe a flight of fantasy into the realms of unreality too far. Still they're going to have to get used to it aren't they?"

"And you Jess? Are you going to have to get used to it?"

Jessica hesitated for a second. "Yes Sarah. Yes I suppose I am. Oh it's easier for me because I know quite a lot of gay people. I have gay friends. It's one thing though to know gay people but it's quite another to suddenly find out that your kid sister you thought you've known all your life is gay. It takes some adjusting to."

"I'm sorry Jess."

"For God's sake stop being sorry Sarah. It's not your fault. If there's any fault to be attached it's to me because I can't just accept it without a moment's hesitation. I'm certainly not going to make moral judgements Sarah and I don't love you any the less because you're gay. I'm not shocked in any bad way just caught by surprise that's all and I need time to digest it. Whatever happens I hope you know that you can always count on me for my support."

"Thank you Jess. That means a lot to me."

"What I can't get over is why I never saw it before."

"I didn't really see it myself Jess. How could you be expected to?"

"The signs were there if you looked for them."

"Jess I'm going to have to sign off. We... we've stopped at a restaurant on the way home for a bite to eat and I think our food is coming out."

"We? Are you with your... well your... friend?"

"Yes Jess. She picked me up at the railway station."

322

"Ok then before you sign off one last thing."

"Yes?"

"I don't know who your friend is Sarah but..."

"My *girlfriend* Jess; call her my girlfriend."

"Ok your girlfriend then. All I want to say is that you ought to keep her out of the way for the moment if you want to avoid any embarrassment."

"What do you mean?"

"I mean that after dinner tonight dad said he intended to drive up to the Toggenburg some time in the next few days. I think he has some fool notion about trying to talk some sense into you. I also think he believes that your girlfriend is in some way responsible for your being gay as if it was infectious or something. I don't suppose you'd relish the thought of him confronting her over the issue so I'd tell her to keep her head down. There's no telling what idiocy dad is capable of doing if he believes he's on a crusade to rescue his darling daughter."

"Oh Christ!"

"Just a sisterly warning kid."

"Thanks Jess. I'll bear it in mind. I have to go now. Thanks for your support and send John my congratulations if he's still at all interested in what I have to say."

"Oh John's cool with it Sarah. He actually stood up for you. I was quite proud of him."

"John stood up for me?"

"Oh yes. Couldn't see what all the fuss was about. He said it was no skin off his nose just because you were gay. I think he was quite pleased that you weren't marrying Alan after all. He can't stand him."

"I wonder if I'll get an invitation to the wedding."

"Of course you will. Mum's hardly going to try to hijack John's wedding the way she tried to yours. For one thing Maria would never let her."

"I'd like to go to John's wedding."

"Maybe you could be one of the bridesmaids. That'd put mum's nose out of joint. Better still dress up real butch and volunteer to be John's best man!"

"Thank you Jess! I think that'll be quite enough poking fun at me."

"Sorry kid. Hey one thing though before I ring off. Can I ask you a question?"

Sarah sighed heavily. "Go on then!"

"Your girlfriend... what's she like? I mean you didn't tell me much at the station and naturally there's been a little speculation over her. Is she really butch?"

"Butch?" Sarah glanced up at Daniela who was sat next to her shamelessly eavesdropping on the conversation. Daniela looked glorious in a soft short pink evening dress, her long blond tresses draped over her bare shoulders and a sapphire necklace about her shapely throat. At the word "butch" she raised an inquiring eyebrow. Sarah bit her lip in amusement. "Why do you ask Jess?"

"Oh it's just the way you've gone all girly and ladylike on us. If you're doing the femme thing I thought maybe it was because you'd got a real butch girlfriend."

"Oh yes she's really butch Jess. Works out all the time, never wears anything but trousers, got tattoos all over, drinks beer straight from the can, goes to football training three times a week and cracks walnuts in her eyelids." Daniela assumed an expression of outrage and made threatening gestures with a fondue fork. "Now I'm *really* going to have to go Jess."

"Ok kid. Talk to you later. Love you!"

"Love you too Jess."

Sarah put her phone away sadly. Daniela rapped a finger on the table. "How dare you tell your sister that I'm really butch Sarah Fuchs?"

Sarah giggled. She couldn't imagine anyone less butch than Daniela. "Relax Danny. Just smokescreen that's all. It sounds like my family are all jumping to erroneous conclusions about you anyway. It won't hurt if they're all pointed in the wrong direction. I suppose you're the last sort of person they'd be looking for as my girlfriend."

Daniela rubbed her chin thoughtfully. "I can't for the life of me decide whether that's an insult or not."

"It's not Danny. I know what my parents will be thinking. They'll be thinking that I've fallen under the control of some horrible butch lesbian who just has designs on my body. It just won't occur to them that my girlfriend is in reality a beautiful, kind, warm hearted woman."

Daniela nodded uncertainly. "Ok Sarah but you ought to be careful filing people into boxes you know. There are lots of butch lesbians who are not predatory skirt hunters you know. Being butch doesn't preclude them from being kind, considerate and loving people."

"I know that Danny. Or at least I can deduce it from my limited experience. Charmaine is quite butch and she's a sweetheart. I'm not expressing my opinion just what my parents will think. They think all lesbians are some sort of macho pseudo males who dress like men, have deep voices and have to shave. My sister's a little more enlightened but even she buys into the idea that there are two sorts of lesbians; butch ones and feminine ones and that butch ones go out with the girly ones as if it was some mirror image of a heterosexual relationship."

"Well I can understand where she gets the idea from Sarah but it's kind of an old fashioned notion nowadays. That was the kind of stereotype that existed among gay women back in the post war years up to around nineteen seventy. That was an age when male and female roles were pretty strictly defined even for straight people and the gay subculture just mirrored it. Back in those days a gay woman had to be either a butch or a femme and those women who refused to assume one role or the other were ostracised in the gay community. Butch girls dating other butches or femmes dating femmes was

325

taboo almost as if they were well... gay or something. Since the nineteen seventies however there's been a lot of change. There was even somewhat of a backlash against the idea of butch and femme roles. It was really just a reflection of the way sexual roles were losing their definition in society as a whole. The gay woman's movement became inextricably linked with the feminist movement and the old idea of butch and femme was seen as merely the propagation of the male dominated patriarchal society that feminism so abhorred. These days I think we have a somewhat healthier model whereby there isn't so much focus on gender identity whether you are straight or gay."

Sarah sighed. "God I feel so ignorant sometimes. Here I am... gay and I know hardly anything about it."

"Maybe that's not such a bad thing Sarah. Perhaps we'll have really crossed the Rubicon when a person's sexual preferences and activities no longer define their identity at all. Now I'm considered gay... I'm openly out... I have large gay following and yet I've never been completely comfortable with the label. Being gay is not who I am. I am the person I am. Strictly speaking you could describe me as bisexual if you wanted. After all I've had relationships with men; I even have a child through heterosexual sex. Nevertheless I am in love with a woman... you."

"I suppose that makes me bisexual as well then Danny."

"Not at all. Why should it make you assume any label at all? Why should anybody have to stand up and define their identity with their sexuality? This is one of the reasons that gay people have such a hard time with bisexuals. Oddly enough there is considerable prejudice against bisexuality within the gay community. I mean standing out and declaring that you're gay is such a life defining moment under present conditions that it's almost as if you draw a line in the sand; this is who I am and this is the way I'll always be. Bisexuality doesn't fit neatly into that. There's a sort of suspicion that bisexuals are people that refuse to be drawn into one thing or another. I say you can't have it both ways... no pun intended. I mean it has been a foundation of gay principle for many years that homosexuality is not a choice; you're just made that way. Now if you insist that your homosexuality is something over which you have no choice about then you can hardly berate the bisexual for not being able to make up their mind about what side of the fence they belong on. Actually I rather suspect that bisexuality is far more common than is normally credited if you assume that occasional attraction for or dalliance with some person outside of your usual sexual identity is assumed to be bisexual. I wonder just how many otherwise heterosexual people have had homosexual experiences or for that matter how many gay people have had heterosexual experiences. I know people prefer to put people into categories; straight or gay but I don't think it's necessarily that simple. There's an awful lot of room for interpretation between those two poles isn't there?"

Sarah nodded thoughtfully. "You know Nicole once argued much the same thing with me."

Daniela glimpsed up at Nicole who was in conversation with Simon and Peter. "I should think it's a subject close to her heart Sarah. After all she's been actively heterosexual all her life. Yet you and I both know that she's in love with you. How does Nicole deal with that seeming contradiction? Now the radically gay viewpoint would say that she's really gay and just hasn't come out and admitted it yet. But what if she really does like boys? Does that conflict with what she feels about you?"

"So you're saying that Nicky is bisexual?"

"I'm saying nothing of the sort. I'm saying that Nicky is Nicky and quite unique and that we shouldn't be trying to put *any* sort of label on her. Every human being is a unique individual and what they feel, do, desire or how they conduct them self is unique to them. Every human mind is such a complex tapestry of so many factors that it's impossible to place it in a simple category. I don't try to split the world into people who take sugar in their tea and those who don't. I don't think there are just people who either adore old Abba songs and those who despise them; most people would be somewhere in the middle. The trouble is that we've politicised our sexuality; drawn up dividing lines. Declaring yourself gay has become a political act; a statement of group identity; a declaration of affinity to that group. That's understandable of course. In previous times there was such antipathy towards homosexuality that gay people naturally gravitated toward each other for mutual support and acceptance. It's sad it had to be that way though. The day we finally come to a situation where we can simply accept every person as simply a person irrespective of whom they fall in love with then maybe we can close the book on this one."

"I think my parents are going to need a fair bit of time to come to that stage Danny."

"Are they really having a hard time with it Sarah?"

Sarah nodded. "Yes! According to Jessica my name was officially unmentionable at dinner in my parents' household tonight."

"I'm so sorry Sarah. Maybe they just need some time to come to terms with it."

"I think they're considering more direct action than that Danny."

"What do you mean?"

"Jessica says that my dad is coming up here in the next few days to talk to me. She says he probably wants to confront you too."

"Is this bad?"

"Yes Danny. He won't be coming in a reconciliatory mood. He's not arriving in a mood of forgiveness and tolerance Danny. Jessica says he's on a mission; a mission to "rescue" me. He's got his dander up by the sounds of things."

"Perhaps it would help if we did talk to him Sarah. Perhaps we could make him see that it's not something terrible after all."

Sarah shook her head vigorously. "No Danny. You've no idea how determined my father can be when he's on one of his crusades. I... I don't want to talk to him. I said everything I needed to say in that letter. I'm not going to sit there and be told off like a naughty little girl and I'm not going to have him talking down his nose to you. I've said what had to be said Danny and if he can't accept that then that's an end to it. My love for you is no longer open to negotiation."

"You're going to have to speak to him sometime Sarah."

"Possibly Danny. But if I do it'll be on my terms, and I'll decide when and where I do it. I'm through with jumping through hoops at my parents' commands. He thinks he can just demand my attendance on him when he comes up and expect me to obey him. Well that's not going to happen anymore. These last few days I saw how close to disaster I came just by bending continuously to my parents' will. Now it ends. *I'll* decide when and under what conditions I'm prepared to discuss the matter further with him."

"So what are you going to do if he just turns up unannounced and demands an audience with you?"

"I... I don't know. Maybe I'll bugger off into the mountains for a few days."

"Maybe we could both go somewhere together Sarah."

"I... I'd like that. Could you do it though? I mean have you got some free time?"

"Sure. I've nothing I can't put off for a couple of weeks. Actually I've been wanting to take you on a little holiday somewhere. This sounds like a perfect excuse."

"Where were you thinking of?"

329

"Ah now that's a surprise. I wanted to take you somewhere special. You've shown me places that are special to you so I wanted to show you a place that's special to me. Would you be up for it?"

"Oh yes!"

"Well give me tomorrow to sort things out and then we'll have a few days to ourselves; just you and me and nothing in the world to care about but each other."

"It sounds heavenly!"

Daniela laughed and leaned over to kiss her. "I think we need a break from all this drama sweetheart. Let's just make some time for love!" She looked up as Magdalena staggered out of the kitchen under the weight of an enormous iron fondue pot filled with bubbling melted cheese. "Hah! Food at last."

The meal was a merry one. Cheese fondue is one of those collective meals designed for companionship and camaraderie. They skewered pieces of bread on their fondue forks, swirled them in the fondue to cover them with rich cheese, seasoned the delicious morsels with a sprinkling of black pepper and washed the whole down with a dry white wine. Frau Elke pushed the party along by insisting that anybody losing their bread in the fondue had to pay a penance by downing a glass of schnapps and also by occasionally enhancing the flavour of the fondue by dropping a shot into the pot.

Sarah, amid the comradeship of her friends, the presence of Daniela and the prospect of an adventure with her, felt suddenly and wondrously happy. The dark depression that had accompanied her on the train on the way home was banished to a nether realm, distant and remote. She laughed at Nicole who was proving to be incompetent at keeping a piece of bread on her fork and was getting steadily tipsier as the night progressed. Simon entertained them with hilarious stories about his own coming out and Peter pompously got to his feet to make a speech welcoming Sarah home and proposing a toast. His speech was somewhat spoiled by the fact that he kept muddling his words up, hiccupping and was continually interrupted by Simon's gentle mocking. The effort seemed to exhaust him for he collapsed back in his chair clutching his glass dazedly and regarding the company with a benign hazy expression on his face. Elke's speech was little better because Angelica kept flicking pieces of bread from her fondue fork at her and the solemnity descended into an unseemly wrestling match between the two women.

At last the party broke up and they made their ways to the car park. Nicole was hanging on Sarah looking bleary and getting maudlin. "I... I love you Sarah." she kept repeating. "I'm so glad you came home. I love you... I..." Nicole hiccupped and stumbled. "Don't go away again Sarah. I love you."

"I love you too you barmy drunken bitch. Now for God's sake get in the car."

Simon laughed. "Come on Nicky I'll help you." Simon had been careful with his alcoholic intake and he was the designated driver.

"But... but I love Sarah." Nicole slurred.

"Yes we know Nicky." Simon told her. "We all do. Now come on and let me help you into the car."

Sarah kissed her with a laugh. "Make sure she gets home alright Simon. She's absolutely bladdered."

With Nicole safely into the back seat, where she promptly fell asleep, Simon and Peter took their leave by kissing the rest of the company and driving away. Elke looked at Daniela. "Are you all right to drive Danny?" she asked concernedly.

"I'll be fine Elke. I haven't had that much to drink and we've only a short distance to go."

"Well you be careful you hear and be careful with that girl of yours. Don't let her out of your sight again."

"Oh I won't." Daniela wrapped an arm around Sarah's waist. "She's stuck with me now."

Sarah smiled sheepishly. "Elke, Angelica, thank you for tonight. I can't tell you how much it means to me."

331

"We're just so happy that you're back Sarah. This valley wouldn't be the same again if you'd left us."

They parted with sweet kisses and Daniela drove slowly back to the house at Oberdorf with Sarah's head resting on her shoulder. They parked the car and carried Sarah's bags to the front door. Daniela opened the door and turned to Sarah. Sarah regarded her in puzzlement. "Aren't we going in?" Daniela grasped her firmly and lifted her. "Eek! What are you doing? Put me down! You'll drop me!"

Daniela laughed, kicked open the door and heaved Sarah bodily through before they collapsed in a giggling heap on the carpet. Daniela took hold of her and kissed her hungrily. "Welcome home my darling."

Chapter Thirty

Sarah woke alone in Daniela's big bed. She took a few moments to luxuriate in the folds of the great soft covers and pillows and stretched languorously. The bed was the most comfortable she had ever slept in. It was like a cocoon of safety and gentleness; the satin sheets and covers like a caress against your skin and scented vaguely with Daniela's perfume. She almost purred with pleasure like a kitten and rubbed her cheek against the pillows. All that was missing was the warm presence of Daniela's body alongside her. As she slowly woke she felt disappointed by that. She wanted Daniela's touch. Slightly puzzled by Daniela's absence she sat up and rubbed her eyes before glancing around the room. They'd come home on fire for each other. Sarah's bags were still unpacked. Their clothes were scattered randomly around the room. Sarah recognised her underwear lying on the floor.

Where was Daniela? The bedroom door was open and one of Daniela's cats had taken advantage of the opportunity afforded and was curled up on the end of the bed. Sarah leaned forward to stroke it and was rewarded with a deep purr of contentment. She listened carefully but the house seemed quiet. Daniela must be up and about however for she could smell fresh brewed coffee. Sarah slipped out of the bedclothes. She was quite naked. One of Daniela's silk dressing gowns was hanging on the wardrobe door so she slipped it around herself and stepped out of the bedroom to look for Daniela.

She found her in the living room with a laptop on her knee and a telephone at her side. She was looking pleased with herself. "Hi little Miss Sleepy Head." she greeted Sarah with a kiss. "Have you any idea what time it is?"

"Er no."

"Nearly eleven o'clock."

"You're joking. Why didn't you wake me up?"

"You looked so peaceful and cosy asleep I couldn't bear to wake you."

"God I slept like a baby. Is there any more of that coffee?" Sarah nodded at Daniela's cup.

"Sure in the pot in the kitchen. The delivery man was here earlier as well so there're fresh rolls and croissants as well."

"After all that fondue yesterday, I could do to go on a diet."

"Nonsense! We can eat in the garden if you want. It's turned out to be a lovely day. Sarah looked out of the window. It was true. The weather seemed to have smiled on her return to the Toggenburg for the garden was wreathed in sunshine."

Sarah nodded at the computer screen. "What's all this about? Business?"

Daniela closed the laptop lid firmly with a grin. "Don't be nosy."

"Oh I'm sorry. I didn't know it was something private."

"It isn't something private. I've just been organising our little holiday is all and it's a surprise."

"Organising?"

"Yes I've been up for three hours. I've been busy."

"It takes you that long to organise a few days away?"

"Well it was complicated. I thought I'd done it pretty quickly."

"Where the hell are we going?"

"Never you mind. You'll find out."

"You've got to give me some sort of clue so I know what to pack Danny."

"Ok you'll need some nice clothes and some sexy underwear because I intend to spend quite a lot of time tearing them off you. Otherwise pack a few old clothes as well and some old trainers."

"Why the old clothes?"

"Well because it's an area of natural beauty and doubtless you'll want to go grubbing about in the wild and get your knees dirty. Pack your binoculars as well and maybe some of your natural history guides. Don't go too mad though. We've only got limited baggage space." Sarah nodded at the wisdom of that. Daniela's Ferrari wasn't exactly roomy in the luggage compartment. "Oh yes.." said Daniela as an afterthought. "You'll need your passport as well."

"My passport? Are we crossing the border?"

"Yes. We probably won't need our passports but it'll be safer to carry them just in case."

"Is it far?"

"It's no good fishing for information Sarah. That's all you're getting out of me. You can bring a couple of bikinis if you like."

"Will it be warm?"

"It might be."

"Oh God I've only got one bikini and Nicole bullied me into buying *that* only this summer."

"Oh Sarah! You're just precious."

"Do I really need to bring it? I mean it's bloody tiny. It wouldn't cover a midget with any decency."

"In that case, I insist that you bring it."

"I'll have to go home to pick up my things Danny."

"Let's get our terminology right Sarah. *This* is your home. What you mean is that you have to go back to your old digs to pick up your things."

"But this is your house Danny."

"No Sarah. It's *our* house. As soon as we get back from holiday we'll start to get all your stuff up here and start making this into our own nest. We've already crossed this line Sarah. We love together, we live together. You're not going to start having second thoughts are you?"

"No Danny. I'm sorry. I'm just in readjustment stage."

"Good girl. Now we'll get something to eat and this afternoon we'll go over to the Alpli and pick up your things to go away with. After that I thought we'd have a quiet evening in and an early night. We don't want a late night tonight. We're on the road at eight sharp in the morning!"

"So early?"

"Hey, it's later than when we went up the Santis. What are you bitching about? You've had a long lie in today."

"Ok ma-am. I'll just jump in the shower. You go grab that coffee pot and some nibbles for breakfast."

They ate in the garden, thankful that the wretched weather of the last few days in the north had broken. It was a glorious day of sparkling sunshine lancing between great banks of cumulus clouds; the big fluffy kind that cartoonists liked to depict angels sitting on playing harps. Sarah had read once that, in the earliest popular register of cloud types, cumulus clouds were the ninth entry on the list and hence, with their heavenly associations of paradise, the expression "to be on cloud nine" had entered the English language as a metaphor for happiness. They were apt accompaniments to the pleasure of this day.

Daniela buttered a roll and helped herself to a slice of ham. "Guess who phoned up this morning while you were idling your life away in bed."

"I've no idea. Who?"

"Rozella no less. She wanted to know if you got home all right."

"Oh God I said I'd phone her once I was on the train home. I forgot all about it."

"Well I reassured her. She seems quite taken by you Sarah."

Sarah blushed. "I'm just another piece of skirt to Rozella."

"You weren't wearing a skirt as I recall."

"What did you say to her?"

"Oh I just thanked her for her concern, for making sure you got on that train yesterday and told her that if she comes sniffing around my girlfriend again I'll take her 500mm telephoto lens and stuff it up her arse for her."

"You didn't."

Daniela laughed. "Relax darling. Rozella and I are old friends."

"I'd better phone her up Danny. I did promise to call her."

"Is your phone switched on honey?"

Sarah shook her head ashamedly. "No. I daren't look what's on it. Doubtless there are reams of bloody messages from the Ticino."

"Well you'd better clear the decks before we do a runner sweetheart."

"I know."

"Are you going to phone Nicole?"

"Yes I'd better tell her that I'm picking up some things this afternoon and that I'm taking off for a few days. I'll have to brief her on a cover story too because my parents will doubtless be trying to get hold of me back at the house. God knows what state Nicky is in this morning though. She was absolutely plastered last night."

"I thought she was quite sweet. More coffee?"

"No thanks. I'd better switch my phone back on and give Nicole a call."

Nicole was still in bed and evidently suffering for Sarah managed only to coax mumbled and uncooperative responses out of her. Eventually Sarah extracted a reluctant promise that Nicole would be up and about and fit to receive visitors sometime after two o'clock which was the earliest she was prepared to commit her hangover recovery time to. At least Nicole had the day free from work, not being required at the hotel until the evening.

After breaking the connection Sarah took a look at her message inbox. It was, as she had suspected, full of communications jostling for her attention. Prominent among them were messages from her father. These amounted for the most part to simple demands that she get in touch with him and contained little of any substance otherwise. Interestingly there were no messages from her mother. One curiosity was a message from her brother. This was unusual, for her brother rarely called unsolicited. Again it was a request for her to get in touch. Her brother did however include the information that he was engaged to be married. Sarah felt strangely moved by John's message. It seemed to be a token of support from her brother and such tokens meant a great deal to her for the moment. She determined to call him but thought it best to wait a day or two until he was back in Appenzell and no longer at her parents' house. There were also messages from both Peter and Nicole but they were dated from the day before and thus obsolete. The most curious message of all read "**Hi How R U Fancy a drink together sometime Give me a call**" The message bore Charmaine's name. Sarah had even forgotten exchanging telephone numbers with her. She mentioned this message to Daniela who raised an eyebrow and sniffed haughtily. "Hmmph! Another of you girlfriends huh? I can't keep up with them all."

Sarah threw a half eaten bread roll at her. "Should I call her do you think?" she asked.

"Sure. Why not? Always keep your options open in case you manage to slip the leash in Winterthur one day. Always keep a harem on standby in reserve." Daniela bent down to stroke Lady Gaga who was rubbing herself against her leg and purring loudly.

"Oh what are we going to do about the cats?" Sarah asked.

"No problem there. We'll call at Elrika's in Oberdorf when we drive over to the Alpli."

"Elrika?"

338

"My cleaning lady. She always looks after the cats when I'm away."

"Oh I see. Does she mind?"

"Of course not. I pay her well enough. She'd probably do it for nothing though. She's a sweetheart and she loves cats. She always protests that I pay her too much. She's an old widow and I don't think she's got much money so I make sure she has enough for her needs."

"Oh I think I might know her."

"I'd consider that overwhelmingly likely. You know just about everyone else in this valley. Certainly she knows you."

"Is her married name Frau Handelmeyer?"

"That's the lady."

"She isn't that old surely Danny. She can't be much over sixty."

"She's seventy two Sarah. She's sprightly for her age though."

"It's good she has some work with you Danny. I know her husband died young and left her with nothing. She can certainly do with the money."

"One of the best things about being rich Sarah is that it affords you the means to extend a little human kindness. Of course being poor doesn't preclude you from generosity but it does limit the amount of assistance you are able to render. Elrika's a lovely lady and trying to eke out her old age on a pittance of a pension. I give her a job well within her capabilities and make sure she earns enough to afford a few luxuries. Actually I'd pay her more if I wasn't concerned about hurting her pride. She's been pretty much essential to me. I have to spend a good deal of time away from home and I can leave my house and my cats under her care without any worries at all."

"Oh will it undermine her position if I move in?"

"Not in the slightest. We might have to invent a few more fictions to justify keeping her on the payroll of course but I'll not see her go without. It's the same with old Hans-ruedi. He's my gardener and handyman. He's a bloody genius around the place. There's nothing he can't fix. He's well into his seventies as well but I'd ten times rather employ him to look after the place than hire professionals." Daniela laughed warmly. "Actually there's a funny story there Sarah. Hans-ruedi's a bit sweet on Elrika but doesn't have the bottle to tell her so. I've caught him pinching flowers out of the garden for Elrika's cottage. I've turned a blind eye to it though. Apparently he's known Elrika since they were kids and always had a thing about her. I think they'd be perfect for each other but Hans-ruedi isn't exactly your original dynamic passionate lover to sweep a girl up off her feet. He's been wooing her in a sort of half-hearted fashion since her husband died about ten years ago apparently. He's confidently expected to pop the question some time over the next decade."

Sarah laughed, charmed by the image of Hans-ruedi's tentative steps into the perilous realms of love. "Maybe it just needs a little pushing along Danny. Do you fancy yourself as a matchmaker?"

"Oh I don't think Elrika would put up that much resistance but she can be a bit impatient with him. No amount of hinting seems to make the slightest difference. He's painfully awkward when she's around. I think if Cupid's arrow is going to hit its mark she'll probably have to drag him bodily into her cottage."

"Poor old Hans-ruedi. I know him as well. His wife left him a long time ago I believe."

"Yes nearly twenty years ago by all accounts. He's lived on his own ever since." Daniela stretched. "Anyway enough gossip. We've got things to do and people to see. Let's clear up these things and get the show on the road!"

For the next few minutes they busied themselves clearing the table and washing the dishes. Dish washing was hardly an onerous chore in Daniela's house. She had an automatic dishwasher and the only work necessary was to stack the dirty plates and cups in the racks and close the door. "I've never seen the point in expending useful energy on tedious household labour when there's an easier alternative." She explained to Sarah.

"That just sounds like a justification for laziness." Sarah told her as she replaced the bread in the bread bin.

Daniela grinned and pinched Sarah's bottom. "Hell if I was that lazy I'd just employ a cute little housemaid with a frilly pinafore to do everything for me."

"Forget it madam. I refuse point blank to dress up in a silly French maid's outfit just for your amusement."

"Meany! You've just punctured one of my favourite sexual fantasies."

Sarah was about to respond when her telephone chimed. She had laid her mobile phone on the kitchen top when they'd come in from the garden and she spun around now to stare at it hesitantly. Daniela raised an eyebrow. "Aren't you going to see who it is?"

Sarah swallowed and picked the offending object up. "Oh shit! It's my dad."

"You're going to have to talk to him sooner or later Sarah."

Sarah shrugged her shoulders helplessly. "I suppose so." Taking a deep breath she fingered the connecting button and held the phone to her ear. "Hello?"

"Ah! At last. I've been trying to phone you all morning. Are you deliberately avoiding me Sarah? I am very disappointed Sarah..."

"I'm fine thank you daddy."

"I beg your pardon."

"I said I'm fine thank you daddy. Thank you for asking."

"What is this nonsense now?"

"No nonsense daddy. I just assumed that you were concerned for my well-being and were desirous of reassurance on the subject."

"Are you being deliberately obtuse Sarah?"

"No father. You told me that you've been attempting to call me all morning and therefore I presumed it was because you were concerned about me."

"Well of course I'm concerned about you."

"Well thank you for your concern father. However let me put your mind at rest and reiterate that I am just fine. I was somewhat upset yesterday but after a good night's sleep I'm in a much better humour today. I trust that both you and mother are well."

"You may trust to nothing of the sort. Your mother and I are deeply disappointed and hurt Sarah. I can't imagine what has come over you. You have seriously offended Alan and your mother is devastated. I think you owe everybody a serious explanation."

"Forgive me but I thought I explained everything in the letter I wrote father."

"You can't possibly expect us to take that wretched document seriously."

"Actually father I do. I wrote that letter in all seriousness after a great deal of thought and soul searching. If you are unable to take it seriously then I see little point in continuing this conversation."

"If you had anything to say Sarah you could have said it to our faces. That way we might have sat down and talked rationally to find a solution."

"A solution? What the hell are you talking about father? Do you think that this is something negotiable? Do you think I'm bargaining with my life? Do you even understand what I said to you in that letter? There isn't any "solution" to this daddy. As to talking to your faces, I spent three days trying to talk to you but you weren't listening. You went right ahead and sold me off to the Bergers against my wishes. That's what talking to your faces brought me. That's why I wrote that letter and left father. I was taking back my life."

"Listen Sarah...."

"No you damn well listen for a change. Have you any idea how difficult it was for me to write you that

342

letter? Have you the slightest notion how much heartache and pain it cost me? I understand that it may have upset you but how do you think I felt? It was the most difficult thing I've ever done in my life and you can't take it seriously."

"How could we possibly do so? Your mother and I never brought you up like this."

"You brought me up to be *honest* father! In that letter I was completely honest but now you are disappointed in me. Presumably you would have preferred me to continue lying. You would have preferred me to lie about my feelings and marry a man I didn't love and never could. You would have preferred me to continue lying so that you could finalise your business transaction and sell me to the highest bidder. Everything I had to say was meaningless to you in the light of that goal. My feelings and considerations were an irrelevancy weren't they? Just so long as you and Herr Berger could shake hands over the deal then what I wanted didn't matter a fig. Since you wouldn't listen to me I was forced to take my life into my own hands. If that "disappoints" you then I'm sorry but it is no longer open to discussion."

"That is unfair Sarah. We wanted nothing other than the very best for you. We have gone to enormous trouble to ensure your future happiness and prosperity and you have thrown it back in our faces with contempt. If you had had some concerns about anything then we could have sat down and ironed the problems out without this display of petulant histrionics. As it is I don't know how we're going to repair all the damage that you've done. Yes I raised you to be honest but by that I meant that you would be able to voice your concerns rationally and maturely and not throw a tantrum and run away just because you thought you weren't getting your own way. I don't know how you could be so selfish Sarah. Your mother is heartbroken."

343

Sarah gripped her forehead desperately. "Father I expressed more in that letter than just a few "concerns" about my bloody marriage."

"I don't think we need to discuss the other wild notions at this point Sarah."

"Don't you? Well then in that case I see no earthly reason why we are talking at all."

"We're talking because we need to sort this out Sarah."

"I think you need to go back and read the letter again daddy. It is quite obvious that you haven't taken a single word of it on board. Go back and read the letter. Once you have absorbed the content then perhaps we can talk."

"I am fully cognisant of the contents of your letter Sarah."

"Then why the blazes can't you understand it? I realise that it possibly wasn't the most lucid and or diplomatic letters I could have written. I wrote it hastily under some considerable pressure but nevertheless I believe I covered all the salient issues concisely. I am *gay* father."

"Sarah stop it now I..."

"I am gay, lesbian, homosexual, queer, a dyke, call it what you will. I am not going to marry Alan. In fact I am not going to marry *any* man because I am gay. Now until you can get your head around that there is no point in discussing the matter further. This is not a bargaining position. I am gay and I am in a relationship with a woman I happen to love. I would have hoped for some support and understanding from my family but clearly that is not the case. Nevertheless I cannot change who I am or how I feel. If you believe that my expressing such a difficult confession to you, a confession that afforded me such pain and heartbreak is merely me throwing a tantrum then this discussion is at an end."

"Like hell it is Sarah."

"What else is there to talk about?"

344

"Well clearly nothing sensible in your present mood. Nevertheless talk we must. We, your mother and I that is, are coming up to the Toggenburg Sarah. I'm not happy about that. I'm a busy man and I can ill afford to have to take the time to drive up to the Toggenburg when if you'd stayed here we could have talked at our leisure. Nevertheless it seems I have no option and I am prepared to go the extra mile to sort this out for once and for all."

"Please don't put yourself to any trouble father."

Sarah's sarcasm was wasted it seemed. "I am prepared to go to a good deal of trouble Sarah. I will not stand by and watch this ridiculous spat destroy my family. We'll be in the Toggenburg the day after tomorrow. In the meantime I want you to consider your position very carefully and rationally. I want us all to be able to sit down and discuss this matter calmly and without dramatics."

"And just where is this pivotal conference supposed to take place father?"

"Why at your house of course. I don't think this is a matter we should discuss in a public place do you?"

"I see. So is my girlfriend invited to this discussion?"

"Don't be ridiculous Sarah. This is a family matter. You can hardly expect your mother and I to meet this woman in a family capacity. If there is some problem with this woman you are seeing then perhaps I can meet her privately at some future date to come to an arrangement with her."

"I don't believe I'm hearing this. Are you saying that you'll buy her off? I think you'll find she's a pretty difficult person to buy father."

"I'm saying nothing of the sort. All I mean is that we might have to make some sort of agreement or accommodation with her but that will depend on the discussion we have the day after tomorrow."

345

"I'm afraid you won't be able to exclude her from that discussion father."

"I don't see why not Sarah. This is a private matter within the family. I consider that it is none of her business."

"In my house?"

"Well yes."

"Father let me put this on the line for you. I no longer live in the house at Alpli."

"What do you mean?"

"I mean father that I now share a house with my girlfriend. I am talking from that house right now. This is *her* house. If you wish to pay a visit to talk to me then you will have to do so under *her* roof and therefore she has every right to insist that she be privy to any such conversation. Furthermore she has every right to be party to any conversation that affects our relationship. If you come to the Toggenburg you will have to come to our house and that means you will have to talk to both of us. You cannot in courtesy expect her not to be present at any discussion regarding her relationship to me conducted within the walls of her own home."

"I don't believe this. Are you saying that you are living with this woman?"

"I would prefer it if you could find some other form of address other than "this woman" whilst referring to the person I love but yes, those are the salient facts."

"Oh good God Sarah! You can't be serious."

"Oh but I am serious father. I am so serious in fact that I have moved in with my girlfriend; so serious that I want to share my life with her."

"Only a few days ago you wanted to share your life with Alan."

"No father. You wanted that; not me."

Sarah could hear her father taking several deep breaths on the other end of the line. Finally he mastered himself. "Well we'll just have to meet in some neutral place after all."

"I'm sorry father but that is not going to happen."

"What?"

"For one thing father I'm not prepared to talk about my girlfriend with you in her absence and secondly I'm afraid that the day after tomorrow will not be convenient in any case."

"I beg your pardon."

"I said it won't be convenient. I won't be here. We are going away for a few days. This has been a very stressful few days for both of us and we've decided that we need some time to ourselves to take stock and relax."

"You can't do that Sarah. I forbid it."

"I'm over twenty one father. You have no right to forbid my movements. I went to considerable trouble to attend upon you in Ticino but now I'm afraid I'm through jumping through hoops at your command. If you wish to arrange a meeting with myself and my girlfriend at some future time then we will out of courtesy try to accommodate some date that is convenient to all parties concerned. I am no longer, however, at your beck and call and I'm damned if I'm going to postpone the holiday that my girlfriend has arranged at such trouble just to listen to you and mum lecturing me on my moral reprehensibility."

"Where the devil are you going?"

"I have no idea. It's a surprise."

"I demand to know Sarah."

"Haven't you got this yet father? You can't *demand* anything. I don't know where we are going and in any case it's not your business. Now if you don't mind I have things to attend to."

"We are not finished young lady!"

"As far as I'm concerned we are father. I see no point in protracting this. I am gay and I'm happily living with a wonderful woman that I love. Now either accept that or get out of my life!"

"Sarah wait..."

"Goodbye father!" Sarah thumbed the button to disconnect the phone and threw the apparatus onto the kitchen top before collapsing onto a chair at the kitchen table, burying her face in her hands and bursting into tears.

Daniela dashed across the kitchen and grasped her tightly. "Oh Sarah! Don't cry my love."

"They're never going to accept it Danny." Sarah sobbed. "Never! Oh God! I didn't want this to happen. I love them Danny. I really do. Why can't they just accept it? It's not as if I can help what I am."

"It's always hard for parents to accept that their children are gay Sarah. They'll remember that they love you in the end and that that is far more important in the long run."

"I've never disobeyed my dad before Danny. Oh God! I feel like I just tore my family apart."

"You haven't sweetheart. Hush now. It'll be all right." Daniela stroked Sarah's hair fondly. "Look we don't have to go on this trip if you don't want. If you like we'll arrange to meet your parents and talk to them. Maybe if we meet them they'll see that I'm not such a horrible person after all and come around to accepting our relationship."

Sarah shook her head vigorously. "No Danny! I want to go away. I want to spend a few days with you and you alone. My parents can be rotten to me but I'm not going to have them be rotten to you."

"I'm a big girl Sarah. I can look after myself."

"No Danny. I know you can look after yourself but I don't want us to have to start out just pandering to my parents' wishes. If we ever get to meet them together then we'll meet them on our own terms, when and where it's convenient for us. They've got to accept that I have my own life now; that *we* have our own life and that it's not conditional on their approval or otherwise. If we let them dictate terms then we'll never be free. We're going on holiday and that's an end to it." Sarah sniffled and managed a watery smile. "Anyway I'm looking forward to it. I just want to be alone with you and the devil with the rest of the world."

"That's my girl. Come on dry your eyes now. We're through here so let's jump in the car and drive over to Alpli to pick your things up. We'll treat ourselves to a big slab of Apfelstrudel with custard at Elke's on the way back."

Chapter Thirty-One

Considering her level of intoxication the previous day, they discovered that Nicole wasn't in too bad a shape. She was pottering around the house half-heartedly. Sarah observed that the house was in need a good tidying up and it was all she could do to prevent herself for admonishing Nicole for letting the place get into such a mess. She bit her lip instead. She didn't live here anymore. It was hard to let go however. Nicole suggested a cup of coffee and Sarah very nearly jumped up to make it. It was odd to be a guest in your own home.

Once they were settled with a cup of coffee at the kitchen table Sarah approached Nicole tentatively. "Has my dad phoned up this morning Nicky?"

"I've no idea."

"What do you mean?"

"I mean the phone's off the hook. I sort of retained enough sense last night to realise that there'd probably be a thunderstorm breaking out in Ticino and I was liable to be receiving the lightning bolts over the phone at some point during the day. I didn't fancy having to deal with your parents in full flow so I disconnected the phone. Fortunately they don't have my mobile number."

"Oh God no wonder my dad thought I was avoiding him. My mobile was switched off too."

Nicole pulled a face. "I can't keep the bloody phone out of commission indefinitely though Foxy. What am I supposed to tell your parents when they finally do get through?"

"I don't think it will be too much of a problem Nicky. I told my father earlier that I didn't live here anymore. He's under the impression that I've moved out. I suggest we stick to that story. If he calls you just tell him that I'm no longer in residence here and that you

350

don't know the number of my new house. If he wants to call me he'll have to use my mobile number."

"What if he wants to know the identity of Danny here or her address?"

"Tell him to mind his own business. If he asks, tell him that I have only told you in confidence and you are obliged to respect that confidentiality. If he really wants to know he can ask me. Actually he doesn't seem too interested at the moment. He just assumes that my girlfriend is some horrible woman that's stolen his precious bloody daughter. I don't think he cares who she is."

Nicole snorted theatrically. "That'll soon bloody change when he comes across a photo of the pair of you in the gossip columns in the Blick."

"We'll cross that bridge when we come to it."

"We may have to cross it earlier than you think Sarah." Daniela pointed out. "We're going on holiday tomorrow. The chances are pretty fair that we'll run across some paparazzi at some point. I mean where we're going is pretty secluded but we still have to appear in public to get there."

Nicole blinked. "What's all this about?"

Sarah answered. "Oh Danny and I are going away for a few days Nicky. I was just coming here to pick up a few things really. Can you hold the fort whilst I'm away and field any inquiries as to my whereabouts in the meantime."

"Sure. Where are you going?"

Sarah glowered at Daniela. "She won't tell me."

"Nowhere exotic Nicky." Daniela told her. "Just somewhere a bit quiet where we can regroup and chill out for a few days."

"Ok so I take it the official line is that you're at a secret location and don't wish to be disturbed."

Sarah nodded. "Yes. That sounds about right."

"Ok cool. Leave it with me." Nicole paused. "Why are you looking at me like that Danny?"

"I was just thinking what a pretty girl you are Nicole."

"Eh?" Nicole took a double take.

"I'm sorry Nicky I wasn't trying to be familiar. It's just that it brought to mind a conversation I was having over the phone this morning."

Nicole frowned uncertainly. "Er what kind of conversation?"

"Oh with an old friend of mine. She's a photographer; my photographer for my album covers and publicity shoots. Sarah met her when she was in Ticino didn't you Sarah?"

Sarah's face had assumed a mask like expression. "Oh er yes. Yes I did meet her briefly."

Nicole looked puzzled. "Well what's this got to do with me?"

"Well this friend of mine was asking if I knew any pretty girls who might be interested in making a little money on the side doing a bit of part time modelling. I think she's on some project photographing a representative collection of natural Swiss girls so she's looking for amateurs rather than full professionals. Of course she insists that she'll pay competitive rates. Anyway, looking at you, it occurred to me that you might just be the kind of girl she's looking for. Should I mention your name? It might be a chance to earn a little extra pocket money."

Nicole looked interested if a little uncertain. "Er what kind of photos?"

"I don't really know Nicole. You'd have to discuss that with her. I think they might be a little on the saucy side but I don't think they'd be offensive. She's very professional and she's a very talented photographer."

"She's the person that did your album covers?"

"Yes. I use her all the time."

"The photos on your albums are fantastic."

"Well as I said she's very talented."

Nicole bit her lip. "But you weren't wearing a stitch on your last cover shot."

Daniela laughed. "Yes I know. I was a bit embarrassed about that but she put me at my ease and I think the photos came out really well. Mind you I was bloody nithered. The water in that waterfall was sodding freezing."

Nicole scratched her head hesitantly. "You think she might want to do that sort of photo?"

"Possibly. I don't know. I'm sure they would be very artistic and flattering. She doesn't do pornography. Certainly you've got the figure for it as long as you're not too shy."

Nicole grinned. "That's one of my lesser faults. Anyway, if she's looking for pretty girls from Switzerland, why doesn't she photograph Sarah? Sarah would be sensational."

Daniela glanced at Sarah who was having a hard time keeping a straight face at Daniela's audacity. "Well, to be truthful Nicky, Sarah was the first person this lady enquired about. She met Sarah in Ticino on the beach in her bikini and was sufficiently impressed by her that she asked me if she thought Sarah would be interested. Sarah told her she was my girlfriend after learning that Rozella (that's the lady's name) was my photographer. I said I'd bring the subject up with her but there might be a problem there."

Nicole frowned. "What kind of problem? Do you mean you wouldn't like her to?"

"Not at all. I'd be delighted if Sarah agreed."

"What?" declared Sarah in horror. "Have you told Rozella that I'll pose for her?"

"No I just said I'd ask you. No the problem is that, although Sarah is a beautiful girl, she also happens to be hopelessly shy in front of a camera lens."

Nicole giggled. "That's true enough. She's bloody terrified of people photographing her.

"Whereas you Nicky..." Daniela pointed out, "have just the right amount of sass to pull it off. It didn't occur to me until I saw you today but now I think you might be just perfect. Of course Rozella might want you to dye your hair back to its natural colour."

Nicole fingered her hair still bearing the shocking hues that had been such a bone of contention between her and Sarah all summer. "Well I was getting fed up of it anyway."

Sarah snorted. "Well at least some good might come out of the whole mad scheme then."

Daniela shook her head. "I don't think it's mad at all Sarah. Nicky can earn some good money doing easy fun work and who knows it might lead to greater things."

Nicole was starting to look excited by the prospect. "Well if you think this lady might be interested then..."

"Oh I'm sure she would be. Shall I give her your number then? Perhaps the two of you could get together and discuss the matter."

"Yeah! Yeah sure. No reason why I can't talk to her about it."

"Excellent. Now are you going to get your things together Sarah?"

Sarah and Daniela took their leave sometime later with Sarah's holiday necessities filling most of the limited available luggage space in the Ferrari. Daniela drove down the Alpli looking thoroughly pleased with herself. Sarah wagged a finger at her. "Daniela Devin! You are a wicked, evil, manipulative bitch."

"To what pray do I merit this unwarranted slur on my character Sarah dearest?"

"You know bloody well what I'm talking about. Letting bloody Rozella loose on Nicky."

"My motives were purely philanthropic."

"Bollocks! You're setting Nicky up like a bloody duck in a shooting gallery."

354

"Why ever so? All I've done is offer Nicky the chance to make a bit of money and have some fun."

"Is Rozella really looking for girls like Nicky for her photo shoot?"

"She will be once I mention the fact to her."

"Do you mean to say you made the whole thing up?"

"Let's just say I was a little creative."

"I don't believe this. Was the whole thing a cock and bull story?"

"Not entirely. Rozella mentioned some time ago making a photo collection along those lines but never got around to it. I thought perhaps I might push the thing along. I think it's a good idea and would give her plenty of scope to be creative. I thought perhaps I could sponsor it and we could produce something really beautiful."

"And at the same time throw Nicole to the tender mercies of Rozella."

"Rozella's always looking for new talent Sarah."

"I'll bet she bloody well is!"

"What are you worried about? I'm sure Nicole can look after herself."

"Not in this case she can't. She won't stand a bloody chance against Rozella and you know it."

"Well good."

"What the hell do you mean?"

"I mean it's about time our dear little Nicole took a walk on the other side of life. She's been a disaster with the boys for long enough. I think it's time we pointed out forcefully that she's been chasing the wrong gender. If anybody can take a sledgehammer to the closet door it's Rozella."

"Oh God! So you're after outing Nicky."

"Oh come on Sarah! Let her have a little adventure. She's been repressing this thing inside of her for too long. A little tumble in the photo studio isn't going to do her any harm. It'll do her the world of good in fact; take away all the confusion and make her come to terms with her sexuality. Once she comes to accept who she is we'll find her a nice girl to settle down with."

Sarah leaned back in her seat and groaned. "Oh my God! You're something else. You really are." She shook her head with a laugh. "Mind you I'd give anything to be a fly on the wall the day that Nicky meets Rozella."

"So I take it you approve then?"

"No I bloody well do not! I've never heard such a foul conniving scheme in all my life. I'm going to spank your arse till you scream for mercy when we get home."

"Is that a promise?"

Sarah pulled a face. "I don't know. It seems pointless trying to correct your behaviour with something you're going to enjoy too much."

"Oh go on Sarah. Please give me a spanking. I'll be ever such a bad girl... I promise."

"Well it can wait until after you've bought me that Apfelstrudel you promised me. I prefer to discipline my girlfriends on a full stomach."

Chapter Thirty-Two

Elke was pleased to see them at the Hotel Toggenburg, for the hotel was quiet and she had time on her hands. Angelica, it seemed, had taken off into town for the afternoon and, with most of the staff running on a split shift and not due back in again until the evening, the entire personnel manning the hotel, apart from Elke, consisted of one bored waitress and one of the sous-chefs in the kitchen playing games on his telephone. The only customer present was a middle aged man, with interestingly wayward, greying hair, nursing a beer on the back terrace. He'd evidently just descended from the Chaserugg for he was dressed in hiking gear and his alpenstock was leaning against the flower boxes on the terrace.

Elke sat the two girls down, brought them coffee and jarred her idling sous-chef into action to rustle up the hot Apfelstrudel the girls had set their hearts on. The Toggenburg hotel was justly proud of its homemade Apfelstrudel. Apple strudel was not strictly speaking a Swiss speciality for it originated in close by Austria but it was popular in eastern Switzerland as one of those indulgent afternoon treats liable to make young ladies agonise about their waistlines. Although it was popular and common in Switzerland the Hotel Toggenburg was undeniably blessed in this regard for the pastry and dessert chef in the hotel was a young Austrian man with a fanatical devotion to upholding the reputation and purity of his native land's traditional cuisine.

He was a young man with very strong views on the proper means of preparation for Apfelstrudel. The secret, he insisted, was in the making of the dough. Typically he would roll out a sheet of strudel dough to the size of a bed sheet and so thin as to be virtually transparent before rolling it around his mixture of tart Winesap apples, raisins, cinnamon and brown sugar and baking the lot in the oven. A slice of the juicy result and its heavenly puffy pastry had earned a well-deserved reputation locally and was popular, especially on those wet cold days when a person was looking for warm comfort food. In Austria, Apfelstrudel was commonly eaten just as it came but in Switzerland it was more usual to eat it with a topping; thick whipped cream or a dollop of ice cream. In the Hotel Toggenburg however the most favoured topping was hot vanilla sauce or, to be more accurate in this case, Sauce Anglaise, which was, to all intents and purposes, pouring custard. Daniela and Sarah, with their English backgrounds, thoroughly approved of this variant and they devoured their afternoon treat with a relish that bordered on greed.

Elke sat with them as they ate. She was interested to hear the story of Sarah's confrontation with her father on the telephone earlier that day. Sarah told her that she had refused to make herself available to her parents the day after tomorrow and that she and Daniela were going away for a short break instead. Curiously Elke seemed rather thoughtful and dubious at this point although she kept her peace. Finally Sarah pushed her plate aside regretfully. Had she been alone at home she would possibly have licked it. As it was, she had to restrain herself from scraping her spoon across its surface to extract every last remaining morsel so diligently that she would have been in danger of removing the pattern. At this point, Daniela picked up her bag and excused herself to visit the ladies. Elke put down her coffee cup and lit a cigarette pensively. "So you won't be seeing your parents then this week?" she asked Sarah.

"No I told them it wasn't convenient. They can bloody well ask me in future before demanding my presence."

Elke nodded thoughtfully. "Well of course you're perfectly within your rights to demand that they respect your convenience and private life Sarah. If you and

Danny have arranged to go away then you are certainly under no obligation to alter your plans in order to accommodate them. I can't help feeling however that it's a bit of an opportunity missed."

"How do you mean?"

"Well you insisted that any discussion concerning you and Danny had to take place with Danny present. I thought that was brilliant. They'd have to meet you as a couple. You couldn't underline your commitment any better."

"Elke I can't expose Danny to my bloody parents and their medieval bigotry. It would be awful."

"Has it occurred to you, Sarah, that, rather than expose Danny to your parents, what you would really be doing is exposing your parents to Danny?"

"I'm not following you."

"Think it through Sarah. Daniela is a remarkable woman."

"I know that. It's why I'm in love with her."

"Yes, of course you are, but sometimes you fail to see how other people see her as well. Daniela is a very, very difficult person to dislike."

"I know Elke. Everybody loves her. I still can't quite believe that out of all the people that adore her she's chosen me."

Elke smiled. "I can." Elke took a pull from her cigarette with a grin. "Why do you think your parents would be any different?"

Sarah furrowed her eyebrows. "Different from what?"

"Different from everybody else in the world that falls in love with Daniela the minute they meet her."

"Everybody else in the world doesn't have a daughter in a lesbian relationship with her." Sarah pointed out.

"I honestly don't think it would make any difference Sarah. Look your dad's imagining some terrible scarlet lesbian woman who's stealing his daughter away. How long do you think that misapprehension is going to last once he's confronted with Danny in the flesh? I'd give him about ten seconds tops. One moment of magic and she'll have him wrapped around her little finger and you know it."

"There's still my mother Elke."

"Hmmph! No problem there. I hate to say it Sarah but essentially your mother is an insufferable snob. Believing that her daughter is having an affair with some unknown nobody is one thing; being confronted with the fact that her daughter's girlfriend is not only fabulously rich but also one of the most celebrated and famous stars in central Europe quite another. She'd be fawning over her sickeningly."

Sarah frowned uncertainly. "I don't know Elke. I don't like the idea."

"You ought to think about it."

"What if they were awful to her?"

"Good God Sarah! Danny could charm the pants off a three day old corpse. Your parents' resistance wouldn't stand a chance in hell. She'd have them wagging their tails like besotted puppy dogs within seconds. Your dad would come over all gallant and deferential and discuss the financial stability of the music industry with her while your mother would be planning her next soiree to introduce her daughter's girlfriend to her star-struck circle of intimates. Job done. The real trouble is you isn't it?"

"What do you mean?"

"I mean the only person who is going to have a problem with Daniela meeting your mum and dad is you. As sure as hell Danny wouldn't be fazed by the prospect. But you? You would have to introduce your parents to the woman you are sleeping with. I think you're as scared as hell about that."

Sarah sighed. "You're probably right."

Elke leaned forward and tapped a finger on Sarah's hand. "Sarah this isn't something to be ashamed of you know. You have a girlfriend to be proud of. You shouldn't try to hide her."

"I *am* proud of her Elke it's just that..."

"Just that you still haven't come to terms with your own sexuality yet?"

"I suppose that's it. I guess there's still a part of me that thinks it's wrong; still ashamed. That's crazy isn't it? I suppose it's my parents that have made me think that being gay is something to be ashamed of. That's why I can't face them with this. I'm such a coward."

"You're no such thing Sarah. I realise that this is all very new to you. You've done amazingly so far. Just take one step at a time but remember your parents are going to learn the identity of your girlfriend some time or other."

"Please don't tell them Elke. Not yet."

"I'll say nothing Sarah but if they make a determined effort to find out it won't be difficult you know."

"Maybe they're not interested."

"They will be."

Chapter Thirty-Three

The following day dawned bright and sunny although there were still clouds about clinging to the sides of the mountains. Sarah was up early; jumping excitedly out of the bed she shared with Daniela at five o'clock, like a big kid on Christmas morning, as Daniela observed in amusement. Sarah couldn't help it. It was a morning of departure that stood in stark contrast to her last leaving of the Toggenburg. Then she had left in a doom filled cloud of melancholy and fear. Today however the promise of the forthcoming journey was anything but. She was excited and eager to be away. She'd spent the evening before animatedly packing her bags in preparation and continuously nagging Daniela for advice. Daniela had teased her mercilessly until, finally exasperated by Sarah's agonised indecision, she had dragged Sarah down onto the carpet in a wrestling match that had culminated satisfactorily for both of them. But Sarah's excitement grew by the minute. It did not matter where they were going. Anywhere with Daniela would be an adventure even if all they were going to do was stay in a little country hotel for a few days. *Life* with Daniela, Sarah was beginning to learn, was an adventure.

Daniela refused to be moved out of bed at such an unholy hour so Sarah padded through into the bathroom to take a shower alone. The bathroom was somewhat messy. They'd made love among the bath suds the previous night and it had had a somewhat deleterious effect on the usually meticulously tidy bathroom. Sarah showered happily, tingling in anticipation. She dried her hair carefully and wrapped a robe around her before re-entering the bedroom. Sitting at the dressing table she applied cosmetics to her face. She had never in her life put her make up on so early in a morning, she reflected. Daniela emerged sleepily from the bedclothes. "For

Christ's sake come back to bed Sarah. We've got ages yet."

"I can't. I'll spoil my make-up."

"Why the hell are you getting tarted up so early? We haven't even had breakfast yet."

"I just want to be ready so we can go as soon as we can."

Daniela sat up in bed with a sigh. "Oh well it looks like there's going to be no lingering in the bed this morning. I'll go and put some coffee on." She heaved herself out of bed, grabbed a robe and, pausing to kiss Sarah in passing, walked out of the bedroom. Sarah paused in her preparations to regard her choice of costume for the day hanging on the wardrobe door with pleasure. Daniela had insisted on her wearing it today and Sarah had put up a certain degree of resistance to the order. It was a short summer dress in violet and white and belted with a gold sash, bearing the name Gucci on the label and with a ridiculously expensive pair of matching gold, high heeled sandals to match. It was daringly short. Sarah had protested that it barely covered her bottom with any decency and that the material was so light that even the merest puff of breeze would threaten to serious compromise her modesty. But Daniela had made her try it on and she'd been so effusive in her praise that Sarah's resistance had crumbled. It was stylish and sexy and even Sarah had had to admit that it flattered her figure and her shapely legs. It made her look, she realised ruefully, like a pop star's girlfriend. There were a dozen more comparable outfits jostling for space with her old blue jeans in her bags as well. Daniela was evidently intending to introduce the new love of her life to the public eye in style it seemed.

If Sarah was eager to be away then the same did not seem true of Daniela for she insisted upon taking a leisurely breakfast and spent so long on her own preparations that Sarah began to gnaw at the bit in frustration. As the final preparations dragged on interminably, she began to chivvy Daniela impatiently. "For God's sake Sarah calm down." Daniela told her from her position at her dressing table. "There's still plenty of time."

"Shall I go put the bags in the car?"

"No honey. Now just take a seat for a few minutes and settle down."

But it was hopeless. Daniela was apparently never going to be satisfied with her make-up and Sarah began to pace the room. "It's nearly eight o'clock Danny. I thought you said we were setting off at eight."

Daniela packed her cosmetics away and took a last critical look at herself in the mirror. "And so we are. Our car should be here in a few minutes."

"Our car? What do you mean?"

"We're getting picked up Sarah dearest. You didn't think I was going to drive did you?" She was interrupted by the sound of a car hooter from the drive in front of the house. "Ah that'll be our car now. He's a bit early. Grab the bags sweetheart and we can get under way."

Perplexedly Sarah picked up her bags and walked to the front door. To her astonishment there was a large silvery limousine parked in the front drive with a uniformed chauffeur standing alongside in a dignified fashion. Daniela emerged behind her and greeted the driver warmly. "Morning Joe." She placed her bags on the doorstep. "Joseph will put our bags in the boot Sarah." she told Sarah.

Sarah was still blinking in shock. "You mean we're travelling in that?"

"Some of the way sweetheart."

"Does this guy work for you?"

"No he's an employee with a private car hire firm darling but I always use him when I need a driver." Joseph stowed their bags away smartly and then held the car door open for them. Sarah sidled into the roomy interior self-consciously and gazed around in amazement at the luxurious upholstery, drinks cabinet, television set and stereo system. She'd never been inside such a classy automobile in her life, not even when she'd been a bridesmaid for one her school friends a couple of years before. Joseph climbed behind the steering wheel and the big car purred smoothly out onto the little road to Schwendi.

Sarah was still shocked by the unexpected mode of transport. "Where is he taking us to then Danny?" she inquired agitatedly.

"Just to get our connection Sarah."

Sarah's astonishment grew. "Our connection? You mean he's driving us to the station? Are we going by train then?"

"No darling he's driving us to Kloten."

"Kloten?" It took a second to register in Sarah's brain. "*Kloten*! You mean the airport? He's driving us to Zurich airport?"

"Well honey apart from the constant jet noise I'm sure that Kloten is a very pleasant suburb of Zurich but, with all due respect to the people that live there, I shouldn't imagine that there are many other things to attract the traveller in Kloten."

Sarah grew pale and her mouth was suddenly dry. "You... you mean we're going on an aeroplane?"

"What else do you expect us to do at Zurich airport? Spend the day browsing around the kiosks?"

"Oh God!"

"What's the matter honey?"

"Danny I... I've never flown in an aeroplane before."

"You have got to be joking."

"No seriously. I've never been on a plane in my life."

Daniela leaned back in her seat and laughed until the tears ran down her cheeks. "Oh God Sarah! You are just priceless. This is delicious. I'm taking you on your first aeroplane flight. This is going to be even better than I thought. Oh Sarah. Life with you is just so much fun."

"Don't laugh at me. I'm scared."

"I'm not laughing at you darling. I'm just laughing for the sheer joy of you. Don't be frightened sweetheart. I'll hold your hand. It'll be fun you'll see. You'll enjoy it."

Sarah was not convinced. The car wound its way sedately down the hill from Schwendi to Unterwasser, attracting the notice of the local people with its regal passing. Sarah found herself cowering down in the interior out of embarrassment every time they passed someone she knew and Daniela's amusement grew. Sarah felt a degree of relief when they finally hit the main road at Unterwasser and began to pick up speed along the valley bottom. They made good time through the towns and villages of the Upper and Lower Toggenburg and near Wil they joined the autobahn heading west and the driver eased the big car up to an effortless one hundred and twenty kilometres an hour. Sarah's earlier excitement had been replaced with trepidation and she grew silent as they sped past the turn offs for Winterthur, bypassing the city to the north and drawing closer to the outlying districts of Zurich. Soon there were large overhead signs across the motorway bearing the stylised silhouettes of aircraft as symbols to indicate the nearing proximity of Switzerland's largest airport and Sarah's nervousness became tangible. Daniela took her hand in the car and perused her anxiously. "You're really worried about this aren't you honey?"

"I... I can't help it Danny. The thought of flying in a plane just seems to terrify me."

"Darling the most danger you are in over this trip is right now. You're statistically hundreds of times more likely to be killed or injured driving in this car than you are in an aeroplane. Relax sweetheart. It'll be just fine.

366

What is it you always say on the mountains? It's not as hard as it looks."

"If I'm climbing in the mountains my life is in my own hands Danny not those of somebody I don't know and can't even see."

"You do that all your life Sarah. Every time you board a train, a bus or a taxi you're placing your life in someone else's hands. Even if you're just crossing a street, eating a meal in a restaurant, walking across a bridge, sitting down in a cinema or buying a product in a shop your health and safety is dependent on the competence and trust of complete strangers. That guy in that BMW right alongside us could suddenly go mad and drive straight into us but we trust him not to. Yet the pilot who will fly our plane is almost certainly far more skilled, competent and trustworthy than him. He's probably logged tens of thousands of flying hours with absolute reliability and without incident. Air travel is statistically the safest mode of transport on the planet. You'll be safer than walking along a promenade."

"I'm afraid logic hasn't got a lot to do with this Danny."

"It'll be fine Sarah. Trust me."

On the outskirts of Zurich the road system became complicated and the autobahn divided in several places and the traffic became heavier. Their driver was experienced in the route to the airport however and he wove through the streams of traffic onto the Unterlandautobahn, the stretch of motorway that serviced the International airport at Kloten. Their proximity to the Flughafen was underlined by a deep rumble above. Sarah glanced nervously out of the window. A large jetliner was on its final approach, so low above the road that Sarah could read the writing on the fuselage. She shivered involuntarily. It seemed impossible that this great metal monster could stay aloft on its thin looking wings. As they pulled off the autobahn Daniela reached in her handbag and pulled out two pairs of large dark sunglasses. "What are these for?" asked Sarah.

"Elementary anti-paparazzi precautions sweetheart. We're coming up to the terminal now so let's keep a low profile shall we. I don't imagine for an instance that there's any advance news of our departure but there's no need to draw attention to ourselves. We don't want to be swamped by casual travellers with cameras on their mobile phones either so let's keep it tight."

"Does it matter if any old person photographs us?"

"Sure it does. Last year some arsehole with a camera got a hugely embarrassing shot of me. I had this low cut top on and I was bending down to pick up my bags and suffered a costume crisis. There was a picture of my right tit all over the papers the next day."

"Well if we're trying to sneak through the airport inconspicuously why are we both dressed up in a way that would start a riot in a monastery?"

"A sort of compromise dear. We don't want to be seen but if we are we have to make damn sure we're looking our best."

"That's completely illogical."

"That's life at the top darling. Nobody said it had to make sense."

"Good grief. This is weird."

"Heads up Sarah. Here's the terminal now. Let's get ready to rock."

The car pulled up by the terminal entrance and Sarah was surprised to see two uniformed baggage handlers make a direct bee-line for the limousine. Almost as soon as they were stopped their luggage was loaded onto an electric motorised trolley and they were whisked away into the airport. It was not the first time Sarah had been to Zurich airport. She had visited several times before, fascinated by the bustling conglomeration of airy light filled buildings crowded with travellers. She had lingered among the cafes, bars and restaurants or wandered about the boutiques and kiosks. She had taken drinks in the panoramic cafeterias on the upper floors and watched the aircraft landing and taking off in a seamlessly endless stream. The airport had seemed like some magic portal to her; a gateway to a world beyond she had rarely glimpsed.

It wasn't just that the aeroplanes were flying to exotic destinations far beyond the limited confines of her life but also that they were climbing up into a medium of which she had no experience. Only stood atop a high mountain had she come close to the rarefied element into which these machines ascended daily. She had watched them in bewitchment feeling curiously dull and earthbound set against the magnificence of their flight. She had watched parties of travellers, of obviously long experience, waiting for their planes, impatiently or bored, and wondered how they could ever lose their thrill of adventure in stepping aboard such incredible machines or find their achievement mundane. She had often come away from the airport feeling oddly dissatisfied and unfulfilled as if the sky and the horizons beyond it had called out to her and she had turned away timidly from their siren's enticement. She could not imagine an aeroplane flight as being routine. She had vowed to herself that one day she would dare to step aboard one of those great shining metal birds and find the sky for herself. She just hadn't expected it to happen so soon. She had awoken this morning with no idea that such a chapter in her life was about to open and that a great adventure long dreamed of and feared was about to begin. She felt her senses enhanced by excitement and dizzy with approaching panic.

Given her choice she would have preferred to have arrived at the airport hours in advance of her scheduled flight and spend her time drinking in the atmosphere and preparing herself mentally for the experience. As it was they were rushed through the terminal so quickly she barely had time to take anything in. She had the vague impression of crowded waiting lounges and long queues at the check-in counters, huge electronic information boards and tannoy announcements and everywhere a bustling purpose and seething mass of people with places to go. They were ushered through the terminal with quiet efficiency accompanied by two baggage handlers and, to Sarah's shock, an armed security guard. They sidestepped the big check-in counters with their long lines of patient travellers clutching their bags and trying to keep the children from running astray and found themselves instead at a small reception in a quiet corner where a smiling girl in a smart uniform took their bags on a conveyor belt and issued them with their tickets and passes. They were the only customers at the counter and the whole process took seconds before they were whisked away once more through strange back corridors of the building, into a lift and finally into a spacious and luxurious departure lounge.

After the busy hustle of the more public areas this lounge was almost tranquilly quiet. A few gentlemen in business suits were sitting around in comfortable chairs looking through papers from their briefcases and a small group of Japanese businessmen were gathered around a laptop in one corner. Sarah felt as if she'd stepped into some bizarre fantasy. The lounge was surrounded by great glass windows and afforded a panoramic view over the tarmac of the airport aprons. Spread out across this vista were dozens of enormous jetliners in every hue and livery; Swissair, Lufthansa, Air France, British Airways, KLM and many more besides. It seemed incredible to Sarah that her fellow passengers could so ignore this extraordinary scene laid out before them. Sarah couldn't tear her eyes away.

Their arrival in the departure lounge had not gone unnoticed for, as soon as they were ushered in, two remarkably beautiful young women in uniforms detached themselves from their stations of duty and intercepted them half way across the lounge. Their spokeswoman, an exquisitely lovely oriental girl, smiled in greeting. "Good day Miss Devin. We will be boarding in about one hour. May I offer you and your companion some refreshments in the meantime?"

"That's very kind of you." Daniela told her with a returning smile.

"Then if you would step this way ladies."

The girl directed them to a table by the window. There was a bottle of champagne cooling in an ice bucket on the table. Sarah took a seat and regarded it with exasperation. "Champagne? At this time of the morning?"

Daniela laughed. "Why not? We're on holiday."

"God I must have soaked up more champagne in the last week than I have in the last five years." Sarah grumbled. "Do you always serve champagne?" she asked their hostess.

The girl fought back a smile. "Only for very special clients Miss." She explained as she began to unravel the foil on the bottle.

"Er I'm a regular customer with the company Sarah." Daniela told her. "They like to pamper me." Sarah suddenly felt a little gauche and unsophisticated so she held her peace as the girl poured the wine into two flutes. Daniela picked one up and raised it in salute. "Here's to a safe journey and a happy landing Sarah."

Sarah swallowed. "Now there's a toast I can sympathise with." They touched glasses and sipped at the chilled champagne before Sarah's eyes were drawn once more to the view beyond the window. "Where are our bags anyway Danny?"

"Hopefully being loaded on the bloody plane."

Sarah squinted through the glass. "Which one is our plane then?"

"I don't think we can see it from here Sarah."

"What are all these aeroplanes anyway?"

"Well that one over there is a Boeing 767, that Swissair jet on the far side is an Airbus 310, that Lufthansa plane is another Airbus, the 320 and that

American Airlines one is a McDonnell Douglas MD-11..."

Christ I thought *I* was supposed to be the geek."

"I've spent an awful lot of time hanging around in airport lounges Sarah. I once bought myself a book on aircraft recognition in an airport kiosk to while away the hours waiting for my plane and got interested in them despite myself."

The hostess who was hovering in the background to see if there was anything else required interrupted apologetically. "Excuse me Miss but if you're interested in aircraft then you might like to watch the plane just arriving. It's just landed and I believe they're parking it at the gate opposite. We don't get many of them here and they always draw a crowd." Interestedly they turned to watch. They didn't have long to watch for a minute or so later an enormous great white machine turned the corner off the taxiway and trundled heavily into the space between the terminal buildings. To Sarah's eyes the thing was colossal and seemed to fill the gap out onto the airfield beyond. There were small trucks scurrying about its feet like pilot fish and it dwarfed all the other aircraft on the apron.

"My God!" breathed Sarah. "What the hell is that?"

Daniela looked impressed. "It's an Airbus 380 Sarah. It's the largest passenger aircraft in the world. I've only ever seen a couple before."

"How the hell can something that big fly?" asked Sarah desperately.

Daniela grinned. "With engines and wings Sarah sweetheart. Aerodynamics isn't your strong suit is it?"

Sarah shook her head in wonder. Even the other occupants of the lounge seemed to have put aside their papers and laptops to watch the newcomer's arrival. "God! It's enormous. Please tell me that we're not flying on that thing Daniela."

Daniela laughed. "No I think our plane will be a bit smaller Sarah. That's a Singapore Airlines 380. It's probably just here for a fuel stop."

"Just how big is our plane Danny? There don't seem to be many passengers here waiting for it."

Daniela grinned. "Oh I think we'll have plenty of space. Come on have some more champagne."

"Won't I get airsick? You *can* get airsick can't you?"

"I'm sure the flight will provide ample sicky bags darling."

At this juncture, a hostess walked over to address the party of Japanese businessmen. They all bowed politely and, putting away their laptops, rose to accompany the girl to a departure gate. Sarah jiggled Daniela's arm nervously. "Oh look. Everybody's leaving. Our plane must be ready to go."

"No honey. They're catching a different flight from ours."

"How do you know?"

"Let's just call it an inspired guess. Relax darling. They'll let us know when it's time for us to board."

Sarah sat back and tapped on the table top nervously with her fingernails. "How can you be so calm about it?" she asked.

"I *have* done it before sweetheart."

Sarah bit her lip. "God this is torment."

Daniela was having a hard time to prevent herself from laughing out loud. "Oh God!" she breathed. "I'm glad I thought of this. You're just a treasure. It's so much fun travelling with you and we haven't even got on the plane yet."

Over the next half an hour, several more people from the departure lounge left, until Sarah and Daniela found themselves sharing the big lounge with only half a dozen remaining passengers. Sarah's mystification grew by the minute. At last the hostess arrived back at their table to announce that they were ready for boarding.

Sarah nearly jumped to her feet in agitation. The hostess led them calmly through the lounge and through a departure gate with a brief stop for a cursory examination of their passports. They then descended down a long sloping tunnel. Sarah had seen these tunnels before and assumed that they led straight to the cabin door of the aircraft but she was mistaken. Instead they emerged into daylight straight out onto the tarmac. The airport noises had been muffled and muted in the quiet calm of the departure lounge but out here in the open air Sarah was assailed by the sounds. Even as they stepped blinking into the sunshine there was a thunderous roar from the runways beyond and Sarah saw a large aircraft climbing away from the runway into the sky leaving a trail of smoky exhaust behind it. As its thunder receded, the whining of numerous turbofan jet engines ticking over on idle insinuated themselves into her hearing mingled with the alarm notes of airport maintenance vehicles rushing about in urgency. It was hot on the tarmac and the air shimmered around the heat generated by the aircraft engines. Sarah glanced behind her, wondering where the other passengers were but she and Daniela seemed to be alone following the stewardess. She gripped Daniela's arm. "Where's everyone else Danny?" she shouted above the din. "We seem to have lost them."

Daniela fought with her laughter. "Oh Sarah! You're just adorable." They rounded a parked aircraft and in front of them, squatting on the tarmac was another aeroplane. "Well this looks like ours darling." She cried.

Sarah froze in horror. "You are pulling my pisser!"

"I didn't think you had one honey; not an external one anyway. I'm sure I would have noticed."

"We can't possibly be flying on that."

"What's wrong with it? Looks fine to me."

Sarah seemed to be hypnotised with shock. In front of them was what apparently, by far and away, the smallest aeroplane in the whole airport with its engines running and its navigation lights blinking. It was quite jaunty in its blue and white livery but it was quite odd looking for its two engines were mounted on pylons on top of the wings and there were large flanges on the tips of the wings and a T-shaped tail plane configuration. It was tiny with only three windows to a side along its cabin and it looked like a toy compared with the large airliners around it. "Where are the other passengers Danny?" cried an alarmed Sarah.

"We're both here darling."

"What? Just the two of us?"

"How many people do you think we're going to get on that plane Sarah? It only takes a maximum of four passengers and the crew."

"You mean we've got a whole plane to ourselves?"

"What did you expect us to do? Ride economy on Easy Jet or Ryanair or something? It's a private chartered business jet honey. We're not mingling with the riff-raff today. Now stop gawping and get aboard."

The stewardess led them aboard by way of a small ladder and into a small cabin just a few feet wide in soft beige tones with two seats on either side facing each other. It was cool in the interior and the noise from the airfield was thankfully muted. It seemed as if the oriental girl from the lounge was not only their airport hostess but also their in-flight stewardess as well for she boarded with them and closed and sealed the cabin door behind her. Beyond, through a hatchway, they could see the pilot making his last minute preparations for departure. The seats were surprisingly comfortable and Daniela settled down at once. She looked highly interested. "This is great. I've never flown on one of these before."

Sarah took a seat on the other side of the narrow gangway. "You mean you haven't flown on such a little plane as well before?"

"Oh no. I often take chartered business flights. How do you think I get to more distant gigs? I've certainly flown in small business jets before. I've never flown in this mark of aircraft before though. They're brand new. I didn't even think they were in service yet."

"What is it?"

"It's a HondaJet HA-420. They're supposed to be a revolutionary new design of light business aircraft. Isn't that right miss?" Daniela directed this last to the stewardess.

The stewardess smiled. "Yes Miss Devin. We're very proud of our new additions to the fleet. The new HA-420 can carry five passengers and two crew members to a maximum range of one thousand four hundred nautical miles. We have a top cruising speed of 420 knots. That's around 778 kilometres an hour and our service ceiling is around forty three thousand feet. The type achieves this performance because of the revolutionary anti-drag features in the aerodynamic design. It also means we have a 30 to 35 percent greater fuel efficiency compared with other comparable aircraft, with the lightweight composites used to construct the aircraft, the efficiency of the HF-120 engines and the aerodynamics all contributing to that. We also have a state of the art Garmin G3000 glass cockpit system with all instrument readouts on flat screen displays."

Sarah gaped at her. "Do you have to learn all that?"

The stewardess smiled disarmingly. "Let's just say I like to know what I'm flying on."

Daniela grinned. "Don't be dissing other people's assimilation of useless facts Sarah. It's no worse than you knowing the bloody Latin names of every flower in the Toggenburg."

The stewardess shrugged with a smile. "I've been flying for ten years miss. I love aeroplanes and everything about them. You tend to pick up that sort of thing with the job."

Sarah blushed. "I'm sorry miss. I didn't mean to be rude."

"Please don't concern yourself Miss. By the way my name's Mae. It's short for Mae-ying-thahan."

Daniela furrowed her brow. "That's Thai isn't it? Do you come from Thailand?"

"Originally Miss but I have American citizenship now although I live most of the time in Switzerland. My name is Thai for a female warrior."

Sarah smiled politely. "I'm pleased to meet you Mae. I think you have a lovely name. My name's Sarah by the way."

The girl smiled radiantly at her. "I know Miss Fuchs. I know your name from our passenger manifest of course. Now ladies excuse me but we'll be departing in a few minutes so may I ask you to fasten your seat belts?"

Sarah became instantly flustered. "Oh I don't think I know how these things work."

Mae grinned at her. "Please let me help you." She leaned across Sarah to reach the seat belt and quickly fastened it about Sarah's waist. For several seconds Sarah was terribly conscious of the warm proximity of the beautiful Thai girl inches from her face. Her perfume was subtle but pleasant and Sarah stared at the smoothness of her skin in fascination. She seemed satisfied with the buckle on Sarah's seatbelt and raised slightly to look Sarah in the face. "There you go Miss. All snug now."

"Thank you Mae. You're very kind."

"It's my pleasure Miss. Let me know if there's anything else I can do for you. Now if you ladies will excuse me for one moment I'll just have a word with our pilot before we depart."

As she left to go forward to the cockpit Daniela leaned across to wag a finger in Sarah's face. "You can pop those eyeballs straight back in your head Miss Fuchs." She whispered fiercely.

"What do you mean?"

"I mean I've got enough to worry about with all the other pieces of fluff you've already got on your phone list without you starting to flirt with the stewardesses."

"I wasn't flirting."

"Bullshit! I saw you fluttering your eyelashes at our little Miss female warrior."

"She's probably straight Danny."

"Oh yes? She was giving you a hell of a come on for somebody not interested in girls Sarah. If she'd got any closer while fastening your seatbelt she'd have been sitting on your lap."

"You mean she's..."

"I'd be prepared to bet money on it." Daniela giggled and leaned forward to whisper. "Mind you if you want to earn your ten mile high badge we could always ask the pilot to close the cabin door for an hour or so and invite Miss Mae-yin-thahan for a high altitude threesome at 43,000 feet."

"You're a bloody disgrace Daniela Devin."

Daniela laughed as Mae reappeared. "We're about to depart ladies. May I run through the emergency procedures with you?" Sarah didn't enjoy this part of the proceedings as Mae pointed out the emergency hatch, the position of the life rafts and the correct usage of them and the location and usage of the emergency oxygen supply in case of cabin decompression. Sarah was certain she wouldn't remember a damn thing if there really was an emergency. As Mae ran through the procedures the aircraft lurched and began to move along the ground. Sarah glanced out of the window and saw the tarmac moving beneath the wing tips. It was bumpier than she had imagined and she was alarmed to see that the wings seemed to be waggling up and down in a most disturbing fashion. As Mae took her own seat facing forward at the front of the cabin Sarah patted Daniela on the knee. "Is that normal Danny?" she muttered anxiously, pointing out of the porthole. "Are the wings supposed to bounce up and down like that?"

"Of course it's normal honey. You have to have some flexibility in the wings. If they were too stiff they'd break off under the stress of flight."

"Oh thanks Danny. Now you'll have me staring out of the window the whole way convinced that the wings are about to break off."

"Strictly speaking it's a porthole Sarah. Aircraft use nautical terminology on board so the front of the plane is forrard and the back is aft. You're sitting on the port side of the plane and my side is starboard."

"Are the windows on your side called starboard holes then?"

"I'll have to tell Mae you said that. We might get our flight free for you being the one millionth paying passenger to have cracked that joke."

"How much are we paying anyway? This must cost a fortune."

"Not as much as you might think. We're paying a tad over three thousand francs for this plane today. I've spent more than that on a dress before today!"

Sarah blinked in surprise. It was a lot of money but nothing like as much as she'd expected. "Really? I thought it would be more. Actually when I first saw it I thought it must be your own private plane or something."

Daniela shook her head regretfully. "I'm afraid not. I mean I'd love to have one of these but rich as I am I couldn't justify the expense of this machine. These things cost over three and a half million new! If we want to have our own private jet one day I'm sure there are more economical alternatives; a used Lear jet or something. Then again it would be better to have something a bit bigger for practical purposes; something big enough to carry the whole band."

Sarah took a breath. "God I can't even imagine owning my own jet aeroplane. I don't even have a bicycle anymore!" She gazed out of the window; she begged its pardon, the porthole. They were passing the huge Airbus 380 on the apron. It towered over them. They could have almost slipped underneath it without being noticed Sarah thought. Then the aircraft was free of the terminal buildings and taxiing out onto the open airfield. At this juncture the pilot addressed them on the internal PA system.

"Good morning Miss Devin and Miss Fuchs. Welcome aboard and thank you for flying with us today. We have clearance from air traffic control and so we should be able to depart on schedule. Our scheduled flight time is about one hour and twenty minutes and we should be arriving in Hamburg around twelve thirty. Our in-flight hostess will be serving a light luncheon as soon as we reach our cruising altitude. On behalf of the crew we wish you a pleasant flight. Thank you."

Sarah looked at Daniela in surprise. "Hamburg? We're going to Hamburg?"

"No darling that's just where we're catching our connecting flight."

"So we have to catch another plane? Why can't we go all the way on this one?"

"Er it's complicated sweetheart. You'll see."

After a short pause at the beginning of the taxiing track the aircraft was moving again and it was evident that they were moving around the airfield perimeter towards the main runway. Sarah gripped the armrest of her seat and felt her heart beating rapidly. She was becoming disoriented as to their position and wished she could see forward from the cockpit. Then the aircraft swung out onto a broad expanse of tarmac. This Sarah realised was the runway and they were moments from take-off. There was a short pause and Sarah felt the aircraft shake as the engines built up power and then they were moving once more. Her mouth dry, Sarah watched the tarmac racing ever more quickly below them and the whole plane rattled as the wheels sped along the uneven surface. Then suddenly the rattling stopped and Sarah felt herself pushed back in her seat with the acceleration as the pilot applied the throttle. The ground fell away from them and in a remarkably short period of time the whole airport was laid out below them and then the suburbs of Kloten and finally the city of Zurich was spread out in panoramic display as the aircraft banked to port and climbed into the sky.

Chapter Thirty-Four

Sarah's nose was glued to the Perspex of the porthole and she watched in astonishment as the towns and villages dwindled to toy like proportions in the landscape below her. Her fears forgotten, she felt a rush of exhilaration quite unlike anything she had known before. She was flying. It felt like the most wondrous thing in the world to her; a miracle almost unimaginable. She had never known anything so exciting. Then suddenly the extraordinary view was blotted out by whiteness. "We've flown into a cloud Danny." she exclaimed.

Daniela was watching her with pleasure. "That does tend to happen quite often Sarah. Aircraft usually have to fly through the cloud base to reach their cruising altitude."

"How can the pilot see where he's going?"

"I think we have radar for this sort of eventuality Sarah darling. Don't worry. We'll soon break out of the top of the clouds."

Daniela was right for after a short passage through the cloud they broke free into the upper sky and Sarah caught her breath. A radiant sunshine was gleaming down on a cloudscape stretching away into the distance; great ranks of clouds silvery white beneath a deep blue sky above. In the distance to the south she could see the mountains peaking above the clouds and glinting in the morning sunshine. It was indescribably beautiful and she felt her emotions choke in her throat. It was better than she had ever expected; a spectacle which she knew would live with her the rest of her days. In that wonderful moment she was hooked on flying for life. To crown the magnificence of it she looked below and saw the shadow of the aircraft on the cloud below and it was surrounded by a circular halo of rainbow. It was a remarkable phenomenon and she excitedly pointed it out to Daniela who had to lean far across the narrow aisle to see it. "It's a glory Sarah." Daniela told her. "You see it quite often when flying on the opposite side of the plane from the sun."

"I've seen something like it before from a mountain top Danny."

"Yes I think there's a name for it in that instance. The Brocken spectre. That's it. It's named after a mountain in the Harz where you can often see it surrounding your own shadow cast on the cloud below."

"It's wonderful."

Daniela smiled enigmatically. "It's even more wonderful through your eyes Sarah."

And still the aircraft climbed; climbed so high in fact that soon the undulations of the clouds below became flattened by perspective and the sky above deepened in colour to a deep azure. Sarah felt overwhelmed. They were sitting in a tiny box surrounded by the sheer vastness of the sky. She knew that, beyond the thin few inches of the Perspex, there was a completely hostile environment where the air was so tenuous that she would not be able to survive in it for more than a few seconds. It seemed a miracle to be alive in this alien world; sitting comfortably and warm, separated from the rarefied, frigid void beyond by only the fragile thin skin of the aeroplane's hull; a couple of centimetres of material between luxurious life and certain death. How lucky she felt to live in an age where this incredible journey into this extraordinary other dimension was possible and even routine.

Their soaring ascent finally levelled out and, at the sounding of a discreet tone in the passenger cabin, Mae unbuckled herself from her seat and turned to her two charges with the captivating smile that seemed to be permanently built into her facial features. "I'll be serving lunch in a few minutes ladies. We have a full onboard lavatory in case you ladies wish to make use of it."

Daniela turned to Sarah. "How about it honey? If you need to use the loo I'd do it now because I don't know if we'll have time in Hamburg and our connecting flight won't have toilets on it. Anyway it's an opportunity not to be missed. How many chances do you get in life to piss all over Germany?"

"I'm fine thanks."

"I'll see to lunch." Mae told them.

Mae brought them lunch on lightweight trays. It was the oddest meal in Sarah's life. She had no idea that, although a cold meal, it contrasted well with the normal standards of airline food for the private charter company with which they were flying prided itself on its gourmet in-flight catering. Sarah was hardly in a position to do it justice though. She was so distracted by the view from her window that Mae could have put a bowl of gruel in front of her for all she would have noticed. She had the vague impression of some delectable Parma ham wedded with slices of ice cold honey melon, slivers of smoked salmon topped with shallots, capers and spoonfuls of caviar on brown bread and a delicious Salad Nicoise with tuna, anchovies, hard boiled eggs and tomatoes on a bed of iceberg lettuce. Mae served a light fruity white wine to accompany the meal. Mae leaned across Sarah to pour her wine. "Is this really your first flight in an aeroplane then Miss?" she asked.

"Yes. Yes it is. This is all new to me. I suppose you've seen it thousands of times in your job though."

"Yes I have. I never get tired of it though. I love flying."

"I wish I had your job Mae. It must be a wonderful life."

"Well it can be harder work than you think but yes I love it. Perhaps you ought to try for an air stewardess job yourself Miss. You've got all the qualifications. You're friendly, charming and very, very pretty. You'd be a shoo in."

"Thank you Mae. It's sweet of you to say so."

"Not at all Miss. Just stating the obvious! I'll put the wine back in the fridge to keep chilled."

Sarah watched her walk forward easily. Mae's shapely legs were just about the only thing that could drag her attention away from the window view. At this point a sealed portion of butter hit her on the end of her nose. Daniela was glaring at her. "Oh sorry honey. We must have hit a spot of turbulence." she told Sarah sourly. Sarah dissolved into giggles.

All too soon, the pilot announced that they were beginning their descent into Hamburg. Until then, Sarah had had virtually no notion of movement other than a few bumps and vibrations. Certainly she had no feeling that she was travelling faster than she had ever done in her life. The plane just seemed to be hanging in the blue void and the only indication of forward movement had been the occasional wisps of cirrus cloud drifting past. Now however the engine noises seemed to change and the aircraft vibrated more as it began to descend into thicker air below. Two or three times the pilot manoeuvred, banking the plane in descending curves. The ground which had been only a vague impression from twelve miles up began to show more detail as she glimpsed it through the breaks in the cloud. Occasionally the aircraft shuddered alarmingly and Sarah glanced anxiously at Daniela and Mae to reassure herself that they were not finding the experience to be anything to worry about. Soon they were close to the cloud tops and the pilot, with the maddeningly matter of fact voice endemic to all airline pilots, was informing them that they were on schedule, due to land in a few minutes and that the weather was fine in Hamburg.

Sarah swallowed. She knew that, statistically, landing was the most dangerous moment of any aircraft flight. She turned to Daniela to speak for the sake of it. "What's Hamburg like Danny."

"Oh it's a big bad city Sarah. I love the place but it's not everybody's cup of tea. We won't be seeing any

385

of it on this trip though. That's probably no bad thing. I don't think an innocent little country girl like you is quite ready for the wicked decadence of a place like Hamburg."

"You make me sound like a hick from the sticks. I have been in cities before you know."

"With all due respect Sarah, Zurich and Bern aren't exactly in Hamburg's league."

Sarah turned back to the view from the aircraft. They were noticeably closer to the ground now and the clouds had cleared sufficiently to afford a fine view over the North German countryside. Sarah saw the great sprawling mass of Hamburg abaft the River Elbe as the aircraft began its approach to the airport. Sarah felt the bump as the pilot lowered the landing gear and she saw the flaps on the wing lowering to increase their drag. Soon they seemed to be apparently landing in the middle of the city for they were skimming so low above the suburbs that Sarah could pick out traffic on the streets and even pedestrians. They passed low over a major highway and a band of woodland by now so low that Sarah began to feel beads of perspiration on her forehead from anxiety. They were nearly on the ground but there was no sign of an airport. There was a patch of open land beneath them and Sarah saw two young girls with bicycles lounging against a fence. Incredibly the two girls were waving to them as they skimmed low above. Then they passed the perimeter fence of the airport and, a second later, the pilot was easing the aeroplane onto the runway. The aircraft jolted as the wheels touched the tarmac and the engine noise changed dramatically as the pilot braked their momentum. Then they were bumping along the runway and slowing. Sarah gulped in a gasp of air. She had been holding her breath. It suddenly felt marvellous to be on the ground once more.

Mae detached herself from her seat and thanked them for flying with the company as they taxied toward the terminal buildings. The pilot was on the PA system thanking them also. "You won't have any delays with your connection." He assured them, "I've been advised that your connecting flight is ready and cleared for immediate departure once we disembark and transfer your luggage."

Daniela nodded in approval. "That's what I call service Sarah. Looks like we'll be down and straight back up again."

Sarah felt giddy with the elation of being safely on the ground and she was a little disappointed to learn that they were taking off again almost immediately. Much though she had felt exhilarated with the experience of flight she had wanted to savour the comforting sense of terra firma for a while longer. "Do we have much further to fly Danny?" she asked.

"No honey. Only another hundred and twenty kilometres there or thereabouts."

Sarah was puzzled. She had calculated that the distance between Zurich and Hamburg was about seven hundred kilometres. Mae had told them that the maximum range of the aircraft was one thousand four hundred nautical miles which was something over two thousand five hundred kilometres. So, since they had easily the range to cover an extra one hundred and twenty kilometres, why the devil did they have to change to another aeroplane? Why couldn't they have flown directly to their final destination? "Why do we have to change if it's only another hundred and twenty klicks Danny?" she asked.

"Er technical reasons Sarah. The airfield where we're going's not big enough to take jets."

"Where the hell is it you're taking me?"

"Somewhere *small* Sarah."

"Are we taking a propeller driven aeroplane then?"

"No actually. We're taking a helicopter."

"You're kidding me!"

"Not at all. Oh we could have taken a light prop plane but that would have meant booking with another charter company. As it is this company charters private helicopters as well so we could have an instant connection without waiting at Hamburg."

"Oh God! A bloody helicopter. I'm certainly getting a thorough initiation into the mysteries of aeronautics today."

Daniela laughed. "We'll turn you into a budding little Amy Johnson in no time."

The aircraft slowed onto a parking apron and finally halted. Mae unsealed the cabin door and, to Sarah's surprise, the pilot himself came to the door to shake their hands, thank them once more for flying with him and wish them a safe journey. Mae graced them both with a radiant smile as she took their hands and bid them farewell. Sarah thought that she held her hand just a little longer than convention required and she gave her such a lingering look of appraisal that Sarah felt quite flustered as she disembarked onto the tarmac. They were given the VIP treatment as soon as they touched the ground for there was a small minibus and two porters awaiting them as they alighted from their aircraft. Their luggage was off loaded in seconds and they were whisked away with admirable efficiency to a corner of the airport serving as a heliport. Their helicopter was indeed waiting for them. It was a modern looking machine and comfortingly new in appearance with its blue and white livery. Daniela told her that it was an American built aircraft, a McDonnell Douglas MD 902 Explorer.

Curiously Sarah felt more at home with the idea of a flight in a helicopter then she had in a jet. Helicopters were familiar machines in the Toggenburg where they were used to service the mountain huts or for mountain rescue services and in use by the forestry management. She had been close to helicopters before and their low operating height was more in keeping with her altitudinal experience from the mountains. She doubted if the helicopters in the Toggenburg had quite such a luxurious interior as this machine however. She wasn't quite sure what to expect but the passenger cabin with its big comfortable seats, plush carpet, drinks cabinet and even a television set was not what she had anticipated. Best of all from Sarah's point of view was the huge window on the side away from the door where Sarah took her seat. The view would be magnificent.

Daniela seemed fascinated by the helicopter. Sarah had never seen this side of her girlfriend before. She genuinely loved aeroplanes of all descriptions and knew enough about them to threaten to be boring on the subject. She was telling Sarah that the machine was an innovative design for it didn't have a conventional tail rotor. Sarah was a bit hazy on the technicalities of helicopter flight but even she was aware that most helicopters had a large rotor to lift it off the ground and fly with and a smaller stabilising rotor on the tail without which the aircraft would simply spin around its own axis. From Daniela's description, however, it seemed that this aircraft dispensed with the tail rotor by the expediency of venting its exhaust out through the tail and using the thrust of that to combat the torque effect of its main rotor. It was all a bit black magic to Sarah but she was reassured to learn that the system not only enhanced performance and reduced noise but was also safer than conventional designs.

No sooner had their bags been stowed away aboard their new aircraft than the pilot powered up his engines and lifted the machine clear of the tarmac. Sarah learned one new thing almost immediately. Flying in helicopters was a far noisier experience than in jet planes. But the flight was wonderful. The sun was out in glory over North Germany and they flew low enough to provide extraordinary views over the landscape passing beneath. The whole of the city of Hamburg was laid out in panorama below them; a vast urban conglomeration and the biggest city Sarah had ever seen. It seemed enormous. Sarah could not imagine living in such a place. It would take hours to get out of town.

Unless of course you had a helicopter at your disposal. The aircraft soon left the outlying suburbs behind and then they were out in open country. It seemed as if the pilot was intent on following the scenic route for the helicopter was tracing along the course of the River Elbe as it wound its way through the billiard table flat landscape of the North German plain. Sarah's geography was becoming somewhat scrambled by the whirlwind course of events of the day for she didn't, at first, appreciate the consequences of following the river. She didn't even make the connection when she looked down and saw great ships winding their way up the river. She knew that Hamburg was one of Europe's largest ports but it lay far inland. Then sometime into the flight the reality struck with the most awesome experience of the day so far. The land suddenly fell away at a sharp edge of sandy shoreline fringed with white waves and away to the horizon stretched a vast expanse of blue water.

Sarah gazed in awe at the spectacle. "Oh my God!" she breathed. "The sea!"

Daniela reached over to take her hand, her eyes shining as she watched Sarah's dumbstruck astonishment. She had been waiting in exited anticipation for this moment and Sarah's reaction. "That's the sea all right Sarah honey; lots and lots and lots of salt water. That stuff covers three fifths of the planet's surface. I couldn't believe it when you told me that day at Bollenwees that you'd never seen the sea. I wanted then to be the first person to show you the sea."

Sarah felt tears pricking at her eyelids. "It's so... so *beautiful*!"

"It sure is honey and you're going to see a lot more of it over the next few days."

Sarah shook her head and tried to put her brain into gear. "But where the hell are we heading Danny? You said we only had a hundred and twenty kilometres to fly. I know my geography of this part of the world is a bit

390

vague but as far as I can recall there's nothing between the North German coast and England and England's surely a hell of a lot further than that."

"Ah that's the best surprise of all. Wait and see."

Sarah looked down and saw a large red and white container ship leaving a white trail in the blue ocean surface. Surely they weren't going to land on a ship! But the helicopter flew on and soon the land behind had vanished over the horizon. Sarah's puzzlement grew. Daniela was eagerly peering forward and finally she gripped Sarah's hand in excitement. "Look out this side Sarah. You can see our destination."

Sarah squeezed over Daniela and looked. On the horizon there was a sliver of land rising from the sea. As they approached it resolved itself into a pair of islands. On the left was a larger island that rose up in red sandstone cliffs and was dominated by a huge wind turbine. Slightly to the east, separated by a narrow straight was a smaller much lower lying island that seemed to be mainly sand. The pilot flew a circuit of the islands to afford his passengers a view and Sarah gasped in wonderment. The larger of the two islands had a large village on its sheltered side and an extensive harbour. To Sarah's surprise half a dozen large white passenger ships were anchored offshore in the lee of the island and the place seemed to be full of people. The cliffs of this island were quite remarkable for they were a deep brick red and, even from their height above, Sarah could see that they were full of seabirds. The top of the island was a verdant green apparently flat plateau and Sarah could make out parties of people walking about the edge of the cliffs.

But the pilot made no attempt to lower his aircraft onto this island. Instead he banked over and crossed the narrow strait to the smaller of the two islands. Even from the air this island looked barren; just scrubby sand dunes of hardy grasses and thorny bushes. In shock Sarah looked down and saw the runway of a tiny airfield laid out among the dunes as the pilot descended. They had, it seemed, arrived. They alighted on the ground with the down draft of the aircraft's rotors blowing loose sand away in a wicked flurry and a group of men were darting out from some low building toward them. The helicopter co-pilot opened the door for them and assisted them out where, stooping beneath the spinning rotors and their hair lashing about their faces, they were ushered quickly away from the helicopter. Two men were already manhandling their luggage from the aircraft. One man, clutching his cap to his head, addressed them with some importance. "Guten tag meine Frauen. Wilkommen auf Helgoland."

Chapter Thirty-Five

Strictly speaking, they weren't actually on Helgoland for that was the name of the larger island although Helgoland was the generic name for the pair of islands too. The smaller island was called Dune and, as they walked away from the tiny collection of buildings, not much more than a cafeteria, following a pair of young men bearing their bags, Sarah reflected that the place could hardly have had a more apt name. The entire island it seemed was simply a few hectares of scrubby sand dunes rising a few metres out of the North Sea. The island had a few tracks on it but nothing resembling a road and, after a day of being conveyed around in luxurious private transport, the two young women found themselves obliged to cover the last leg of their journey on foot.

Under normal circumstances this would hardly have been an imposition because there was just about nowhere on the island more than one kilometre from anywhere else. Sarah discovered, however, that high heeled shoes were not only a pain for getting in and out of aeroplanes in, they were also just about the most impracticable form of footwear ever designed for walking in sand. Sarah's short dress was also displaying impracticalities. It had been downright embarrassing as it whipped around her thighs under the hurricane like blast from the helicopter rotors and it was continuing to demonstrate its less than adequate resources for the maintenance of decency in the stiff breeze that blew across the island. Daniela's outfit for the day was not a whit more practical but at least she had the sense to ameliorate the worst failings. She bent down to unfasten her shoes. "Take your shoes off Sarah." she told her.

Sarah nodded, seeing the sound reasoning in the advice immediately. "Where are these guys taking us?" she asked in puzzlement.

"To our digs."

"Our digs." Sarah looked around in bewilderment. Apart from the little low building that served as a terminal for the little airport the only man-made structures she could see were a somewhat derelict looking concrete object that looked like a bunker from World War Two and a wooden observation platform. "What bloody digs? The place looks deserted."

"We've got a chalet a little further along. It's not exactly five star accommodation but it'll be perfectly comfortable. I've stayed in them before."

"You mean people live on this island?"

"No. All the inhabitants of Helgoland live on the main island. All there is on Dune is the airfield and a handful of holiday chalets. I hope you weren't harbouring any hopes of mingling with the madding crowds Sarah because we're going to be pretty much on our jacks for most of the time."

"Will there be other people in the other chalets?"

"Shouldn't be. I've rented the whole lot for the week. We'll be the only residents on Dune."

"You mean we're going to be completely alone?"

"Most of the time. Let me tell you about Helgoland. The islands are a big tourist destination. You remember those ships we saw anchored offshore as we flew in? Well they arrive every day and offload about six thousand tourists on the islands. They can't actually get into the harbour on the main island so they anchor offshore and all the fishermen of the island go out to them and offload the passengers into their fishing cobles and ferry them to land. Those ships come mainly from Busum and Cuxhafen on the mainland and take about two and half to three hours to make the crossing to Helgoland. So they arrive each day around lunchtime and re-embark their passengers and depart around teatime. Most of the tourists are day trippers so, for a few hours in the afternoon, the main island is a madhouse. After about five o'clock the place quietens down dramatically. Now there is a ferry service taking day trippers from the main island over here to Dune although with only a few hours to spend on the islands not many trippers take advantage of it. Mostly during the day the visitors on Dune are people staying in hotels on the main island. They don't stay long either because the last boat back to the main island is around six o'clock. That boat takes all the personnel from the airfield and cafe as well so, from that moment on until say ten o'clock the next morning, the only people that will be on this island will be me and my girl Friday."

"You're kidding me. Are you saying that we're literally going to be marooned on a desert island?"

"Well there is a small pond in the middle of it but those are essentially the facts yes."

"But what the hell are we going to eat and drink?"

"Oh we can go over to the main island during the day to stock up with provisions Sarah. Also I've got an ally on the islands. One of the fishing lads called Rudi has been madly in love with me since the first time I ever came here. He'll drop everything at the drop of a hat to ferry us between the islands in his boat whenever we want. In fact I called him up yesterday and asked him to stock the chalet up with some provisions for when we arrived so hopefully there'll be something for tea this evening. Rudi's a pearl and absolutely invaluable so we have to cultivate him properly. Of course I pay him well for his trouble but he does need a bit of female flattery and pampering as a pat on the head as well so remember when you meet him to flutter your eyelashes at him and tell him how big and brave and wonderful he is and he'll swim across from the main island if you ask him to."

"How long have you been coming here Danny?"

"Years Sarah. I found this place when I had my own demons to face honey. This was the place I ran off to

395

when I needed to get away from the world. I once thought of living here but it was impractical for a number of reasons. Thank God I didn't. I'd have never have met you."

"You might have met someone like me."

Daniela shook her head firmly. "There's nobody like you."

The small collection of wooden chalets lay in a sheltered depression among the dunes and, from their location, Sarah could hear that most evocative of all sounds; the rhythmic cadence of the surf on the foreshore just a couple of hundred metres away. It was a sound Sarah had never heard in her life and it was all she could do to prevent herself from rushing through the dividing dunes to stand at the water's edge. She willed patience upon herself. There would be time enough. Their chalet was a single story wooden building with a living room, two bedrooms, a bathroom and a kitchen. It was basic but comfortable and at least the kitchen was modern. The furniture was simple and without much in the way of luxury but perfectly adequate. There was an ancient looking television set in the living room as a concession to contemporary communications technology and an old radio in the master bedroom with its double bed. The major let down was the bathroom for there was no bath and only a sink and a shower that provided a feeble trickle of water to bathe under. "Fresh water is a valuable commodity on Helgoland." Daniela explained. "The only fresh water sources are rainwater and desalinated seawater. All that has to be lighted across from the main island to provide fresh water on Dune, so it's not something to squander lightly by soaking up the suds for hours. We can get a proper bath at the spa on the main island if you want or otherwise, if you want to bathe thoroughly well..." Daniela jerked a thumb, "there's the sea just over there."

"I'm sure we'll manage Danny but where's the loo?"

"Outside in that shed. It's a bit er primitive and smelly but it'll do in an emergency. Just a bit uncomfortable if you need to go in the middle of the night and there's a bit of a blow. I'm sorry if it's all a bit basic Sarah."

Sarah grinned delightedly. "I think it's heavenly. I thought we'd be staying in some posh hotel or something but this is much more fun."

Daniela grinned in return and kissed her. "I think so too. Come on let's see what Rudi's left us for tea tonight." The kitchen was reasonably modern although the cooker was powered by bottled gas which presumably had to be transported from the main island as well. There was however a microwave oven, a fridge, a coffee maker and even a toaster.

"Where does the electricity come from Danny?" Sarah asked.

"By cable from the main island. There are two electricity generators on the main island. There's a little oil powered generating station and you probably saw that big wind turbine as we flew in."

"Oh yes of course."

"It's a pain in the neck that wind turbine though. It's forever breaking down and the locals are always moaning about it. I think they'll probably get rid of it." Daniela was opening cupboards and the fridge. "Well looks like we're not going to go hungry tonight. Rudi must have thought we were bringing half a dozen friends or something. There's enough food here to keep us most of the week by looks of things." It was true for their provider had done a sterling job of provisioning the chalet. There was a loaf of fresh dark bread of the German style and a packet of black pumpernickel bread as well as a pack of salty butter, half a kilo of soft cheese, some Danish salami, fresh milk, a dozen eggs, packs of tea and coffee, some tins of soup, fresh tomatoes, onions, some German cured bacon, a big jar of pickled herrings, a bottle of vegetable oil, sugar, a bag of potatoes, a sausage of liver pate, some smoked ham, a tub of strawberry yoghurt, tins of sardines and mackerel fillets, carrots, a packet of biscuits, a small jar of German caviar, half a dozen lemons, some small apples, a couple of fillets of what appeared to be smoked haddock, some links of sausages, two peppered beefsteaks, a small bottle of vinegar, a head of lettuce, one large, rich looking fruit cake, six bottles of white wine, a crate of Holsteiner Pils and a bottle of schnapps.

Sarah blinked at the riches on offer. "My God! I presume your friend Rudi is not a great believer in the efficacious benefits to health of a frugal diet."

"He's just *German* Sarah. Germans just blink in confusion when you start talking about calories and weight control. Dieting went out with post war rationing in Germany."

Sarah rubbed her hands together. "Well I'm ready to put a hole in our rations for today. I know we ate on the plane but I'm famished again."

"It's the sea air Sarah. You always get a big appetite at the seaside. I eat like a bloody ravenous mule whenever I'm on Helgoland but I never seem to put weight on. I think the air just invigorates you and keeps you active so you burn all the calories off."

Sarah ran a hand through her hair. "I know what you mean. I can't decide whether I want to stuff myself or go outside."

"We can do both Sarah. We've got a table outside behind the chalet so here's what I suggest. We can eat something cold now and have a bottle of beer. We can just chill out until the last of the trippers bugger off and then, when we've got the place to ourselves, we can take a turn around the island and go dabble our feet in the sea. When it starts to get dark later on we can light a fire in the grill place outside and grill those steaks and sausages and maybe bake a couple of potatoes for our supper. If it's not too cold we can then go and make a disgrace of ourselves on the beach by starlight. I want you to go down on me while I look out to sea. I hope you remembered to pack your toothbrush. Oral sex is not without its hazards on the beach. You get bloody sand between your teeth."

"Too much information!"

Daniela laughed and smacked Sarah affectionately on the bottom. "Let's go look at the garden if that's the right word."

At the back of the chalet was a small flat area of very short grass surrounded by Buckthorn bushes and sheltered from the breeze by surrounding dunes. A rough wooden trestle table and benches held pride of place in this little sheltered haven and there was a concrete fireplace covered by an iron grid as a grill in one corner. At the far end was their lavatory in a small hut. Sarah, being Swiss, regarded this with trepidation and insisted upon examining it. To her pleasant surprise there was a roll of lavatory paper hanging on a nail inside. Rudi, it seemed, had thought of everything. There was another thing that surprised her for as she walked around the little garden area a small brown animal exploded from nearly under her feet and dashed away. "Danny!" she called excitedly. "Did you see that? It was a rabbit."

"Nothing unusual there Sarah sweetheart. The islands are infested with rabbits."

"I've hardly ever seen a wild rabbit before Danny!"

"Oh come on now! You must have done."

"No really. Rabbits are really rare in Switzerland. We've got plenty of hares and mountain hares, yes, but not rabbits. There's only one wild colony of rabbits anywhere in Switzerland and that's on an island in Lake Biel called St Peter's Island. I actually went there especially to see them. I spent all day trying to find them. I didn't realise that they come out mostly in the evening."

Daniela laughed, charmed at the thought of Sarah stalking around an island in a Swiss lake trying to obtain a rare sighting of the elusive rabbit. "Well you'll hardly be able to avoid seeing them here Sarah. The islands are crawling with them."

Sarah looked thrilled. It was the first intimation that she'd had that these islands perhaps contained some really interesting wildlife. She was already beginning to take notice of the dune vegetation and some of the characteristic flowers and plants of this unfamiliar type of habitat. She was hoping to see some seabirds too but she had not expected to find much in the way of mammalian life. "I suppose that rabbits are just about the biggest wild animals on the islands aren't they Danny?"

Daniela grinned mischievously. "Not at all. That's why I wanted us to wait until the place quietens down before we go for a walk around the island. I have something *really* special to show you."

Sarah span around in a pirouette of sheer delight. "This place is wonderful. Thank you for bringing me here Danny." She paused to draw a deep breath into her nostrils. "Even the air smells different."

"That's the smell of the sea honey. Actually it's not. Sea water doesn't actually smell of anything. What you can smell is the seaweed along the shore line. It gives that characteristic tang to the air along the coast."

Sarah bit her lip suddenly. "Oh God I know nothing about seaweed."

Daniela laughed delightedly. "Why would you want to?"

"Don't laugh at me Danny. I've always prided myself that I can identify most of the plants and animals around me and know something of them but here I'm a complete dumbo. This is entirely new territory for me. I've no idea what's on these islands. There could be entirely new ecosystems to explore and I've not the faintest idea about how to go about and identify all the things in them."

Danny nodded with a smile. "Oh yes there will be new things for you to moon over Sarah. Have you ever looked through a rock pool?" She shook her head. "No of course you haven't. Silly of me. You've never even seen one have you?"

Sarah looked at her. "Rock pools?"

"When the tide retreats it leaves behind pools of water among the rocks Sarah. They're absolutely teeming with life; crabs and other crustaceans, fishes, seaweeds, shellfish, starfish, sea anemones, sea urchins... all sorts of stuff. I don't know much about them but even I can spend hours rooting around in them to see what they hold. They're like little miniature worlds full of life. They're fascinating."

"There're rock pools here?" Sarah asked uncertainly.

"Not on Dune Sarah because this island is all sand but on the main island yes. In fact the rock pools on Helgoland proper are renowned. Apparently there are all sorts of rare species to be found in them. There's a centre for the study of marine biology on the main island and they bring parties of students here to Helgoland on field trips to study the marine life. You'll be like a pig in shit here Sarah!"

"But I don't have any field guides to marine life Danny. I've brought guides to the wild flowers, insects and birds here but I just don't have anything in my collection on marine life."

"That's not a problem honey. We can buy some books on the subject on the main island."

"They have book shops on the main island?"

"Oh hell yes. Helgoland is a big tourist destination and it's also has tax exempt status which means that it's full of shops to cater for the tourists. You can buy all sorts on Helgoland because day trippers come out from the mainland to buy luxury items that would normally carry a high purchase tax on them. There are shops to buy duty free cigarettes and booze but also all sorts of shops for expensive high tax value items. I bought my camera here on Helgoland and I was going to buy myself a pair of binoculars when we go over to the main island tomorrow. I can't keep using yours all the time."

"There are shops where you can buy binoculars?"

"Oh yes. There are at least two shops dealing in high quality optical equipment Sarah. I know for a fact that they have Zeiss binoculars in them because I nearly bought a pair the last time I was here."

"But surely field guides on marine life are a bit specialist for the average tourist Danny."

"No of course not. Lots of people come to see the sea life. I've seen books on shellfish and marine life in the shops. I don't know if they're any good but the marine biology centre sells books and things at its kiosk so you might well be able to find something a bit better there."

Sarah's eyes were shining brightly. Here was a whole new adventure she had not anticipated; a whole new environment; an ecosystem completely unfamiliar to her to examine. The sea held wonders in store she was only just beginning to comprehend the diversity of. A week or ten days alone on holiday with Daniela was thrilling enough but this sudden potential explosion of the boundaries of her natural history knowledge was an intoxicatingly new possibility to put the icing on the cake. She could barely contain her excitement. She felt something of what Charles Darwin must have felt the day he set foot on the Galapagos Islands.

Daniela was watching her closely and loving her for the quickening of her enthusiasm and the restlessly questing thirst for knowledge that so defined her. She blessed once again the inspiration that had come to her to bring Sarah to this place. Gripped in a wave of love that was almost unbearable in its intensity, she took Sarah by the waist and kissed her. "Come darling." She said hoarsely. "Let's pack our things away and then get something to eat."

The meal behind the chalet was simple but deeply satisfying; cheese, liver pate, cold meat and salami with tomatoes on pumpernickel bread. Sarah loved the dark heavy rye bread of coarse rye flower and rye berries, slightly sweet and yet sour simultaneously. They spread the salty butter on the breads and ate it in little squares with pieces of cheese or cold meats on it. They tried the German caviar which wasn't caviar from sturgeon but the roe of a common inshore fish called a Lumpsucker, dyed black to resemble proper caviar and much cheaper than the real thing. With a squeeze of lemon it was delicious on the black bread and a thick layer of butter. Daniela opened a small tin of mackerel fillets and they ate them on bread with relish washing it all down with draughts of good German beer. It was a little feast and a feast made all the better by the incessant sound of the nearby surf and the cry of the seabirds overhead.

Sarah ate with her binoculars on the table next to her and, throughout her stay on Helgoland, they would rarely be out of reach of her hand. They had not begun to explore but already Sarah was adding new species to her lists of natural observations. The seagulls were mostly herring gulls which were rare in Switzerland where they were replaced by their southern counterpart the Yellow Legged Gull. One huge brute of a gull did fly over that Sarah recognised as a Greater Black Backed Gull. It was not a new species for Sarah for she had seen one before; once and that had been a young bird in immature plumage that had turned up unexpectedly on Lake Constance some years before. This was the first adult she had ever seen. Then, wheeling in small flocks were the terns. Sea terns in Switzerland were normally all Common Terns that bred on the lakes. Just once, on a shining day in the Rhine delta on Lake Constance in early September, Sarah had been privileged to see a pair of Caspian Terns that had gone somewhat astray on their migration. These terns above her however were entirely new to her for they were Sandwich Terns; a bird she had never seen before. Her excitement grew. If these were the wonders to be seen in the confined range of view from the outside of their chalet what extraordinary things were to be found once they ventured abroad. She found herself gobbling her food eager to be away.

"Relax Sarah." Daniela told her with a smile. "We've got all the time in the world to explore. We'll give it an hour or so yet and then we'll take a look round."

"I can't help it Danny." Sarah told her sheepishly. "I've hardly ever been away from Switzerland. This is all so new and wonderful for me."

"We've got time on our hands to take it all in Sarah. Pass me the bread will you?" Daniela took another slice of bread and spread it with butter contentedly. "Do you know how pumpernickel gets its name Sarah?"

"Nope. That piece of useless information isn't in my data banks."

"Apparently it's a composite of the German word pumpen referring to the unfortunate effects of flatulence and the name Nick which is an old term for the devil. So the word means farting Nick or farting devil. Presumably it refers to the devastating impacts on the digestion of eating dark rye bread."

"I shall remember to avoid pulling the bedclothes over my head tonight."

"By the way have you got your mobile switched on?"

Sarah shook her head. "I switched it off when we got on the plane this morning and I haven't turned it back on yet. Not that I give a monkeys about it. I'm not really in the mood to converse with the outside world for the moment."

"Me neither but we ought to have at least one phone up and running so we can call Rudi when we need him and so on."

"That's a point. How will we charge our phones up? The power sockets are different here."

"Relax. I have an adapter with me. Maybe it's not a bad idea to keep your phone off though. That way we won't have our holiday ruined by your parents harassing

404

you. If we need to phone anybody in the Toggenburg we can use my phone."

"How long exactly are we staying here Danny?"

"I don't really know honey. We'll give it a week and then see how we feel."

Sarah frowned. "You mean we haven't got a flight home booked?"

"No not yet. We can call up and book a flight when we feel like honey. There's no pressure. We've only got the chalets booked for a week though so we might have to think again after that."

"I can't believe you booked all the chalets on the island just so we would be completely alone!"

"I know. It was terrible of me. I'm so selfish and greedy. I feel ashamed of myself."

"Liar."

Daniela giggled girlishly and stood up. "I'm out of beer. Do you want another one out of the fridge as well?"

"Yes please but *then* can we go for a walk?"

"Aber naturlich Fraulein Fuchs."

Chapter Thirty-Six

They struggled with the inadequate shower and changed clothes before they set out to explore the island. Sarah had brought her hiking boots with her but, extracting them from her bags, she frowned and could think of no justification for wearing them. She had a pair of Adidas trainers with her as well but it all seemed somehow in contravention of the protocols of being marooned on a desert island. She pulled out her beach sari and went barefoot instead. Daniela considered that to be a fine idea and did likewise. She tied a gauzy wrap about her waist and turned to Sarah. "Come on let's go. Have you got your binoculars with you?"

Sarah stared at her. "You are not proposing to step out of the house dressed like that are you Miss Devin?"

Daniela looked puzzled and regarded herself critically. "What's wrong with me?"

"Nothing if you happen to be within the privacy of a Sheik's harem! I believe virtual nudity is perfectly acceptable private evening wear within that context."

"I'm not wearing anything less than you are."

"Yes but in my case I have wrapped my sari about me in such a fashion as to at least afford some degree of modesty whereas you have just sort of tied yours about your waist as an afterthought and show every intention of stepping abroad naked from the waist up."

"Nobody here but us chickens Sarah. The last boat for Helgoland left twenty minutes ago. Now stop griping. The only reason I'm wearing anything at all is in case I need something to sit on."

"God! Remove the last veneer of civilisation and you revert to a cavewoman. A Polynesian islander has more decorum than you."

"Well I would have hung a garland of flowers about my neck but the local flora seems to be a bit thin on the ground and those bushes look prickly."

Sarah laughed. "Ok desert island babe. Let's see what this place has to offer."

They walked across the centre of the island to the west picking their way through the overgrown dunes. There were surprisingly a lot of birds among the dunes; Meadow Pipits, Linnets, Sparrows and White Wagtails but Daniela dampened Sarah's enthusiasm. "This is nothing!" she said. "You ought to see this place and the main island in spring or autumn. It is absolutely crawling with birds then; great flocks of them all over the place. Apparently these islands are one of the best bird watching sites in all Germany during the migration season. At those times of year, Helgoland attracts birdwatchers from all over because the islands are a major gathering point for migrating birds and there are always rare birds to be seen."

Sarah nodded. "Yes it makes sense. I know from my reading that coastal peninsulas and offshore islands form important migration points. I've never seen that of course but we have similar places along the migration routes in Switzerland. I'd love to be here in spring or autumn though."

"No reason why we can't have a week or so here come September Sarah. The weather usually stays nice right into the autumn here."

Sarah stopped suddenly, her eyes gleaming. She had sighted a small pink flower growing in a tuft in a little damp patch of sandy salt marsh. "Oh look Danny!" she enthused as she pointed it out.

Daniela smiled at her sudden excitement. "Er... pretty! I suppose you're going to tell me that it's something rather more than just pretty though."

"I wasn't expecting to see it Danny but when I think about it, it's logical. We have this flower in the mountains in Switzerland. It's Thrift or Sea Thrift I

407

suppose. The sort we have in the mountains is a sub-species; Mountain Thrift or *Armeria maritima alpina.* This must be the nominate species. I know they grow in saline coastal habitats."

"Well trust you to find at least something familiar."

"There're a lot of familiar things Danny. Those bushes there are Sea Buckthorn for example and they're another plant associated with coastal dunes but they also grow on rough ground or by the sides of rivers in Switzerland."

Daniela nodded thoughtfully. "Yes I know something about those bushes. One of the wardens here once told me that they're often planted to stabilise the dunes in coastal habitats. It's the same thing apparently with that tall rough grass there which, if memory serves me correctly, is called Marram Grass."

"Hell I never even though to bring an identification guide to grasses."

"Well shouldn't be a problem sweetheart if you're interested in them. We can photograph them or even take some dried samples back with us and you can pore over your books to your heart's content once we get home. I should think there's a whole load of plants here you've never seen before." Daniela cast her eyes around and pointed. "That one there for example. That's pretty common on Helgoland but, apart from the Yorkshire coast, I've never seen it anywhere else."

Sarah looked in surprise. "God you're right! I *haven't* seen that before." The plant was an odd looking blue grey object with very spiny leaves growing among the dunes. "What the hell is it?"

"I think it's called Sea Holly or something like that Sarah because the leaves look like holly leaves. I may be wrong though."

"I've got my Collins' guide to the Wild Flowers of Britain and Northern Europe back at the chalet. I'll look it up when we get back."

Daniela grinned in pleasure. "I might have known this holiday would turn into a naturalist field trip."

"I'm sorry Danny. I don't want to be boring but all this is just great for me."

"Hey honey. I'm not complaining. On the contrary, I think it's wonderful. I've always loved nature but I've never known much about it and that frustrated me. Now I've got an expert observer at my disposal and you've opened my eyes. You've really made me look at the natural environment around me and see it through your eyes. You're not boring me. I can't listen to you enough."

Sarah flushed with pleasure and excitement. Impulsively she wrapped an arm around Daniela and kissed her. "Thank you for bringing me here Danny."

"I wouldn't have missed it for a peerage sweetheart. Come on. There's loads more I want you to see."

Their route brought them out on the western shore of the island facing across the strait to the main island less than a thousand metres across the water. Sarah scanned the main island with her binoculars. She could see people walking about along the shore of the larger island. There seemed to be a lower level to the island before a line of red cliffs reared up behind. There were houses and larger buildings and a harbour full of boats. The island looked populous and busy. It felt bizarre to be completely alone on an island and yet separated by such a narrow body of water from civilisation.

In front of them, on their own shore, was a small harbour that Daniela told her was the embarkation point for the boats ferrying passengers between the two islands. It was completely empty of boats but Daniela had seen something floating in the water. "Look Sarah. A jellyfish."

Sarah peered over the edge of the concrete quay and saw it immediately. She had never seen a jellyfish in the wild and she'd always had a feeling that they were odd amorphous masses of gelatinous appearance and fairly unpleasant. This creature was a revelation. It was curiously and strangely beautiful as it pulsated slowly in the rocking motion of the water. Most striking of all were the four purple rings in its hood that gave it a remarkably unworldly appearance; almost alien and strange. "Wow!" breathed Sarah. "It's amazing. I've never seen anything like it. What a weird animal." She shook her head in despair. "God we've hardly begun to explore and I'm clueless already. I don't know the first thing about jellyfish. It never occurred to me that we might actually see one. God! I'd love to know what it is."

Daniela looked smug. "Well you can try asking me because this one I *do* know. It's a Moon Jellyfish."

"What a lovely name. How do you know that?"

"No big deal. They're dead common. I don't think the Emperor Hirohito would have got too excited by them."

Sarah blinked. "Emperor Hirohito?"

"Japanese Emperor between 1926 and 1989 Sarah honey. He was the emperor that ruled over Japan during World War Two."

Sarah put a hand on her hip exasperatedly. "I *know* that Danny. I do have a degree in history you know. Why would he be excited by a jellyfish though?"

"Well apparently Hirohito, when he wasn't indulging in calligraphy, esoteric poetry or trying to subjugate the entire Pacific Ocean under Japanese rule, was a keen student of marine biology and the world's foremost authority on jellyfish."

"Seriously?"

"So I've read."

"So when did you become an authority on jellyfish?"

"I didn't. I just like swimming in the sea and those things swarm in their thousands from time to time. A lot of species of jellyfish have pretty potent and dangerous

410

stings so I wanted to know if they were dangerous before sharing the water with them. So I asked about them."

"And are they... dangerous I mean?"

"No they're completely harmless. They do have stings but they can't penetrate human skin apparently."

Sarah sighed. "I wish I knew more about them. It makes me feel so ignorant."

"That's the last thing you are darling." Daniela pointed at the long breakwater jutting out from the south of the island. It was lined with roosting large black birds, some holding their wings out as they perched. They were curiously primitive, almost reptilian looking creatures. "Are those cormorants Sarah?"

Sarah nodded and placed her binoculars to her eyes. "Yes Danny. We get loads of them on the Swiss Lakes as well. Fishermen hate them because they think they eat all the fish. You see how they're holding their wings out? That's to dry them. They actually get waterlogged when they're swimming and so they have to come to land to dry out. They can get so waterlogged that they actually sink otherwise. Sometimes you see them swimming with just their head above water because they've taken so much water on and... oh wow!"

"What is it?"

"Just a moment." Sarah was staring intently at the roosting birds. Finally she took her binoculars from her eyes and handed them to Daniela. "Take a look at the bird about six from the end of the wall Danny!"

Daniela looked carefully with a frown. "It looks just like the others Sarah, just a bit smaller."

"It's a *shag* Danny. I've never had one before."

"With all due respect Sarah I would have to dispute that. Whatever your previous history I'm pretty certain that we have done sufficient since becoming acquainted to disqualify you from the sisterhood of Vestal Virginity."

"The *bird* is a shag you half-witted slut. It's a close relative of the cormorant. I've never seen one before."

"How the hell can you tell the difference? It looks just like a small cormorant to me."

"Well it's smaller, less robust and more slender but the diagnostic features are the feathering on the face and the shape of the forehead. See how steep the forehead is and if you look closely you'll see the eye is completely surrounded by feathers whereas on a cormorant it would be bare flesh."

"I'll take your word for it. Personally I think they're all peculiarly unattractive birds. I hate to be anthropomorphic about it but there's something just a bit sinister about them... like emaciated vultures or something."

Sarah giggled. "Hey, don't tell your friend Rudi that our favourite vulture in the Toggenburg has the same name as him."

"He'd probably just laugh." Daniela hefted Sarah's binoculars in her hand. "I have to buy a pair of these tomorrow."

Sarah looked at her with a wry smile. "Well let's hope that everybody else on the island over there hasn't had the same idea because if they're stood over there scanning this island they're currently enjoying a perfect view of you naked to the waist."

"Ok! I take the hint. Let's get out of the public eye and walk around the beach to the north."

If Sarah was already beginning to fall in love with Helgoland it was that magical walk along the north beach of Dune that really cemented that love. This was the real sea, crashing onto the beach and hissing as each wave receded to be followed by the next. Sarah was entranced. They walked to the edge of the surf line and let the breaking waves wash over their bare feet. Daniela cast her wrap aside and walked naked into the surf to her waist letting a roller fall across her and emerging with water streaming from her and her hair hanging wetly on her shoulders. Sarah was not so daring but she sat on the sand and watched Daniela in pleasure thinking she

412

looked like some enchanted mermaid emerging from the sea. Sarah dug around in the sand and found it full of seashells; razor shells, clams, whelks, oysters, tellins, winkles, limpets, cockles, scallops, mussels and so many more. She desperately wanted to know the identity of all these diverse sea creatures. She vowed that tomorrow she would return to the beach and bring a plastic bag and start collecting samples. There were so many and so exquisitely beautiful in their diversity. Then there were the sea weeds washed up along the tide line; great fronds of brown kelp and smaller species of greens and reds. Sarah felt her head swimming. How could she ever begin to sort them all out?

Daniela was dabbling about along the water edge. She picked up a couple of things and padded back up the beach toward Sarah. Her naked body was glistening with water in the evening sunlight and she looked heartbreakingly beautiful. She squatted down by Sarah and kissed her. Sarah pulled a face. "Urgh! You taste salty."

"Er that's pretty understandable Sarah I have been splashing around in salt water you know."

"I didn't think the sea was *that* salty."

"God! What are you like? Surely you knew that sea water is salty."

"Well yes... I suppose so... like mineral water contains salt or something. I didn't think that it would *taste* so salty though."

Daniela lay back on the sand and laughed. "Oh God I just love being here with you. You're just precious. Did you actually think that sea water was going to taste like Perrier or something?"

Sarah slapped her thigh. "Stop laughing at me. What are those things you've picked up anyway?"

Daniela held out the objects in her hand. "Just a couple of things I thought you might be interested in." She held out an odd looking little black roughly

413

rectangular sac with strange appendages protruding from each corner. "What do you make of that?"

"I don't know. What is it; some kind of seed pod or something?"

"It's a mermaid's purse Sarah."

"Right! So they carry their credit cards around in those things right?"

Daniela laughed delightedly. "Actually it's the egg case of a fish, either a ray or a dogfish. I think you can tell the difference by the shape of these tendrils on the corners but I'm not sure how."

Sarah took the little sac in astonishment. "My God! You mean a fish hatches out from one of these?"

"That's right. Weird isn't it?"

"It's marvellous. Jesus! There's so much to learn. What else have you got?" In reply Daniela held out a hard white sliver of some spongy looking material a few inches long. Sarah looked with interest. "I know this one Danny. It's a cuttlefish skeleton isn't it? People put them in their bird cages for their budgies to gnaw on."

"Exactly. It's amazing what you can find washed up along the shore line Sarah; shellfish, dead crabs, the shells of sea urchins... all sorts of stuff."

Sarah shook her head. "This is just incredible. I feel like I've walked into another world."

"We've hardly begun Sarah!" Daniela sprang to her feet. "Come on. Let's walk further around the beach. I want to show you my all-time favourite."

"Hey! What about your wrap?"

"Carry it for me. I'm too wet."

Sarah followed Daniela along the beach. Daniela seemed excited and she skipped before Sarah like an animated child completely uninhibited in her nudity. At last she stopped and clasped her hands together in glee. "I knew they'd be here." She waved Sarah forward. "Look."

For a moment Sarah was nonplussed. Ahead on the beach were several large, apparently inanimate lumps.

414

Then one of them moved and raised its head. Sarah stared dumbfounded. "Oh my God! They're seals."

Daniela grinned, her expression the one of somebody who has just provided a wonderful surprise. "They haul out on the beach nearly every day Sarah. Once all the trippers have gone they come out of the sea to rest on the beach."

"God! Can we get a bit closer?"

"Sure as long as we don't get too close. They're pretty used to people but they'll spook if we try to get right up to them."

"This is wonderful! I've only ever seen them in a zoo before. What kind of seals are they?"

"Look through your binoculars Sarah and look at their noses. Rudi taught me about these animals. There are two species you might see; the Common or Harbour Seal and the Grey Seal. You can tell the difference from the shape of their noses and the nostrils. These are Grey Seals. You can tell because they've got longer more pointed snouts and their nostrils are nearly parallel to each other where they'd form a V shape with a common seal."

As they approached one of the animals raised its head and grunted loudly at them. Sarah was fascinated. "This is fantastic! Why didn't we bring a camera?"

"Darling we've doubled back on ourselves. The chalet is only a couple of hundred metres back of those dunes. Why don't you wait here while I nip back and grab the camera and we can sit and watch them awhile?"

"Yes! Oh yes!"

Sarah sat down on the sand, less than a hundred metres from the nearest seals, completely enthralled. Daniela was soon back but, as she cautiously approached the beach, she saw Sarah gesticulating excitedly. She stalked up to Sarah in interest. "What is it honey?"

"Fish Danny...big fish! They must be sharks or something... look just off the beach maybe a hundred metres out. They keep breaking the surface with their fins. Is that why the seals are out of the water?"

"Where Sarah? I can't see them."

"Look! There. There must be five or six of them."

"Give me your binoculars." Daniela looked at the creatures breaking surface just off the beach. "Oh Sarah you muppet. I thought you were supposed to be the naturalist. They're not sharks you barmy bitch. They're porpoises."

"*Porpoises*!" Sarah squealed.

"Sure. I've seen them before. I think they're called Harbour Porpoises in some places. They're quite common and you can often see them from the beach. Don't confuse them with dolphins though although they're quite closely related. They're mammals like very small whales."

Sarah ran a hand through her hair. "Oh my! This is amazing!"

"Yes I've seen a few of them now and I've seen dolphins and pilot whales from a boat a bit further offshore. Maybe we can get Rudi to take us out one day and see if we can see any."

Sarah sat back on her haunches and took a breath. "Danny I can't believe you brought me here. I just love it here."

Daniela looked at her and loved her. "Hey! I brought a couple of bottles of beer from the chalet." She wielded a bottle opener and passed a bottle to Sarah. "Here's to us darling."

"To us!"

Daniela took a moment to bask in Sarah's radiant smile; so childlike and joyful on the beach of Dune. She grappled for a moment with her breath. "Sarah" she said at last, "Do you know something?"

"What Danny?"

"I have never, ever, been so happy in my life as I am at this moment."

Chapter Thirty-Seven

The next days were sheer bliss; an almost enchanted interlude in their lives, far from the complexities and anxieties of the preceding days. The Ticino and its attendant worries seemed to have receded to some remote, vaguely troubling location far beyond the horizon. On Helgoland, Sarah and Daniela pared their relationship back to fundamentals; the simple joy of each other's company. The past was adjourned; the future postponed. This was simply a time to be and a time to be in love. Sarah would always feel that it was on Helgoland that she and Daniela formed the unbreakable bonds that would tie them together for life; forever; the place where they became indivisible; the joining point from where their lives henceforth would become a single shared adventure. It was the place that settled all further question or discussion. They belonged to each other and that was no longer a matter for interpretation or negotiation.

In the event, they spent two weeks on Helgoland for Daniela was able to lease the chalet for a further week, so reluctant were they to leave their desert island. Throughout those two weeks, they were quite literally inseparable. Sarah had never in her adult life been so continuously aware of another person's presence. They were very seldom out of each other's sight and on the rare occasions that one of them did wander out of sight they became restless and unhappy until they were reunited. Otherwise they stayed always where they could see each other and usually within touching distance. So reluctant were they to be separated that even when one of them was obliged to use the outside lavatory the other would follow them out and sit in the chalet garden outside to continue their conversation while the other attended to their toilet. They slept together, bathed together, ate together, walked hand in hand everywhere together and made love everywhere they could think of. They almost became appendages of each other; a single unit incomplete without the other; a happiness and deep satisfaction neither of them had ever experienced before.

On their second day on Dune, when the trippers had vanished for the day, Daniela dared Sarah to walk around the entire island with her completely naked and that became their daily routine whenever the weather was fine. They collected shells from the beach, drilled little holes in them and, with the aid of some old fishing line, fashioned them into necklaces and bangles to decorate their naked bodies with in some strange kinship with some primitive past. Even when there were people about they wore little other than a bikini or a beach wrap and Sarah discovered for the first time the pleasure and comfort of her own skin. Only on the occasions when they crossed the strait to the main island or the days when the weather turned poor on them did they dress more modestly.

For the most part the weather stayed fine and warm but one day a storm flared up and for two days the sea was too rough to allow boats to cross between the islands so that they were completely isolated on Dune. They were delighted. They had enough provisions in the chalet to weather the storm and there was a delicious sense of adventure in being so totally cut off from civilisation. They walked among the dunes with the gale whipping through their hair or staggered along the beach with the surf crashing in white fury onto the sand and felt vibrantly and exultantly alive. It was heavenly too to lie snug abed in each other's arms and listen to the wind howling about the chalet and hear the roar of the surf on the foreshore a little over a hundred metres away. Life could not get much more basic or richly satisfying than that.

The only irritation in their existence was paradoxically the one thing that helped it be such a pleasure; sand! The stuff got everywhere. It got in their shoes, it got in their clothes, it got in their hair. It even managed to insinuate itself into their food. They had to shake their bedclothes out each day just to try to rid themselves of it and no amount of care and attention seemed to be able to eliminate it from the carpets. Sarah declared that the stuff must have physical properties quite unique in the natural world. It apparently attached itself to any part of your body that came into contact with it with the tenacity of a limpet only to shed itself gleefully onto any surface it could find as soon as you stepped indoors. It was ubiquitous; as unavoidable as death and taxes. Sarah had never encountered such a tenaciously persistent substance. Even weeks after they returned to Switzerland, she would be finding grains of Helgoland lingering among her possessions. It was a minor grumble however and one easily tolerated in their happiness. Dune after all was made of sand. It was a part of life on the island.

They didn't confine themselves to Dune of course for they were both eager to explore the main island as well. In this respect Rudi, Daniela's friend and ally, was quite simply indispensable for he was willing, indeed eager, to act as the girls' private inter-island ferry service whenever prevailing conditions and the obligations of his other duties permitted. Rudi turned out to be a tall good looking young man with a shock of unruly blond hair, a deeply tanned complexion, an amiable demeanour and a nearly incomprehensible Frisian dialect. He was not, it must be admitted, an intellectual giant for he was of simple fishing stock but he was clever in the ways of the sea and expert with his boat. He was also totally devoted to Daniela and Sarah. In fact they were just about the best things that had ever happened to Rudi and he worshipped the two girls unreservedly. Privately, amid much giggling, they wondered between them if Rudi actually ever realised that they were anything other than good friends. He certainly never seemed to realise it and they were careful to conceal the true extent of their affections for each other whenever he was around.

Rudi did everything for them. He ferried them supplies from the main island whenever they asked. He was willing to carry them between the islands at whatever time of day or night they requested. He took them for trips out in his boat and never complained. Any outrageous demand they made of him he complied with, his ubiquitous broad grin never failing him; a faithful servant ardently devoted to the two young women in his life. He imagined himself their protector and champion. The day following the passing of the storm he was the first person back on Dune terrified that his two charges must be in mortal danger after being cut off for two days. They wondered if he had actually managed to sleep through worry during the storm. He was so happy to find them in good health and unharmed that they thought he was going to burst into tears. Rudi was priceless. The girls exploited him ruthlessly, teased him mercilessly and adored him.

Rudi's main duties for the day during the tourist season were in ferrying tourists to and from the ships anchored offshore. On her first trip to the main island Sarah was able to observe this process more closely. None of the ships actually docked in the harbour at Helgoland. Instead they dropped anchor in the lee of the islands a few hundred metres from shore and a positive swarm of fishing cobles raced out to divest them of their human cargo. Thus the habitual tranquillity of the islands was shattered each day in the early afternoon when the first of the big ships hove into view over the horizon. Then all the fishermen would drop everything and hasten out in their boats to begin the task of bringing the day trippers ashore, bodily heaving people into the cobles from large hatches set in the side of the ships. Considering that, on an average day in the summer months, up to six thousand people were transferred in this manner the whole procedure was executed in a remarkably short period of time. The fishermen had the process down to a fine tuned art. Once, presumably, the community on Helgoland had depended on fishing for its livelihood but this daily influx of tourists was a far better harvest from the sea it would appear and now fishing was of secondary importance. Or so Sarah thought. Daniela gave her another slant on things however as they watched the tourists arriving. "Tourism has quite a long history on Helgoland Sarah." she told her. "When this was a British colony the place was well known for tourism."

Sarah started in surprise. "A British colony? You're joking."

"Not at all. Britain captured the islands from Denmark during the Napoleonic Wars in 1807 and it was formally ceded to Britain in 1814. Under British rule it became a popular spa resort for wealthy people and a refuge for dissident artists and writers from Germany especially during the revolutions in 1830 and 1848. Also Britain had liberal gaming laws so this place was a big gambling den in those years and full of casinos. There was a lot of money coming into the islands."

"God I never knew this! When did it become German then?"

"In 1890 as part of the Helgoland-Zanzibar treaty in which Britain ceded control over Helgoland in return for German possessions and a free hand in Africa."

"It seems a pretty small place to swap for something as big as Zanzibar."

"It is. It was one of the smallest colonies of the British Empire. In the end though, it was the more important place. Helgoland gave Germany control over the Helgoland Bight and their North Sea coastline during the two World Wars so it turned out to be a vital strategic asset. Britain went to a lot of trouble to try and neutralise this place in the war."

"You mean this island was attacked during the war?"

421

"Hell yes! This place was intensely bombed during the Second World War. There's probably been more tons of explosives expended on these islands than on any other comparably sized patch of ground on the planet. This was an important naval and U boat base. They bombed the shit out of it. In the biggest raid over nine hundred and sixty heavy bombers saturated the islands and turned the place into a moonscape. The whole population was evacuated during the war."

Sarah shook her head in disbelief. "It doesn't seem possible. The place is so small."

"Oh yes. In fact the war completely altered the topography of the islands. You'll see that later."

When the tourists had left the island that evening Sarah and Daniela were able to explore without the inevitable attention they would have attracted otherwise. The main island was divided into several different regions. At the very south of the island was a large open harbour consisting of the South Harbour and Vorhafen bordered by a somewhat desolate landscape dotted with a few buildings. The main village which had a population of some one thousand six hundred people was mostly in a low lying area on the southern edge of the island called the Unterland although there were some houses extending onto the cliffs above. To the north east facing across the strait to Dune was an area of dunes called the Nord Ost Land or North East Land which contained the oil powered electricity plant, the water desalination plant and catchment area, the spa, the youth hostel and the marine research centre.

To the west of the village was an area of broken ground and scrubby vegetation, resembling a large quarry that was named the Mittelland. Sarah liked this sunny sheltered area. She found Traveller's Joy and bushes of naturalised *Rosa rugosa*, the prickly Asian rose bushes that grew freely by the sea. There were Grayling butterflies on the wing and rabbits among the bushes. Daniela had a different name for the region though. "This is the "Big Bang" Sarah." she told her.

"I presume we're not talking cosmology here."

Daniela shook her head. "No. After the war, the occupying Royal Navy tried to destroy the fortifications by detonating 6,800 tonnes of explosives here. It's supposed to be one of the largest non-nuclear explosions in history. What you're standing in is the fucking great hole it left behind."

"My God!" Having lived her life in Switzerland Sarah was somewhat sheltered from the terrible devastation that so much of Europe had suffered during the wars of the twentieth century. It seemed incredible to her that anyone would have wanted to destroy this lovely island.

The village on Helgoland was relatively modern which was hardly surprising since World War Two had barely left one brick standing on another after it on the island. Despite this it was not without its charm. It was almost entirely free of cars. Heavy items were transported on little electric trolleys. The only passenger vehicle on the island seemed to be the little electric police van. Even bicycles were banned it seemed. Thus all the streets were pedestrian streets and they were full of shops, cafes, restaurants, take away food outlets and souvenir kiosks to cater for the tourist hordes. When the tourists were present it was a busy place and Daniela was forced to tie her hair up and don baseball cap and large dark glasses to conceal her identity to prevent their holiday from being ruined by autograph hunters or have their solitude compromised by publicity. Daniela had perfected the art of disappearing into the background in the presence of crowds as a necessary protection of her privacy but it was always a little tense. She wasn't quite as well known here in North Germany as in Switzerland but she was still famous enough to make the precautions necessary and they were always relieved when the last of the tourists re-embarked on the fishing cobles to ferry them back to the waiting ships in the late afternoon. After that they were at leisure to sit outside on the terrace of a restaurant with a drink in the sunshine until such time as Rudi was free to carry them back across the strait to Dune.

To Sarah's delight they found several good books on marine life in the shops and at the Marine Biology centre and she could start to identify the sea life around her with more authority. Daniela, in her turn, boosted the local economy by purchasing an expensive pair of binoculars; Zeiss Ikon of the same mark as Sarah's own. They further returned some of Daniela's considerable amount of disposable income into circulation by buying a telescope. At home in Switzerland Sarah had her own field telescope but it was a bit old and battered and in many ways unsatisfactory. Thus, whilst they were buying Daniela's binoculars, she covetously admired a seriously expensive telescope made by the Austrian firm of Swarovski on display in the same shop. Daniela saw her looking at it. "What's up Sarah?"

"I'm just thinking I wish I'd brought my telescope. It would have been just the thing for seeing the birds and animals around the islands."

"Is it like this one?"

"Good God no! I couldn't begin to afford one of these! This is a Swarovski HD STM 80 with a 20 to 60x zoom eyepiece, carrying bag, tripod and lens cleaning kit."

"So a pretty good piece of kit then?"

"Brilliant! They're among some of the best spotting scopes in the business; second to none."

"Ok we'll take it then."

"You're mad! With all the accessories it's nearly three thousand Euros."

"Ach a pittance. Call it an investment. We'll set it up on the cliff top to look at the birds on Lange Anna, charge the tourists a Euro a time to look and we'll make our money back in no time."

Sarah laughed. "God I bet you could do too."

"Sure you could. Tourists are custom designed to be divested of their money. There's a lass that has a stall on the path up to the Oberland selling pieces of the red flint you find here on Helgoland. It's a characteristic stone you find in the red sandstone and very unusual. She sells pieces of the flint by size and weight. She charges up to twenty odd Euros for the bigger pieces and the tourists snap them up. It never occurs to them that with a hammer and a bit of work they could dabble around the bases of the cliffs or on the rocks and pick up the stuff by the bag full for nothing."

Sarah grinned. "Oh God! What a way to make a living. We could set ourselves up as a pair of nature guides, do three or four hours of work a day when the tourists are ashore and be perfectly well off."

"Except sweetheart we don't need to. We're *already* well off. So well off, in fact, that we can afford to hire a private jet to fly us here and buy ourselves a new toy to play with for no other reason than that we can. So come on let's buy this beauty and hump it up on the Oberland to try it out."

"Oh God Danny! Are you sure?"

"Of course I am. I was sure the minute I saw that avaricious look in your eyes. You really want this baby don't you?"

"I've always wanted one Danny but I could never afford one. It doesn't seem right though."

"Why?"

"Well because without your money I wouldn't be able to. I've always wanted to have a telescope like this but it was always one of those things you dream about. Now you can just come along and buy it on a whim and it doesn't seem right."

"Sarah darling I was being facetious before. Yes money does allow you to buy things that you would only be able to dream about without it but it's not just a casual whim. Why do you think that thing's on display here?

There're lots of rich people that visit these islands many of whom would pick up that thing just on a whim. They'd probably play with it a few times and then it would be relegated to some cupboard somewhere and hardly ever get used again. With you that's not the case. You'd treasure it and use it. With you, such a high quality instrument would be put to the purpose for which it was made. I've never known eyes like yours. You're a fantastic observer Sarah. You and that telescope *deserve* each other. So stop bleating and let's buy the bloody thing."

And so they did. There were still a lot of visitors about so Daniela insisted on going for a beer in a congenial pub before they set out to try out their new purchases. Sarah almost groaned in frustration as she crooned over her new telescope but Daniela made her wait patiently until the island was quiet once more. Then they set out up on to the Oberland.

The Oberland of Helgoland was a plateau ringed by red sandstone cliffs. To the south and east these cliffs fell down to the low lying areas of the island but on the west and north they plummeted fifty metres down into the sea. The top of this plateau Sarah had thought was flat but in fact it was deeply pitted by huge holes a legacy of the ferocious bombing the island had endured during the war. All over it was carpeted with short grass kept short by the characteristic breed of black Helgoland sheep that grazed up here. Sarah looked around the strange bomb pitted landscape sadly. "It seems awful that people would want to bomb somewhere like this."

"People do a lot of stupid things in wartime Sarah."

"Was Dune bombed as well?"

"Yes Sarah. It wasn't as badly hit as the main island of course because most of the important installations and the naval base were over here but certainly there were guns and what have you on Dune so it would have been targeted. It was also hit by accident on at least one occasion."

"Accident?"

"Yes. Apparently in 1944 the Americans hit it by mistake. They had this bloody mad scheme called Operation Aphrodite that consisted of loading a stripped down B17 Flying Fortress with explosives and flying it by remote control to a target and crashing it deliberately. Well they tried the idea a couple of times on Helgoland but on one occasion the guy operating the radio control got the islands mixed up, missed the U boat pens on the main island and only made a big hole in the sand dunes on Dune. You can't see the damage as much on Dune of course because it's all sand and any holes quickly fill up with blown sand."

"Good God! I still can't get my head around why anyone would want to despoil a place like this in a war."

Daniela looked grim. "You were brought up Swiss Sarah. Switzerland's hardly ever been touched by war for over a hundred and fifty years. You know what I missed when I first came to live permanently in Switzerland?"

"No."

"It was something odd; something you don't really notice until they're not there; war memorials! Every city in Europe, every town, every village has memorials to its dead in the world wars. You can walk into the tiniest village or hamlet and somewhere on a little patch of grass you'll find a little stone memorial commemorating the people of that village who died in the wars. They're ubiquitous, a part of the daily background of life, a constant reminder of the untold millions of Europeans who were slaughtered in the wars of the twentieth century. Except in Switzerland. You don't see war memorials in Switzerland."

Sarah felt a cold chill in her spine and the echoes in her mind of the thunder of guns and bombs where there was now only the sound of the sea against the cliffs. It seemed an obscenity that people had died in violence on this tranquil island. She had studied history at university

427

but here the scars and ghosts of history seemed very close indeed. She was Swiss but she was also English and European. Europe was a paradox. Few places on earth had contributed more to human civilisation and culture than Europe and yet nowhere else on earth was the ground more stained with the blood of barbarity. For thousands of years people had murdered each other by the millions in conflict over this appendage of the great Eurasian landmass. Nowhere else could boast quite such a violent past and here, on this tiny little patch of land, the very physical scars of that violence could still be seen. She shuddered and shook her head to clear the uncomfortable burden of history from her mind.

If any evidence was present that the sound of the guns had been silent now for over sixty years then they found it on the cliffs of Helgoland. These cliffs on the north and west of the island were extraordinary to Sarah. She was, of course, entirely familiar with cliff faces but she had never seen cliffs like these before. For one thing they were sea cliffs, plunging fifty metres down directly into the foaming surf. They were of the curious brick red sandstone that was the characteristic rock of Helgoland but the red colour was not uniform for it was everywhere streaked with white. The white streaks and blotches on it were not the result of geological modification however. They were rather more recent and biological in nature.

"Bird shit!" Daniela told her when Sarah wondered about the discolouration. It was true too. The cliffs were heavily fouled with guano. It was easy to see why for hundreds upon hundreds of sea birds were roosting on the ledges of the cliffs and filling the air with a cacophony of guttural and wailing cries. Sarah was astonished at the spectacle. Birds of course nested and roosted on cliffs in the mountains as well but not in these sort of numbers. Some ledges just seemed to be full of birds virtually brushing wings with each other and Sarah wondered how they all managed to occupy the same tiny spaces without continual conflict between them. She expressed amazement at the sheer number of birds. "This is nothing Sarah." Daniela told her. "You ought to be here in the spring or early summer when all the birds are breeding. There's three or four times as many then and you can hardly hear yourself think for the racket."

"Jesus! How do they all nest on these cliffs?"

"A lot of them don't. Some birds just lay their eggs on the rock ledges. The eggs are specially shaped so that they don't roll off. Having said that, a lot of them do roll off or get knocked off by squabbling birds. In the springtime the rocks at the base of the cliffs must be Germany's biggest omelette."

"It's amazing." Sarah declared. "I've never seen so many birds trying to fit into so little space."

"These cliffs here at the north west are called the Lummelfelsen, Sarah, and they're apparently the smallest nature reserve in Germany. Lummel is the German word for a guillemot it turns out so it translates as Guillemot cliffs. A birdwatcher guy gave me a tour of the cliffs and he told me that there are about two and a half thousand guillemots that breed here. They'll have all finished breeding by now though so I suppose most of them are back out to sea."

Sarah was scouring the cliff faces excitedly with her binoculars. "Not all of them Danny. Look there's a bunch of them about half way down that bit sticking out over there."

Daniela raised her own binoculars to look. "Oh yes! I see them. Hey, let's set up the telescope and take a close look at them." In the telescope the birds were a wonderful sight. Their backs which appeared black at any range were now revealed to be a dark chocolate brown colour. They were stood along the ledge in a group perhaps twenty strong, uttering harsh growling noises. Sarah was entranced. "Have you ever seen one before?" Daniela asked her.

"No never Danny. We don't exactly get many of them in Switzerland you know!"

429

Daniela was peering through the telescope in fascination. "This thing was a good buy Sarah! The optical quality is fantastic."

"It's a class instrument Danny. You've only got it at twenty times magnification there as well. If you turn the eyepiece you can zoom up to sixty times."

Daniela tried it and whistled in appreciation. "My God! I could nearly count the feathers on their arses." She seemed entranced by the birds. "They're weird aren't they? Some of the ignorant tourists think that they're penguins."

Sarah laughed. "Don't be too harsh on them Danny. Technically they're correct."

"Oh come on now Sarah. I may not be much of an ornithologist but even I know that you only find penguins at the south pole."

"Well the southern hemisphere any way although there is a species of penguin called a Galapagos Penguin that lives on the Galapagos Islands which are dead on the equator. The most northerly of their breeding colonies is on the north end of the island of Isabella which is just in the Northern Hemisphere so technically they're a North Hemisphere breeding bird."

"Now you're just being bloody pedantic. You will concede, I presume, that most penguins are south of the equator and, even if a few do creep into the Northern Hemisphere, that's only on the Galapagos islands which, if my shaky geography isn't letting me down, I recall are in the Pacific Ocean and pretty far removed from here. In any case, the only other thing I can say with certainty about penguins is that they can't fly! Now those things are half way up a bloody great cliff and, without the use of ropes and rock climbing equipment, I can't see how they could possibly scale that cliff without the power of flight."

"Well of course guillemots can fly Danny. Nevertheless they are technically penguins."

"Ok little Miss know-it-all. Explain."

430

"Etymology Danny. It's all in a word. Where do you think the word penguin comes from?"

"I have no idea."

"It's an old word, probably Gaelic but incorporated into French and borrowed from there by English and it was the old word for birds of the Auk family especially Razorbills. There was a flightless member of the auk family that's extinct now called a Great Auk which was even known as a King Penguin and an island off America where it bred is still known as Penguin Island. Penguin was just the generic name for auks. When European sailing crews, especially the crews of Magellan's ships, entered waters around the South Pole they encountered flightless birds that looked, to their eyes, just like auks and so they called them penguins which was their name for auks and we've been stuck with the name ever since. So technically those birds there don't look like penguins. They *are* penguins and the birds of the family Sphenisicidae look like them."

Daniela groaned. "I wish I'd never mentioned the name. Considering you've never seen them before you already appear to be an expert on them."

"I'm not an expert on them Danny but of course I've read up about them. There's loads of things here I've never seen before but I've read about."

"Such as?"

"Well those seagulls for instance."

"We get seagulls in Switzerland Sarah."

"Yes but some of the gulls here are species you never see in Switzerland."

"Well which ones? There are bloody thousands of them."

"Those little ones with the yellow bills and black legs. They're just about the most numerous gull on the cliffs.

"So what are they?"

Sarah laughed happily. "If you listen they're telling you their name!"

"Being with you can often get pretty weird Sarah but I'm not about to hold a conversation with a sodding seagull."

"It's their calls Danny. They have a call which gives them their name; Kittiwake. Listen. They sound like they're calling out kitti-wake!"

"I see what you mean. You've never seen those gulls before?"

"Hell no! There was one immature bird turned up at Romanshorn on Lake Constance a couple of years ago but I never got to see it. I never thought that the first time I'd see one I'd be seeing literally hundreds of them. This is just amazing to me. Then there's the pigeons."

Daniela looked around the cliffs in surprise. In fact there were quite a few pigeons roosting on the cliffs but she could see nothing particularly interesting about them. "But they're just ordinary pigeons aren't they Sarah?"

"Well yes they are but it depends on what you mean by ordinary. Actually they're no different from the pigeons you see in nearly every city in Europe or the ones people keep in lofts. What most people don't realise is that, originally, the common old garden pigeon was in fact a bird that nested for the most part on sea cliffs. The truly wild form is called a Rock Dove. All the domestic forms and feral pigeons in towns are in fact descendants from these wild Rock Doves. These birds here are the wild ancestors of every pigeon you ever fed in the local park."

"Why would they take to city life so well then?"

"Cliffs Danny. When you think about it, to a bird, a city, with all its tall buildings, is really just an interlocking collection of convenient cliffs full of ledges and holes to nest and roost on. Loads of birds we think of as city birds actually started out as birds that nest on cliffs; seagulls, sparrows, Jackdaws, swifts, swallows, martins, Kestrels, Peregrine Falcons and yes pigeons."

"Sparrows nest on cliffs?"

"Yes the common House Sparrow originally nested on sea cliffs. They still do. I've seen half a dozen flitting around this cliff while we've been stood here."

"So why don't guillemots breed in cities then?"

"Because they're sea birds Danny and they feed on fish from the sea. You don't get sand eels in park lakes."

Daniela shouldered the telescope tripod. "Ok Miss Clever Pants. Let's walk further along. There's a couple of birds on here I do know something about that I want to show you."

They saw the birds almost immediately. They were on one of the broadest ledges of the cliff they had seen; a jutting terrace perhaps half way up the cliff where Daniela had seen them on previous visits. Daniela clapped her hands in pleasure. "I knew they'd be here. I just knew it."

Sarah was staring in astonishment. The birds were quite the most spectacular sea birds anywhere on the cliffs; great white, sleek looking creatures with a yellow tinge to their heads, large robust sharp bills, black wing tips and oddly maniacal looking blue grey eyes. They were huge; dwarfing the surrounding Kittiwakes and predatory looking. Three of them were roosting on the ledge and, even as they watched, a fourth bird came arrowing in from the sea for all the world like a fighter bomber on a strike mission. Sarah let out her breath. "Gannets! Bloody gannets. I've always wanted to see a gannet."

Daniela was looking unbearably smug. "Cool huh?"

"They're fantastic."

Daniela nodded. "I've seen them before Sarah. There's a place in Yorkshire on Flamborough Head called Bempton Cliffs where there are thousands of them. It's supposed to be the largest mainland gannetry in England. I went there when I was a teenager and it's an amazing place. There aren't many gannets on Helgoland though. They've only been breeding here since 1991,

I'm told, so the colony is still rather small. Still they're amazing birds. I think they're one of my favourites."

"They're wonderful Danny. I've seen films of them and pictures but I've always wanted to see them in the wild. This is just brilliant." For the next few minutes Sarah enthused over her gannets but Daniela seemed distracted. She was using their new telescope to search the ledges of the cliffs meticulously. At last Sarah tore her eyes away from the little group of gannets. "What are you doing Danny?"

"There's another bird I'm trying to find for you Sarah. That bird watching guy who gave me a tour of the cliffs pointed these out to me and showed me how to identify them. They're not as cool to look at as those gannets but I thought you might be interested." Suddenly she yipped in triumph. "Aha! Found one." She stepped back from the telescope. "Take a look Sarah and tell me what you think of this."

Bemused Sarah stepped up to peer through the eyepiece. For a moment she was puzzled. The bird crouched up on a ledge below was peculiarly unattractive at first glance like a somewhat scruffy looking gull in dull grey with an odd looking bill. "What is it?" she asked.

Daniela punched the air triumphantly. "At last! A bloody bird that I know the name of and you don't. It's a Fulmar Sarah."

The fog cleared from Sarah's brain. "Oh of course! My God I couldn't think what it was to begin with. Wow! What a strange looking bird."

"The beaks are weird aren't they?"

"Yes they're tube noses Danny. They're related to petrels and albatrosses. I didn't expect to see these. I read somewhere that they've only really colonised Europe over the last century."

"I don't know Sarah. You see how there are no other birds next to them on their ledges? That guy told me that they're very anti-social birds. Apparently they've got this endearing habit of puking up on any bird that encroaches on their territory so the other birds leave them well alone."

"These cliffs are just mind blowing Danny. I've never seen anything like them. What's all that rubbish around the gannets?"

"Old discarded fishing net by the look of it Sarah. It's a big problem on Helgoland they tell me. The gannets collect it for nesting material and they're always getting tangled in it. They've even had to send rock climbers down the cliffs to disentangle struggling birds. I wouldn't fancy it myself! Can you imagine having to wrestle with a bird the size of a gannet dangling on a rope half way down that sodding cliff?"

"God no!"

"Let's go look at Lange Anna."

"Who or what the blue blazes is Lange Anna Danny?"

"You'll see."

Lange Anna was a famous landmark on Helgoland; a large sea stack at the very North West corner of the island separated from the main body of the cliffs by the erosive action of the sea. The isolated tower of sandstone stood in splendid isolation some 47 metres in height; a great rock column alive with roosting seabirds. They found Herring gulls, Kittiwakes, cormorants, shags and, for a new thrill, even a couple of Razorbills near this stack to complete their day… a wonderful day on Helgoland.

Chapter Thirty-Eight

There were more such days and they seemed to blend one into another as the two young women lost themselves in the magic of the islands. They found wading birds in plenty on the islands and some of these were familiar to Sarah. The Redshanks, Dunlin and Curlews were all regular visitors to Switzerland in winter or on migration and even the little Sanderling which raced up and down the beaches in front of the waves like comical little clockwork toys were common passage migrants on the Swiss lakes. So too were the Ringed Plovers they frequently came upon along the beaches but there were some waders that Sarah had not encountered before. There were the odd little Turnstones among the rocks and along the beaches for instance which became favourites for them and the big, flamboyant black and white Oystercatchers. The ones they loved the most, however, were the unassuming little dark waders with yellow beaks and legs that they found along the rocky shore at the north end of the main island. They were Purple Sandpipers and, in strong sunlight at close quarters, there was indeed a subtle purple sheen to their mantles. It was easy to get to close quarters as well for they discovered that Purple Sandpipers were ridiculously tame. They would often dabble around among the rocks within a couple of feet of you and they seemed to have no fear of people whatsoever. They loved them because they were their companions among the rocks when the tide was out and allowing them to explore the rock pools on the northern shore.

Sarah and Daniela quickly became enthusiastic rock pool collectors. The wealth of life in these pools astonished Sarah and she could spend hours hunting among them while Daniela sat on a rock and watched her with deep affection. They early acquired a pair of children's fishing nets and a couple of glass jars and a plastic washing up bowl to examine their catches in and would fish among the pools as happy as children, whooping with glee whenever they found something new. They found the common Green Shore crabs to be abundant and they found Velvet Swimming Crabs and even a largish Edible Crab. It was the little Hermit Crabs they adored the most though and these were so abundant that it seemed that every discarded whelk or periwinkle shell had its Hermit Crab lodging in it. There were all sorts of shrimps and prawns to test their identification skills, sea urchins and sea anemones. They found common starfish, a Common Brittle Starfish and one spectacular species of starfish with ten arms they learned was called a Common Sun Star.

To begin with Sarah was overwhelmed by the diversity of sea weeds they found. It was a whole class of plant life for which she had no prior knowledge of and she despaired at ever being able to sort it all out. But Sarah had the kind of mind that looks for order and categorisation. She quickly realised that these diverse marine algae could be roughly divided into three sorts; brown ones, green ones and red ones. The brown ones were the big rubbery tough things that washed up all over the place and made underwater forests of thick fronds and stems. The green ones were usually smaller and more delicate rooting among the rock pools and, most delicate and attractive of all, were the red species which could be exquisite little adornments to the pools. Once she had narrowed it down to these three major groups it was then just a matter of elimination before she could arrive at a guess at the species but it was often a long process of consultation with their nature guides before they were fully satisfied that they had identified one.

Sarah's collection of seashells was growing by the day in the chalet and they would often eat outside in the garden of an evening with shells scattered about on the table and discuss their day's haul of shellfish over a couple of open identification guides. Sarah had never had such an inclination that there were so many different species of shellfish in the world; some one hundred thousand known species by one account. It was a huge, diverse phylum of the animal kingdom which, other than a passing interest in freshwater snails, she had scarcely touched before. Sometimes she felt an almost despairing sadness that life never could never be long enough to truly appreciate all the wondrous diversity of life in the world. Here everything seemed new; completely different to her own range of knowledge. For most of her life she had been content with the natural riches of her homeland but now, just a small distance in global terms from that homeland, she was confronted with a new, bewilderingly complex and unfamiliar ecosystem that took her breath away with its beauty and alien fascination. She felt frustrated by her lack of knowledge and greedy for the new horizons opening before her. She could pick up and finger one of her new prize possessions; a chiton she was almost sure was a Coat-of-Mail Chiton, and know that although she loved Switzerland, and always would, it would never be quite enough for her again.

There were fish too in the rock pools; often odd little fish of curiously ugly yet endearing appearance. Sarah had bought a field guide to European fish species among her new acquisitions but even so she found many of the fish to be difficult identification problems. For instance they caught a little brown spiny thing that was evidently a species of Goby but that was about as far as Sarah could pin it down with certainty. Judging by the distribution maps in her guide Sarah guessed it was either a Common Goby or a Sand Goby but, to be honest, it was hard enough to tell the two species apart on the illustrations in the field guide let alone on a small wriggling creature in the bottom of the plastic bowl. She also came upon a Shanny or at least what she assumed

438

was a Shanny although the Blenny family was another one in which it was difficult to separate species. One rather spectacular species in this group she did feel confident about was a long eel like little fish about twelve centimetres long that she discovered after turning over some rocks. This particular specimen didn't take kindly to capture for it flapped around furiously in the bowl and vanished like quicksilver when re-released into the rock pool but at least Sarah was able to put a name to it; a Gunnel. Compounding the problem was another species of small brown bottom dwelling fish that Sarah was aware that she might come across. From her reading she was aware that Weevers were common along the shallow fringes of the North Sea and they were not dissimilar from Gobies and Blennies. The trouble was that Weevers had seriously poisonous spines on them and that made Sarah cautious about picking up small unidentified fish to examine them more closely. In the end she never found a Weever although she did catch a small fish that she was fairly sure was a Short Spined Sea Scorpion. Sea Scorpions were not poisonous; they just looked as if they ought to be. Whatever the fish were however Sarah found them fascinating. It was another new exciting realm for her.

There were some odd encounters too for her. For instance they came upon another species of quite tame bird among the rocks below the North Cliffs that, on the face of it, was peculiarly uninteresting. It was a little brown pipit; quite drab and not distinguished by any particularly attractive feature of plumage. But it was strangely familiar for it was a Rock Pipit and a close relation of the ubiquitous Water Pipits that were such constant accompaniments to the Alpine meadows in Switzerland. It was so closely related, in fact, that, until a few years previously, it had been considered as co-specific with a Water Pipit. Yet it was now regarded as a completely different species. It was a bit like bumping into someone you thought you knew but then

439

discovering they only spoke Swahili or something. It was a long lost relation from the mountains.

The two young women took more than an academic interest in the sea life around Helgoland; they also formed a more basic attachment to it for it became a major component of their diet. In many respects the food on Helgoland was Sarah's biggest challenge. It would of course have been entirely possible for Sarah to stick with relatively familiar food or at least food items that were not quite so challenging but Daniela, as always, was eager to explore Sarah's zest for adventure and new experiences and she openly dared Sarah to try the more startling of maritime cuisine. It was hard for Sarah because sea food did not feature heavily in Swiss cooking and many items were completely strange to her. Nevertheless she tried them all bravely with mixed results. Prawns and shrimps she had tried before and they were less of a challenge. Shellfish on the other hand were something she had virtually never tried. To her surprise she found that she enjoyed the mussels she ate in a white wine sauce and other shellfish, such as cockles and clams were quite tolerable. Oysters, however, she was far less sure about and she was at a loss to see what all the fuss was about with these luxury shellfish. She likewise had mixed feelings about fresh crab and on one occasion Daniela took her to an expensive restaurant on the main island and insisted she tried lobster. Daniela loved the stuff but Sarah could have taken it or left it.

There was one major item of marine food however that was awarded an unreserved seal of approval... fish. Sarah had always liked fish but the variety of fresh fish in Switzerland was generally pretty limited. Her experience of fresh fish was mostly confined to the fresh water species harvested from the Swiss lakes or farmed in fresh water such as trout, perch or whitefish. Marine species were largely frozen, smoked or otherwise processed and then only in a limited variety.

Furthermore she had rarely had chance to experiment with cooking fish back in the cottage in the Alpli for Nicole was an unenthusiastic fish eater at best. On Helgoland however she had virtually unlimited supplies of fresh fish to hand and she could quite happily have lived on little else. By far and away her favourite were the marinated herring filets served up with North German style fried potatoes that were a stock item in the cuisine of North Germany. Herrings she discovered were not only a part of the cuisine and culture of this part of the world but also a major dynamic in its history. There had actually been *wars* over the herring fisheries in these regions, so important were the little silvery fish to human economy in Northern Europe. Sarah tried herrings raw, pickled, cooked in vinegar, smoked, garnished with sour cream and fried. She loved them all.

Daniela loved fish as well and they became adventurous in trying out as many types as they could. Another great favourite of theirs was fresh mackerel which was virtually unknown in Switzerland and Sarah enjoyed the fresh plaice that Rudi brought them one day. They made a habit, when on the main island, of stopping by the harbour whenever any fisherman was returning with his catch and buying any fish that took their fancy. On one occasion they tried Dover Sole which was delicious but their best buy, as far as flatfish were concerned, was a sizeable turbot they found among one catch which they feasted on that evening and unanimously declared to be the tastiest fish they had tried so far.

They were not merely passive consumers of fish however; they were active hunters too for, one day, in the late afternoon after the departure of the day's tourists, Rudi took them fishing in his boat for a few hours. Sarah viewed this excursion with trepidation for, until now, her seafaring experience had been confined to boat trips on the Swiss lakes and Rudi's short ferry journeys between the islands. "I'm sure I'm going to be sea sick." she declared with conviction and only consented to the adventure after Rudi promised faithfully to instantly transport her back to terra firma should she become queasy. In the event the sea was calm and her fears ungrounded and she enjoyed their trip out on the open sea, where the boat was surrounded by sea birds and they were lucky enough to see a flight of Brent Geese flying by offshore, several Red Throated Divers and even a small pod of Pilot Whales.

The fishing method caught them by surprise however. Rudi provided them with rods and reels and monofilament line to which was attached the bait. The bait was unconvincing, however, for it was a heavy, silver, vaguely fish shaped slug of metal armed with a fearsome looking treble hook. "Why," wondered Daniela aloud, "would any fish be stupid enough to try and eat a pound of stainless steel?"

"I think it's supposed to look like a fish Danny." Sarah observed dubiously.

"Ye Gods! I knew that fish never had much of a reputation for intellectual prowess but they must be absolute morons to mistake one of these bloody things for lunch. Do you really think we're actually going to catch anything Rudi?"

Rudi was astride the tiller of the boat posing it up dreadfully for the benefit of his two charges. The water was choppy enough to force the girls to sit down on the benches in the coble but Rudi was stood with his legs apart, one hand resting gently on the tiller and the other clutching a can of beer. His only concession to the movement of the boat was to occasionally wipe the spray from his sunglasses. He was evidently running on testosterone. He grinned hugely. "We're gonna catch fish you see." he reassured them. The girls were unconvinced.

At last Rudi picked out a likely mark some way off the northern end of the islands and instructed them to lower their lures over the side of the boat. He showed them how to allow their lures, which he called pilkers, to drop to the bottom and then work them up and down by lifting their rods in a rhythmic fashion. It was surprisingly hard work and the girls remained pessimistic. "I could quickly get bored with this." Daniela grumbled.

"Well think of the workout our upper arms are getting." Sarah laughed. "We might not catch anything for tea but we're sure as hell getting fit trying."

"I honestly can't think of a more ridiculous way of...EEK!" Daniela squealed and the rod was bucking alarmingly in her hands. "There's something pulling on the end Rudi."

"Ah you have fish. Bring him up then."

"I can't! It's pulling too hard." The rod was curved over and bouncing up and down and Daniela looked so thoroughly terrified that Sarah burst out in laughter. "Stop laughing Sarah. The sodding thing nearly had me overboard. Help me Rudi."

Rudi left his station at the tiller with a grin and grasped Daniela by the shoulders. "Come now. Reel him in. I have you safe."

"Put your back into it Danny." grinned Sarah. "That could be our tea tonight." Daniela shot her a poisonous look and hauled away bravely. Inch by inch she dragged the hard plunging fish toward the surface.

Rudi peered over the side of the boat as a flash of colour appeared in the water below. "Jawohl! Eine gutes Dorsch."

"What the hell is a Dorsch?" asked Daniela acerbically.

"You call him cod in English."

Sarah's interest perked up. "You've caught a cod Danny? Wow don't let him drop off. I've never seen a live cod."

Daniela uttered an unfortunate epithet. "I haven't caught the bloody thing yet Sarah, however, assuming my arms don't actually separate from my shoulder blades, I will endeavour to satisfy your naturist curiosity."

At last the fish was floundering on the surface. Sarah yipped excitedly. "Wow! It's a big one Danny."

Rudi nodded and picked up an evil looking gaff. "Ja he is not so bad; two and a half maybe three kilo."

With an expert quick snatch with the gaff Rudi hauled the fish inboard. Daniela collapsed exhausted on the bench. "I am absolutely knackered!" she declared feelingly but she looked pleased with herself.

Sarah was examining the fish with interest. From pictures she had seen she had always thought that cod were quite ugly fish but this creature was handsome with its yellow and brown mottled flanks catching the sunlight and its thickset head. It seemed almost a shame to kill it even though it would be a welcome guest at dinner that evening. "It's a beauty Danny." she enthused. "My God! Look at the size of the mouth on it." The fish had a huge gaping mouth. The big pilker was dwarfed in that yawning gape.

Rudi meanwhile was attending to necessities. With a flourish he produced a flask from his box by the tiller and three small cups. "Your first fish." he boomed. "We go have a drink to celebrate." He poured three small shots of schnapps and handed them around before raising his cup. "Petri Heil!" The girls decided unanimously that Rudi's schnapps was quite the foulest, most evil alcoholic beverage that either of them had ever had the misfortune to pour down their throats in their lives but Rudi would not let them dwell on the malodorous effects on their livers for long. "Come now. Get your lines back in the water. There is plenty more fish."

And so it proved for the mark was a productive one and before Rudi finally set course back to land Sarah and Daniela had taken a dozen codling between them from perhaps a couple of pounds in weight up to nearly seven. They lay back in the boat exhausted with the effort and sipped at cans of beer they had liberated from Rudi's stash. "I never knew fishing was such hard work." Daniela observed. "I always thought people did this for relaxation." But she looked triumphant. "I tell you what Sarah. It's fish and chips English style for tea tonight. We'll whip up some batter and deep fry them. Shame we can't get mushy peas here."

"What the hell are mushy peas?" asked Sarah in mystification.

"Hmmph! Call yourself English. You've been exiled from Blighty for too long Sarah dear. Mushy peas are dried marrow-fat peas soaked overnight and then simmered until they make a sort of lumpy puree; absolute essential accompaniment to fish and chips."

"It sounds disgusting!"

"Well to be honest it looks pretty disgusting too but it's delicious; part of our great Yorkshire culinary heritage. Mind you they do make you fart something rotten."

"I think we'll stick to an accompanying salad ok."

Back in harbour on the main island Rudi cleaned and filleted the fish and, since there was too much for the two girls, they shared their catch with him. Then they took him for a beer and his preening pride in being seen in public accompanied by the two beautiful girls was richly comic. Daniela bought him a bottle of good Scotch to thank him for the day out. It would, Daniela pointed out, be far better for his liver than the toxic schnapps he had inflicted on them that day; a distilled beverage that Daniela theorised was probably derived from extracted sting-ray venom.

Back on Dune that night they had their best meal yet. Daniela sacrificed a bottle of beer to make beer batter to coat the thick cod fillets while Sarah peeled potatoes for chips and tossed a salad. They deep fried the battered fish to a golden brown and fried up a mound of chips. The day out on the open sea had given them an even better appetite than usual but it was dark by the

445

time their preparations were complete. They ate outside in the garden nonetheless for they had purchased a bottled gas lamp for such eventualities and it hissed away on the rough wooden table attracting moths and bathing the little garden in soft light as the beams of the lighthouse on the main island swept regularly overhead. The fish was superb with big firm white flakes that crumbled in your mouth with a buttery after taste and they gorged themselves on it.

Sarah pushed her plate aside with a sigh of replete satisfaction. "You know something Danny?" she said, "That was the first time I ever in my life actually ate something that I caught and killed with my own hands. It feels kind of odd."

"Why Sarah?"

"I don't know. I guess I'm just not comfortable killing anything. I felt really sorry killing those fish today. I don't even like killing insects or anything. But that's hypocritical isn't it? I mean I eat meat and fish and so on. Somebody has to kill the animals I eat but I'm squeamish about doing it myself."

Daniela nodded and poured another glass of wine. "I know what you mean Sarah. It does seem sad to kill a beautiful fish. There's another thing though. Somehow I find it more satisfying that we actually took our food with our own hands. You feel more connected to the animal you're eating. It's not just an anonymous slab of flesh on a supermarket counter that somebody else killed for you. You participated in the process. You actually had to work for your food. Somehow it feels more ethical. You feel that if everybody had to kill their own meat it might make them more appreciative of it and more sympathetic to the animals that had to die to provide it."

"Yes I feel a little like that too. I've eaten game during the hunting season but it makes me wonder what it would feel like to actually have to go out and hunt a

446

deer to eat myself. It's all very well when somebody else shoots it for you."

"Well we can always try and catch a rabbit for our supper tomorrow."

"Oh God! Don't say that. I couldn't do it. They're too cute."

"I don't think I could either but I've eaten rabbit and it's nice. Double standards I suppose. I can just about get my head around killing a fish for supper but cute little bunnies are a different matter aren't they?"

"I suppose so. What are we going to do tomorrow?"

"Well the forecast says it's going to be breezy tomorrow."

"So?"

"Well Sarah there's something I want to do that's really silly but it's something I've never done in my life."

"What is it?"

"You'll laugh."

"I won't. I promise."

"It's something I saw in a shop today before we went out with Rudi."

"Go on."

"They were selling kites. I've never flown a kite in my life and I've always wanted to. You promised you wouldn't laugh!"

Sarah wiped her eyes. "I can't help it. I think it's a brilliant idea. Tomorrow we'll go fly a kite."

Chapter Thirty-Nine

The next day they flew a kite.. Giggling like a pair of small children, they ran out a long length of line along the beach and after many aborted efforts finally managed to get their new toy aloft. It was a colourful design in yellow and scarlet and they managed to raise it to a prodigious altitude, gasping as it receded into the blue above to nearly vanishing point; as happy as a pair of schoolgirls on their summer holiday.

They spent a good deal of time on the beach in the evenings for Daniela, it seemed, had some mermaid blood in her and adored to be by the water side. The seals on the beach became their familiar companions and some they came to recognise each day; often giving them silly names. One particularly corpulent bull reminded Sarah irresistibly of Herr Berger and so they called him Bruno. They would frequently picnic along the beach among their seals and Sarah would recline on the sand in perfect contentment and watch Daniela disport herself among the waves.

Daniela had one thing in common with Nicole for she was a superb swimmer and any body of water held a siren's call to her. Sarah was at best an indifferent swimmer. She had, it is true, learned to swim at school but that had been in a nice controlled and heated swimming bath. She was unlikely to be tempted into swimming in the alpine lakes and tarns of the Toggenburg and she was afraid of their cold depths. If the idea of swimming in a mountain lake made her nervous then the thought of merrily floundering out into a dirty great ocean filled her with horror. Daniela did manage to lure her into the sea on a few occasions but never beyond her depth or even much above waist height and then only when the surf was gentle. Daniela on the other hand seemed utterly fearless in the water and on occasions swam so far offshore that Sarah became agitated and begged her to be careful. Despite her nervousness Sarah enjoyed watching Daniela in the water. She seemed so graceful and strong and Sarah envied her for her confident familiarity with the water. Also Daniela apparently regarded swimming costumes as pure vanity for she nearly always bathed nude and the sight of her emerging naked from the waves with the water running off her never failed to take Sarah's breath away.

On one occasion they invited Rudi along for an evening picnic on the beach by way of thanking him for his unstinting efforts on their behalf. It was as if all Rudi's birthdays and Christmases had come at once and he threw himself into the preparations for the party with unfettered glee. They planned to light a fire of driftwood on the sand and grill food to eat and Rudi moored his boat in the little harbour on Dune and proceeded to unload a formidable quantity of edibles. The girls helped him carry the load in something approaching disbelief as Rudi quite happily shouldered a crate of beer and beamed in delight at the prospect of having the two loves of his life at his exclusive disposal for an evening.

It was a merry picnic. The girls learned that what they considered to be a wantonly extravagant quantity of comestibles was simply regarded as mere survival rations in Rudi's view. His large athletic bulk, it appeared, required an inordinate amount of calorific intake to maintain. A plateful of food that the girls would have quailed at would disappear in a twinkling when confronted with his appetite and he guzzled the beer down with the alacrity of a parched wanderer happily chancing upon a brewery in the middle of the Gobi desert. They watched the contents of the beer crate disappearing alarmingly but Rudi was not fazed. He had a spare crate still in the boat.

In deference to Rudi's presence the girls adopted more modest dress for the evening; which meant that they wore their bikinis. They'd picked a spot on the sheltered lee of the island and it was idyllic in the in the late afternoon and evening. The tide was a small one that day and as it flooded Daniela took to the water whilst Rudi initiated Sarah into some other mysteries of the art of fishing. He'd brought a pair of shore casting rods with him, accompanying accessory gear and a collection of freshly garnered invertebrate marine life to act as bait. Whilst Daniela kept a cautious distance from their efforts he attempted with mixed success to teach Sarah the basics of casting six ounce leads and streaming trails of baited hooks out into the surf. They propped the rods up on a sturdy stainless steel tripod and Rudi sat back on the sand to open another bottle of beer with the aid of his cigarette lighter. The fishing could have been better for the crabs were active and if any fish were not quick enough to seize the bait they would find the hooks stripped clean in quick order by the hordes of rapacious crustaceans. Nevertheless the hungry crabs had serious rivals for their voraciousness for the sandy ground to the south of the island was thick with flatfish; Dabs ranging in size from little things that would have fitted easily onto a postcard to some credibly large specimens nearly a pound in weight. Rudi taught Sarah how to tell a Dab apart from the very similar Flounder by the arch of the lateral line and Sarah found a certain affection for the rather silly looking fish.

She was learning a lot from Rudi. For instance she learned that flatfish actually swim on their sides and not as, she had previously imagined, their bellies. They were actually laterally flattened. Rudi told her that different species of flatfish swim with different sides of their bodies facing upwards. For instance Turbot and Brill swam with their left hand sides up while plaice or Flounders or Dabs presented their right hand sides up. When they were young, Rudi told her, their eyes started on one side but as they matured the blind side eye migrated around the head until both eyes were on the side looking up. Sarah was astonished. She had underestimated Rudi. His knowledge of the sea and the creatures that lived in it was encyclopaedic. She could have listened to him for hours. All the smaller fish they returned to the sea but there were a few that were big enough to eat and Rudi taught her how to clean the fish and they grilled them over hot embers. Sarah found them sweet and delicate albeit a little thin and bony.

Daniela had brought her camera and insisted on taking some photographs as a souvenir. Sarah was losing her timidity in front of a camera even in her bikini for Daniela had taken several photos of her during their Helgoland sojourn of her wearing considerably less. Nevertheless, she was shy posing before the camera in her bikini with Rudi present. Daniela however determined that they should all have a picture together and, to that end, she found a solid mounting for the camera and set it to take a shot on automatic. They placed Rudi in the middle and the result was just priceless. Rudi's face on the photograph with his arms about the two lovely bikini clad girls on either side was such a comical picture of pride and goofy happiness that it reduced the girls to tears of laughter. Before they left Helgoland they printed the picture off and gave the copy to Rudi as a memento. It would hang on his wall as one of his most precious possessions the rest of his days.

But at last they had to leave. Helgoland had been a little dream; a time out from reality; a pause to gather their breath before attending to the unfinished business that awaited them back in Switzerland. There was no sadness in their leaving. The islands would not go away. They could return when they wished. Helgoland would be a little private place to escape to whenever they wished. But the mountains were calling too and both of them were eager to go back to the place they would make their home together. Rudi was distraught however and they took him to dinner on their last night on Helgoland and cherished him greatly. He was devastated to be losing his own little harem of spectacular beauties and, incidentally, disappointed in losing a lucrative side-line to his normal work for Daniela had been generous to the point of lavishness in remunerating him for his efforts on their behalf. They told him he was welcome to visit them in Switzerland although they knew that he would never leave his islands. It didn't matter. They would see him again and maybe by then, hopefully, he would have finally understood that that pretty little red headed girl, that worked in the spa and had waited so long for him to notice her, was all that he needed to complete his life and contentment on the islands he loved. They wished her well in her wooing of this gentle shy giant. The day that he realised that she was everything his ambition could require and tentatively open his heart to her mercurial sparkle and wicked teasing then these islands would be more blessed than ever.

But Sarah and Daniela had to go home. And now they both knew that it *was* a home; a home for both of them. Helgoland had provided the honeymoon. Now it was time to go home and forge a future. There was one last blip on that future however; one last piece of unfinished business to attend to before they could truly return home in triumph. Sarah had no inclination of this until their final day on Helgoland. Daniela had spent time on the telephone arranging their return. They took a last beer in a favourite restaurant on the main island. Sarah felt gently sad about leaving although she looked forward to being back in the Toggenburg. "So we're flying out tomorrow then Danny?"

"Yes sweetheart. Our chopper's picking us up in the morning."

"I'm going to miss Helgoland."

"So am I darling. It's been wonderful."

"Will we come back someday?"

"Of course we will. These islands are part of us forever now. We'll come again when the birds are migrating and then you'll have all sorts to keep you amused."

"Thank you for bringing me here Danny. I love this place. I love you too."

"And I love you. There'll always be part of us we'll leave on Helgoland Sarah. We just have to keep coming back to find it."

"It feels weird to think we'll be back in the Toggenburg tomorrow."

"We won't."

"I beg your pardon."

"Oh darling we're not going straight back. We have to make a detour en route. We have some unfinished business to attend to."

"What business? What are you talking about?"

"You've sort of lost track of time here on Helgoland haven't you darling?"

"Well in a way I suppose. But what do you mean?"

"I mean that there's something you've forgotten; something special. I haven't. I've been keeping track of the dates. Two days after tomorrow there's something very special we have to do. Something just for you."

Chapter Forty

Sarah had ended up in front of Rozella's camera lens after all but not quite in the manner that Rozella would have wished, Sarah suspected. Nor was Rozella's the only camera currently trained on Sarah. In fact she was facing a positive barrage of them and looking comically self-conscious about it. Rozella was the official, professional photographer but there was also a good contingent of amateurs to record this milestone in Sarah's life. Daniela had been busy over the telephone from Helgoland and Sarah was coming to realise that her girlfriend excelled in the covert organisation of surprises. This time she had pulled off a monumental coup. Sarah had had no inkling of what Daniela was up to until their private jet had landed at Kloten. There'd been a big limousine waiting for them but once away from the airport, instead of taking the autobahn eastwards toward the Toggenburg, the car had turned onto the west bound lane. Sarah had been totally mystified until they'd left the autobahn and she'd realised their destination. Then her memory had jolted and comprehension had swept over her in a blinding rush.

They'd stayed overnight in a large and very luxurious hotel in the city centre and the next day a small convoy of cars had arrived at the hotel. Rozella had driven up from Solothurn in the official capacity of designated photographer. Nicole had arrived with Peter in her old Renault for it appeared that Simon was travelling independently. He was driving straight from Winterthur on some clandestine mission of his own that Sarah was still puzzled about. Just for devilment Daniela had asked him to bring Charmaine along if she was free and agreeable. "After all Sarah," she'd said with a wicked grin and a pat on the bottom, "We can't be neglecting any of your personal harem now can we?"

Charmaine had enthusiastically joined the excursion. Elke and Angelica had driven up for the event as well, looking glorious in their best clothes. In fact everybody was well groomed for the day. Sarah had blinked in astonishment when Nicole had arrived in a brand new dress she'd bought especially for the occasion and with her hair back to its original honey blond colour. She looked lovely.

Sarah's own outfit for the day had required some panic last minute preparation and the acquisition of some startling new items in her wardrobe. Sarah had expected to hire these afore mentioned items but Daniela had insisted on buying them. It had seemed a bit ridiculous to Sarah since this would be the only day in her life that she would actually ever wear them but Daniela had said that they would want them as a memento and Sarah had surrendered to the inevitable. A memento was all they would be thought Sarah to herself with a small grumble. The bloody clothes had been giving her grief all day so far. They were surely not the kind of things she'd have any hankering to put on again in the future. It was roasting hot on the hotel terrace where she was posing for photographs and the heavy black gown was not exactly designed for cool summer wear. At least the hat was staying in place now though. She'd been terrified before the ceremony that it was going to fall off as she made her curtsy but Angelica had performed some black magic involving hair pins and the thing was now fastened to her head with the tenacity of a limpet.

"Just one more Sarah." demanded Elke wielding her camera.

"You can't possibly want more Elke. I look like a complete clown."

"You look wonderful Sarah."

"Come off it. I look like Batman's evil twin sister."

"Stop moaning Foxy." Nicole told her. "You look just perfect. Hold your diploma up where we can see it."

"It's only a piece of paper Nicky."

455

Elke shook her head decisively. "That piece of paper took you three hard years of sweat to obtain Sarah. Hold it up and be proud. You're a woman with letters behind her name now."

With a rueful smile Sarah held up the simple document declaring for the world that she was now a Bachelor of the Arts First Class. It was true she conceded. She *had* worked hard for this moment. She *ought* to be proud of her achievement. It was strange though. All through university she had looked forward to this day and yet, in the end, after the upheavals of this summer, she had almost completely forgotten about her graduation day. Only Daniela had remembered that this was the day to crown her years at university and arranged this surprise for her. Sarah had never imagined her graduation like this. She had always thought that this day she would be honoured for her achievement in front of the proud eyes of her parents. She had dreamed of making them proud of her. But they were not proud of her it seemed. They were not here. Nothing underlined her alienation from her parents more than that painful absence. She'd had two tickets for the graduation ceremony especially for her mother and father. They'd had to pull a few strings to let Daniela and Nicole take their places instead.

Perhaps she ought to have phoned them to remind them that she was graduating but she hadn't dared. They would have had to meet Daniela. Sarah wasn't ready for that; not even on such an important day as this. She'd thought of calling her brother and sister but it had seemed exclusive and divisive to invite some of her family and not others. They all knew her graduation date in any case. She'd received no messages of inquiry about it. Nobody had called to ask whether she was attending the graduation or what her plans were to celebrate it. The familial silence had been sonorous. It marked the pride of this day with sadness.

Daniela, bless her, *was* proud however. Her eyes were shining with that pride as Sarah self-consciously posed for photographs. In fact all her friends present were proud. Even Charmaine and Rozella who she knew so little were grinning in delight. Angelica was gushing all over her, Elke was quite obviously thrilled, Simon was looking uncommonly smug and Peter was staring at her in her cap and gown as if he'd suddenly seen her for the first time. Nicole had been priceless all day. She'd been strutting around in Sarah's wake visibly excited and absolutely beglamoured by her academic old housemate. She'd fussed over Sarah's appearance before the ceremony with such petty detail that Sarah had been tempted to slap her.

Rozella was putting away her camera at last. "Ok Didi." she said to Daniela. "I think we got good pictures enough less of course you are wanting I take some more private ones back in your suite."

"Behave yourself Rosy. This is supposed to be a solemn celebration of Sarah's academic achievement. I'll get back to you on that one." Daniela turned to the company. "Ok if everybody's got enough photos I suggest we take a break for refreshments. Simon see if you can grab that waitress and tell her to roll out the bubbly?"

Sarah was relieved that the photo session was finally over although doubtless there would be other photos throughout the evening. The whole party was staying at the hotel for the night. That must be costing Daniela a small fortune thought Sarah. She'd booked two double rooms and three singles for the rest of the company as well as an enormous, hideously extravagant suite for herself and Sarah. That would not be cheap. The Hotel Bellevue Palace was the only five star hotel in the Swiss capital of Bern. Rooms *started* at three hundred Swiss francs a shot and Daniela had not booked them into the cheap rooms. Then there was the five course celebratory dinner she had booked for the evening. That was another item not likely to be on the economy side of the budget. Then there was the room service, the beauty salon they'd used to tart Sarah up that morning, the drinks reception, the private party in the hotel disco that evening and heaven knew what else. God only knew what the final bill was going to come to. This was one serious hotel. Visiting heads of state stayed at the Bellevue Palace when they came to Switzerland on official business. It was handy for them. The Swiss parliament building was right next door.

Sarah cringed at the thought. Daniela had insisted on being photographed with her arm around Sarah in her cap and gown on the very steps of the Parliament on their way back to the hotel. A couple of tourists had looked bemused. Sarah hoped to hell that nobody outside of their party had taken a clandestine photograph because if that made it into the morning papers there'd be an explosion in the mega-tonnage category in a certain villa in Ascona.

They gathered around a table set on the terrace overlooking the deep valley of the Aar river that flowed through Bern as the waitresses laid champagne buckets out and nibbles. The hotel was quite a contrast with the more austere accommodation Daniela and she had enjoyed on Helgoland. It was all neo-classical pillars and statuary, great vaulting ceilings with dome skylights and enormous chandeliers over marble floors and plush furnishings. The suite that she was sharing with Daniela was nearly big enough to set a volleyball court out in.

Sarah looked around at her friends nervously. For the first time in her life she realised she was actually out with a group of friends who were all gay. Well all gay apart from the problematical case of Nicole, that is, who, theoretically, was still officially straight. Sarah wondered how long that particular question mark was going to remain however. Nicole didn't seem at all put out by the situation. In fact, as Sarah glanced at her covertly, she was showing Charmaine the video of Sarah's degree ceremony on the video camera since, as one of the only guests present in the hall, she had had a camera thrust into her hands and charged with the responsibility of recording the occasion for posterity. Charmaine looked interested; not so much in the rather wobbly images on the video screen, but in their enthusiastic displayer. In her new dress Nicole looked as pretty as Sarah could ever remember seeing her and Charmaine was trying not to drool. She would have serious competition Sarah realised. Rozella's antennae had zoomed in on the available single girls in the company within seconds and she was already displaying that smoky look in her eyes indicating that she was in hunting mood whenever she drifted closer to Nicole. Nicole was in for an interesting evening Sarah thought. She wondered with a giggle if she ought to feel jealous.

There were some other undercurrents going on. Sarah frowned as she saw Daniela and Simon in a clandestine huddle, obviously having a quick secret conference. They were hatching something Sarah was sure. Simon made his excuses and left for a few minutes. With narrowed eyes Sarah kept a close look on him surreptitiously as he returned and saw him pass some small object furtively to Daniela. They were definitely up to something.

Daniela had been superb all day. Curiously she had almost faded into the background at the award ceremonies but her presence had not gone unnoticed among some of Sarah's university friends after the ceremony. Sarah had been a bit uneasy about that but Daniela had dealt with the situation with her customary grace, signed autographs congratulated Sarah's academic colleagues and given nothing to suggest that she was anything other than a dear friend of Sarah's.

Slightly more worrying was the fact that Daniela had also been spotted by a reporter from the local newspaper, the Berner Zeitung, who blessed his fortune at sighting a popular celebrity on the otherwise fairly

459

dull assignment of covering the university graduation ceremonies. Fortunately Sarah had been able to vanish into the crowd at that moment and Daniela had endured having her photograph taken and she had finessed his questions by merely stating that she was present in honour of a family friend. As luck would have it, the young reporter was a relatively inexperienced journalist whose usual task was the reporting of just such limited local news as the graduation day at the university. Had he been one of the more aggressive tabloid reporters with a truffle pig's nose for a lurking story for the gossip columns then he might have dug deeper and started to put two and two together. As it was Daniela's photograph became merely a footnote among the dignitaries attending the ceremonies and there was no hint of exactly who it was who Daniela had come to witness being honoured. It was a breathtakingly close call however. There was information to be had in abundance had the reporter cared to follow it up, not least of which was Daniela's presence, with Sarah, at Bern's most esteemed hotel. They wouldn't always be so lucky Sarah realised. The day had been an enormous risk but, so far, they seemed to have got away with it.

There was a part of Sarah that almost wanted to say, "The hell with it!" and declare to the world that she was Daniela's lover. She guessed it would not faze her proud girlfriend in the slightest but she herself was not ready for such an overt declaration. Certainly their theoretical reporter would have had material enough had he wished to interview the personnel of the hotel for Daniela was not particularly hiding her affection within the public, if rather exclusive, domain of the Bellevue Palace. Even now, as Sarah nursed a glass of champagne, Daniela drifted over to wrap an arm around her waist. "Well sweetheart you're *officially* a bachelor now then."

Sarah grinned. "I think I've been that ever since I told Alan what to do with his engagement ring Danny; a spinster at any rate."

Daniela rubbed her chin thoughtfully. "God no! I don't think you qualify for the term spinster until you're over forty. Shall we just refer to you as a bachelorette?"

"I don't know Danny. Don't you think it makes me sound like a drunken floozy on a hen party?"

"Well we can't call you a maiden since you are quite clearly not one. What *do* you call a single woman that isn't actually insulting and suggesting that she's been left on the shelf and somehow to be pitied? Are we seeing a fundamental gap in the English vocabulary here?"

"I don't know Danny and it's irrelevant in any case. I'm *not* single. I'm in a committed relationship with a wonderful, beautiful and infuriatingly devious woman. Why exactly have you invited Charmaine to this shindig Danny? Are you just trying to do a number on Nicole?"

Daniela laughed gaily. "No honey, although I'm interested to see what develops there. Charmaine seems quite taken with your old housemate and I haven't seen Nicole looking discomfited by her attentions as yet. Who knows? Maybe Charmaine's the girl to tease the closet door open a fraction."

"Well you'd better divert Rozella away then because she looks as if she has ambitions in that regard."

"Rozella looks like that every time she looks at *any* potentially available female Sarah. If you let Rosy loose in Amish country they'd have to lock up their wives and daughters and run her out of town on a rail."

"Well I'd already gathered that Danny but you haven't answered my question. Why did you invite Charmaine?"

"Well apart from the fact that I thought it was good that you had other gay friends I did have an ulterior motive."

"Which is?"

"She's a bass player."

"Sorry?"

"I said she's a bass player. I need a bass player. Mine just quit."

"Oh God! Seriously?"

"Oh nothing acrimonious Sarah. His wife is having a baby and so he wants to take a time out to hold her hand as it were so he's dropped out of our touring schedule this winter. I've heard excellent reports about your Charmaine. She played in a band called the Weisse Stern and they were red hot."

"Yes I know that. I've even seen them play. They were really good."

"Well there you are. I need a bass player to fill in over the winter and I'm a great believer in giving raw untapped talent a chance. I was going to offer her an audition to see whether she can step in."

"Oh wow! She'll be thrilled. Do you think she'll be good enough?"

"I don't know until I hear her properly but I've had good reports as I've said. She'll have to be good though. Geo's an extremely talented bass player. He's going to be a hard act to cover."

Sarah giggled. "My God I could just imagine Nicky being a groupie."

"Early days Sarah. Let's just see what pans out." Daniela paused for a moment looking troubled. "Have I made a mistake Sarah?"

"Whatever do you mean?"

"I mean this... this whole thing... coming to Bern for your graduation and everything."

"Why no. Why should you think so?"

"I just wanted to celebrate you and your achievement Sarah; to throw a little party to tell you how proud I am of you. I didn't want to upset you."

"Danny I'm not upset. Really I'm not. It was very sweet and thoughtful of you. I'm touched; deeply touched."

"You've been looking sad all day Sarah."

462

"It's not your fault Danny. Really it isn't. It's just that..." Sarah tailed off helplessly.

"It's just that your mum and dad aren't here right?"

Sarah nodded miserably. "Yes! I know it seems childish Danny but you always want your parents to be proud of you when you graduate from university. Mine don't even seem to care though." Sarah laughed bitterly. "My dad spent a lot of money to send me through university. You'd have thought he'd have wanted to see at least *some* return on his investment."

"You've been out of touch with your folks for two weeks Sarah. Maybe they just forgot. Perhaps we should have called them and reminded them."

Sarah shook her head. "I sent them the details of my graduation as soon as I had my results Danny. They knew full well when my graduation was. I just don't think they were interested. They tolerated me going to university just because it was something I really wanted to do but they didn't think it important. As far as they were concerned, marrying Alan was my life defining career move. University was just a hobby they were prepared to indulge me in before marrying me off. My dad as much as said that I didn't need a degree to be a good wife and mother. I'm just a disappointment to them now. They couldn't really give a toss about how clever I've been at university."

"I'm sure that's not true Sarah. I'm sure your parents would have been proud of you if they'd been here. Possibly they didn't even know if you intended to attend your graduation. You haven't exactly been keeping them informed of your intentions."

"I know Danny but I don't think they would have come in any case. There were an awful lot of bridges burning behind me when I left the Ticino. They sure as hell wouldn't have come if they'd known you were going to be here."

"I could have stayed away Sarah if that's what it would have taken."

Sarah shook her head. "No! I wouldn't have let you. You're my life now and if they don't want to see that then I'm not going to bend over backwards to accommodate their bloody bigotry. I love you Danny. I'm not going to pretend you don't exist for their benefit. I'm happy that you were here today; more happy than I can say."

Daniela kissed her fondly and then lowered her head looking shy. "Er Sarah I hope I haven't made another mistake here but I've got you a little present for your graduation." Timidly she reached into her handbag and held out a small gift wrapped box.

Sarah took one look at the small box and instantly jumped to a conclusion concerning its contents. "Oh Danny you haven't been buying me expensive jewellery again have you?"

"No honey. It's not jewellery honestly. Actually it's something I think we both need."

Puzzled Sarah opened the box. Once she regarded the contents for a second she was more puzzled than ever for there was an odd plastic electronic fob in it attached to a key ring. Curiously she turned it over. There was a round medal on the key ring sporting a circle divided into blue and white quarters. There were three letters above the circle.... BMW. Sarah gasped. "Oh Danny! You have *got* to be kidding."

Simon drifted up behind with a grin on his face. "She's not kidding Sarah. I drove it up here this morning. It's in the hotel car park. You want to have a look?"

Sarah felt her head swimming. "Danny.... you are just.... just *impossible*!"

Daniela looked sheepish. "We need a new car Sarah so I asked Simon to pick out something suitable. He might have gone a bit over the top though but that was my fault for allowing such a generous budget."

"But... a BMW... I ... I mean..." Sarah was speechless.

"I asked Simon to pick us out a four by four for the winter Sarah. I didn't spend as much time as I'd have liked in the Toggenburg last winter but what time I did have showed me that a bloody Ferrari is just about the least practical vehicle you could have on snow bound mountain roads. I thought Simon would pick out a Toyota or something but he's got this thing about German cars."

"Come on." urged Simon. "Let's go look at her."

A minute or two later they were stood around the imposing, dark metallic blue vehicle with Sarah looking decidedly scared of it. "It's a new generation BMW X5 SUV" Simon told her proudly. "It's a diesel version but she'll still tip toe up to two hundred and twenty klicks with your foot on the floor and go nought to a hundred in just over eight seconds. It rides beautifully too and the four wheel drive gives you good off road performance. She'll be just the thing in the Toggenburg in winter."

Sarah had gone pale. "It's bloody huge Simon. I don't think I can drive something like this. I wouldn't even know where to start."

"Don't worry." Simon reassured her. "I'll coach you. You'll soon learn the ropes."

"You'll have to coach me as well Simon." Daniela observed. "I'll probably end up driving the damn thing as much as Sarah."

"Is this really mine?" whispered Sarah in shock.

Daniela grinned. "Oh yes darling. All yours. We still have to complete all the paperwork but you can drive it home in the morning with Simon to coach you along."

Sarah let out her breath. "My God! I've never had my own car before. Dad kept saying he was going to get me a little car but he never did. Jesus! I never thought my first car would be something like this. God knows what the insurance will be. And the running costs. How the hell can I afford to run this?"

"Well it is a bit thirsty." Simon conceded, "But it's a diesel so it's more economical than you might think. I think it does about fourteen kilometres to the litre. You've got a three litre engine with something like 286 brake horse power twin turbo on these new variants so that's not bad."

"We'll certainly solve our luggage storage problems with this beast!" Daniela observed bemusedly. "God you could get a travelling circus in that boot."

"Oh yes," said Simon. "You've got even more space too because this is the five seat option. They offer a seven seat option as well. I think the storage space comes to about 620 litres and an additional 90 litres under the seats. You can get a lot of kitchen sinks in there. Got all the bells and whistles too including Sat Nav, air bags on all seats, head up display, automatic air conditioning and a few technical gizmos such as iDrive control interface, Dynamic stability control and some gadget that controls your downhill handling which doubtless you'll learn all about in due course. She's got a five gear automatic gearbox which takes a bit of getting used to but, all in all, you've got a hell of a car there."

"And if BMW ever want a sales rep then they can find a world beater in you Simon." observed Daniela sardonically. "What I want to know is, is it practical and is it safe."

"Sure it is Danny. It trumps your Ferrari on both those counts although it's not as much fun. Still it's a hell of a sporty machine for an SUV and comfortable too. Sarah will have to learn how to handle it but once she's got the hang of it she'll have an eminently suitable vehicle for the kind of terrain in the Toggenburg."

"My father's got a BMW." Sarah noted. "He swears by them but God knows what he'd say if he saw me driving about in that thing." She shook her head. "God in heaven! How much did you pay for it?"

"Er nearly seventy thousand francs with the extras." Simon confessed. I hope that's all right Danny."

"It's fine Simon. I just didn't expect you to come up with such serious machine. I was thinking along the lines of a little four wheel drive runabout that Sarah could get up along the mountain roads in with her field gear and still use to drive down to town in. You seem to have exceeded your mandate somewhat."

"It's a good car Danny. I know I'm a bit of a petrol head but it really is a thoroughly top notch car."

"I'm scared to death of it." Sarah confessed.

Daniela put an arm around her waist. "We'll give it a try on Simon's recommendation honey. If it's too much for you we can always trade it in for something a little less authoritative."

Sarah nodded but deep within her there was the stirring of excitement. It was true that the imposing motor car filled her with trepidation but the thought of driving around in this for all the world to see gave her a thrill of anticipation. You couldn't ignore somebody in this car. It was big, in your face and had two hundred and eighty plus snarling horses under its bonnet. You couldn't describe it as beautiful or elegant. It was a bloody great behemoth of a machine, intimidating and masculine. You couldn't make it girly if you sprayed it pink. It was beginning to grow on her. Suddenly she wanted more than anything to tame this monster. They couldn't call her a lipstick lesbian in this baby. She'd show the diesel dykes in Winterthur a thing or two.

"Why don't you sit behind the wheel for a minute?" Simon suggested. "See how it feels."

Sarah nodded numbly and allowed herself to be coaxed into the car. The interior was surprisingly luxurious, in an understated sort of way, but the car felt even bigger from the inside. The interior was huge. She felt like she'd stepped into the Tardis. Everything about this car seemed over the top. Even the steering wheel was massive and robust. In a sense it was everything her conservative and reserved nature stood against and yet it felt exhilarating and liberating as if she had newly

467

discovered her secret dark side and rather enjoying it. It was the heady sense of power. She wondered idly if the car was touching her inner masculine side. She grasped the wheel with mounting excitement.

"Shall we take her for a turn?" asked Simon hopefully.

Daniela laughed. "No Simon. We've got to get back to the others. There'll be time enough for you and Sarah to play with it tomorrow and the coming weeks." She turned to Sarah. "Well? Do you like it?"

Sarah's face was flushed. "Oh God! It's amazing Danny. I don't know if I can deal with this much car but I'm dying to find out. Thank you Danny... I ... I'm overwhelmed."

Daniela was watching her in amusement. "Well it's time to get back darling so stop crooning over it for the time being. You can renew your affair with your new love in the morning! I'm glad you like it though."

Sarah flung herself out of the car into Daniela's arms. "I don't know how to thank you Danny."

"By being damn careful Sarah. I don't mind if you trash the car but please don't harm a hair on your head in the damn thing."

"I'll be careful honestly. Oh thank you Danny."

"Hey, we needed a new car. Maybe this thing will fit the bill." She stopped with a grin. "You looked good in that car. I think it might just suit you."

Chapter Forty-One

When they had returned to the hotel terrace, Nicole intercepted Sarah alone. "Where the hell have you three been?"

Sarah held up her key ring with a grin. "Just taking a look at my new car Nicky. Danny's bought me a car for my graduation."

"Oh wow! What did she get you?"

"A bloody great big BMW four by four built like a main battle tank and enough power to pull an intercity express."

"Oh what! Brilliant!"

"It's massive Nicky." Sarah whispered, casting covert glances aside at Daniela who was talking to Elke. "You could fit your Renault in the bloody boot."

"Fantastic! Can we go see it?"

"Later maybe. Right now though we ought to stay around or we'll look rude."

"We've got to try it out Sarah."

"What do you mean by "we"?"

"Well you'll let me have a go won't you?"

"In your dreams. It's brand spanking new and I'm damned if I'm going to let a lunatic like you get your paws on it."

"Don't be tight Sarah."

"Forget it Nicky. You'd trash it in no time. You don't exactly have an exemplary record when it comes to paying due care and attention behind the wheel."

"Meanie!"

At this point Charmaine drifted over to join them. She looked smart and chic in a light grey trouser suit over a simple black sleeveless top; her short dark blond hair coiffed boyishly but stylishly. "Hey what's happening?" she asked.

Nicole pulled a face. "Sarah's just been gloating over her new car."

Charmaine grinned. "Yeah Simon picked me up in it in Winterthur. Sharp set of wheels there Sarah."

Sarah smiled. "I'm sorry Charmaine but it's been so busy today I haven't really had the time to thank you properly for coming."

"I should thank you Sarah. I don't often get the chance to hobnob with the high society in places like this. This is quite some hotel."

Sarah laughed. "Well it's a bit more ostentatious than the digs we had on Helgoland."

Charmaine grinned at her. "Pretty rudimentary huh?"

"Well I wouldn't say that exactly. I mean the chalet was quite comfortable and at least we had a whole island to ourselves more or less."

"Wow! Cool. The whole girl Friday sort of thing then?"

"Something like that." Sarah hesitated. "Er Charmaine have you spoken to Danny yet?"

Charmaine looked startled. "Hell no! Well just to say, "hello and by the way you're my idol" and other such small talk."

"Well I think she wants a word with you if you can spare her a minute."

"With me? What the hell for?"

"Why don't you ask her? I think you might find it interesting."

Charmaine looked confused. "Why sure... I mean of course... I'll do that." She wafted her hands distractedly and drifted over to where Daniela was in conversation with Elke.

Nicole raised an eyebrow. "What's all that about?"

"Charmaine is a gifted bass player Nicky and Danny needs a replacement bassist for her winter tour. She's after giving Charmaine an audition."

Wow! No shit?"

470

"Absolutely. It could be a big chance for Charmaine." Sarah gave Nicole a sideways glance. "She's a nice girl Charmaine."

"Yeah she's nice."

"She's also gay Nicky."

"Erm I'd sort of figured that Sarah."

"Are you comfortable with that Nicky?"

"Why should it bother me? Everybody else seems to be gay although I'm not sure about that Italian chick Rozella."

Sarah snorted. "Oh she's gay all right Nicky. She's gay with a vengeance. Tread carefully around her Nicky. She's nitro-glycerine."

Nicole looked concerned. "And this is the chick that wants to use me as a photo model?"

"Oh God! Have you talked to her about it?"

"Yes sort of. She was talking about taking few trial shots next week in fact."

"I see. Well do be aware that Rozella is a very wicked girl Nicky. I'd take a chaperone if I was you."

"Hell Daniela said she was professional Sarah. She's only taking my photograph for heaven's sake. It's not like she's going to be able to drag me into bed."

"Nicky listen to me. Listen to me seriously. If Rozella decides to drag you into bed then she's going to drag you into bed. You're out of her league Nicky. She's a powerful seductress. You won't stand a chance." Sarah paused thoughtfully. "Maybe I'll ask Danny to tell her to back off and treat you professionally."

"Why this sudden concern for protecting my innocence Sarah dearest?"

"I'm just worried about you Nicky. I... I don't think you're ready for the likes of Rozella."

"What *am* I ready for Sarah?"

"I don't know Nicky. I'm not sure how to say this."

"Say what?"

"Daniela thinks you're gay Nicky."

"Does she?"

471

"She thinks you're gay but not out in the open with it."

"Really?"

"And you did kiss me once and... well say that you... well that you had a thing about me."

"And?"

"These monosyllabic responses are not helping me here Nicky."

"What do you want me to say?"

"I am just aware Nicky that you happen to be in the company of gay people and you are after all unattached and that two of the company present are equally aware of your single status and very interested in it. It's likely that at some point during the evening one or both of them are going to make their intentions clear."

Nicole blushed. "What if they do?"

"Well exactly. What if they do? What are you going to do about it?"

Nicole bit her lip. "I don't know. What should I do?"

"That depends Nicky doesn't it?"

"On what?"

"On whether or not you want them to make an approach to you."

"So you think I'm gay too?"

"I don't know Nicky. Until that day you asked me for a kiss and told me how you felt about me I'd have said absolutely not. Now I'm not so sure. I don't even know whether you know yourself. I guess it's something you have to work out for yourself. I just want you to know that everybody else here probably thinks you're gay and it's something you should be aware of. I don't want you to feel uncomfortable."

Nicole cast her eyes down. "Is this why you sent Charmaine off on an errand to see Danny?"

"You were getting kind of friendly with her Nicky. I just wanted to make sure that you were aware that she's

472

gay and interested in you so that you could avoid any embarrassment if her attentions were unwanted."

"You think she fancies me?"

"I'm sure of it Nicky."

Nicole swirled the liquid in her glass around thoughtfully. She was having trouble meeting Sarah's eye. "I'm sure I can look after myself Sarah." she mumbled at last. "Anyway have you spoken to your dad in the last few days?"

Sarah was taken by surprise by Nicole's rapid change of subject. "No I haven't. I did have a couple of messages from him on my phone but they're over a week old. He didn't say anything and there's not been a peep out of him since."

"He probably got fed up of talking to your answering machine Foxy. I know I did. What was the matter? Don't they have cellular radio-telecommunications on Helgoland or something?"

"Er actually I had my phone switched off most of the time Nicky. I forgot to take my charger so we used Danny's phone mostly."

"You do-nut! No wonder he thinks you're ignoring him."

"You mean you've spoken to him?"

"He's called twice in the last week Sarah. He sounds well miffed with you."

"Oh God! What did he say?"

"Well he wanted to know where you were and what you were doing essentially."

"What did you tell him?"

"Not a lot. How could I? I didn't even know where you'd gone myself. I just told him that you'd gone away on holiday with a friend and that I didn't know when you'd be back. He wanted to know if I knew who you'd gone with Sarah."

"Hell! What did you say?"

"I told him that I did know but that it was confidential and that I wasn't at liberty to breach that confidentiality. He got pretty stuffy about that."

"Oh Jesus! Did he say what he wanted?"

"No. He just told me to tell you to phone him urgently as soon as you were back and had come to your senses. He started to make some observations about your conduct so I told him I had pressing business to attend to and cut him off."

"Did he say anything about my graduation?"

"Not a damn thing but he sounded like he was in a hurry to speak to you."

Sarah grimaced in guilty anxiety. "Oh God! Maybe that's why he wanted to talk to me. Maybe he and mum were going to come after all and they couldn't get hold of me. For all they knew I might still have been on holiday. I just thought they didn't care. I might have been doing them an injustice. Oh damn! What a mess."

"Maybe you'd better call them Sarah."

Sarah nodded, racked with guilt. "Yes I suppose I ought to. Oh hell! I don't know what I'm going to say. I've well and truly screwed this one up haven't I?"

"It's understandable Sarah. You hardly parted with them on the best of terms after all."

"I know Nicky but I've spent the whole day so far thinking that my parents couldn't give a damn about my graduation and couldn't be bothered to turn up and maybe it was my fault after all. I feel like a worm."

"He probably thought you weren't going to attend graduation Sarah."

"Well he wasn't far wrong Nicky. It was only because Danny remembered it that I'm here at all. What the devil am I going to say to him?"

"Well if that's true then maybe you should apologise Sarah. You're big enough to know when you're in the wrong."

Sarah nodded abjectly. "You're right Nicky. In fact I'll call him now. Can I borrow your phone? Mine's got no charge on it."

"Bloody hell! That sounds expensive. I've just put some credit on my phone too. Why can't you borrow Danny's?"

"Give me a break Nicky! I'm not about to transfer Danny's mobile number to my dad's sodding SIM card. I'll buy you some more credit don't worry."

Nicole handed over her telephone. "Go on then but don't spend all night dragging the family's dirty laundry out into the open."

"Thanks Nicky."

Discreetly Sarah walked through the open veranda doors into the interior of the hotel's bar to make her call. She took a stool at the bar and held the phone in her hand in indecision. "Can I get you something Fraulein?"

Sarah started and glanced around. The barman was waiting patiently and smiling at her. "Oh er yes. Yes you can. I'll have a stiff brandy please."

"I have an excellent Remy Martin XO cognac you might enjoy Fraulein."

"Yeah sure. That'll be fine."

With an air of satisfaction the barman produced an enormous brandy snifter that looked like an undersized goldfish bowl and carefully measured out a double shot of the dark amber liquid. "I've slightly cooled the cognac Fraulein." He told Sarah. "Many people drink cognac at room temperature or slightly warmed but I think that a fine cognac is best served slightly cool. That way the alcohol does not vaporise as much and overwhelm the aroma and flavour. You get a much smoother flavour and less burning sensation on the palate when the alcohol is more viscous." Sarah blinked in surprise. She hadn't expected her impulsive buy to be such a connoisseur's event. The barman pushed the bill over to her. "Are you charging this to your room bill Fraulein?" Sarah took a horrified glance at the bill and decided that she'd better. Her dose of Dutch courage was setting her back well over a hundred francs! Hopefully this little item would be well buried in the astronomical bill that Daniela would be picking up in the morning. Swallowing hastily Sarah signed the bill and clutched her drink. It seemed obscene that a hundred millilitres of liquid could cost so much. But the brandy was smooth and rich and the warm glow of its aftertaste bolstered her resolve. She dialled her father's number.

Her father sounded puzzled as he answered. Presumably he didn't recognise the number paged up on his phone. "Hello?" he ventured tentatively.

"Hello daddy it's Sarah."

"Ah! Finally! So you have decided to re-establish communication after all then Sarah."

"I'm sorry that I haven't returned your calls father. I've been away and my phone has been out of commission."

"I'm sure you were capable of at least letting us know where you were Sarah. It is too bad of you to disappear without trace for a fortnight without affording us the courtesy of informing us of your whereabouts. Where the devil have you been anyway?"

"North Germany father. We spent some time at the seaside."

"By "we" I am presuming that you were accompanied by this woman you have been involved with Sarah."

"Yes father. I did tell you before I left that I was going away with my girlfriend."

"This nonsense has got to stop Sarah."

Sarah blinked disbelievingly. "I beg your pardon!"

"I said Sarah that you have got to put a stop to this nonsense. Your mother is deeply distraught Sarah. I won't have you breaking your mother's heart like this."

Sarah felt her mind churning in bewilderment. "Just what is this nonsense you want me to stop father?"

"I think you know that very well Sarah. I asked you, before you went gallivanting off, if you could meet up with your mother and I so that we could sit down and discuss things rationally and sensibly. You chose instead to throw a tantrum and run off somewhere with this woman instead. I'm hoping now that you've calmed down and come to your senses. The situation is not unsalvageable but it is time for you to stop acting like a spoiled child and behave responsibly." Sarah took several deep breaths and a gulp of cognac that probably cost around fifty francs for a single swallow. "Are you still there Sarah?"

"Yes I'm still here father. I'm just trying to keep a grasp on my credulity. You telephoned Nicole twice this past week I understand. Was there any specific thing you wished to talk to me about or were you just desirous of spouting more sanctimonious bullshit about my moral reprehensibility?"

"There is no need for that tone Sarah. I have, in your absence, been working industriously on your behalf and little thanks I seem to be getting."

"Working on my behalf?"

"Yes Sarah. I have had several long talks with Alan and I must say that he has been very mature and understanding about the situation. He was very angry and upset about the situation to begin with understandably but after due reflection, and not a little diplomacy on my account I might say, he is prepared to at least discuss the matter with you and see if there isn't some way of coming to an equable agreement and putting this sordid episode behind all of us."

Sarah felt a cold chill of deep anger begin to course through her. Her voice was dangerously calm and measured. "I see father. So you believe that Alan might be prepared to forgive and forget do you?"

"If you were to demonstrate suitable contrition then yes I believe he might. Naturally of course he would expect some guarantees that there would be no repetition of this behaviour but he has shown a remarkable degree of understanding and extenuation considering that, after all, you have been unfaithful to him. He has accepted very gracefully that there may have been faults on his side and he has voiced his willingness to redress those faults. Nevertheless he feels, quite rightly, that he is the wronged party and he will require appropriate remorse and penitence on your behalf and a firm commitment that such a thing will not happen again. If that were forthcoming then he is prepared to bury the past and move on."

"Move on?"

"Yes. He still retains his affections for you and he would even now be prepared to forgive your indiscretions and take you back."

"That sounds terribly charitable of him father." Sarah's voice was like ice.

"I thought so too Sarah. I have to say that not many men would have been so forgiving and prepared to overlook such a major breach of trust."

"Not many men are looking at the prospect of losing a multi-million franc town house as a dowry either." Sarah mumbled.

"What was that? What did you say Sarah?"

"I was just thinking aloud father. So let me get this straight. All I have to do is crawl back to Alan on my hands and knees, beg his forgiveness and he'll nobly grant me absolution and magnanimously consent to marry me after all?"

"Well there's no need to put it as dramatically as that but those are the essential facts."

"Well that all seems simple enough father. Just when and how are you proposing that this beneficent reconciliation should take place?"

"That is why I have been trying to get hold of you Sarah. The week after next Alan is obliged to return to America for some weeks on business and so there is not a moment to lose. I propose therefore that we meet with Alan and yourself and have a long serious discussion."

Alan is returning to America? I thought he was remaining in Switzerland until at least the autumn. Wouldn't his business arrangements have clashed with the previously proposed date of our wedding?"

"Well obviously that provisional date has had to be postponed now Sarah in view of all that has passed. Should we be able to effect a reconciliation and persuade Alan that you are truly contrite about your conduct we would be looking at a new date some time next year I presume."

"And this meeting father; this public repast of humble pie I'm expected to dine on, that will be when?"

"Within the next few days Sarah. I presume you are back in Switzerland now so there is no reason why we can't get together as soon as possible."

"And that was all that you wanted to talk to me about father?"

"Well yes. Isn't that enough?"

"There was no other thing that you might have wished to discuss with me or arrange with me?"

"Well obviously I have some private issues to discuss concerning your recent conduct Sarah but I think this is the most important matter don't you?"

"I suppose that I'd better see Alan then father."

"I'm pleased that you are seeing sense Sarah..."

"Yes since he doesn't seem to have got the message from my earlier conversation with him I suppose it is incumbent on me to tell him once more that I am not going to marry him, that I never would marry him and that I wouldn't marry the sanctimonious, pontificating bastard if he was the last man left on earth. He can take his nauseating, hypocritical, exonerating clemency and shove it up his arse. The only way I'll appear in a church with him is if it's his funeral and then only because I'll want to dance on his fucking grave."

"Sarah!"

"Oh shut up father! I can't believe that you're doing this to me. How dare you go behind my back and tell Alan that I'd be ready to come crawling back to him like a dutiful, subservient little plaything and beg for his forgiveness? Have you completely lost your mind? Did you know that after I broke off our fictitious engagement that this bastard had the effrontery to phone up my close friends to threaten and abuse them? If you arrange a meeting between us then I shall take the opportunity afforded to slap his face for him. You can further tell him that if he ever dares to threaten or harass any of my friends again I shall take legal action and don't let him kid himself that he can hide behind his father's dodgy wealth and influence. I'll drag the bastard into court and let it all out into the open. And as for you father I would be obliged if you never ever mentioned that man's name again in my presence or ever even obliquely referred to any impossible fantasy of my marrying him."

"I am very disappointed in you Sarah!"

The word "disappointed" was ill advised. Sarah's anger rose to boiling point. "Oh so you're disappointed are you father? Today of all days you are *disappointed*?"

"What do you mean Sarah?"

"I mean father that today I have endeavoured to publicly uphold the pride of our family. I now discover that I was wasting my time. My family obviously has no pride in me and never has. All my family was interested in was pimping me off to the Bergers for financial gain."

"That's a monstrous thing to say Sarah."

"Is it? Well just for the record father, although you are quite evidently disinterested, I have to inform you that I have performed my public duty creditably today and did not disgrace the family name during the ceremony."

"What on earth are you talking about?"

"Do you know where I am father?"

"Well I presumed you are in the Toggenburg."

480

"Wrong! Actually I'm sat at the bar in the Hotel Bellevue Palace in Bern. It's quite a posh place actually. I believe that Queen Elizabeth and Winston Churchill among other people have stayed here."

"I know the Bellevue Sarah. What the blazes are *you* doing there?"

"Just sat at the bar sipping very expensive cognac and trying not to lose my temper whilst listening to my father talk complete garbage to me and tell me that he's "disappointed" whilst wearing academic robes that I, in my ignorance, had thought would afford him pride rather than shame."

"Academic gowns...you mean..."

"It was my graduation today father! I have achieved the distinction of a First class Bachelor of Arts degree; the only person among my year group in my faculty to have done so."

There was a long pause on the other end of the line. "Oh Sarah.... I... didn't realise...I..."

"No you didn't father. I had thought that the reason you were trying to call me was because you were aware of my graduation today. But no. You were too busy trying to recoup your investment with the Bergers. Naturally you overlooked something as trivial and unimportant as the fruition of my three years of dedication and diligent effort in academic study."

Mr Fuchs sounded subdued and remorseful. "I...I'm sorry Sarah... I would have... I mean I would have wanted to be there but...."

"Please don't concern yourself father. I can understand how awkward it would have been for you to so honour a daughter's achievement who has brought such *shame* on you because of her unforgivable sexual orientation. Of course you wouldn't have wished to be seen publicly acknowledging your parentage of a lesbian, however clever she might be."

"That is unfair Sarah. I would have wanted to be there."

481

"What and have to meet my girlfriend father? I don't think so. In any case I am sorry that you are so ashamed of me. Fortunately my girlfriend and my good friends are *not* ashamed of me and they stood in for you at my graduation. Now if you'll excuse me father I really do have to return to my girlfriend and I'm afraid this conversation is becoming painful for me."

"Wait Sarah...."

"For what father? To listen to some more of your denial and bigotry? I'm sorry but I can't do that. I'm gay father. I'd hoped that you were beginning to come to an acceptance of that but every word you say tells me that you haven't. I can't do anything about that. You're just going to have to live with it father because I'm not going to change however distressing and shameful it is for you. I'll understand however if you don't ever wish to speak to me again."

"Sarah don't sign off while you're so angry."

"I'm not angry any more father... just sad. Goodbye father."

Sarah slammed Nicole's phone down on the bar and buried her head in her hands. A small scraping sound caught her attention. She glanced up with tears in her eyes. A balloon shaped glass full of cognac was being pushed next to her elbow. She blinked hastily and looked up. The barman was regarding her compassionately. "Your drink Fraulein."

"I... I didn't order another drink."

"Please Fraulein it's on the house. Actually that's not true. It's on me."

"I can't let you offer me another drink. This stuff is expensive. I know they don't pay you enough to just splash out like that."

"I'm sorry Miss but I couldn't help overhearing your conversation on the phone. Please accept this drink from me. I know how it is and you look like you could do with another drink."

"You know how it is?"

"Of course! I'm gay too." He winked at her. "Don't worry about the cost. I sell a lot of this stuff and I did a little creative manipulating with the measures. Don't tell a soul."

Sarah managed a watery smile. "Thank you... er..."

"Ricardo Miss."

"Thank you Ricardo. Tell me something. Were your parents hard work when you told them you were gay too?"

The boy laughed. "You have no idea darling! I thought *I* was supposed to be the drama queen."

"Thank you for the drink Ricardo."

"It was entirely my pleasure Fraulein."

"There you are!" Sarah span on her stool at the sound of the voice behind her. Daniela was stood next to her looking worried. "Is everything ok sweetheart?"

"Not really Danny. I just had a torrid conversation with my dad."

"Oh!"

"I've broken my parents' heart Danny. I... I didn't mean to do that."

"Sarah! Don't say things like that. Tell me what happened." In a few brief words Sarah described the conversation she had had with her father. Daniela took her hands gently. "Sarah you haven't done anything wrong."

"It feels like I have Danny. My father told me that my mother was heartbroken and he sounds the same himself."

"Sarah was it hard for you to accept that you're gay?"

"You know it was."

"Well it's no different for your parents honey. They'll go through all the usual "Oh where did we go wrong; why did this happen to us; why is our daughter different: are we such terrible parents etc, etc" but sooner or later they'll remember that you're the daughter they love and they'll come to realise that you are who you are and that is the beautiful girl they've doted on since she was a baby. It's hard for parents to adjust Sarah. You just have to be patient with them and understanding."

"Will they ever understand *me*?"

"Yes they will Sarah. Believe me they will."

"And us?"

"That too Sarah. One day we'll sit down with your parents for dinner together and we'll laugh about all this. It just takes time."

"Oh Danny I love you."

"I love you too Sarah." Daniela pointed a finger at Sarah's glass. "But don't be hammering that stuff back too much all right. We've got a long night to get through and don't forget... you're driving back in the morning.

Chapter Forty-Two

The next day, for the second time that summer, Sarah came home to the Toggenburg from Bern. That sentence essentially covers the only similarity between the two home comings for two more different returns it would be hard to imagine. Early in the summer Sarah had been returning to a Toggenburg whose welcoming embrace had been clouded with uncertainty. She had been none too sure just how long she had left to enjoy her beloved valley and the future lay dominated by a marriage she had already begun to dread. She had returned home alone on a railway train to no job and uncertain prospects other than those afforded by the imminent loss of her liberty. There had been no such person as Daniela Devin in her life, no realisation of her sexual proclivity and certainly not the slightest foresight among the wildest realms of her imagination of the bomb that was about to explode in her life within a few short weeks.

How things had changed. For one thing she was no longer an anonymous figure peering out of the windows of an Inter-city express train. There was an officious piece of paper to say that she was a lettered woman, honoured by her university for having achieved a Bachelor's degree, and that with distinction. She was somebody; one of the top percent of people in society with a university degree and she had raised that bar even higher with the attainment of a first class degree. It would not be the end of her academic climb. She had bumped into her old tutor at the graduation. "Give me a call." He had said, "We need to talk about your future plans."

Daniela had been quietly satisfied. "We'd better get your application forms sorted." She'd noted. "We'll make damn sure your parents turn up for your doctoral graduation." There was a new plan therefore. Not a plan to become Mrs Berger but instead a measured route to the title of Doctor Fuchs. There was a shining castle on the hill and Daniela made it all possible. Daniela made a life possible; a life of happiness, high achievement and freedom. The woman that had fallen so dramatically into Sarah's world had changed her life forever.

Sarah was honest enough with herself to confess that she had the great good fortune of being loved by a very wealthy woman. Not every gay person emerging from the proverbial closet could have hoped for such fortune. Many a young, newly emergent person might have had to face alienation from their family and friends alone and without the comforting cushion of such unlimited wealth. Yet it is hard to escape the feeling that such great fortune could scarcely have happened to a better person or one more determined to prove herself worthy of it. Wealth comes to many people who do not deserve it but, just once in a while, it falls into the lap of a person who truly merits it and has the seeds of greatness in them to best utilise it for good. Sarah was one such person. Wealth would never corrupt her nor ever change her fundamental virtue. Like the woman she loved, Sarah was a phenomenon; one destined to touch the lives of many and make the world a better place for her having graced it with her life.

That new life was just beginning as she returned in triumph to the valley that held her heart. The very newness of it was in no better way underlined than through the mode of her return. She was no second class passenger on the east bound express this time. Their return from Bern had taken a somewhat convoluted route for Simon had driven them out of the city and then onto a quiet set of country roads where he had handed control over the big BMW to Sarah and coached her for two hours as she gingerly steered the machine around and tried to master it. Peter and Daniela had occupied the back seats as Simon patiently instructed Sarah from the front passenger seat. He had been pleasantly surprised by Sarah's progress although apt to smile at her timidity with the powerful car. Nevertheless it was plain to see that Sarah was a competent if somewhat cautious driver. Although Sarah had never owned a car before she had sufficient experience behind the wheel, combined with a certain natural ability, tempered with a great deal of responsibility and care.

Sarah found the big car a challenge. Its sheer size took some getting used to and on tight corners and narrow lanes she had to bear its dimensions in mind constantly. She made a hash of her first few attempts to park it and reversing was a nightmare. Also she was shocked by the sheer power of the car whenever Simon cajoled her into treading a little more heavily on the accelerator on the open road. It was like unleashing some primeval beast from under the bonnet as the car leaped forward with a feral growl from the big engine. Oddly however, once her confidence began to grow and they eased the car away from the country lanes, she found the car more comfortable at high speed on the open autobahn. Somehow it seemed smoother and more manageable once given its head on a broad fast road and she tentatively allowed the speedometer to creep above a hundred kilometres an hour and began to enjoy herself. Simon smiled in satisfaction. "You're a good driver Sarah." he told her. "I'm impressed."

"Thank you kind sir. That's true praise. Do you need dropping off in Winterthur?"

Simon glanced back at Peter in the rear seat behind him. "Oh we forgot Sarah. You're not up to speed on developments are you?"

"Developments?"

"I've moved to the Toggenburg full time Sarah. Pete and I took up our new house last week."

"Why that's wonderful. Congratulations."

Peter looked sheepish. "Thanks Sarah. You're officially invited to our house warming party."

"I look forward to it. Where is the new house?"

"Well actually it's a pub Sarah." Simon told her with a grin.

"A pub? Seriously?"

"Yes, and not too far from you. You know the little pub at Eggenwaldi at the bottom of the chairlift up to Oberdorf? Well we've taken a lease on it. Originally we were going to buy a cottage over near Starkenbach but it was proving to be a bit of a nightmare regarding financing. Anyway this place came up on the market and it seemed too good to miss."

"This is wonderful. Are you going to run it as a pub?"

"Well that's the idea." Simon frowned. "Why are we trailing behind this truck Sarah?"

"Er we're doing nearly a hundred and ten Simon."

"So? We've got clear road behind us and you've got two hundred and eighty six horses at your disposal. Stop being a wimp and lose the fucker."

Sarah smiled uncertainly. "Yes sir." Tentatively she applied her left hand indicator and pulled out into the overtaking lane. The big car seemed to growl in pure satisfaction as she pressed on the pedal and they coasted past the big lorry with alacrity. The power of the car almost frightened Sarah. "Jesus this thing's fast." she breathed.

"That's the sport part of the Sports Utility Vehicle designation Sarah. You've got a twin turbo, six cylinder, three litre diesel under that bonnet. Sure she's fast."

"I don't think I've ever driven anything with this much power before."

"Wait till you try out Danny's Ferrari."

"Oh God! I wouldn't dare."

Daniela leaned forward. "You're going to have to Sarah. If we're going to have two cars in the family we'll both have to be able to be proficient on both of them."

"Christ! You mean you'll let me drive your Ferrari Danny?"

"Sure. You'll probably be better at driving it than me."

"God I'll be scared to death."

Simon grinned. "Don't panic. I'll teach you Sarah. It'll be a thrill for you." He smiled wickedly. "You can ease off the gas now Sarah. You're over the limit. I'd hate you to get your first speeding ticket on your first day in your new car."

"Oh shit!" Sarah relaxed her tread on the pedal. "You just don't realise how fast you're going sometimes in this thing."

Simon patted her on the knee affectionately. "We'll take her over the border one day if you want to see what she's made of. We'll cut her loose on a German autobahn and let her show you what she's got."

"Do you always feminise your cars Simon?" Daniela asked with a laugh.

"Sure. Cars are like ships and women; beautiful, expensive and completely unpredictable."

Sarah glanced at him inquisitively. "Are you *sure* you're gay Simon?"

Simon threw his head back and laughed richly. "Let's just say that cars bring out my masculine side. I can get downright hetero with my cars but I don't want to sleep with them."

Sarah's mobile phone, resting at the side of her seat, chimed. "Oh God! Who's that?" she wondered aloud.

Daniela reached forward and picked it up. "It's Nicky Sarah. Do you want me to answer it?"

"Yes please. I need both hands for driving."

Daniela keyed the button. "Hi Nicky! It's Danny... no we're not home yet. Sarah's been playing with her new car all morning! Where are you?" Daniela grinned mischievously and winked at the other occupants of the car. "Oh you're still in Winterthur then? You dropped Charlie off then?" Nicole had taken it upon herself to

489

drive Charmaine home that morning. The blossoming friendship between Nicole and Charmaine had been the subject of much amused speculation the evening before. Charmaine had even dragged Nicole out onto the dance floor in the hotel disco and Nicole's look of self-consciousness had been just priceless. "So where are you in Winterthur then Nicky?" Daniela continued. "Oh I see. The Planet huh?" Sarah raised her eyebrows. The Planet was the name of the bar she had first met Charmaine in. Daniela was in one of her teasing moods. "Better be careful Nicky." she warned. "The Planet's a gay bar. We'd hate you to taint your reputation." Sarah glanced behind her and shot Daniela a look of pure venom. Daniela ignored her and laughed. Nicole had made an opprobrious remark. "Ok Nicky. If you're setting off now you'll probably beat us home. We're just coming up to Zurich. You want to meet up in Unterwasser for a drink?" Daniela paused to listen. "Ok. The Sternen then... don't know but we won't be far behind you unless Sarah manages to wrap her new toy around the central reservation. Wait for us ok. See you then." She signed off and replaced the phone with a grin. "Well that sounded very cosy. Charlie and Nicky are having a little drink together in Winterthur."

Peter shook his head in bemusement. "Do you really think they shared a room together last night?"

Sarah grinned. "I don't know. I couldn't get a word out of Nicky at breakfast this morning."

Daniela leaned back in her seat in smugly. "There was an awful lot of meaningful eye contact and blushes over the breakfast buffet Sarah and they did have adjoining rooms."

Sarah nodded. "Yes and when I offered to drive Charlie home today Nicky nearly dropped her orange juice."

Simon rapped on the dashboard of the car sharply. "You're a bunch of gossiping old women. Leave poor Nicky alone. I'm sure she'll tell us in her own good time if there's anything going on between the pair of them. In the meantime give her some space. It's not easy coming out as I'm sure we all know."

Daniela smiled. "Oh I'll give her all the space she needs Simon. I think Charlie's the best thing that could happen to her."

Simon nodded in agreement. "Charlie's cool Danny. I like her a lot."

"Of course," noted Daniela, "Sarah might be jealous of Nicky pinching one of her personal harem."

"Any more remarks like that Miss Devin and I'll pull over and you can take the bloody bus home." Sarah remarked acerbically.

"What did Charlie say about your offering her a job Danny?" inquired Peter.

"Well I haven't promised her anything Pete but she's coming up to the studio next Thursday for an audition so we'll see then. She's familiar with most of our stuff so that's a bonus and she sounds very keen."

Simon laughed. "I'll bet she does. It's a big chance for her."

Daniela nodded. "Yes and she's a nice girl and she'll look good on stage. If her playing's up to scratch I think it might work out well. I'm not promising anything yet though. We'll see on Thursday."

Sarah grinned wickedly. "Hey, will me and Nicky get special groupie rates at your next concert then?"

Daniela regarded her sourly. "You'd be getting a special slap if you weren't driving about two tons of German automotive technology and my life didn't depend on your unwavering concentration."

Sarah grinned and eased the car up to a cruising speed, just under a hundred and twenty kilometres an hour. She was beginning to lose her fear of her new car. It was fun. They ate up the kilometres until all too soon they were on the outskirts of Wil where Sarah steered off the motorway and onto the main road up the Thur valley. Suddenly she felt excited and impatient; wanting to be home. But the road along the valley was not conducive to impatient driving for it was frequently narrow, bendy and passed through a collection of villages and small towns; Bazenheid, Ganterschwil, Butschwil, Lichtensteig, Wattwil, Ebknatt-Kappel and Nesslau. Sarah negotiated the road with caution biting her lip in concentration. It would be unthinkable to mess up her arrival back at the last hurdle.

Beyond Nesslau the course of the valley took a sharp kink to the east, narrowed and became walled in by the mountains. This was the Upper Toggenburg; Sarah's domain. She slowed the car so markedly that Peter looked at her in puzzlement. "What the hell are we doing; kerb crawling?"

Sarah shook her head slowly. "I'm just taking it in Pete. This is important to me." And it was. The line of the Churfirsten mountains were shimmering in the autumn sunshine on the southern side of the valley and the peaks of the Santis massif were hazy to the north. Sarah felt a deep satisfaction that she was unable to articulate; a sort of completeness as if finding her mountains again at last and this time for good. All summer long she had faced the possibility of losing this, her homeland, for alien exile. It had been a struggle and it was a struggle not yet over for there were many issues as yet unresolved but she knew now with certainty that nobody could take her away her beloved Toggenburg again. Her life had changed unrecognisably since that day in early summer when Nicole had picked her up on her return from university in Nesslau but the Toggenburg; that had not changed. Here it was in all its glorious constancy. She knew she would travel more in her life now for that was something that would come with a life shared with Daniela but she also knew that she was more rooted in this valley than ever. She belonged here.

Nicole was waving to them as they pulled into Unterwasser alongside the terrace of the Hotel Sternen and there was a rightness to that as well for Nicole had

492

always been here; as part of the valley as the brooks and meadows; as firmly constant as the sound of the cowbells in the alps. Sarah parked her car triumphantly in the big car park on the opposite side of the village street from the hotel and she and her passengers alighted stretching after the long drive. "Well done Sarah!" Simon told her. "You picked that up really quickly. You drive well." Sarah smiled with pleasure and took a moment to indulgently stroke a hand over the bonnet of the car. The metal was smooth and warm to the touch under the hot sunshine. This car was hers now. She had driven it home to her valley herself. It belonged to her. She raised her eyes, drank in the vista around her and flared her nostrils at the scent of the valley; happy to be alive. Daniela was watching her carefully with delight. She snaked a hand around her waist. "It's good to be back huh Sarah?"

Sarah nodded, not wanting to speak for the moment; her mind on a high plain among her mountains. Peter was concerned with more earthly matters. "What are we waiting for?" he asked. "I could do with a beer."

Before Sarah could answer, her telephone chimed. She took the apparatus and glanced at it. "You guys go ahead. It's my sister." As the others drifted away toward the hotel Sarah lingered and keyed the response button. "Hi Jess!"

"Hi kid! Mum and dad phoned me last night. They said you were back in Switzerland for your graduation."

"That's right Jess. It was yesterday."

"Hell I'm sorry Sarah. I had no idea it was your graduation. I would have wanted to be there."

"It's fine Jess honestly. I'll send you the photos if you like and if you really want to see me looking like something out of a Gothic fantasy in a cap and gown."

"I'll bet you looked great. Dad was well miffed that you hadn't told him that you were attending your graduation."

"Dad's well miffed with me for a lot of reasons Jess."

"Yes I gathered that Sarah. He was er... quite outspoken in his opinions regarding your life choices. I told him to button it and let you get on with it. Where the hell have you been for the last two weeks anyway? Dad said something vague about Germany or something."

"Actually I've been stranded on a desert island."

"Come on Sarah. Tell me where you've really been."

"I'm serious Jess. My girlfriend and I spent two weeks alone on a little island of sand dunes in the North Sea."

"Really?"

"Absolutely! It was heavenly."

"My God! Did you tell dad that?"

"I just said we'd been away to the seaside which was technically correct."

"When did you get back?"

"The day before yesterday. We flew into Zurich and went straight to Bern for my graduation."

"Dad said that you called him from the Bellevue Palace. Surely you didn't stay there."

"Well yes actually. It was a bit grand for me though."

"Er just about one of the top hotels in the country Sarah. It must have cost a fortune."

Sarah grimaced. She wondered what Jessica would say if she knew about the private business jet, the helicopter flights and the fact that Daniela had effectively booked the entire island for them exclusively, not to mention her new car. "Er well it was a bit pricy Jess but it was a special occasion." she prevaricated.

"This girlfriend of yours must be loaded Sarah."

"She's comfortably well off Jess."

"I've just got to meet her."

"I think you'd like her Jess. I'm sure she'd like to meet you."

"Where are you now anyway kid?" Sarah took a deep breath and glanced around at the glory of the Toggenburg in the afternoon sunshine. Her eyes drifted up the hillside opposite to Schwendi clinging above the valley and along the valley side to Oberdorf, in the distance, where she would sleep in Daniela's house this night.

"I'm home!"

(To be continued.)

Postscript

The characters in this novel are entirely fictitious and bear no resemblance to any persons dead or alive. The locations in the story, on the other hand, are all real places. The locations in Switzerland, including the various places described in Ticino, Bern, the regions of central Switzerland and, of course, the Toggenburg valley itself will be recognisable to anybody familiar with them. So too will be the islands of Helgoland and Dune that form a part of this story. The cover photograph of this volume is a panoramic view of the Toggenburg taken from the mountains of the North East and looking westwards along the Toggenburg valley. This is Sarah's domain sandwiched between the mountains of the Santis massif to the north and the row of peaks, known as the Churfirsten, to the south.